"Why didn't you tell me th

Riley snorted. "I mean, really! This is so not a topic for casual conversation. I was supposed to tell you that my dead husband is now a demon, he visits me, and we make love. Was I supposed to tell you that?" Her hands began trembling, then her whole body shook . . . She started crying.

"It's okay. It's a normal reaction," Malik soothed.

"I was almost killed!" She looked up at Malik, her eyes glistening. "You saved my life."

"It's okay," he murmured.

"Why would he want to kill me? Does he hate me that much?"

Malik bit back a retort. "Demons have an exaggerated sense of power. They think they're invincible."

"Aren't they?"

"About as invincible as a wet piece of tissue," Malik answered.

Riley gazed into Malik's blue eyes. *He's cute, really cute.* Her throat went dry when Malik winked at her. *How can I possibly be thinking about Malik like that after Bradley's murder attempt?*

Also by Desiree Day

Crazy Love

Cruising

One G-String Short of Crazy

SPIRITUAL
SEDUCTION

DESIREE DAY

G

GALLERY BOOKS
New York London Toronto Sydney

Gallery Books
A Division of Simon & Schuster, Inc.
1230 Avenue of the Americas
New York, NY 10020

First Gallery Books trade paperback edition April 2010

GALLERY and colophon are registered trademarks of Simon & Schuster, Inc.

For information about special discounts for bulk purchases,
please contact Simon & Schuster Special Sales at 1-866-506-1949
or business@simonandschuster.com.

The Simon & Schuster Speakers Bureau can bring authors to your live event. For more information or to book an event contact the Simon & Schuster Speakers Bureau at 1-866-248-3049 or visit our website at www.simonspeakers.com.

Designed by Renata Di Biase

Manufactured in the United States of America

10 9 8 7 6 5 4 3 2 1

Library of Congress Cataloging-in-Publication Data

Day, Desiree.
 Spiritual seduction / by Desiree Day.
  p. cm.
1. African American women—Fiction. I. Title.
PS3604.A9865S65 2010
813'.6—dc22   2009031258

ISBN 978-1-4391-2678-3
ISBN 978-1-4391-7108-0 (ebook)

To Dad, thank you for your constant support.

acknowledgments

First of all, I would like to thank my readers, I really appreciate you all. Thank you, Megan, for all your hard work. Thanks, Bob, for your continued support.

Many thanks to: Yasmin Coleman of APOOO, Radiah Hubbert of Urban Reviews, Tee C. Royal of Rawsistaz, Ella Curry of EDC Creations, Stacey Dilliard of Unique Styles Magazine, and many others who have helped me on this journey. I couldn't have done it without you all.

Enjoy.

SPIRITUAL
SEDUCTION

Riley Tyson primped and styled in front of the mirror as though she were on her way to the Oscars, but the outfit she had on screamed PTA meeting.

"I don't know why you're getting dressed, you know your sorry-ass husband isn't taking you anywhere," her younger sister, Tamia Stewart, said bluntly.

Riley gave a sigh, a long-suffering one that said she had heard her sister's comments before. "Don't you have a man you want to go out with tonight?"

Tamia grinned. "I have *many* men that I can be with tonight, but you're more fun," she teased. "Seriously, I don't know why you bother. I don't remember your silly husband ever taking you out for your anniversary. Why do you keep setting yourself up?"

Riley turned away from the mirror and looked at her sister. "He said he'll take me out and I believe him. Besides, I called him earlier today to confirm."

Tamia narrowed her mascaraed eyes at her sister. "Did you talk to him?"

"Well . . ."

"You got his voicemail didn't you? Didn't you?" Tamia pressed until Riley nodded. "That man is harder to catch than a straight man in San Francisco."

"Not true," Riley said with a laugh. "He checks his voicemail all the time. And I *know* that he got my message and we will be going out tonight."

"You're delusional," Tamia muttered, low enough for Riley to pretend not to have heard her. "Why hasn't he called you back? It's almost six o'clock. If I were you, I'd stick on a sweat suit, heat up a Stouffer's dinner, pull out the Ben and Jerry's, and plop down in front of the TV. Because that's gonna be your dinner and a movie."

"We're going out," Riley stated firmly. She primly patted her slicked-down hair. "It's our fifth anniversary. How can he not want to celebrate it?"

Tamia tilted her head in amazement, as if to say, What planet do you live on? "The same way he didn't want to celebrate the other four," Tamia mumbled.

"I heard you," Riley said. "He always had a good reason."

"Yeah, right. He had to work," Tamia said with a snort.

"He did," Riley said quickly, defending her husband. "And he always made it up to me."

"That's right, I forgot," Tamia replied sarcastically. "He gave you wilted roses on your first anniversary. For your second he was gracious enough to give you a card, two weeks late, and it looked like he had picked it up off the bathroom floor. And—"

"He took me to the Bahamas," Riley interjected, cutting her sister off.

"Yeah, but you admitted that you never saw him. He spent his days on the golf course and his nights in the clubs."

"He bought me diamond earrings," Riley protested while reaching for her jewelry box.

"Forget it . . . you don't have to show me. They're no bigger than a crackhead's brain. I wouldn't be surprised if they're fake." Tamia was silent, then, "And he treats you like his personal maid. I can't believe you clean up after him like he's a two-year-old. This room looked like Aretha Franklin was in it getting ready for an awards show before you cleaned it up."

"I don't mind," Riley blurted out. "We're like yin and yang, he's a slob and I'm a neat freak," she said.

"Yin and yang? Is that what it's called? You two are more like the Ying Yang Twins, bizarre."

Riley ignored her again as she moved from the mirror and sat next to her younger sister. They looked so much alike that it was obvious they were related. Each with skin as smooth as toffee and the color of toasted cinnamon, behinds that were compared to perfect peaches, and breasts that would never see the inside of a plastic surgeon's office because they were so full and perfect. Riley glanced at her sister. "Why do you hate Bradley so much?" she asked quietly. Tamia had been making the same remarks ever since Riley had introduced them to each other.

"Because he's a fucking jerk!"

"Tamia! Watch your mouth! The children might hear you." Riley glanced toward the open door. Even though they were across the hall, Brie, her one-year-old, and four-year-old Carter had bionic hearing.

"I'm sorry," Tamia replied contritely. She tried another tack. "I don't think he's good for you."

"Tamia, why do you keep pressing this? It's been the same thing for the last six years."

Tamia scrutinized her sister. "Because something's going on with you two, I can tell. I don't know what it is, but something is off. You two are off."

Riley quickly averted her eyes. "There's nothing wrong." She picked up a scarf and absentmindedly began twisting it.

Tamia grabbed the scarf. "Are you sure?" Riley nodded. "You'd tell me, right?"

"I would."

"Promise?"

"Promise. He's a very good man. He takes very good care of me and the kids. You just refuse to see it."

"In six years I have yet to see Mr. Nice Guy."

Riley studied her sister and cast her gaze downward, then out of the blue she said sadly, "Who'd want a lady with two kids?"

"So that's it—you're staying with him because you're afraid of ending up alone?"

"A little," Riley admitted. "Sometimes I just think about what would happen if I left. I'm not delusional. I know what a jerk he is and that he isn't perfect, but who is? And I do love him," she said honestly. "I have two kids to think about; it'd be selfish of me to take them away from their father just because he's a jerk."

Tamia snorted. "He's more than a jerk. Anyway, he could always visit them," Tamia added.

Riley shook her head. "I don't want that. It would be too unsettling and confusing for the children."

"They'd adjust; children are very resilient. I hate to see you married to somebody who doesn't appreciate you."

Riley squared her shoulders. "I'll deal with it; I just want things to work out . . . for the kids." She stood up. "Do you like my outfit?" she asked, changing the subject. She twirled around.

"I still think it's a waste," Tamia muttered. "I don't think his trifling behind is taking you anywhere."

"Tamia!" Riley warned.

"Okay, okay. I'll let it go," Tamia relented. "And you look aw'right."

"Just all right?" Riley asked, exasperated. "What's wrong?"

"Well, you look like a mommy."

"I am a mommy."

"Yeah, but everybody doesn't have to know that. And if you want to go out tonight, you should want Bradley to want to take you out . . . to show you off."

"I think I look good," Riley decided and returned her attention to the mirror. She paused. "What? Do you think I should change?" she asked hesitantly.

Tamia bit back a smile. Her sister had as much fashion sense as a nun. She strutted to Riley's side. "The first thing you can do is let your hair down," she answered while tugging at her sister's ponytail. "What the hell did you do, slather it with Super Glue?" Riley's reddish-brown shoulder-length hair was slicked to her scalp. "If it was pulled any tighter, your nose might end up where your eyes are," Tamia joked.

"It's easier this way," Riley explained. "With two kids . . ."

"I know, I know." Tamia had been hearing the same excuse ever since Brie was born. "You won't have them tonight. Let it loose." Tamia rolled the rubber band off her sister's hair and ran her fingers through it. "Now, doesn't that feel better?"

"Yeah," Riley admitted, suddenly feeling as though her head had been released from a bear trap.

Tamia grabbed a comb and dragged it through her sister's hair until silky smooth tresses caressed her shoulders. "Perfect," she said, taking a second to admire her work. "Now we have to find you something sexy to wear."

"This is sexy enough," Riley protested as she ran a hand over her long-sleeve, knee-length dress and her confining pumps with their conservative two-inch heels.

"Yeah, if you're dead," Tamia called over her shoulder. She had sauntered over to her sister's walk-in closet and was thumbing through her clothes. "This is going to be a challenge."

"What's that?" Riley eyed the garments her sister had slung over her arm. Victorious, Tamia scooted away from the closet carrying her selections.

"Girl, your closet is worse than a contestant on *What Not to Wear*. I had to dig deep to find this stuff. *Very deep.*" She held up a pair of black leather pants, a silky black camisole, and a black-lace cardigan. Dangling from one finger was a pair of black, strappy, four-inch heels.

Riley blushed. "I can't wear that!"

"Why not? It was in your closet. So obviously you've worn them before," Tamia quipped.

"Yeah, but not together," she sputtered. "I'll look like a whore!"

"Well, whores get sex and get taken out. Change!" Tamia ordered.

Riley sighed and quickly did as her sister had told her to do.

"You look hot!" Tamia said as soon as Riley slipped on a pair of oversize sterling-silver hoop earrings. "Hot! If you weren't my sister and I was into girls, I'd take you out."

"Thanks!" Riley's eyes were bright as she studied her reflection. "I do look good, don't I?"

"Yeah. Too good for Bradley."

"Tamia!"

"Okay. I'll shut up." She grabbed her purse. "I'ma say good-bye to my niece and nephew then hit the road. I think there's a bed somewhere in Atlanta that needs warming."

"And you're just the body to do it?"

"You got that right," Tamia quipped before sauntering toward the bedroom door.

"Tamia!" Riley called. "Who are you going out with tonight?" She couldn't resist asking. Her sister's proclivity for eclectic men always amused her. There was Todd, the saxophone-playing vegetarian; Marcus, the seven-foot-tall bald Buddhist; and Alvin, the professional student who had more degrees than she had fingers. And none of her boyfriends lasted more than a month.

"Oh, I have a new one. You'd like him." She winked.

"I bet." Riley grinned as her sister jetted out the door.

Three hours later when Bradley strolled into the house, Riley was in the living room, her gaze bouncing between the TV and the children. Their eight o'clock bedtime had long since passed, but Carter wanted to stay up to see his daddy, and fortunately it just happened to be Brie's feeding time. Without a word or a glance to his wife, he made a beeline for Carter.

Grabbing his son by the waist, Bradley hoisted Carter into the air and spun him around until he screamed with laughter. When he could no longer stand it, he begged to be let down. *This is the side of Bradley that Tamia never sees,* Riley thought happily as her husband gingerly returned Carter to the floor. Carter adoringly hugged his father's leg, and Bradley lovingly patted his head. Riley's gaze shifted from father to son. Carter was the spitting image of his father. Both had hazel-colored eyes that changed colors depending on their mood, sandy-colored hair that, like their skin, turned golden in the summer, and long limbs that made it hard for either of them to find clothes that fit properly.

Brie solemnly watched the action from her mother's lap. Bradley didn't say a word before plucking Brie from Riley. Brie immediately erupted in tears and Bradley drew his lips back in a snarl before depositing her back in her mother's lap.

Twenty minutes later, with Carter trailing after him, Bradley headed toward his son's bedroom. Riley followed silently while carrying a now-cooing Brie. He glanced over at his wife, his gaze running coldly over her outfit. "Why are you dressed like some bitch ready to hop on the back of a motorcycle?" he asked, his lips twisted into a sneer.

Riley's eyes widened at his harsh words. "I'm dressed like this because we're going out to dinner."

"Who's going out to dinner?"

"We are. Don't you remember? It's our anniversary . . . and you promised," Riley said at Bradley's blank look.

He shook his head. "I didn't promise you a damn thing. I have a meeting tonight. I just came home to change."

"Bradley!" Riley protested. "I got all dressed up, and the babysitter will be here soon to watch the children."

"You'd better call her and let her know that we won't be needing her tonight."

"But it's our anniversary. Our *fifth* one."

"And?" Bradley said with a snarl. "Like I said, Riley, I have to go back to work. If you want to celebrate our anniversary, fine, go for it! But you're on your own." He stepped into Carter's bedroom.

"Hey, little man, put your pajamas on and hop into bed."

Carter looked up expectantly at his dad. "Are you gonna read me a story tonight?" he asked, his voice hopeful. Months ago Bradley had read him a bedtime story, but he hadn't cracked a book since. Riley had been reading to him ever since, picking up where Bradley had left off.

"I don't have the time, little man. Daddy needs to get back to work."

"But, Daddy," Carter whined.

"I need to go. Go to bed!" Bradley roared so loudly that Carter jumped.

"Yes, Daddy," he whimpered as soon as he found his voice.

Bradley stalked out of the room.

"I'll be right back. Here, take your little sister," Riley whispered to Carter before placing Brie in his arms and racing after her husband. "Bradley!" He stopped and Riley heard him sigh before turning to her. "Come on, your work will be there tomorrow. We don't even have to go out. You can read Carter a story, then we can order in and rent a movie. Just spend the evening with me," she pleaded softly and reached for his hand.

Bradley glanced down at their intertwined hands, then into his wife's eyes. All her longing, hurt, and love stared back at him. His gaze guiltily shifted away.

"Just stay with me, Bradley. Okay? Just stay. Are you going to stay?" Riley begged her husband as tears began running down her face. Bradley just rolled his eyes and turned away. Wanting him to stay with her, Riley dropped to the floor and wrapped her arms around his legs.

"What the fuck!" Furious, Bradley looked down to find his wife tearfully peering up at him.

"Tell me that you want to celebrate our anniversary with me," she begged.

Bradley shook her off as though she were an overaffectionate puppy. "Get off me!" he ordered.

Suddenly Carter ran out of his room. "Leave my mommy alone!"

"Go back to your room!"

"Leave her alone!" Carter demanded.

"Carter, go back to your room. Otherwise be prepared to get in line for an ass whipping. You'll get yours right after your mother's."

Carter's presence sobered Riley. She sniffled and pushed herself up to her knees. "Go back to your room, baby. I was just playing with your father." Carter's worried gaze went from his mother to his father. "Go on back to bed. I'll be there in a minute. Have your book out, baby."

With an eye roll to his father, he reluctantly backed his way into his bedroom while keeping his gaze fixed on his parents.

As soon as Carter was out of sight, Bradley slapped Riley across the face and she fell to the floor. "Don't you ever do any of that ghetto shit to me. Grabbing my legs like you're crazy." A whimper squeezed past Riley's lips, but she pressed back the scream that threatened to erupt. *The children.*

Bradley left her on the hallway floor as he went into their bedroom and quickly undressed, dropping everything on the carpet for Riley to pick up later. After throwing on a clean set of clothes, he stalked out of the bedroom.

"Bradley!" Riley called, stumbling after him. The sandals her sister had picked out slowed her down. "We don't have to go out, we can stay home. I have a steak in the freezer; it'll only take twenty minutes if I microwave it. Come on, baby, stay with me."

Bradley suddenly stopped and studied his wife. The right side of her face was red from the slap, mascara ran down her cheeks like black tar, and her once neat hair hung sadly around her face. "You look like a shitty whore." He slammed out of the house. Riley fell against the door.

Loud banging snatched Riley from a restless sleep. She tiredly reached for Bradley but found herself groping air. Her eyes popped open and she turned toward the clock: 3:00 glared at her. "He must've lost his keys." She threw on a nightgown, stumbled down the stairs half asleep, and pulled open the door. "I see you forgot your ke—" She stopped when she saw the two police officers standing in front of her.

"Mrs. Tyson?" Riley nodded. "Wife of *Bradley Tyson?*" Riley's hand went to her mouth as she began to tremble. She nodded. "May we come in? We have some bad news."

chapter TWO

Riley sleepwalked through telling friends and family members about Bradley's death, stumbling through the process of making Bradley's funeral arrangements and the days leading up to his burial. The only things that pierced her cocoon of desolation were her children.

Riley woodenly walked around her living room greeting her guests and accepting their condolences. *I wonder if everybody would be here if they really knew how Bradley died. Would they waste their time on a man killed by a pimp after refusing to pay for a blow job?* The thought lazily flitted in and out of her mind.

Bradley's mother, Ophelia, had insisted that Riley host everybody at her house after the funeral, and Riley hated herself for letting Ophelia bully her into doing it. All she was aching to do was crawl into bed and never come out.

Bradley's friends and relatives filled her house, laughing, eating, and talking as though they had just spent the last two hours at a club and not a funeral. A couple of her colleagues and a smattering of her family were there, watching the scene with a mixture of horror and amusement.

"Riley! Riley!" Bradley's mother yelled from across the room. "We're out of dip; can you run into the kitchen and get some? And while you're in there can you bring out some more Kool-Aid? Oh, yeah, and we're all out of Chee-tos."

Riley momentarily stiffened before extracting herself from her group of friends and dragging into the kitchen.

Tamia watched her sister crawl back into the living room laden down with items. "This is it. It's time for her to sit down," she said quietly before carving her way through the guests and sidling up to her sister. She gently took the items from Riley's hands. "I got this. Go sit down," she whispered in her ear.

Riley slowly turned to look at her sister through flat eyes. She blinked as though trying to force herself awake from a bad dream. "Why do you want me to sit down?" she asked, her voice thick with grief.

Tamia's heart lurched, and tears stung the back of her eyes, threatening to spill over. "You look tired," she answered helplessly, aching to take her sister away for a week at the beach.

"Oh, okay," Riley replied, her voice a monotone. She stiffly turned around, fumbled through the crowd, and plopped down in an empty spot on the couch.

Tamia placed the items on the table and elbowed her way into the dime-size space next to her sister. She wrapped her arm around her waist. Riley rested her head on her sister's shoulder. "How ghetto is Bradley's family? *I mean really,*" Tamia said in an undertone, "can't they at least *fake* looking sad? Instead of looking like they won a ticket to an all-you-can-eat buffet."

"Do you want to know how he died?" Riley asked softly.

"I thought he was mugged?"

"Kinda. He had refused to pay a prostitute for a blow job she had given him. He said that she didn't do a good job," she whispered in her sister's ear.

"No shit!" Tamia murmured.

"I know that prostitutes are into servicing customers, but not customer service. So she called her pimp and I guess Bradley still refused to pay, so the man killed him and took all his money," she said in an undertone.

"How did the police find out?"

"A homeless man had seen the whole thing. He'd never liked the man who killed Bradley; I guess he was a tyrant to the homeless in the area. And do you want to know the kicker?"

"What?"

"The detective who's investigating this case said Bradley had DNA from two different women on his dick."

"Oh no! You'd better get tested."

"Oh, I did, trust me," she answered quietly. "And I'm fine. Instead of spending our anniversary with me, he was screwing around with two different women."

"I'm sorry." Tamia tightened her grip around her sister and let her have her little bit of peace in the sea of madness swirling around her.

Malik Davenport, Riley's boss and vice principal at her school, glided into Riley's house. He hated this part, but he knew it was necessary. He had ignored the tradition of wearing black, instead opting for all gray, which looked like ice against his almond-colored skin. His naturally curly hair was cut close to his head. At six foot seven he easily stood out among the crowd. He slipped off his sunglasses even though he hated removing them. The reaction was always the same, and this time, like in the past, it hadn't changed. During Bradley's funeral he had stayed in the shadows, but he couldn't hide his eyes in the broad daylight; the sun flickering through the open blinds seemed to enhance them. Vibrant blue eyes framed by inch-long eyelashes coolly searched the room for Riley.

Having sky blue eyes isn't that unique, but being a black man with blue eyes is. Growing up he had hated his eye color, a bright blue with flecks of silver that, depending on his mood, could make a person's heart melt with desire or freeze with fear. Kids had made fun of his eyes, and having skin the color of an almond just made his eyes stand out even more. The good thing was that his eye color was a family trait that all the Davenport men shared. And it wasn't until he became a teenager that he appreciated the power of his eyes. Ladies young and old all flocked to him like gold diggers to millionaires.

After spotting Riley across the crowded living room, Malik sliced his way through the patches of people, oblivious to the admiring stares from the women. His unwavering gaze remained glued on Riley as he made his way to her side.

He hugged her tightly before releasing her, but one of his arms remained loosely roped around her waist. "I am so sorry for your loss. How are you doing?"

Riley forced herself to smile. Malik ignored the bags under her eyes, big enough to hold a pair of Gucci boots; her gaunt figure, which looked like she hadn't eaten in days; and her disheveled appearance. Even though she had on the standard widow's uniform of all black, her outfit looked as though she had pulled it off the closet floor. Her dress had more wrinkles than Phyllis Diller and her shoes were more run down than a fifty-year-old aging rock star.

"I'm fine," Riley replied woodenly. "I'm doing fine. We had a good turnout. All of Bradley's friends and relatives came," she said. "Everybody looks so nice." Malik listened quietly, a little startled by the randomness of the comments. Riley sounded as if she was talking about an afternoon brunch with friends rather than her husband's funeral.

Riley didn't tell Malik that among Bradley's *friends* was a woman with a one-year-old baby who was the spitting image of Bradley. And his relatives included two drug dealers, a nit-picking mother, and a brother who'd rob you blind while staring you in the face.

"I see. You're so fine that you put on two different shoes," he said quietly.

Riley furrowed her brow with confusion and Malik nodded toward her feet. She glanced down then let out a groan. Malik was right. While they were both the same style of pump, one was black and the other was navy. "Why didn't anybody tell me?" She turned to the crowd. "Why didn't any of you tell me that I was wearing two different shoes?" she shouted. "You could have told me instead of having me walk around like some crazy person." The room went quiet as all eyes turned to Riley. She glared back at them.

"Let's get you a drink, something strong," Malik decided as he grabbed Riley's arm and guided her over to the buffet. The talking resumed quickly, as though someone had turned the volume up on a CD player. He grabbed a bottle of wine then arched a questioning eyebrow at her. "Where would you like to go to get away for a minute?"

It took her a moment to brush the cobwebs off her brain. "The basement," she finally decided. "It'll be quiet down there." They slinked along the fringes of the clusters of guests to the main corridor of the house. Three doors lined the hallway. Riley opened the one closest to her, flicked on the light, and then they slipped unnoticed down the stairs. As soon as he hit the bottom step, Malik froze for a second then started swatting the air.

"Are there bugs down here? I hope nobody left a window open," Riley said nervously. Too embarrassed to look at Malik after her outburst, she walked toward the windows and busied herself with checking them. "The windows are all closed," she said. "I don't know how they got in." She looked worriedly around the basement.

"I think I got them all," Malik said casually.

"Great!" Riley glanced at Malik before shyly looking away. "I'm sorry about upstairs. I don't know what's wrong with me. That wasn't me."

Malik grinned. "I know," he said, quietly taking in her face and glad that he'd suggested they get away. They hadn't been in the basement long, but the sad, pinched look she'd worn upstairs was gone. "Remember, we've been working together for the past six years. So I *know* the real Riley. You're under a lot of stress and you're grieving."

"Thank you," Riley said gratefully.

Malik finally took the time to look around the basement and felt as though he had entered a sports bar.

Nine luxurious leather recliners were neatly aligned in front of a sixty-two-inch plasma TV. A hot dog machine sat in one corner; a popcorn machine and even a counter filled with the standard movie theater candy hugged a wall. Next to that was a fully stocked bar. Malik slowly turned around and saw a pool table at the other end of the room.

Riley saw the look of admiration flash across his face. "Quite the playroom, huh? This was Bradley's home away from home, his man cave. He came here to get away from it all," she said, her voice hollow. "I guess a family is too much for some men. Have a seat."

Malik grabbed two glasses from the bar before settling on a leather sofa next to Riley. He poured the drinks and pressed a glass into Riley's hand. "Drink this; it'll make you feel better," he ordered.

Riley arched an eyebrow at him. She had never known alcohol to do any good. "I don't know . . ."

"Come on, I'm not asking you to drink the whole bottle, just a little sip . . . to calm you down a bit," Malik coaxed.

Riley pushed the glass away. "No. I don't want it to become a crutch."

"One glass is hardly considered a crutch."

Riley eyed the glass with doubt. She had heard stories of people who turned to alcohol in their grief and then couldn't stop.

Malik sighed. "You'll be okay, I promise," he said gently as he looked into her eyes. "You're more than a colleague to me; you're my friend and I care about what happens to you. I just want you to relax."

"Okay, just a little sip," she acquiesced. She tentatively brought the glass up to her lips and sipped. The wine tasted like fruit punch with a kick. "Hmmm, this is good." She took another swallow.

"I guess you don't drink much."

Riley nodded her head. "Maybe once or twice a year, and even then it was always just a sip. Bradley was the drinker." She jutted out her chin at the bar.

"They say that a little wine is okay for you. So drink up."

Two glasses later, Riley's mismatched shoes were on the floor and her feet were tucked under her as she shared stories of her and Bradley's dating days. "He was so nice; every time he picked me up for a date he gave me a dozen roses and chocolate. It was so sweet, I really felt like I was being courted," she said. "And he used to cook for me, nothing fancy, just steak and potatoes, very simple food, but I really appreciated the gesture."

"It sounds like you two had some good times."

Riley nodded her head. "We did. We used to take weekend getaways to Savannah, Charleston, and Hilton Head. It was all his idea; he was spontaneous like that. He used to surprise me by showing up at my apartment and telling me to pack a bag for the weekend. After the fourth time, it wasn't that much of a surprise, but I loved it anyway. He was so spontaneous; I loved that about him," she said.

"Who doesn't like spontaneity? It keeps things fresh."

"It does," Riley agreed. "And gifts, when we were dating he used to always give me gifts. The best gift he gave me was a Coach bag. I had admired it while we were out shopping and later that week he surprised me with it. I still have it," she admitted and smiled wistfully. "Things were good then."

Malik smiled at her indulgently. He had never seen this side of her; he liked it, and even though it was alcohol induced, it was endearing. "And they weren't right before he died?"

Riley flushed. "They were okay," she confessed. "Sometimes people change," she said, then an epiphany hit her. "Maybe people really don't change, maybe they finally pull off their masks and show their true faces." She shrugged. "I don't know, that's just my two cents."

"Two cents? That sounded like an Oprahism, and you know her words are worth at least a million a piece. So if we add up what you just said"—Malik repeated her words and pretended to calculate—"I think you just spouted a cool five million dollars' worth of words," Malik joked, trying to lighten the mood.

Riley blinked at him before throwing her head back and laughing; she liked this side of Malik. It was rare for her to see his playful side, and she loved it. But just as quickly as it had changed, her sad mood abruptly returned. Her face went blank, as though someone had flicked a switch.

Sensing her mood change, Malik sobered up. "What's wrong?"

Riley's eyes watered. "I shouldn't be acting like this. It's not right."

"All you're doing is laughing."

"Yeah, I'm laughing. But three hours ago, I was burying my husband and crying so hard that my stomach hurt. This is *soooo* wrong," she moaned. "I'm going to hell for this."

Malik made his hands into fists, wanting to encourage her to lay her head in his lap, something he had been dreaming about for a long time. "For laughing?" Malik asked quietly.

Riley gulped. "Who carried on this way after losing a spouse?" she asked. "A mean-spirited one, that's who."

"You're one of the nicest people I know," Malik said in her defense and watched her struggle with her feelings and his words. It appeared to be a tie. "All you're doing is catching pieces of joy. And there's nothing wrong with that. A lot of people can't do it. They become stuck in their pain and can never move forward." Riley laughed bitterly and before he could stop himself, Malik grabbed her hand. "Don't ever be ashamed of your feelings. Revel in them."

"That's such a girlie thing to say," she teased. She squeezed his hand. "Thanks," she said softly. "I really appreciate that. I feel like I'm betraying his memory, that by feeling good, I'm not mourning him," she admitted.

"That's not true," Malik insisted. "Mourning doesn't automatically equate with respect. Some people mourn because they feel obligated, even if they don't feel sad. What they really want to do is dance on that person's grave. Some mourn because they are unsure about how they should really feel. And there are some people who genuinely mourn their loss, but slivers of happiness slip through and they're thrown for a loop. And that's normal. Stop being so hard on yourself. You're human. If you weren't, you wouldn't care about this stuff."

Riley smiled. "I'm so glad you're in my life. You're a good friend."

"You're welcome." Malik hugged her, feeling her breasts pressing against him. He sighed softly, then the unthinkable happened. *Oh shit! Think about her dead husband, think about her dead husband,* he silently chanted until his body returned to normal. "Everything will be okay," he managed to squeak out.

"I know," Riley murmured, oblivious to Malik's dilemma. "It's just hard right now. Carter is devastated, and there's so much I have to organize. I always thought Bradley was so organized, but I found out that he wasn't. He left a lot of unfinished business."

Malik wanted to ask what, but he held his tongue. "You'll get it done. Let me know if I can help."

"I will."

"Riley, are you down there? Riley!" Ophelia's voice cut through them, slicing them apart. Riley jumped up, her face flushed with guilt.

"Oh my God! It's Bradley's mom. She'll kill me if she finds us down here by ourselves."

"What's wrong?" Malik's brow crinkled. "We're not doing anything."

Riley jumped up and frantically paced in front of the sofa. "I know that, but she'll see it differently. She'll say that we sneaked off to be alone," she hurriedly explained.

Malik shrugged. "Well, we did." He kicked at the air.

Riley stopped pacing long enough to glare at him. "Would you stop with all that damn kicking?" she hissed. "There aren't any bugs down here."

Malik blinked. Her moods changed faster than Beyonce's hairstyles. "I'm not killing—forget it, you wouldn't believe me if I told you," he said solemnly.

"I'm sorry. I just buried my husband, but my biggest worry right now is trying to hide my friend so my mother-in-law won't think I'm trying to hook up with him. How sick is that?" She placed a trembling hand to her cheek. "I can't think straight, there's too much going on."

Ophelia called Riley again. Malik watched Riley going into meltdown mode.

"It'll be okay, all we're doing is talking, anyone can see that."

"But she won't," Riley muttered as she shot a panicked look toward the staircase, half-expecting to see Ophelia lumbering down.

Two days later, after the children were in bed, Riley ventured down to the basement again. She thought about the crisis that had been averted two days earlier when Ophelia walked in on her and Malik.

Malik's quick thinking saved them. By the time Ophelia made it to the bottom of the stairs, Malik had squeezed out enough tears to instantly become the grieving friend. And after giving her a convoluted excuse about being too embarrassed to cry in front of the others, Ophelia decided that nothing was going on between the two and left them alone. But it didn't stop her from telling everybody that the fine blue-eyed brother was a pussy.

What should I do with all this stuff? Riley thought, looking at a box she had taken from the trunk of Bradley's car. *I guess I'll start small.*

She grabbed the box, placed it on the couch, and sat down. She hesitated before tentatively lifting the top. Bradley's scent wafted up to her and tears stung her eyes. "I will not cry. I'm too strong for that." She pulled out a sweater, held it to her nose, and savored his scent. "I miss you so much." She folded the sweater and placed it on the arm of the couch to keep as a reminder of her dead husband. She rooted around until she found his wedding ring. "I'll save this for Carter," she decided. It took her fifteen minutes to reminisce over each piece before deciding if she wanted to donate, save, or pass it to Carter or Brie.

The last item in the box was his laptop. Knowing that the kids were fast asleep, something made her pull it out and power it up. She studied the icons. The words MY BLOG immediately caught her eye; she furrowed her brow in puzzlement. "Bradley kept an internet blog?"

Against her better judgment she clicked on it and scanned the headings. MY WIFE THE BITCH, MY WIFE THE DICK LIMPER, I'M A NEW-MILLENNIUM TYPE OF PIMP. With shaking hands Riley clicked on the most recent posting. Her stomach roiled with nausea with each word she read. Every sentence about her was laced with hatred. By the time she read the third post, she was sobbing and could barely read the text.

According to Bradley, she was so boring in bed that he had to look for pleasure somewhere else. And she no longer kept herself up. Especially in Atlanta, where women got their hair and nails done *every* week; she was barely passable, so much so that he hated taking her out in public. He was ashamed to be seen with her. She gasped when she saw an old picture of herself and she remembered the occasion. It had been taken three days after Brie was born, and she still looked nine months pregnant. Her hair looked as if she had seen a ghost, because with a newborn baby she hadn't had time to comb it. Rings the size of China outlined her eyes. He had told her that she was beautiful and he'd wanted to take the picture so that he could remember this moment. After much protest she had let him do it. "Oh no!" she cried.

He had given explicit details in the blog on how he would concoct stories to meet his mistresses and what they had done together. And if his readers didn't believe it, he had videos proving it. Horrified, Riley watched one video as one of his mistresses fellated him while he reclined on a bed with his hands behind his head. He arrogantly stared into the camera while occasionally throwing out instructions. Riley wanted to vomit on his laptop. She began shaking with hurt and anger.

Riley covered her face with her hands and sobbed. Gut-wrenching sobs cut through her, shattering her soul. "I loved you so much!" she croaked. "I ignored how you treated me. I ignored your cheating, telling myself that you were just being a man and once you realized what you had at home, you'd appreciate me. But I was wrong."

Sometime later, she pulled herself off the couch. "You deserved to die, bastard. You're nothing but an evil piece of shit!"

She jogged up the stairs for an oversize garbage bag, hurried back to the basement, gathered up the laptop, and tossed it in the bag.

chapter THREE

"You doing okay, girl?" Tamia whispered, even though she didn't need to. The voices surrounding them swallowed up anything she said. She hadn't seen her sister since Bradley's funeral, one month before.

"What?" Riley shouted.

So much for privacy. "How are you doing?" Tamia yelled in return.

"I'm fine."

Tamia rolled her eyes. "I don't know how you can eat in here every day; I haven't been here ten minutes and I've already got indigestion." Tamia frowned as she glanced around the teachers' lounge. "They're worse than the students." At a table to their left were three teachers not so quietly tearing apart a coworker. And tucked away in a corner was a couple pawing at each other as though they were newlyweds; her sister informed her that they were, but just not each other's.

Riley shrugged. The cliques and constant feuding between the teachers at Booker T. Washington Middle School were worse than those of the cast members of a Disney show. Fortunately, after six years she'd learned to keep herself out of the fray. "You get used to it."

Tamia grabbed her sister's hand. "Come on, this noise is driving me crazy. Let's go outside." Riley glanced over her shoulder at the clock. "Do you have time?"

"Yeah, just barely," she answered. Her forty-five-minute lunch break went by faster than a fuck session with a seventy-year-old man.

"You sure? I don't want you to be late."

"We're fine. I'm monitoring study hall after this. And half the kids don't even show up. And the ones who do spend more time listening to their iPods or trying to get a date for Friday, so they pretty much manage themselves. Come on." They gathered up their trays and picked their way through the teachers' lounge and headed outside. They settled on a bench near a tree. Riley raised her face to the sun as though inviting it for a kiss. "This is wonderful. I love September in Atlanta. It's so beautiful. You were so smart to suggest that we come outside. This is exactly what I needed. Mmmmm."

Just then Malik strolled up to their table. "Ladies."

Riley smiled brightly, unable to help herself. Even though they'd been friends before Bradley's death, their friendship had deepened since then. Every morning he stopped by to see how she was doing and whether there was anything he could do for her around the house. "Mr. Davenport," she said for appearances' sake because there were students sitting nearby. "We're enjoying the weather. You want to sit with us?"

"No, just stopping by to see how you're doing and checking to see if there's anything you need help with." Riley stared up at him, mesmerized by his eyes. It felt like she was looking into a storm of blue water and a wave of heat washed over her body, hardening her nipples. "Riley?"

"Um, no, we're fine, I mean, *I'm* fine," she stuttered as she pulled herself out of his gaze. *What the hell just happened?*

"You sure? It won't be a problem."

"You're sweet, but I'm fine. And I'll be sure to let you know if I need anything."

"Cool," Malik said before sauntering away.

"He's cute," Tamia said after Malik left.

"He's very nice," Riley answered, still a little unsettled by her reaction to Malik.

"But his eyes creep me out," Tamia said and shuddered.

At least that's all they do to you. "I know. They used to freak me out when I first met him, but I'm used to them now," she answered with a shrug. "And I think they're unique. You don't meet that many black men who have his eye color."

"That's true, and I've met a *lot* of black men," Tamia said. Riley rolled her eyes. "You should go out with him," Tamia blurted out.

"Tamia!" Riley hissed. "Bradley hasn't been dead that long. I'm not ready to date and won't be for a long time. I need to focus on myself and my children. Besides, who would want to date a lady with two little kids?"

Tamia rolled her eyes. "Oh, here we go. A lot of men would. And I bet one fine vice principal would be very interested in it."

Riley shook her head. Her sister was worse than a professional matchmaker. "Malik and I aren't like that. We're colleagues and we occasionally lunch together, and even though we've become closer since Bradley's death, I think Malik sees me as a friend."

"I doubt it. I think he likes you. Men usually don't volunteer to help unless they have an ulterior motive. Maybe he's just giving you room to grieve and after a respectable period, he'll make his move."

"Would you stop being so silly? Even if that was true, which I don't think it is, I couldn't go for him. He doesn't have any swag."

Tamia cocked an eyebrow. "First of all, what do *you* know about swagger? And I hope you didn't think Bradley had swag. That wasn't swag, that was just damn foolishness."

"No, Bradley had swag; he was confident and cocky. Unfortunately, that's what got him into trouble. But I do like a confident and sexy man. And I just don't see that in Malik."

"Aha! I thought you weren't looking."

"I was looking, but not like *that*," Riley admitted. "Just in a what-if kind of way."

"You keep it up. You're going to *what-if* your ass right out of something that could be nice."

"Why don't you take him?" Riley asked, curious. She hadn't known her sister to pass on a man.

"Because he looks boring as hell," Tamia said with a laugh. "Fineness can only get you so far. I admit, I need the swagger too. And Malik doesn't have it," she said firmly, then, "So, how are you doing? I mean, really doing. And just ignore our previous conversation. I don't think sometimes; I really shouldn't be trying to hook you up."

Riley waved her sister's worries away; Tamia was simply being Tamia. "Actually, I feel wonderful," she admitted before cutting off a piece of steak and eating it.

Tamia looked at her sister as though she had gone crazy.

"It didn't happen overnight; it was a process. But I knew I was truly happy when Mary J. Blige's song, 'Just Fine,' came on the radio and I started bouncing around the house like I didn't have any sense. I was happy again. It was like God had flicked a switch."

Tamia blinked at her sister. "You were dancing around the

house?" she asked. The vision of her sister moping around and mourning her dead husband quickly evaporated.

"Don't judge me," Riley sputtered defensively. "You don't know everything."

Tamia snorted. "Oh yeah I do. He was a jerk, an asshole, a—"

"A wife beater," Riley finished for her, her voice soft with embarrassment.

"That fucking asshole!"

Riley's eyes darted around; luckily no one had heard Tamia. "Sssh, keep it down," Riley scolded her sister.

"Sorry. But he beat you?" Tamia scooted her chair next to her sister's. "Why didn't you tell me? I would've helped you. Shit, I would've killed him!"

"That's why. You would've made my life more miserable than it was. And that would've pissed him off more." Riley sighed deeply. "And I was scared, so scared. He always told me that I wouldn't be able to survive without him. He always called me stupid; not a day went by that I wasn't called stupid or dumb. And I believed him. I was so messed up that if he had told me my shit smelled like chocolate, I would've believed him." She shook her head slowly. "I believed him, T. I was beginning to think I was dumb," she confessed.

"You're not, baby, you know that. You have a master's in education and you've been named teacher of the year three years in a row. You're hardly stupid. It doesn't surprise me. Something about him just left me unsettled. He was fine and all, but I could tell he was a snake. He was slicker than one of those megachurch pastors."

Riley smiled sadly. "I know, you warned me about marrying him. But I didn't think you knew what you were talking about. I was blinded by love for that man."

"I probably wouldn't have listened to me either. He put a glow on your face that was brighter than the sun. Trust me, if I'd had a man who did that to me, I wouldn't have listened either."

"Hindsight is a bitch," Riley muttered. "You know how men always complain that women change as soon as they're married?"

Tamia nodded.

"In this case it was Bradley; as soon as Reverend Brown pronounced us husband and wife, he changed," Riley confessed. "The Bradley who brought me gifts for no reason at all, who called me on the phone in the middle of the night just to hear my voice and who would stop in the middle of the sidewalk and kiss me just because he felt like it, was gone. He had turned into a whole other person. And I kept hoping the Bradley I fell in love with would return."

"I guess that never happened, huh?"

"In bits and pieces, just enough to keep me hoping that he could change. You know that he never let me write a check?" Tamia's eyebrows shot up and she forced herself to remain quiet. "When we first got married, I thought he was so organized; he took care of all the bills. All I had to do was give him my paycheck and I'd tell him the amount of money I needed for the week, but that quickly changed. He started giving me an allowance of what *he* thought I needed for the week. Like twenty dollars for lunch. I can laugh at it now."

"How the hell did you survive on twenty dollars a week?"

"That was my lunch money," Riley answered, chagrined. The whole thing seemed like a lifetime ago, but it really hadn't been that long. "He gave me fifty dollars a week for groceries."

"You fed a family of four for fifty dollars a week? You're fucking kidding me!"

"Tamia!" Riley warned.

"Okay, okay. But how did you manage that?"

"It was easy, Bradley rarely ate at home, Brie drank milk and ate baby food, and Carter was fine with a can of SpaghettiOs. So it worked itself out," Riley answered.

Tamia glanced at the three-inch steak on her sister's plate. She had been eyeing it ever since she pulled it from her lunch bag. "I guess it did work itself out."

Riley blushed. "I deserve this."

"I know you do, sweetie."

"I'm sorry," Riley blurted out.

"What? Why?"

"I feel like I failed you. I'm your big sister, I should've been setting a better example for you."

"You were the perfect example," Tamia said emphatically. "You are the perfect mom and if I'm ever a mom and could ever be just one percent of the mother you are, and then I'd consider myself blessed."

Riley's eyes glistened. "That's sweet." She picked at her potato then said, "If he hadn't gotten killed, I still would've been with him," she admitted. "I never would've left him."

"You don't know that," Tamia protested. "You're a smart lady. You would've realized that you deserved more and that your children deserved to have a father who respects his wife."

Riley nodded. The image of herself on her knees begging Bradley to stay flashed in her head. "I think you're right. I would have gotten tired of being treated like shit." She brightened. "One good thing is that since he was so cheap, he had over three hundred thousand dollars saved. And with the life insurance policy . . ."

"You're rolling in dough," Tamia finished for her.

"Yeah, thanks to Bradley."

"So are you going to stop working?"

"Nope. I enjoy teaching. I'll use some of the money to travel during the summer, but I'll dump most of it into my retirement account and the rest into the children's college fund."

"Cool, we should take a trip to Brazil. The men there are hawt!"

"Maybe we should," Riley agreed, then blurted out, "He didn't even love me."

"Of course he did," Tamia said, soothing her sister. To her own ears her words sounded like a lie.

"No he didn't," Riley said, thinking about the video and the blog. "But the best things he gave me were the kids," she said. "Do you know that he told me what to wear to work every day? Every Sunday he'd assign my clothing for the week."

"Damn, he was controlling."

"Very! And if I didn't agree with him and deviated from his wardrobe suggestions, he'd hit me."

Tamia shook her head sadly. The man was truly a monster.

Riley continued, "It's over. It's finally over. I never realized how bad it was until he was gone. And the funny thing was that his abuse started so subtly. When we first started dating, he would call me at least once an hour and if I didn't answer his call, he would accuse me of cheating on him. I thought it was cute. And when he started telling me what to wear and what to say, I thought he was trying to make me a better person. I really thought he loved me."

Tamia's mouth had dropped open as she listened to her sister's confession. "I'm so sorry. Never in a million years would I have guessed you were going through that, never. You always defended him and you were always so damn happy!" They laughed, lightening the mood. "How's Carter dealing with all of this? He and Bradley were close."

Riley looked off toward the parking lot, where some students were clustered together talking. "Carter is suffering. He really misses his father. And a couple of times —"

"What?"

Riley shrugged. "Nothing. It's just something his teacher said."

"What?" Tamia pressed.

"Well, his teacher heard him talking to himself."

"What's wrong with that? A lot of people talk to themselves."

"That's what I told her. But then she said she heard it again and she asked him who he was talking to and he said his father."

"That's normal. It's just his way of coping with losing Bradley. It's good that he feels comfortable doing it."

"Tamia, the teacher said that she heard a response. She heard a male's voice that wasn't Carter's."

"Maybe it was another student."

Riley shook her head. "They're all four and their voices haven't started changing yet. She heard something and she swears it was Bradley. Do you believe that, Tamia? Carter was talking to his father. His dead father."

chapter FOUR

Riley hugged Brie to her chest and gently bussed her cheek
while inhaling her sweet baby smell. "You're so precious, my little
boo-boo." Brie gave her mother a sleepy grin in response. "I know
you had a long day, sweetie." Riley kissed the top of her daughter's head before placing her in her crib. Two minutes before, she
had hugged Carter good night. She peeked over at him, sleeping
peacefully. After Bradley's death he'd started having nightmares
and she had moved him into his sister's room. He had been sleeping quietly ever since. Turning off the light she tiptoed to her
bedroom.

She mentally ran through tomorrow's to-do list as she undressed. "Not too busy," she muttered to herself once she had com-
pleted the list. "Thank goodness tomorrow is Saturday. It's been
a long week." There had been a field trip to the world-renowned
Georgia Aquarium, the creating of tests, and having to play substi-
tute cheerleading coach while the regular coach honeymooned in
Aruba.

Naked, she strutted to her full-length mirror and studied her
body. Her eyes fell on the Jell-O-like cellulite and the slight
paunch that made her stomach look like she had swallowed an

oversize grapefruit. Bradley's taunts about her body jabbed at her like cactus needles.

"Screw you. So what if my body isn't perfect? Other men will want and appreciate me." She reached for her nightgown and had it over her head before she pulled it off and tossed it to the floor. "Hell, this is my house, I love my freaking body, and I can walk around naked if I want to." She lightly ran her fingers over her body. "See that, Bradley, I'm walking around with no clothes on and you can't tell me to get dressed. I bet it's driving you crazy. You can't do anything to me anymore," she said to her reflection before sticking out her tongue and swaggering downstairs to the living room. She made a quick detour to the kitchen for a snack.

Riley settled on the couch and pulled a thin blanket around her naked body. On an end table sat a bag of Chee-tos and a glass of red wine. Her feet were tucked comfortably beneath her and the lights were dim. "This feels so luscious," she murmured before snuggling under the blanket.

The only noises that cracked the silence were the classroom-trained voices of the news anchors. Their well-modulated tones didn't miss a beat as they delivered the evening news to the Atlanta audience. Riley nibbled on Chee-tos and sipped wine as she watched a group of people cheer on the forty-something blond reporter who was kissing a hundred-pound-plus pig on its snout. The absurdity of it made her talk to the TV.

"Charity shmarity, you won't catch me kissing a filthy pig. Contrary to popular belief, pigs are not the love choice for all southerners," she said, disgusted by the news. Every year it climbed another notch higher on her tacky scale.

Riley snickered to herself. "They only do stuff like that in Alabama; it's a state law!" she sputtered, then laughed uproariously at her joke. If she hadn't been holding the wineglass, she would've slapped her knee in amusement. She had laughed more in the six weeks since Bradley's death than she had in years.

Suddenly her right hand began to tingle and she absentmindedly rubbed it. A ribbon of heat blew over her face. *I'm too young to be having hot flashes.* She shrugged the blanket off, exposing her naked body. Wisps of fire danced over her breasts and she gasped in confusion and looked wildly around. "What the—?" Her bewilderment turned to desire as the wisps began to feel like a dozen hands caressing her. *This isn't normal,* her brain screamed. *It's not natural.* The sensation went to the top of her head and stopped at the tip of her toes, making her feel as though she was getting a full-body massage by six different people. Every inch of her body tingled.

All of a sudden a strip of heat began stroking the inside of her thighs and Riley's mouth dropped open with terror. It lazily inched up to her pussy, where it halted and curled against her skin.

"What's going on?" she shrieked as she tried swatting at the unseen force. When that didn't work she tried rubbing it away. "Just stop," she begged. "Please stop," she cried while frantically patting her leg. "Get away!" She backed up against the couch while clutching the blanket to her breasts, praying that the force would go away, but it didn't.

Instead, the blanket was tugged from her grasp and Riley watched while it floated through the air and landed on the floor. A gentle nudge forced her onto her back. She squeezed her eyes shut hoping that it would make whatever had taken control of her body go away.

It didn't, but a strip of air stroked her cheek as if trying to reassure her that everything would be okay. The tenderness coaxed her eyes open, but she let out a cry of frustration when she saw the empty room. "What is really going on here?" she whispered.

Her question went unanswered. Ribbons of heat began to dance over her cheeks. They cupped her face as wisps of air stroked her mouth. She tentatively puckered her lips. A soft gasp of surprise escaped her when a pair of full lips pressed against hers; she cautiously relaxed her mouth and her unseen lover increased its force until it had Riley eagerly returning its kisses.

A gentle pressure on her mouth eased her lips open and her lover's tongue glided in. Riley reeled back with surprise, and looked wildly around. She was all alone. It felt like she was kissing a real man.

The band of hot air crept down her stomach and breezed over her moist folds then snaked into her pussy. "What the hell?" she muttered. Riley squeezed her eyes and legs shut but the sensation continued. *This is so not natural!* The sliver of heat slowly brushed over her clit as though tasting it for the first time. Riley let out a low groan as she dropped her legs open and began moving her hips. Perspiration glistened on her body. Her lover began lapping at her clit as if it was a juicy mango.

She automatically reached down to cup a head, but all she felt was air and she groaned in frustration. She grabbed a couch pillow instead and held on for life as her climax built. Her body jerked as the explosion took her to the heavens and made her see stars. Wrapping her arms around her hot and sweaty body, she let out loud, heavy sobs of relief. She hadn't had a climax that powerful in years. Bradley's idea of making love was to treat her as though she was a come collector.

"Did you enjoy that?"

Riley's eyes snapped open. She looked up to see Bradley

standing over her. *I must be having an orgasm-induced hallucination,* she thought, then smiled serenely to herself before closing her eyes again. She opened them two seconds later to find her late husband still in front of her, grinning. She froze, too scared to scream.

"Hi, Ri Ri," he said with a grin. Riley gasped. He hadn't called her that in years. Just a couple of months ago, his words of choice were *cunt, stupid bitch,* or *worthless bitch,* depending on his mood.

"Bradley!" Riley finally managed. She rubbed her eyes.

"Yeah, it's me. You're not going crazy, beautiful," he said playfully and Riley blinked. "I'm glad you enjoyed our lovemaking."

Beautiful? "Bradley? That was you? You did that to me?"

Bradley nodded. "I did. It was lovely. Wasn't it?" He winked.

Riley snatched up the blanket and wrapped it around her nakedness. "Bradley?"

"Yep!" he teased, noticing her modesty but ignoring it.

"What are you doing here? We buried you. You're *dead*!"

Her husband grinned. "According to the laws of *this* side, I am dead, but on the *other* side, I'm a newborn. I've been reborn!" he announced. His voice echoed softly, as though he was talking from the bottom of a well.

Riley watched him, her eyes wide. He hovered a couple of inches off the floor, looking almost like the Bradley she had fallen in love with years before. Instead of his hazel eyes, a soft golden glow shined where his eyes should've been. He shimmered as though he had been sprinkled with diamond dust. Being semi-transparent, Riley was able to make out only his clothes, the same ones he had been buried in. When the sudden realization came that she was talking to a ghost, she pressed herself against the couch, too terrified to run or scream.

"Oh my God! Oh my God!" she chanted repeatedly. "You're dead, you're not supposed to be here."

"Oh, I am supposed to be here," Bradley answered and smiled indulgently. "I'm back, Riley, and I want us to be together. I want us to be a family again."

chapter FIVE

A huge grin covered Riley's face as she stepped out of the bathroom and stood at the threshold of her room. Rose petals carpeted her bedroom floor, Chrisette Michele's throaty voice filled the air, and a bottle of wine surrounded by chocolate-covered strawberries sat on the nightstand. Riley sauntered lazily across the room, stopping occasionally to caress the rose petals with her feet before sliding into bed.

Bradley hovered above her, changing colors to the beat of the song. It was like watching her own personal laser light show. Riley smiled up at him. "This reminds me of when we were dating. You were so romantic. Buying me things, pampering me and bathing me." She giggled softly.

After the initial shock, she'd begun to love Bradley's visits; it was like a second honeymoon. For the past month he had been visiting her nightly. Lovemaking wasn't always on the agenda. Sometimes they'd spend hours just talking and rediscovering each other. Riley would sit on the bed with Bradley next to her. Depending on his mood, he showed up as either a bouncing golden orb or the semitransparent version of himself. With their favorite music acting as a backdrop, they revealed things about themselves that they hadn't dared divulge while they were married. Riley had fallen in love with him all over again.

Bradley lay next to her on the bed, nodding his head in time to the music. "I love you," Riley said and meant it.

Bradley turned to her and studied her eyes as if searching for the truth before answering. "I know you do, I can see it all over your face. I love you too."

"May I ask you something?"

"Of course you may."

She glanced into his eye sockets and involuntarily shuddered, still not used to the yellow glow where his hazel eyes used to be. Sometimes he reminded her of a jack-o'-lantern. "I hate to bring this up—it really seems stupid—but I have to know."

"Just ask me. You don't have to be uncomfortable, we're lovers. Better than that," he decided, "we're friends, and friends are always comfortable around each other, aren't they? And they always say what's on their minds," he said with a grin, exposing a ring of yellow.

"Did you really hate me that much?"

"What do you mean?" Bradley asked, feigning ignorance.

"I read your blog," Riley admitted. "It made me ill. I couldn't believe you felt that way about me. Every entry was filled with hate."

"That's not true," Bradley said soothingly. "You read it wrong."

"You called me a 'silly cunt, whose only purpose on earth was to be an incubator for my son,'" she said, quoting him verbatim.

"That was a joke. The whole blog was a joke. I was really hoping that a literary agent would find it and offer me a book deal. You know how they are always on the lookout for fresh new voices. That's all I was doing. I guess I should've told you. I didn't want you to laugh at my dreams," he admitted sheepishly.

I was so messed up that if he had told me my shit smelled like chocolate, I would've believed him. Riley shoved the thought away. "I wouldn't have laughed. I would've supported you," she said earnestly.

"Thanks. I know that now."

"I wish that I could tell everybody about us."

Bradley chuckled. "I do too, baby, but how soon after you start talking do you think they'll take the kids away from you and lock you up?"

Riley sighed. "I know. You're my little secret. I wish I could hold you again." She had been thinking about how nice it would be to wrap her arms around her husband and feel his warm body next to hers.

Bradley thought for a moment before answering. "Why don't you use one of your body-lounger pillows and imagine that it's me?"

Riley glanced at the extra-long pillow, which wasn't as tall as Bradley nor as firm. "I don't think that it'll work," she protested.

"Just try," Bradley coaxed.

Riley shrugged before picking up the pillow. "I guess this is my own version of a blow-up doll," she muttered. Closing her eyes she drew the pillow to her breast and gave it a hard squeeze.

"Harder!"

Riley's eyes flew open. Bradley's gauzy face was plastered on the pillow. She let out a howl of laughter.

"Just pretend it's me."

Riley's face reddened. "I can't. I'm not going to *do* a pillow." A feathery wisp of air stroked her cheek.

"Come on, you want to, I can see it in your face." Riley glanced at the door. Ever since Bradley had returned, she had put a lock on it. Bradley saw the direction of her gaze. "It's locked."

"I don't know. I'll feel a little weird."

"What's so weird about it? Remember when we first started dating, and you insisted that we wait to get to know each other before you gave me some, so all we did was dry-hump each other until you decided to make love to me? It'll be like that."

"I don't know . . ."

"Just put the pillow between your legs. And see, my face is still here."

Riley chuckled nervously. "Yeah. I see."

"Now start moving," Bradley instructed.

"Bradley!" she protested but slipped the pillow between her legs anyway.

"Come on."

Riley grasped the pillow and tentatively moved her hips.

"That's it," Bradley encouraged. "Move that ass a little more!"

"I'm moving," Riley answered self-consciously. *What the hell am I doing?*

"Maybe you need a little help," Bradley whispered right before curls of air repeatedly stroked her nipples. Riley groaned softly. Her hips moved faster.

"Fuck that pillow like it's me!"

The soft cotton swiped over Riley's clit, barely kissing it. "This isn't working." She clutched the feathery-soft pillow and threw it across the room. Her hand quickly took its place.

"Aww, you got tired of me so quickly," Bradley quipped. He hovered over her, occasionally swiping himself across her stomach.

"No, I didn't," Riley denied as her fingers furiously moved in her soft folds. "I can't help it. I just want to come."

"Is that all?" Bradley chuckled. "I'll be glad to accommodate you."

"Uh-uh, I'm almost done."

"Let me do it, please?" Riley reluctantly stopped her self-love session. "Just lie back and enjoy it. You look so hot with your legs spread wide open and your skin glistening as though you just finished making love," he said while admiring his wife.

"I know something that'll make me even hotter."

"What?"

"If you do what you promised to do," Riley said tightly. Bradley chuckled. "There's nothing funny about this. Either you finish it or I will!"

"Feisty! Feisty!"

"Fuck me! Fuck me!"

"I'm going to make this quick and dirty," Bradley promised.

Ribbons of heat slowly traveled up her legs to her pussy. Riley moaned. Dozens of bands of heat zoomed over her cunt, zigzagging over it and sending Riley into a frenzy. She gasped for air as her hips moved in ways she didn't even know they could. Her body had begun to tingle, signaling that her orgasm was close, when she froze. Her mouth gaped open.

"What's happening?" she croaked in surprise.

"I'm fucking you," Bradley said, bemused by her astonishment, "just like you told me to."

"You have a dick. You didn't tell me that you had a dick," she murmured. Bradley's hardness slipped in and out of her, and she eagerly moved her hips, matching his every thrust.

The tingling sensation returned; Riley closed her eyes as a jolt of passion shot through her then the aftershocks of her climax rippled over her. After catching her breath, Riley looked at Bradley. "I don't ever want this to end. Don't you ever leave me."

chapter SIX

The bell rang, signaling the end of the day, and before Riley could say good-bye, the students were running out of the room faster than a group of paparazzi trying to get a crotch shot of a celebrity. "Well, good-bye to you too," Riley muttered after the last student had emptied the classroom. She got up and closed the door. "Finally, peace and quiet." She sighed as she returned to her desk chair and stretched her feet in front of her. Other than her drive to and from work, the patch of time after the students left was the only time she had to herself. "Maybe I should schedule that trip to Brazil. I need a break." A two-inch stack of tests lay in front of her, requiring her attention. But her gaze moved to the classroom. It looked worse than a first-grader's science project that had gone wrong. Candy wrappers, broken pencils, and balled-up paper littered the floor. And suspiciously wet, sticky spots of brown goo spotted the third row. "I'm going to leave the cleaning for the janitor. I'm not in the mood for it today."

She grabbed the stack of papers and her red pen and started reviewing the tests. Halfway through the pile she felt a puff of air on her leg. She brushed it with her left foot. It returned a second time, this time more persistent. "Oh my God! A bug!" she screamed as she pulled her legs up. After a quick examination and finding them bug free, she tentatively lowered her legs. Several minutes later the sensation returned as it tickled its way up her thighs. Her breathing quickened. "Bradley? Bradley is that you?" He pinched her in response and she laughed. "What are you doing here? You've never visited me at work."

Bradley instantly materialized. Riley gasped; no matter how many times he did it, she would never get used to his sudden appearances. "I was in the mood for some afternoon delight."

"Bradley!" Riley gushed. Even when he was alive he never ever showed up at her job for a quickie. She darted a look toward the door. "I guess I should lock it."

"Why? Let's be daring, it'll add to the excitement."

Riley raised her eyebrows. "I wouldn't want any kids to walk in on us."

Bradley sniffed. "Those *kids* see much more explicit shit on TV than what they'll see with us."

"Still." Riley pushed herself out of her chair and was midway up when she felt pressure on her shoulders, forcing her down. "What's wrong? What are you doing?"

"I told you that I didn't want the door locked," Bradley answered. "And it won't get locked," he said firmly.

"But—"

Bradley picked her up and placed her on top of the desk. He pushed her forward so that the stack of tests served as cushions for her elbows and her butt pointed right at him. "Lovely. I've always loved your ass," he drawled while using one finger to keep her in place.

"Bradley, let me go," Riley protested as she struggled against him.

"You're good by asking me nicely. Ask me more nicely and I'll consider it," he teased.

"Bradley," Riley hissed, too afraid to scream. She didn't need a colleague to run to her rescue.

"Come on, Ri Ri, you know the saying: You can always catch more bees with honey than with vinegar."

Riley looked over her shoulder. "I'm not trying to catch any insects. I want to get up!"

Bradley chuckled gleefully. "You've turned feisty. I like it, I surely do." He absentmindedly stroked her back. "Would you like it if I took you right here? Right now? In this position?"

"Bradley, please don't," Riley begged softly. "Let's wait until I get home, that way we'll be uninterrupted."

Bradley stretched his neck, twisting it around so that he could look her in the eyes. "No one will walk in on us. I bet everybody is gone. Would you like me to double-check? I can take attendance. Would that make you feel more comfortable?" Bradley asked, his voice mocking.

"Would you just let me up?"

Suddenly Riley felt a band of tightness around her waist and felt herself being lifted and flipped over as though she was an IHOP breakfast special. This time she screamed, not caring who might hear her.

In the blink of an eye, Bradley darkened, had Riley's dress tangled around her waist, her panties bunched on the floor, and her legs hugging his waist. She happened to glance down and she gasped at what she saw. *I'm in the air. I'm floating. I'm going to fucking fall.* Her stomach clenched, then she began struggling to get her feet back on solid ground. Bradley banded his hands around her waist and whispered in her ear, "Save your strength; you'll need it."

"I don't want to fall!" Riley protested while looking fearfully toward the floor. *We have to be at least ten feet high.*

Riley let out a yelp of fear when Bradley cupped her behind. The panoramic view of the classroom went unappreciated when she howled in objection as he effortlessly lifted her over his head. She was so high that the top of her head scraped the ceiling. "Bradley," she squeaked.

"I'll have you screaming my name," he promised.

"Yeah, with fear. Let me down," Riley insisted.

"I'll let you down after I do this." A strip of warm air breezed over her behind before teasing her clit.

Riley moaned and pressed her hands against the ceiling while wisps of warm air stroked her pussy. Her hips moved languorously. "Oh, Bradley," she groaned, enjoying her aerial lovemaking session. The orgasm sneaked up on her, and its intensity took her by surprise. Riley gulped air as relief electrified her body. Suddenly she went limp and began falling toward the floor. Her eyes widened with comprehension and her body went cold. She began flailing her arms and legs.

Bradley watched her fall and chuckled at her fear. "I was joking." He swooped down, scooped her up an instant before she would've hit desks, and raced back to the ceiling. He snaked his arms around her waist and plunged into her; Riley swooned. Bradley leisurely moved her hips back and forth, her earlier scare forgotten, as she rode his cock. She looked at him through unfocused eyes. "What kind of spell do you have over me?"

Bradley chuckled. "You wouldn't believe me if I told you." He zoomed toward the ceiling and looped through the air, never once missing a stroke. The air kissing her skin, Bradley's slow strokes, and flying over her classroom caused a sensation overload. Riley sobbed and shook as an otherworldly orgasm took over her body.

Tamia pushed open the door. "Hey, girl—" She stopped mid-step and the blood plummeted from her face at the sight before her. Tamia fell against the door and her mouth gaped open and closed with disbelief. Suspended in midair was Riley, with her head thrown back and hips pumping back and forth. Her sister's face glistened and shimmered with ecstasy as she wept. The scent of sex blanketed the room, making it feel more like a strip joint than a middle school classroom. Tamia watched the scene in horror and her eyes stretched to the size of doorknobs when she realized that something was observing her. Eyes, the color of blood, bouncing above Riley's head blinked at her as they dispassionately studied her.

"Oh my God. What the hell is going on here?" Tamia asked, her face ashen and her voice shaking.

"I'm in love with him . . . still in love," Riley admitted.

Tamia's eyes were wide with horror. "He's a ghost, a ghost," she hissed. "How can this be possible?"

"It's possible."

"Tell me why you're doing this. I remember you telling me how he used to beat you. Not only is this sick . . . it's crazy."

"It's not sick and I'm not sick. It's love. He's changed. He's a million times better than what he was like when he was alive. It's like he's been changed into a saint."

"What? Bradley's a saint now? Saint fucking Bradley, so he's right up there with Saint Francis of Assisi?" Tamia began laughing hysterically.

"Stop it! That's why I didn't want to tell you. Or tell anybody. I knew that you'd all call me crazy, but I'm not."

"You're not crazy, I know you're not," Tamia stated. "But this situation is not only crazy, it's so unfuckinbelievable and scary. If I hadn't seen it with my own two eyes, I wouldn't have believed it. Okay, so you told me that Carter was talking to his dad. Strange, hell, it's bizarre, and I admit it gave me the heebie-jeebies. But this thing you and Bradley have going on, his making love to you, if that's what you want to call it, and his having changed, it's bullshit!"

"Would you stop saying that!"

"You listen to me!" Tamia ordered. "That thing is no saint. Eventually you're gonna piss him off and he's gonna turn on you and it's gonna get ugly . . . really ugly," Tamia said somberly.

"You're blowing everything out of proportion. Bradley isn't like that anymore. He can control his temper," she argued. "He's wonderful."

"So what are you going to do? You can't spend the rest of your life with a ghost."

"Why can't I? I don't see anything wrong with that. He provides all my needs. Mentally, physically, and spi—"

"Don't you dare say spiritually," Tamia shot at her.

"Well, it's true. He's a part of me and I'm a part of him. He's probably in the room right now. He can do that, you know, he can be in the room with me and I won't know it unless he makes his presence known."

"If y'all are such a part of each other, shouldn't you be able to sense his presence?"

"I guess," Riley answered, doubt flickering in her eyes. "But it doesn't work like that." She glanced up toward the ceiling. "Right, baby, tell Tamia that it doesn't work like that."

Tamia shrank against her chair. "Don't you dare summon that demon here!" she ordered in a quavering voice, her previous bravado gone.

"I'm sorry. I didn't mean to scare you."

"Yeah, well, this stuff just creeps me out. What are you gonna do? Are you really gonna spend the rest of your life with a ghost?" Riley opened her mouth to respond, but Tamia cut her off. "I want you to think before you answer my question. Are you going to spend the rest of your life living with a ghost?" she asked, emphasizing each word. "Now you may answer."

chapter SEVEN

Riley confidently moved around her kitchen as she gathered the ingredients for homemade brownies. Bradley's visits had continued, leaving Riley more in love with him than ever. She smiled down at Carter. Since Bradley's death, he rarely let her leave his sight. "Wanna help?"

"Okay," he answered eagerly. He loved watching his mom mix the thick gooey batter, but he loved licking the chocolate-covered mixing spoon even more.

"Well, come on then." Riley grinned at her firstborn.

They worked together silently, talking only when Riley gave him instructions.

Now is a good time. "You wanna lick the spoon?" Riley asked Carter.

Carter snatched the spoon from his mother's hand and touched it to the tip of his tongue. She could tell as soon as the sugar hit him; he began bouncing around like a two-dollar rubber ball.

"So do you miss your father?" she asked casually.

"Nope!"

"You don't? Why not?"

"Because," he said with a giggle. He looked up at her slyly.

The hairs on the back of her neck stood up. "Carter Bradley Tyson, what are you hiding?"

"Nothing!" he protested.

"Carter!" she said in a voice that Carter knew meant he had better start talking.

"He told me not to tell. He said that if I did, people would call me a liar. And I'm not a liar, Mommy."

Riley breathed deeply. "Your father told you not to say what?"

"That we talk," he confessed.

Shocked, Riley leaned against the kitchen counter. *So it's true. His teacher was right.* "What do you talk about?" she asked quietly.

"Everything. We talk about everything. How I'm doing in school. How Brie's doing. He said that he visited her, but she's too little to understand."

Riley gripped the edge of the countertop. "Go on," she encouraged.

"He's a lot nicer now."

"Really? Like how? What does he do?" Riley eased over to the refrigerator for a bottled water. She took a long sip.

Carter thought for a moment before answering. "Well, he doesn't yell like he used too and that's good because when he yelled, my stomach felt like somebody was twisting it. And he said he was sorry for hitting you."

"That's nice," she said calmly then took another gulp of water. "What else?"

"And he picks me up."

The plastic water bottle almost slipped from Riley's hands. She set it on the counter. "He picks you up?" she asked, her voice shrill.

"Yeah. One time late at night, while you were sleeping, he carried me to the kitchen and we had cookies and milk," Carter answered, oblivious to his mother's fear.

"He carried you to the kitchen and you guys ate?"

Carter grinned sheepishly. "Well, I'm the one who ate, he watched. Then he carried me back to bed." He set down the now chocolate-free mixing spoon.

Riley closed her eyes then slowly reopened them. Her hands were shaking; she stuck them behind her back to hide them from Carter. "So does your father visit you anywhere else?"

"Uh-huh. He's everywhere."

Riley twisted her hands together. "Like where?" she asked, forcing herself to keep her voice light.

"He visits me at school, he visits me when I'm playing outside, and once he even came to see me while you were driving me to school."

Riley's eyes widened. "How did he do that, I can see—I mean I *can't* see how he did that without me seeing him."

Carter giggled. "He hid under the seat and kept tickling me. I couldn't stop laughing. I told you he was a lot funnier now."

Riley suddenly remembered driving Carter to school and smiling to herself because he was in such a good mood. *I didn't know that Bradley was the source.* She busied herself with putting the brownies in the oven. "So you and your father have a good time together, huh?" she called over her shoulder.

"We do! He's the best father."

"Hmmm, have you told anybody else that you see your father?"

Carter looked at her oddly. "No, just you. Remember, I told you, he made me promise not to tell." Suddenly Carter's face crumpled. "Now he's going to be mad at me," he said between whimpers.

Riley scooted over to Carter and pulled him into an embrace. "No he won't. He won't know."

Carter sniffled. "Yeah he will. He said that he knows everything and sees everything. He said that he's just like Santa Claus."

Riley's arms tightened around her son. "No he isn't," she reassured him, but her eyes quickly scanned the kitchen looking for any sign of Bradley. "You did the right thing when you told me. I'm sure that he wanted you to."

Carter pulled away from his mother and looked up at her with tear-stained eyes. "You sure?"

"I am."

Carter swiped a hand over his eyes. "Good. And you know what else he said?" Carter asked, happy again.

"What, baby?"

"He told me that he's always going to be my daddy, no matter what. He said that I'll never ever have another daddy. He said he'll be mine forever and ever," he chanted in a singsong voice. "Forever and ever."

Riley stared at her son in shock.

Riley sat up on the bed and admired the show. She and Bradley had made love. Bradley split himself into dozens of golf ball–size balls and bounced off the walls, moving so fast that he looked like white streaks. "Do you have something you want to tell me?" he asked and she jumped. It sounded as though he was sitting right next to her.

"Ummm, no." It had been a week since Carter had confided in her about Bradley and she hadn't found the right time to talk to him about it.

"You sure?" Six orbs of light bounced in front of her; they moved erratically around her. Transfixed, Riley couldn't breathe when one of the orbs broke away from the group and began caressing her cheek. "You wouldn't keep secrets from me, would you?" Bradley murmured. Frozen with a combination of fear and fascination, Riley managed to shake her head no. "Good, because that would mean you didn't love me anymore." Suddenly Riley's hand shot up to her face; the orb had turned into a white ball of heat plastered to her cheek, scorching it.

"Bradley!" she screamed in pain. "You're hurting me . . . you're burning me. Stop it!"

Before she could blink, the orb's temperature had dropped, leaving behind an inch-long blister. "I'm sorry," Bradley soothed. "I was sensing that everything wasn't copacetic and it irked me. And you know all I want to do is make you happy. Here, let me make it up to you."

Riley reached toward her face but before she could touch it, Bradley stopped her. "I said I'll take care of it," he said firmly before swiping across her face, instantly healing her wound. Then he changed into a globe the size of a beach ball and floated lazily in front of her.

Riley lifted her hand to touch her face, but dropped it after she felt Bradley zip by. She eyed him with distrust. "Carter told me that you visit him," she said softly.

"Is that all? He's my son."

"True, but your visits can be confusing and very scary. He's still a little boy."

Suddenly Bradley's colors dimmed. "I would never do anything to hurt my son."

"I'm not saying that you would," Riley said quickly. "I would prefer that you not visit him. He's way too young to comprehend what's really going on."

"Oh, but you do?" Bradley barked.

Riley's stomach twisted with fear. "I don't have any idea what's going on," Riley sputtered, "but I can imagine how scary this is for a little boy, and then for you to say that you'll be his daddy forever, that just sets up false expectations."

"So now you're calling me a liar."

"I'm not, I'm not. I'm sure your intentions are true, but you can't be around forever. That doesn't make sense."

Bradley let out a loud laugh that seemed to shake the roof and Riley covered her ears. "So now she's calling me crazy," he muttered to himself. "I wonder if a crazy person would do this?" Riley let out a horrified gasp as her dresser turned upside down, all her clothes and everything from the dresser top tumbling to the floor.

"Stop it!"

"Shhh, or the kids will hear you," Bradley mocked.

"I wasn't trying to insinuate anything. I don't want Carter to get hurt," she said, her tone placating. "I know that you're trying to do what's best for the family."

Bradley changed to a fiery red. "And you'd better remember that." A blink later he was gauzy white. "I want you to take a trip with me. I think you'll love it. It'll be like a second honeymoon." Bradley grinned mysteriously. Riley looked down to find her hands clutching the blankets.

chapter EIGHT

Riley laid her copy of Zora Neale Hurston's collection of short stories on her nightstand. Brie and Carter were tucked in bed. "One more day until the weekend," she muttered.

She snuggled under a thin blanket, savoring the coolness on her skin. Moments later her eyes drifted closed, taking her to a place where she swam in turquoise-colored water and frolicked on the white-sand beaches of Mexico.

The balmy air kissed her skin and the powdery fine sand felt like silk under her feet. Riley alternated between skipping and running across the beach, going so fast that she thought she was flying.

Articles of her clothing began to disappear with every mile she raced over. Soon she zoomed, naked, along the beach. She continued to run for what felt like miles.

Suddenly she froze; something had her feet. For a second she wobbled, like a life-size Bobble Head figurine, before she fell facedown in the sand. Riley struggled to get up, but the harder she thrashed about, the deeper she went. I'm digging my own grave, Riley frantically thought. The sand began to fill every one of her orifices. It clogged her throat, coated her eyes, plugged her ears, and scratched her naked body. A few minutes before, the sand that was so silky was now as heavy as concrete, Riley thought hysterically as she fell.

Wake up! Wake up! she silently screamed into her pitch-black grave. Please let me wake up! She continued to fall through the dark hole with the sand cascading over her. It felt like the sand was scraping off her skin. *I'm going to die in my sleep.*

Oh, God, please wake me up. And just then, she abruptly stopped. Riley blindly reached out and felt solid ground. She hesitantly opened her eyes and looked around. Everything was so green and fresh-smelling and bright. Standing next to her was Bradley. Not the gauzy see-through version, but the flesh-and-bone solid one she had fallen in love with. "Bradley? Where am I?"

"You're in my world, baby, Lavastar, where your every wish is my command. Just tell me what you want and I'll make it happen."

Riley couldn't tear her eyes away from the scene in front of her. "Is this heaven?"

"Better," Bradley answered arrogantly. "This is my world, where everything and everybody is at your beck and call. You don't have to do anything."

Riley continued to stare in wonderment. "This is paradise," she murmured. "This is what I was dreaming about." Pristine white sand hugged an ocean of sparkling turquoise-colored water, palm trees performed a sensual dance, and the balmy air stroked her body. She glanced down, expecting to see her skin in shreds. Instead it was blemish free and rocking a tangerine-colored bikini. "Where did this come from?"

"It's a gift from me."

"What happened? I was asleep in bed. How did I get here? Am I still alive?"

Bradley reached for her hand. "Let's take a walk." Riley stuck her hand in his.

"Oh my God!" she exclaimed and Bradley winced. "I'm actually holding your hand." Her eyes teared up and she giggled. "I'm sorry. We haven't held hands since we were dating and now you're dead and we are. I never thought that I would be touching you again," she said tearfully.

Bradley squeezed her hand in response as she allowed herself to be led off the beach. After ten minutes of walking and talking, the lush plants were becoming scarce. Suddenly Riley looked up and came to a standstill, her heart leaping into her throat. "This cannot be real, it can't be real," she whispered, dumbfounded.

"Believe it. I told you it's my world and I can create whatever I want."

"Oh my God!"

"Don't say that!"

"What? Go—"

"Yes!" Bradley barked. He snatched his hand from hers. "Don't you ever say *His* name."

"I'm sorry. Where am I, Bradley, and why can't I say G—?"

Bradley smiled serenely. "I'll tell you everything, just be patient. Just for now know that you're in Lavastar. All this can be a little overwhelming. Just enjoy it for now." He grabbed her hand and grinned down at her. "Are you okay?" Riley nervously bit her lip before she nodded. "Good, let's go." They continued their stroll, Riley practically skipping.

Peeking out over the horizon was the Eiffel Tower. Riley turned to Bradley. "How did you do this? I've always wanted to visit Paris."

"I knew that, so I brought Paris to you. Welcome to Paris."

Riley flung herself into Bradley's arms. "I love you so much! You are just so wonderful. Thank you, thank you," she babbled, overcome with emotion.

Bradley leaned down and gently kissed her. "You deserve it. Let's go." Two minutes later they were seated at a table at an outdoor café. "What would you like to eat?" Riley glanced around, noticing that they were the only two people in the café and that there was no waitstaff. Bradley saw her look. "Don't worry, everything will be taken care of. Read the menu and tell me what you want."

"Okay, so you got the hookup with the chef?" Riley teased.

Bradley shrugged. "Sure, if that's what you want to call it. Just order."

Riley studied the menu before reciting her order. As soon as the last word was out of her mouth, her complete meal was in front of her. Her brow furrowed with confusion. "How did you do that?"

Bradley sighed as if bored. "I keep telling you that this is my world. You'll save yourself a lot of time by not asking me the same questions. I created everything that's here. The sooner you start believing it, the easier things will be."

Riley and Bradley spent hours traipsing through Paris as though they were honeymooners. While she noticed that the city was empty of people except for them, she kept silent. By the time they got to Bradley's house, a Spanish villa, the sun was high and bright in the sky, as though it was noon. Riley frowned. "What time is it? It seems like it should be dark by now or at least dusk?"

Bradley smiled benevolently before turning his face toward the sky. Moments later the sky turned silky black. Stars twinkled, crickets chirped, and a full moon shone down on them. Bradley placed a finger over Riley's lips. "It's my world," he said before Riley could comment.

She sat down at a table filled with succulent fruit: mangos, papayas, oranges. She suddenly realized that Bradley hadn't eaten anything in the time they had been together. "Aren't you hungry?"

"Hunger is something that happens in your world, not mine."

"But I was hungry. I ate that big dinner or lunch," she answered, feeling confused. "Anyway, I ate in Paris."

"Did you really eat or did you think you ate? And were you really hungry or were you simply eating out of habit and not need?"

"I don't know," she answered, and for the first time, she felt a sliver of fear run through her. "Where am I, Bradley? Really? Don't answer me with a riddle. I really want to know where I am. Is this hell?"

Bradley chuckled. "Baby, this is not hell. Why are you so insistent on calling paradise that? This is simply my world. I can't be more honest than that." He stroked her face and laughed softly. "If you were in hell, you would know it," he muttered.

"This whole thing scares me. It seems unnatural," she said while rubbing her arms. *At least this feels normal.*

Bradley gathered his wife to him and tenderly kissed her. "Does this feel unnatural?" A breathless Riley shook her head. "I want to make love to you."

The idea of hell and food was forgotten as Bradley nudged Riley and she found herself lying faceup on a king-size bed. She didn't bother to comment on the fact that the bed hadn't been there two seconds ago. Bradley laid down beside her and lovingly caressed her body. She glanced down to find all her clothes gone.

"Will we be making love while flying through the air?" Riley asked shakily, still nervous about being with Bradley.

"Not unless you want to," Bradley answered. "We can do whatever you want to, baby."

"Oh!" Riley uttered. Even while they were dating, Bradley was nice, but not this nice. "It's like I'm making love to you for the first time."

"But we make love all the time," Bradley said softly.

"Yeah, but it's not the same. This feels real; the times before didn't," she admitted.

"Really? I thought you enjoyed it. That's what your screams told me."

"I did enjoy it, but you were like my life-size dildo. I was able to come but something special was missing."

"Am I that something special?" Bradley murmured against her cheek.

Bradley rolled on top of her. "Don't move," Riley begged. "Let me touch you, feel you." Her hands roamed over Bradley's body, occasionally squeezing his butt, back, or thigh. She sighed happily. "This is what I'm talking about." She slowly stroked his cock, savoring it as though it was her first time seeing it.

"I guess you were right," he murmured in her ear as he parted her legs with his knee.

"What? I'm right in Bradley's world, how is that possible?" Riley joked.

"Don't get used to it," he said softly. "But you were right about making love. I feel like it's our first time."

Riley giggled girlishly. "Me too." Then she pulled his face toward hers and gently kissed his lips.

Bradley shuddered. "I haven't touched a woman—"

"Since you died," Riley finished for him then quickly averted her eyes.

"Look at me!" Bradley demanded. "I'm not dead, I'm reborn."

"Since you were reborn," Riley repeated. She reached between them and caressed his penis. "You've come back bigger and better than ever."

"Glad to hear it," Bradley quipped before slipping into her. Riley wrapped her legs around his waist. "I missed this." Bradley lazily moved as he savored her moistness. "You're juicy. Are you juicy for me?" Riley nodded as her hands ran up and down his muscular back. "Well, I feel flattered," Bradley said teasingly. "I guess I'd better take advantage of it." He grabbed her behind and gave it a quick squeeze before increasing his speed. Riley clung to him as he thrust into her. "Is this what you miss, baby?" Bradley asked.

"I do. I don't ever want this to end. You feel so good."

Bradley moaned. "Your pussy feels so good. I forgot how good you felt and I want to feel some more." Bradley stopped his movements and quickly moved into a position that he knew would bring Riley instant gratification. With one of Riley's legs hooked over his shoulder he slowly reentered her.

Riley inhaled softly. "You know this is my position?" she said, surprised; after they had gotten married, sex with Bradley was always about Bradley and he did nothing to satisfy her.

"I know; I want to make sure you're happy."

Riley grinned. "I'm delirious," she said then caressed his face while enjoying his long strokes. Moments later he hit her spot and Riley trembled with ecstasy. Through half-closed eyes she glanced up at her lover and immediately froze. Instead of Bradley's hazel eyes, a pair of blood red eyes were dispassionately watching her. Horrified, Riley snapped her eyes shut.

"What's wrong?" Bradley asked.

"Nothing," Riley whispered while keeping her eyes closed.

"Look at me," Bradley ordered. Riley took a deep breath before slowly opening her eyes. "What's wrong?"

Riley blinked. Bradley's eyes were hazel, a cool and calming hazel. "I thought I saw something," Riley said nervously. "I guess I was wrong."

"I need to take care of some things," he said abruptly. "I'll be back before you even miss me. See you." Bradley kissed her quickly on the shoulder before dissolving.

"What have I gotten myself into?" Exhausted, Riley fell into a deep sleep.

The next morning Riley stirred and lazily opened her eyes. Then she shot up in the bed. Bradley's house was gone and instead she was in a luxurious hotel room. The room's contemporary red, gray, and cream color palette startled her, since it was distinctly different from Bradley's original color scheme of all black.

She yelled for Bradley and he instantly materialized at her side. "Where am I?"

Bradley nuzzled her neck. "You'd get an F in geography." He gestured toward the window. "Don't you recognize those mountains, that lake?"

Riley frowned, then smiled excitedly. "We're in Switzerland and those are the Swiss Alps." She stood transfixed at the window; moments later she shook her head and turned to Bradley. "Is this really Switzerland or just your world?"

"What do you think?"

"I think I really need to get back home. I'm sure Brie and Carter are missing me."

"They're fine, I've been checking on them. Tamia is watching them."

"How? She doesn't know that I'm gone. I really need to go," she insisted.

"They're fine."

"How do you know?" Riley persisted.

Bradley sighed. "Come on. I'll show you." Before she could say anything, Bradley grabbed her hand and they flew between worlds. What seemed like seconds later, she and Bradley were hovering over Brie's bed. She was snuggled with her teddy bear. "I told you. Check out my son." Two heartbeats later they were looking down on Carter, who was in dreamland as well. Riley visibly relaxed. "Did you enjoy your visit?" Bradley asked as soon as they returned to Lavastar.

"I did. Thanks for putting my mind at ease. I can't wait to get back home. It's nice here and everything, but I want to be back with my family."

"I'm your family."

"I know you are, silly," Riley said with a laugh. "But I'm talking about my babies and my sister. I miss them so much."

"But you just saw that the kids are doing fine."

"Yes, I did," Riley said slowly. "But that was a two-second visit. I want to be with my kids all the time. Not doing fly-by check-ins like I'm some type of bargain-basement nanny."

"Tamia will take care of them. This is probably the only chance she'll have at being a mommy," Bradley said with a sneer.

Riley's stomach began to churn with fear. "This has been nice, Bradley, but I want to go home. Now!"

Bradley chuckled. "You haven't figured it out yet, have you?" Riley fearfully shook her head. "You're not leaving. You're here forever."

Riley gasped. "You can't do this, Bradley."

"Sure I can," he said smugly. "And I did. Welcome home, Riley. You're not going anywhere. You're staying here with me. Forever!"

chapter NINE

Riley glared at Bradley, which she had been doing ever since he had announced that she was a prisoner in his world.

"I used to love it when you pouted," Bradley taunted. "I thought it was so cute."

Riley turned her back to him and stared out at the turquoise-colored water. "I guess it's not cute anymore, huh?" she called over her shoulder.

"What do you think?"

Riley shrugged and continued to gaze at the water as though it was TV. Suddenly her mouth dropped open. The calming blue-green water was slowly being replaced by thick blood-red goop. Leaning forward in shock she watched as man-size fish popped to the top of the tarlike substance and floated in the blood bath. Turning slowly she found Bradley intently watching her, a smirk on his face. "What the hell are you?"

"I'm Bradley," he answered. "I'm the same person you married, I'm the same person who was reborn, and I'm the same person who brought you here."

Riley stood up and faced him. "Well, I don't like you. You're a bully, Bradley, a mean-spirited bully."

"I guess that's one way to look at me," he said, his voice

thoughtful. "But I consider myself a person who gets what he wants. I've always been like that, remember?" He inched closer to Riley. "You think I didn't know that your sister didn't want me to marry you?" Riley shook her head. "Oh, I knew. But I married you just to spite her."

"What?" Riley stumbled back in surprise. "What did you say?"

"Yeah. You were fine and everything. But nobody looks down on me and thinks they're better than I am. So I married you to prove that I'm just as good, if not better, than she is."

"So you married me to prove a point?" she asked, her voice incredulous. "So you didn't love me?"

"You were cool, but there were so many different women for me to fuck, why settle for one?"

"Asshole!" All of a sudden the lush palm trees shriveled into little black bushes, the pristine white sand turned into bowling-ball-size boulders, and the tranquil blue sky shattered, exposing a urine-colored sky filled with hundreds of black clouds. Riley watched with terror-filled eyes as pieces of the clouds broke apart and morphed into spirits. Soon the sky was filled with thousands of demons, hissing and hovering above her.

"What are those?" Riley croaked as she clamped her hands over her ears. They sounded like a million angry bees.

"That's my army," Bradley proudly announced, "and it's growing by leaps and bounds. Who would've thought that I was military material?" He gave a self-deprecating smile. "Not me."

"Why are they here?" She couldn't help it; she sneaked another look at them. Some were eyeing her with interest, but the majority were studying her as lions do their prey. She knew without a doubt that she was minutes away from her own death.

"I ordered them here. I want them to know their charge. They're going to be my eyes and ears whenever I have to run out," he said nonchalantly.

"Where am I! Where am I," she whimpered.

Bradley dissolved into a fine mist and wove himself seductively over Riley. "You're here, Riley . . . in my world," he taunted. "And you aren't leaving, so make yourself comfortable," he ordered before disappearing.

Riley looked up to find that paradise had been restored. She blinked. "It can't be." She squinted. "Oh my God!" she exclaimed, forgetting Bradley's order that she not voice His name. Off in the distance was a silhouette of a house that looked exactly like hers. She took off across the beach, trudging in the sand. "He's letting me go. He's letting me go home to my babies," she sang as she hurried to the house.

A smile the size of the Atlantic Ocean filled her face as she ran to the front door. "I'm home!" Her heart soared as she pushed it open. She raced to the living room and came to a quick stop. A huge crater-size hole filled with rattlesnakes sat where her living oom used to be.

She sobbed loudly before dropping to her knees. "You crazy bastard!" she shouted. Bradley's laughter reverberated throughout the house. She covered her ears as she sank to the floor. "You're evil, you're evil," she repeated.

"Come on," Bradley cajoled. "Stop being so dramatic."

Riley whirled around and found Bradley standing behind her. "What do you want with me?"

Riley, having lost track of the time, sat on the veranda watching the scenery. So far she had seen the great pyramids of Egypt, Niagara

Falls, the Taj Mahal, and Petra. She didn't know if she had been sitting for two hours, two days, or two weeks. Occasionally she'd spy one of Bradley's soldiers in the distance, watching her. She wasn't sure if he was supposed to be guarding her or if he watched her out of curiosity. Either way she didn't care. Until she was back home with her kids, nothing mattered to her anymore.

Bradley materialized at her side. "Enjoying the view?" he asked with a chuckle.

Riley ignored him as she continued to watch the world fly by. "You fooled me," Riley finally said.

"*Moi?*" Bradley asked coyly. "I gave you what you needed."

"What was that, Bradley? To be fucked? To be taken away from my kids? To be lied to? What part did I need?"

"You needed to be happy. After I left your world, you were miserable."

Riley stood up and faced him. "You mean when you were *murdered*? Were you spying on me? If so, you'd know that I wasn't sad. I was fucking ecstatic!" She laughed at the way his mouth widened with shock. "Aha! That's right. You didn't see me after you *died*, because if you had you would've seen me doing a fucking dance."

Regaining his composure, Bradley fixed her with a piercing stare. She glared back at him and a slow grin worked his lips up as Riley began fidgeting. Laughter echoed as she rapidly hopped from one foot to the other. "What did you do!" It felt as if she was walking over a bed of hot coals. Spikes of heat radiated from the soles of her feet and up her legs.

"I see that you're so *ecstatic* you're jumping for joy," he joked.

"Stop it!" Riley shrieked as she ran around. It didn't matter where she stepped, she couldn't escape the hellish heat. She was stepping so fast that she brought her knees almost up to her chest.

Bradley gave a dismissive wave; he had finished toying with her. The heat subsided; Riley dropped to the ground and gently rubbed her feet. After checking for signs of blistering, she glared at Bradley. "Why am I here? You don't love me."

"I do. I love you," he said, stunning Riley into silence. "It's true, I really do love you."

Riley shook her head in disbelief. "You're crazy, Bradley. You told me over and over again that you don't love me. You can't claim to love me then treat me like shit."

"I'm sorry," he said sincerely. "That wasn't my intent."

Riley was shocked into silence for a second time. He sounded genuine. They stared at each other, Bradley earnestly watching her and Riley intently studying him. Riley mentally squared her shoulders then snapped her fingers, breaking the silence. "So just like that you changed; when did you realize that you loved me?"

"I always did. I guess I haven't been able to show my love for you in the way that I should," he said while he seductively caressed her arm. "Now I want to spend a million lifetimes showing you how much I love you."

Riley vehemently shook her head. "You don't love me. You admitted to marrying me to spite my sister. And if you did love me, you'd let me leave."

"Why would you want to leave? I can expose you to things that people only dream about."

"Why do you want to keep me here, especially if I'm so unhappy?" Riley pleaded.

"You'll come to love it here, just like I did. And I want you with me forever. You're not leaving," he said firmly. "I love you."

Riley stared at him, incredulous. He really believes he loves me; he's delusional. But she knew that his moods could switch from charming to mean in a heartbeat and he wasn't going to let her go home.

"Just leave me alone," Riley said, her voice weary. She returned to her seat and Bradley resumed the show.

Sometime later, Riley felt a small tickle on her neck. She didn't acknowledge it, knowing what it was.

"Stop ignoring me," Bradley hissed in her ear.

"Are you going to let me go home?" Riley asked.

"No."

"Then I'll continue to ignore you."

"No you won't! You're just mad at me right now, but you'll change your mind. We have eternity to be together."

Riley snorted. "Oh what a famous last line."

"Stop being so mean."

"Are you going to let me leave?"

"What do you think?" Bradley asked.

Riley looked into his eyes and knew the answer. She stumbled away from him. Moments later she found herself sitting and watching the crystal-clear water. Again time froze as she blocked everything out.

She didn't move until she caught motion out of the corner of her eye. *He's back.* Squaring her shoulders, she turned to face Bradley head-on. *He's not going to hurt me anymore.* The thought evaporated just as quickly as it had come. Her mind frantically worked to comprehend who was coming toward her. "It can't be. This is one of his tricks. This can't be happening," she stuttered with disbelief. Wave after wave of shock washed over her body as the visitor glided toward her.

The figure came to a stop in front of her. "Mommy?" Riley whispered, her voice trembling. "Mommy?" she repeated. Fifteen years ago her parents had died in a house fire. "Is that really you?"

"It's really me, Riley," her mother answered.

Longing and distrust warred on Riley's pretty face. "How do I know that it's really you and not one of Bradley's tricks?" she asked.

"Because he doesn't know about me, so he can't tease you with something that he has no knowledge of."

That was true, her parents had perished long before she met Bradley. He had only seen pictures of them. "I don't know . . . ," she said, not knowing who to trust. "What are you doing here? How did you get here?"

"I'm here to help you. If I was in cahoots with Bradley, do you think I would try to help you escape?"

Riley began backing away. "You could be a trick. You could be one of his helpers who's come to get my hopes up and then take me to Bradley so that he can hurt me."

"Do you think Bradley would let someone do that? He would love to personally see your expression when he tortures you. He wouldn't have it any other way. He's evil."

Riley ran into her mother's arms, erasing the distance between them. "Mommy! I've missed you so much. Tamia and I think about you all the time. I'm so sad that you never got a chance to know Brie and Carter, they're so sweet—"

Her mother cut her off. "I know them. I visit them all the time, I just don't make my presence known like Bradley does. They're beautiful kids. You're doing a wonderful job with them." Suddenly her words turned earnest. "We need to go. Right now your father and some angels have come down from heaven to rescue you. They're distracting Bradley and his army, but I'm not sure how they're doing. We need to get you back."

"Daddy's here?" Questions swirled in Riley's head. But before she could say anything else her mother grabbed her hand. "Come on, we've got to go." Riley felt herself being pulled off the ground; before she could catch her breath, she was zooming through the air, going so fast that everything looked like one long strip of black.

While in midair, they jerked to a stop. "Oh no! Bradley must have figured out what's going on. Hold on!" her mother warned as they began descending. A hand the width of Texas, with tractor-trailer-size fingers, was pushing them down. Riley clung to her mother as they rapidly approached the ground.

"Why doesn't he just scoop us up?" Riley yelled.

"He likes toying with us; he'll do it soon," she reassured her daughter. "Be prepared."

They continued to drop at an alarmingly fast rate through the air. And just as abruptly as it had started, it stopped and they were floating again. "They must've distracted him again. Come on." They moved, even faster than before. Moments later they slowed to a stop and eased to the ground.

"This is the way out," her mother said, pointing in front of her. All Riley saw was white, sheet after sheet of it.

"It looks so lifeless, like a giant vacuum. Are you sure this is the way out?"

"It is," her mother reassured her. "Trust me and trust Him."

Riley threw her arms around her mother's waist. "I miss you so much. I pray for you and Daddy every night and I think about you both every day."

Her mother kissed her forehead. "I know you do, honey, we hear your prayers. And we're with you all the time. Your daddy and I are always watching over you. That's how we knew you were in trouble."

"Mommy, when you said this wasn't heaven, what is it?" she asked, already knowing the answer.

"A place worse than hell, baby, that evil thing brought you to a place worse than hell."

"Oh my God!" Riley exclaimed. "Worse than hell?" Her legs went weak with shock and she leaned on her mother for support.

"It's okay. I don't have time to explain it to you now, so just trust me," her mother murmured in her ear.

"How are you going to get back?" Riley asked, not ready to let her mother go.

"We'll get back," she reassured her daughter. Just then the sky turned black and the air became as thick as Jell-O, making it hard to breathe. "You'd better go," her mother choked out. "Bradley is on his way and he's pissed."

Loud howls sliced through the thickness and chilled Riley to her bones.

"Come on, slip through here," her mother ordered. She had bent down and lifted a corner of Bradley's world; she had peeled it back as easily as though it was wallpaper. On the other side was Riley's bedroom. "Hurry!"

Riley paused and risked a look over her shoulder, shuddering at what she saw. The sky was black with thousands of evil spirits. Leading the pack was none other than Bradley. She could feel his hate-filled glare on her. "Are you going to be okay?"

"I'll be fine. Trust me. God won't let anything happen to us. Don't worry about me."

"Oh, Mommy, this isn't enough time. And I want to see Daddy."

The air was heating up and Riley found herself fidgeting. Bradley and his army began descending. Her mother looked over her daughter's shoulder. Bradley and his crew had landed and were marching toward them. "We'll come see you, just go!"

"Mom!" That was the last thing Riley said before her mother shoved her and she found herself, for the second time, swimming through space, gulping sand as though it was water. She clawed at her throat as she raced through the air at the speed of a dead body being thrown from a thirty-story building. Then she blacked out.

"What happened?" Riley groggily asked her sister, who was eyeing her with concern. "Am I really home?"

"You're home," Tamia insisted. Riley had been asking her that ever since she'd found her on the kitchen floor a half hour ago. "Tell me what happened."

"I don't know, it felt so real, but I thought it was a dream. I don't know," she said helplessly.

Tamia rubbed her sister's back. "That's okay, take your time. Want some tea?" Riley shrugged. "I'll make you some," Tamia decided.

"What made you come over here?" Riley asked.

"I don't know. I just got the urge to come over and visit my big sis. It was weird. But I'm glad that I did," she called over her shoulder. She was at the sink filling the kettle with water; as soon as she placed it over a high flame she returned to the table to sit with her sister.

"I'm glad you did too," Riley muttered.

"What happened?"

Suddenly Riley's heart skipped a beat. "Where are Carter and Brie!" she shot up from her chair and frantically grabbed her sister's arm. "Where are my babies?"

"They're fine. I checked on them right after I made sure you were okay; they're with Markie."

Riley remembered Markie. She was Tamia's buddy who was allergic to working, but she had a good soul. "Where are they?"

"She took them out for breakfast. I didn't think you'd be in the mood to cook." Riley shook her head. "Tell me what happened. Are you okay?" Tamia asked for the hundredth time.

"I'm fine," Riley answered, looking as confused as a country music fan watching Jessica Simpson sing country. "So you found me on the kitchen floor when you let yourself in?" she asked, looking at her sister for confirmation.

"Yeah. Just tell me what happened. You scared me, girl. You were lying so still . . . ," she said, gulping, "that I thought you were dead."

"Mommy pushed me down here. I thought I was going to my bedroom, but I ended up here," she mused.

"Stop it right now!" her sister ordered. "You saw Mommy?" she asked as a lump formed in her throat.

"I did. She looked so beautiful and so peaceful. At first I didn't think she was real, you know, that she was something Bradley had created to fool me. It took a minute, but she convinced me she was real. She saved me."

"Did you see Daddy?" Tamia asked breathlessly.

Riley shook her head. "He was with the angels, helping to distract Bradley so that I could escape," she explained.

"So Mommy and Daddy are angels?" she asked.

"No, I don't think so," Riley answered. "But I bet they will be after this. I just hope that they escaped," Riley said, remembering Bradley's army. "It was horrible, Tamia. So horrible . . ."

Tamia's eyes widened with fear. "Tell me *everything* that

happened. *Everything!*" Just then the whistling from the kettle interrupted then. "Hold on a sec. Let me fix our tea." In one minute flat, two cups of hot tea were on the table. "Okay."

"Bradley had taken me to his world," Riley started.

"What? He did what?"

"Not my body, but my spirit. I thought it was a dream, but I don't know, it felt so real."

"It sounds like you had a nightmare and were sleepwalking."

"It was all so real."

"Okay, just tell me what happened."

In meticulous detail, Riley told her sister everything; when she finished, Tamia's arms were covered with goose bumps. "I can still see the pit of snakes," she said before taking a sip of tea. "As soon as I discovered that it was all a ruse, he showed me what he really was."

"So Bradley is evil?"

"He's *very* evil. I'm sorry that I didn't believe you before."

"What are you going to do? Do you think he'll leave you alone?"

Riley shrugged. "I don't know."

"Well, he did let you leave. And if it was really his world, like you said it was, he didn't have to let you leave, he could've killed you."

"Don't be making him seem like an angel. Weren't you listening? Mommy and Daddy rescued me. I was this close," she said, illustrating by putting two fingers close together, "to getting caught. He was so close that I could smell him. I was so lucky. He almost had me."

"Do you think he's going to force you to go back?"

"I don't doubt it. Bradley hates the word *no*. But he might surprise me and let me live my life."

"I would be so scared if I were you," Tamia admitted.

Riley looked at her sister. She never imagined her as being afraid of anything, and that terrified her. "Do you really think I should be worried? Maybe he got it all out of his system." The statement sounded stupid even to her.

"I don't know," Tamia answered; just then Markie stepped through the door holding a bag filled with their breakfast.

"Let's eat and talk about it later," Tamia said.

Riley leaned over to whisper in her ear. "Mommy said that she and Daddy visit us all the time. They were with us all this time and we didn't even know it." She grinned at her sister.

After Tamia and Markie left, Riley walked upstairs to her bathroom. She stumbled at the threshold then shrieked. The stench of death filled the room. A shriveled black flower lay on the countertop. Written out in petals was: YOU WILL BE MINE! DON'T FIGHT IT! Riley screamed and screamed until she was hoarse.

chapter ELEVEN

Riley and Malik sat in her classroom as they reviewed the status reports of her students. It was a monthly activity that Malik did with all his teachers. That way no student slipped through the cracks and every student got the help he or she needed.

It was October in Atlanta, a transitional time before winter, when hoodies and flip-flops were standard outfits for teenagers and where some evenings were just as sultry as a June day.

Riley was happy to be back at work. The episode with Bradley had left her terrified. Fortunately, he hadn't reappeared.

"I think Troy and Deanna are going to need a tutor," Riley said; she glanced up when she didn't get a response. Malik was staring at her as though she had tatted up and begun singing Lil Wayne's latest song. "What's wrong, you're looking at me like I smell or something."

Malik jerked back, ashamed that he had been caught staring. "You're fine. I was daydreaming and you got caught in my line of vision." He glanced down at the sheet of paper in front of him. "You're right, let's sign those two up for tutoring. They can benefit from the extra help."

"Terrific. I'll coordinate it." Riley scanned the paper. "I can't read this, what does it say?" She handed the paper to Malik. His eyes widened and he pushed away from the table as though she was handing him a grenade. "What's wrong?"

"I have to use the bathroom." He ran out of the classroom before Riley could say another word.

"That was so bizarre, running out of here like he was running from a bill collector. I hope he's all right," she muttered before returning to her stack of papers. Five minutes later, she heard the door open. "Welcome ba—" The words stuck in her throat. Malik's face was twisted in horror. He flew across the floor, pushed Riley down, and a sound like a roaring train reverberated through the room. She clamped her hands over her ears. A streak of yellow almost like a lightning bolt flew out of Malik's hand. It shattered the windows. Riley gasped.

"Shit!" Malik's eyes narrowed as they locked on his target. Riley felt a cold wind skate over her scalp and she shivered. "Don't move!" Malik barked. "Gotcha!" A flash of yellow came within a hair of her ear and shattered her desk into a million pieces. Malik whipped around on his heel and aimed his hand at a spot over her. She heard a loud crack and then peeked up to find the bulletin board splitting into two.

"What is going on?" she screamed.

"Just be quiet and stay still," Malik ordered as a flash of lavender bounced off the walls and hovered above her head. It radiated so much heat that it caused her to sweat; it trickled down her face and into her eyes. She didn't dare move. Malik swung his hand out, aimed, and shot. "Shit!" Plaster from the ceiling rained on Riley's head.

"You can't hurt me," the thing taunted. Riley's eyes grew to the size of tires as the entity zoomed toward Malik.

"Oh, God, somebody please help!" she cried as it sheathed Malik in a violet-colored bubble. She lurched forward as Malik's mouth widened then let out a deafening howl. She clamped her hands to her ears. "I need help."

Riley breathed deeply then twisted her lips with disgust. She had a mouthful of goo. The thick mass slithered down her throat, cutting off her air. She clawed at her throat, trying to pull the mess out. She jumped up and staggered toward Malik. Their eyes locked.

"Don't panic!" he commanded. "The more you struggle, the worse it gets. Just let it slide down your throat; it won't hurt you if you swallow it." Riley vehemently shook her head. "Just pretend that it's ice cream. Remember, the more you fight it, the thicker it'll get."

Forcing her body to be still, Riley closed her eyes and envisioned a big bowl of her favorite ice cream, strawberry daiquiri. After what felt like hours, it began to thin and slide down her throat. Riley hungrily gulped in air.

Malik reached into his pocket and drew out a pair of nail scissors. Pulling his arm back, he stabbed at the bubble, puncturing it. A bright purple blast filled the room, followed by a loud groan. Riley saw the face of a young man, his mouth stretched in pain, zooming toward the ceiling before exploding. Indigo dust rained from the ceiling. Riley slid to the floor.

"It almost got you," Malik growled.

Riley peeked up at Malik. "What the hell are you? Who are you?" she asked.

"I'm a warrior," Malik replied calmly.

"Like the ghost busters? From the movie?" she asked, shaken.

Malik snorted. "That movie is based on some people my family knew. They were just as inept as they were portrayed as being in the movie. I'm the real deal," he said arrogantly.

"What happened?"

"A demon was here to poison you."

The blood drained from Riley's face. "Poison me. What? Why?"

Malik shrugged. "All I know is that he was trying to kill you."

"Trying to kill me?" Suddenly Riley's eyes widened. "Bradley. Bradley did this."

"You're probably right."

"How did—I mean, how did you know?" Riley stuttered.

"You're covered in black dust," he said with disdain.

Riley looked down at her clothing. It looked just as spotless as it had this morning.

"You can't see it, it's invisible to the human eye. You're covered in it. It's all over your face, your hands, and your hair."

Riley blushed. "Bradley visited us . . . I mean me."

"So you saw him?" Malik asked and Riley nodded. "Did you two talk?"

"We did."

"Did you two fuck?" he asked casually.

"Malik!"

"I'm sorry," he said, softening. "His dust is all over you; it's their DNA. And I'm guessing that you guys went there. Demons can be very seductive. Only a jealous male demon or mortal will do what he did."

"We had sex," Riley admitted. "I was falling in love with him all over again, but he showed his true self and I stopped."

"Why didn't you tell me this was going on?" he asked.

Riley snorted. "I mean, really! This is so not a topic for casual conversation. I was supposed to tell you that my dead husband is now a demon, he visits me, and we make love? Was I supposed to tell you that?" Her hands began trembling, then her whole body. She was shaking more than a hypoglycemic on a sugar low. When she realized what had almost happened, she started crying.

"It's okay. It's a normal reaction," Malik soothed.

"I was almost killed! If it hadn't been for you, that thing would've killed me." She looked up at Malik, her eyes glistening. "You saved my life. You saved me!" she sobbed.

"It's okay," he murmured.

"Why would he want to kill me? Does he hate me that much?"

Malik bit back a retort. "Demons have an exaggerated sense of power. They think they're invincible."

"Aren't they?"

"About as invincible as a wet piece of tissue," Malik answered. "Speaking of tissues." He plucked some out of the tissue holder and handed them to her.

Riley blew her nose. "We need to clean this up." Riley looked around the classroom; it looked like it had been used for hockey practice. Every piece of furniture was smashed to little bits.

"I'll have someone take care of it," Malik said absentmindedly.

Riley gazed into Malik's blue eyes. *He's cute, really cute.* Her throat went dry when Malik winked at her. *How can I possibly be thinking about Malik like that after Bradley's murder attempt?* "I don't think the janitor can take care of this," she mumbled.

Malik gave a dismissive wave. "No, no. I have special people who are used to cleaning up after fights like this. They'll be here as soon as we leave and the room will look exactly like it did before."

"Oh!" By using magic? she wanted to ask, but kept silent instead.

"My main concern is Bradley, he's powerful. He hasn't been in the other world for long, but he's already gotten soldiers. And I want to know if it's only a few or if he has developed an army. If it's the latter, we're in a shitload of trouble."

chapter TWELVE

Riley looked around Malik's study, still amazed by his house. *He certainly didn't afford this on his vice principal's salary.* His Tudor-style home wasn't a wannabe mini McMansion type of mansion, it was a real to-die-for mansion. Driving up she had counted what she believed to be four distinct wings. Every room she had peeked in was decorated with priceless pieces of art and über expensive furniture. Even the den had more artifacts than the Metropolitan Museum of Art. She had a pretty good idea that the leather sofa she was sitting on wasn't from Sears.

It had been only a couple of days since the demon attack, but they hadn't talked about it. School wasn't safe, Malik didn't want to talk about it over the phone, and he didn't want to meet anywhere except his house. She didn't understand why until a few minutes later.

"This house is demon proof. There's an impenetrable force field surrounding it," Malik explained as soon as they were comfortable.

"Is that something I can buy from the store?" she quipped as she surreptitiously studied him. His stuffy suit and tie were gone, replaced by a pair of loose-fitting jeans and a muscle-hugging Ralph Lauren polo.

He cocked an eyebrow at her. "It depends on where you go." Riley gasped with surprise. "I'm joking," Malik said. "The force field was specially designed for us. There are only a handful of them in the world."

"And no demons can penetrate it?" she asked, still unconvinced that any place was safe after the demon attack.

Malik shook his head. "It's impenetrable," he said firmly.

"What are you? And why do you have a force field surrounding your house? We're in Atlanta, for Pete's sake! What can I do to protect myself and my family against more attacks?" she blurted out. Ever since the attack, she had been looking over her shoulder and sharing her bed with Brie and Carter.

"Calm down. It'll be okay. That's why I invited you over. I want to explain everything to you. By the way, you can buy ghost repellant at the store."

"Is it called ghost repellant? And is it by the bug spray?" Riley retorted.

Malik laughed. "I'm joking, ghost repellant doesn't exist. But we have something better than repellant, we have paladins. They're our support. We have hundreds of them throughout the world who aren't warriors but who support us."

"Oh!" Riley said. A second later she asked, "So how do you know who's a paladin?"

"It's easy. They have our family crest tattooed on their necks. Or some of them have chips with three-D images of the crest embedded in their necks."

Riley winced. "What? That sounds painful." She stroked her Adam's apple. "I don't think I can do that."

"We don't put them there." Malik lifted her hair off her neck and gently traced a circle under her ear. Riley trembled. "This is where they're inserted." Malik glided his finger lightly over her skin. "Your skin is so soft, it'll be easy to put a chip in you. Right here." He leaned down and gently blew on her neck as he made small circular movements. Riley sighed softly as her body relaxed against his. "Would you like me to insert it?" Malik whispered in her ear.

"Oh, yes!"

"Maybe after a couple of dates," he said with a smirk.

Riley blushed. "What? I didn't mean that," she lied. She looked at him with new eyes. She liked this *new* Malik. He was assertive and sexy. And he had swag. Riley pulled away, putting some space between them. "But how can you see an image that's covered by skin? Don't tell me you have X-ray vision?"

Malik shrugged as he grinned sheepishly. "I kinda do." Riley shielded her breasts with her hands. "I can't see through clothes, of course. There are only certain things I can see that the human eye can't. And the chips are such that they were designed that way."

Riley began unconsciously sliding away from him. "So you're not human?"

Malik saw her movements and laughed to himself. "I'm human, very human," he clarified, "but with extraordinary skills."

Riley eyed him suspiciously. "What does that mean?"

"The story goes that my great-great-grandfather's great-great-great-grandfather saved the life of an Outsch man's, only son."

"A what?"

"I guess what you would call a witch doctor," Malik explained. Riley nodded and he continued. "And he was so thankful that he gave him some special powers. And those powers are inherited by the men in the family. The firstborn sons are the most powerful and the rest are all mediums."

"Just the men?" It was Malik's turn to nod. "How very misogynistic," she drawled. "So what can you do?"

"I can communicate with the dead and terminate demons. When I go into attack mode, watch out."

"I saw you. But it felt like I was watching a movie, not actually in the middle of it all. I can't believe that demon slayers even exist."

"We do. My family isn't the only one. Others are scattered throughout the world. But we are some of the most powerful."

Riley felt light-headed and slumped down. "I don't believe this. I don't know what to think anymore. Evil spirits and demon slayers, and I've met both? Oh, God!"

"Relax," Malik soothed. "It'll be okay."

It took Riley a few minutes to compose herself. "Were you scared when you discovered your powers?" Riley asked when she found her voice.

"A little. I destroyed my first ghost when I was seven."

"Oh. So while other little boys were playing with Hot Wheels and G.I. Joe, you were hunting for ghosts?"

"Pretty much. My father used to take me to the racetracks; there were always tons of ghosts there."

Riley's brow furrowed. "The racetracks?"

Malik nodded. "Yeah, bad spirits like to hang out where desperate people go. Nowadays it's the poker tournaments. But they floated around the racetracks in packs; sometimes they were so thick that I couldn't see the clouds. Anyway, the ghosts preyed on those humans for sport. They sensed their desperation."

Riley shuddered. "Oh my God, what did they do?"

"It depended on their mood. Some of the ghosts, called Inhibitors, temporarily took possession of bodies and forced the human to make crazy bet after crazy bet until he lost everything. As soon as the human hit rock bottom, the Inhibitor would disappear, leaving behind an empty shell."

A wide-eyed Riley shook her head in disbelief. "You're kidding, right?"

"I wish," Malik answered. "There are a lot more, but then there are the evil ones who have the impulse control of a toddler. Anything can piss them off. And when they are, whoever upsets them is going to have one hell of a time trying to evade them."

"Like me, huh?" Riley asked fearfully.

Malik squeezed her hand. "Yeah, like you." Malik saw the fear in Riley's eyes. "It'll be fine." He took a deep breath and said, "The worst demons of all leave a residue of black dust on every human they come in contact with. It's their DNA. Truly evil ghosts use it as a weapon. They have soldiers who spend an eternity harvesting dust. And it can be deadly for me, if I'm exposed to it. Fortunately, I have an ointment that's an antidote."

"Oh no! I came into contact with Bradley. Am I okay? I mean, are you okay?"

Malik gave her a reassuring smile. "I slathered myself with the ointment. I'm okay."

"Oh good. How was I able to see Bradley and not the demon who tried to kill me? I mean, I got a glimpse of it, when you stabbed it. But if you hadn't done that, I wouldn't have known it was in the room. And how did you destroy ghosts without causing a riot?"

"First of all, not everybody can see demons. Humans can see demons only when they make themselves visible, but then there are demons who go into stealth mode and only people like myself and mediums can see them. So we can have a fight and to some people all it would look like is we're swatting at bugs. And the mediums who can actually see the fight are so used to it that it doesn't even bother them. They just get out of our way."

"So there's a war going on between the dead and the undead?"

"Yep."

"And Bradley is very dangerous?" Riley squeaked.

"Yeah. He's got powers that are unbelievable. I consulted my father about it. He had some of his friends who can communicate with ghosts do some research on Bradley. And I'll tell you, he's a bad brother. The spirits were afraid to talk to my father's friends. They were that scared of Bradley."

"What can he do, put a hit out on them?" Riley half-joked in a trembling voice.

Malik pulled Riley into his arms. She gratefully rested her head on his chest and he flinched against her; she pulled back. "It's okay, just a knee-jerk reaction. The ointment is still working. But getting back to Bradley, remember that there are demons who kill other demons."

Riley snuggled against Malik, feeling safe from the spirits. "Do they go to hell?"

"No, they go to a place worse than hell. It's called Lavastar and it's rumored that hell is a playground compared to it. Even Lucifer won't go near it. The most depraved, evil, and unfortunate souls end up there."

"That's where I was. That's what Bradley called it when I asked him where I was."

"And you made it out?" Malik asked, amazed. "No one has ever made it out alive."

Riley finished digesting this information before she spoke. "Thank you," she mumbled against his chest.

"For what?"

"For saving my life. Even saying thank you sounds so inadequate."

"It's fine."

Riley pulled away and caught Malik's gaze. "How come you never told me about this?"

"I guess I could've squeezed it in right after our curriculum-planning meeting," he joked.

"But we've been friends for years. You could've told me," Riley insisted.

"Just like you could've told me that Bradley beat you," Malik said softly.

Riley gasped and her face reddened with embarrassment. "You knew?" she asked, her eyes shining with unshed tears. Malik nodded. "I guess everybody knew."

"No, they didn't. Nobody said anything about it to me, and you know how they gossip. If they'd had a tiny taste of what was really going on with you, it would've spread like a pregnant woman's ass. And I would've heard it."

"How did you know? What made you suspect? I was so careful," she muttered to herself.

Malik cleared his throat. "Because I couldn't take my eyes off you," he admitted.

"What?"

"I've always had a crush on you. But you were married and I respected that. Then after Bradley died, I thought I could say something, but then I saw you covered in dust and suspected that you two were still sexing. So I backed off and gave you your space."

Riley blushed. "So all this time you liked me?" she asked, her voice filled with wonder. "You had a crush on me?"

"I did," Malik answered softly.

"Wow!"

"Yeah, wow." Malik gently cradled Riley's face in his hands as he tenderly kissed her eyelids, stroked her cheeks with his thumbs, and grazed her lips with his. He abruptly pulled away and smiled at her apologetically. "We've got things to do and I need to stay focused." He strolled over to his computer.

"Sure, focus is good," she muttered, shocked by Malik's confession. Riley spied a gold ring encrusted with jewels lying on the floor. "What's this?" she asked, scooping it up. "It looks expensive."

Malik glanced over his shoulder. "My royal jewelry," he answered nonchalantly.

"Royal . . . jewelry?" she asked, chopping up the two words as though they didn't belong together. "Why do you have royal jewelry?"

"I'm the prince of Ulgani."

"You're a prince?" she asked.

"Yep, my grandfather Bayard is the king."

"A prince?" Riley gulped.

Malik nodded. "That's right . . . a prince saved your life," he joked.

"Stop joking and tell me how serious this is. How come you don't have a crown?"

"We don't respect crowns, they're too ostentatious." Malik shrugged. "It's not like I can wear it every day."

Months ago, if anyone had told her she would be talking about demons as nonchalantly as though she was talking about a pair of shoes, she would have told them they were crazy.

"What are you doing working as a vice principal if you're a prince?"

Malik smiled. "I love children. And I know that being a vice principal isn't as glamorous as being a prince. But I decide the children's curriculum and assist with selecting their teachers. There's no job more rewarding than guiding someone's future. Other than being a mommy," he added with a grin.

"That's so sweet and true. That's why I love teaching so much. The kids, the feeling you get when you see your students excel and realize that they are able to soar because of you. And you never know if you're teaching the next Barack Obama or Robert L. Johnson."

"Exactly! You understand."

Riley glanced at him. "Is there anything else you want to tell me?"

"I was married," Malik announced.

"What?"

"I was married, about a hundred years ago. She was murdered."

"You're over a hundred years old?" Riley sputtered. "So you're a century-old demon-slaying prince."

Malik smiled wryly, having expected her shell-shocked response. "Yep. Anyway, her name was Aldornia. A demon killed her. And the horrible part was that he killed her for fun. So I killed him. I fucking destroyed him," he said angrily.

"I'm sorry about your wife." She knew beneath his rage was pain. "Are you okay?"

"I'm fine. I've a long time to grieve," he answered, then refocused on the computer screen.

Riley moved to a chair closer to Malik. "Tell me more about this war between the dead and the undead. I kinda always believed in ghosts. And when Bradley showed up, I thought I was going crazy and then realized I wasn't. When I saw the fight between you and my almost murderer, I thought again that I was going crazy. What's going on?"

Malik turned away from his computer and slid closer to her, but then quickly scooted away; the ointment was wearing off. "I'm going to have to answer your questions while I'm bathing you. You're still covered in Bradley's dust."

"What?" she squeaked.

"Yeah, my skin is starting to tingle. Soon, it'll be itching like crazy, then it'll start blistering then . . ." His omission said it loud and clear.

"Didn't I get it all over your furniture and stuff?" she asked, hoping to mask her nervousness at the thought of him bathing her.

"You did, but it's only trace amounts; I'll have some paladins come in and sanitize it later tonight. I'm okay for a little while, but I can tell that the ointment is wearing off. Come on."

Riley followed Malik down the hall to a bathroom. It had marble tile, granite vanity tops, soft lightning, and a huge sunken tub.

"This is gorgeous," Riley said in a hushed voice. She had only seen bathrooms like this in magazines.

"I like it too. Take off your clothes and leave them outside the door; someone will pick them up and destroy them. There'll be a new set of clothes waiting for you once we're done."

"You have paladins living with you?" She knew he had the room. With a mansion this size, he could easily house twenty or more people.

"Nope. I live here with my grandfather, father, and cook, Tao. My father will pick up your clothes."

Riley gulped. "I don't know. I don't feel comfortable with your father picking up my *undergarments*."

Malik laughed loudly. "I can't wait to tell him that, he's going to get a good chuckle. It's okay, really it is. I guess I should've told you there's a special bag for you to use." He pulled open a drawer in the vanity and pulled out a black velvet drawstring bag. "Here, stick your stuff in here. He's going to pick it up and burn it. So your *undergarments* will be safe."

Riley snatched the bag from him. "You should've explained it better," she snapped, embarrassed by the misunderstanding. She looked at Malik. "Umm, I need some privacy."

"Why? I'm going to bathe you, right?"

"Give me some space," Riley said firmly.

Malik reluctantly walked out of the room. "Call me when you're ready," he said.

Riley slowly undressed then held up a pair of lacy boy shorts. "He'd better not look at my panties," she muttered before stuffing her clothes inside the velvet bag and setting it outside the door. "Okay, I'm ready," she called down the empty corridor. She slammed the door shut and glanced around the bathroom. There was no towel in sight. "Crap! Crap! Crap!"

"I'm coming in," Malik announced before entering. She unsuccessfully tried to cover herself with her hands. She finally settled on covering her crotch. Malik had removed all of his clothes except his boxers. Riley took in his chiseled pecs, tight eight-pack, and muscled legs. *Wow! Malik's got more muscles than the rapper Nelly.*

"Where are your clothes?" she squeaked; she couldn't tear her eyes off his body.

"I can't give you a bath while I'm fully clothed, can I?" he asked with a smirk.

"Sure you can. I do it all the time with the kids."

"I hope I'm not making you uncomfortable; all I want to do is bathe you, that's all. What do you think I want to do?"

"Of course I'm uncomfortable, I'm standing naked in front of my male friend, *who I think is fine as hell.* I have my dead husband visiting me, unbeknownst to me I'm covered in his dust, which is, by the way, fatal to you, and I was nearly killed by an evil spirit," she said. Suddenly she began whimpering as she blinked back tears. "I'm sorry."

"No, I'm sorry," Malik said softly. "If you want, I can put something different on."

Riley sniffed. "No, no, don't change. I'm just stressed. That's all."

"That's understandable." He went to the vanity and pulled out a thumb-size vial and a slip of plastic. Malik motioned toward the bathtub. "Hop in."

Riley eyed the empty basin. "Don't we need to fill it with water?"

Malik held up the small tube. "Water and this liquid don't mix, sort of like how oil and vinegar don't."

"Oh, okay." She stepped into the bathtub and for the second time tried unsuccessfully to cover her breasts and the spot between her legs.

Malik gazed at her body and whistled softly; he loved a curvaceous woman. "You're hot!"

Riley blushed. "Thanks," she stammered. "What do you want me to do? Stand or sit?"

Malik chuckled as though she had said something funny. "Why don't you sit? I can't have you slipping and hurting yourself."

Riley shot him a wary smile before lowering herself into the tub. "It's cold," she grumbled, "and clammy."

"I'll fix that." Malik's hands disappeared to the side of the tub and seconds later it began vibrating and getting warm.

The tension melted from Riley's face. "Oh my God! This is heavenly," she moaned as she eased herself back and rested against the now warm marble. "What did you do?" She closed her eyes.

"It was magic," Malik whispered in her ear. Her eyes snapped open; she hadn't heard him get in.

"What are you doing?" His normally vibrant blue eyes had darkened to a smoldering navy. "What happened to your eyes?"

Malik winked. "They change colors when I get excited."

"I'm not ready for this. I'm just not! I'm here so you can protect me from Bradley's army . . . nothing more. I can't handle getting involved with anyone right now."

"I'm not asking you for anything."

Malik opened the thumb-size vial and upturned it. A thick copper-colored liquid flowed out. In the blink of an eye the tub was full and Malik's underwear was on the floor.

"How did you do that?" Riley breathed. She scooped up some of the fluid and let it slip through her fingers; it felt like talcum powder. "This is crazy."

"Magic," he teased. "Ready?"

Riley nodded, still dazed by everything.

With his plastic square he dipped into the liquid before wiping it over Riley's arm. She tingled.

"What's going on?" It felt as if a hundred little fingers were massaging her. "Why do I feel like this?"

"If you're feeling all tingly, like you're getting felt over by a dozen people, then it's working. This is a deep-cleaning method that neutralizes the dust, making it possible for me to touch you."

"Does it have to feel so good?" Riley moaned. Malik had done her other arm and face and had moved to her breasts.

"It has different effects on different people. Some people don't have skin as sensitive as yours." Riley groaned in response.

After some quick maneuvering, Malik faced Riley. Malik gently ran the plastic wipe over her feet, paying special attention to her toes. He placed her legs over his shoulder and tenderly cleaned her calves. He caressed the inside of her thighs with his scrap of plastic as Riley shivered. He leisurely inched his way up and Riley shook uncontrollably with anticipation.

He tenderly swiped the swatch of plastic against her vagina's lips. Riley's back arched toward his hand. "What are you doing? You're supposed to be bathing me, not seducing me. Stop it!"

"I could stop," Malik said smoothly, "but then you would miss this." He glided the plastic over her moist lips, cruised it over her clit, and massaged it over her butt. Riley clutched the edge of the bathtub.

"Don't stop." It felt as if four pairs of hands were pleasuring her.

"I don't plan on doing so," Malik said as he slowly moved the scrap of plastic over her stomach.

Riley whimpered as her eyes fluttered shut. "Oh, Malik!"

"I love how you say my name. Say it again," he whispered as he gently flicked the plastic against her clit.

"Malik!" Riley chanted as she writhed with desire. "Malik, what are you doing?" she asked between pants. "It feels like I have three men down there. Oh, Malik!"

"Just me. I can do the work of six men." Malik chuckled. "Get ready, baby."

"For what?"

"I'm going to take you someplace you've never been before," he promised right before he slid the swatch over her clit, bringing Riley to immediate orgasm. She shuddered and mewled softly. "We're all done," Malik said.

Malik scooped Riley up, draped a towel over her, and pushed his way through the door.

"Where am I?" she asked, gazing around.

"This is my room. You're in my wing of the house."

"It's so nice." The normally harsh and cold gray, black, red, and icy blue subtly formed a harmonious blend of colors. Vibrant cherry furniture made the room even more inviting. Taking up most of one wall was a double set of French doors that led out to a balcony. Riley caught her reflection in the mirror. Her skin sparkled as though she had been dusted with gold flecks.

Malik set her down and the towel fell away. Riley stood on tip-toe and boldly placed a kiss on Malik's lips. "I like your swag," she whispered.

"I thought you liked my lips," Malik murmured as he brushed his mouth over Riley's. All of a sudden, Malik pulled back and gazed down at her naked body.

"What?"

"Now I need to decide whether I want to make love to you or plan my battle against Bradley," Malik drawled.

chapter THIRTEEN

Riley and Malik were in Malik's sitting area enjoying dinner. "I want to know more about you—your history, Ulgani, everything," Riley said.

Malik reclined in his chair, stretching his long legs in front of him and crossing his arms over his chest. His biceps bulged under his shirt. "Where would you like me to start?"

"Tell me about your country."

"It's in Africa, and that's where the majority of my family is."

"What's it like?"

Malik smiled. "Beautiful. It's so green, and the beaches there are phenomenal. And they sunbathe topless," he said with a wink, causing Riley to blush.

"Tell me something else about it besides its topless beaches."

Malik grinned. "Bayard likes telling stories about how it looked when he was growing up. Back then it was acres and acres of jungle. He used to go hunting, fishing, and horseback riding."

"That sounds like so much fun. So different from children growing up today," she said, thinking about the kids she taught, who thought any form of outdoor activity was as uncool as their parents singing along with a Kanye West song.

"It was. My childhood was very similar. I told you about fighting demons at the racetrack. But I also did the fishing and hunting thing. There's nothing more exhilarating than hunting the king of the jungle."

Riley dropped her fork in shock. "You killed a lion?"

Malik smiled sheepishly. "Well, I didn't actually kill him, but they let me come along," he admitted. "I didn't bag my first lion until I was twenty or so."

Riley shuddered. "How barbaric."

"That's what we did for fun. We didn't have skateboards or video games. Nature was our playground."

"How poetic," Riley said with a laugh. "Tell me more."

"Over the years the jungle got smaller as the village morphed into a huge city."

"How big is Ulgani?" She had picked up her fork and resumed eating.

"It has about two million people and it's about the size of Dallas."

"Do you miss it?"

Malik shrugged. "A little. But I go home once or twice a year. Bayard and my father go much more frequently."

"Are they scared of you guys?" Riley asked tentatively.

Malik laughed at her. "They're used to us. You've got to remember that we've been ruling the country for centuries."

Riley shrugged. "That doesn't mean anything. There are a lot of countries that have had the same rulers for years, but that doesn't erase the inhabitants' fears. Look at North Korea."

"Touché. They really aren't afraid of us. Don't you think that if they were, the world would know all about the demon slayers?"

"What happens if somebody gets pissed off at your family? I find it hard to believe that after all this time no one has told any outsiders."

"Don't get me wrong, there are occasional leaks; we can't prevent that. But no one believes them, especially when the story ends up on the cover of the *Moonie*, that supermarket tabloid. No one reads that stuff," he said with a snort.

"So why the undying loyalty?"

"We take care of them. I don't mean to brag, but my family is rich. I mean crazy rich and we're the government. My grandfathers lived a long time, and during their lifetimes they accumulated a lot of money. There are no poor people in Ulgani. We made our country rich, we've recruited and created new businesses in the country. We pay for their health care, schooling, and vacations. Everybody has a job, even if it's only sweeping sidewalks; everybody who wants to work does so. So why kill the golden goose?" Malik finished.

"That makes sense. Now tell me more about your history."

Malik grinned. "You know, you would make a good investigative reporter. How did you end up as a teacher?"

Riley pointed her fork at him. "Hey, this is about you. Don't try to change the subject," she said playfully. "Keep talking."

Malik grinned. "Once we hit forty we stop aging. Our organs age but at a snail's pace. We could live forever."

"Are you immune to our diseases?"

"Pretty much. We don't catch colds, and our cells fight off cancer. But we can die from conventional methods, like fires, bullets, or a drowning."

"So how long have you guys been here in Atlanta?" she asked then took a bite of food.

"Oh, a long time, about a hundred years. Atlanta wasn't always so crowded. The ninety-six summer Olympics brought with it a boatload of people. There were a lot of desperate ones looking for a fresh start. And you're learning that wherever there are desperate people, demons are sure to be in the mix. After Los Angeles, San Francisco, New York City, and Chicago, Atlanta's got the highest demon population. There are so many desperate people here and the demons love them," he said sadly. I guess they feel that they are a lot more fun to manipulate than people who have their stuff together."

Riley shuddered. "That's sad."

"It is," Malik agreed. "Anyway, this city has gotten so big that we were able to move to different counties. And for the past twenty years, we've been living here. We're so far away from anyone that we don't even know our neighbors, so we can come and go as we please without anyone asking us any questions."

"What about school? Aren't you nervous that people at school will find out?"

Malik shook his head. "Not at all. I really enjoy working with kids. I'll probably be there for another twenty or thirty years."

"But how?" Riley asked. "You'll age. I mean, come on, eventually black gotta crack."

This time Malik laughed heartily. "We have makeup for that. Over the years we've gotten quite good at that too. We have paladins who can age me. They can give me a receding hairline, sagging skin, a little fat around the middle. After I *retire*, then I can move on to another district."

"Unbelievable," Riley muttered. "But after a while, won't people recognize you? The teaching community is pretty small, and even smaller for the administrators. I know Atlanta is big, but it really isn't *that* big!"

"You'd be surprised. People in Atlanta are so self-centered and self-absorbed that they never look beyond their designer shoes.

And if that one lone observant person notices me, I can tell him that I'm Malik's grandson or nephew or whatever is appropriate. A paladin will provide me with a new ID and credentials, everything I'll need to be a vice principal. Or I might not want to do that, I might want to do something else. That's one of the good things about living as long as we have, you acquire so many different skills."

"Amazing!" Riley shook her head. "Never in my wildest dreams would I ever have believed this." She picked up a croissant and bit into it.

Suddenly, Malik nonchalantly said, "I want you to move in with me."

Startled, Riley dropped her croissant. "What? What did you say?" When he had called her yesterday and invited her over for dinner, she'd jumped at the chance. She had expected exquisite food and a couple of hours of stimulating conversation. Moving in with Malik was the last thing on her mind.

"I want you to move in with me," he repeated. "This place is big enough for you and the kids."

It had only been a week since he had bathed her and made her come so hard that she still got wet from the memory of it. "Why do you want me to move in with you? Is it because of what happened in the bathtub?" she asked shyly. "Because that really isn't me. It's like you cast a spell over me or something."

Malik chuckled. "Trust me, that was all you. Magic wasn't necessary." His voice turned serious. "Please move in with me."

Riley shook her head. "I can't. The only man I ever lived with was Bradley, and I was married to him. I don't plan on marrying you."

"I didn't ask you to," Malik retorted. "This is the safest place for you and the kids. Neither Bradley nor any of his minions can get to you here."

Riley picked up her croissant and resumed eating. "Bradley won't do anything to me or the kids," she replied confidently. There hadn't been any evidence of Bradley since the incident with the dead flower.

"He's no longer the man you married. He's evil," Malik said, his voice ominous.

"I know, I've seen it with my own eyes. I've been to Lavastar, remember? He hates me, but he won't do anything to his kids."

"Oh, *really?*"

"Yeah," Riley said, suddenly unsure. "Why did you say it like that?"

"Because Bradley's been around the kids."

Riley's heart pounded. "I know that he occasionally visits Carter. I don't like it but I can't stop him."

"He not only visits him," Malik said slowly, "he takes him on trips."

"He takes him on—" Riley's eyes widened with comprehension; she slapped a hand over her mouth to stop the wail she was sure would come out.

"Are you okay?"

Riley nodded before lowering her hand. "Why didn't you tell me? Why didn't you tell me this before?"

"I just found out, only hours ago."

"Tell me everything."

"My father's been communicating with spirits who have seen Bradley and Carter. Bradley's been bragging to everybody about how he's going to bring Carter to live with him . . . permanently. He doesn't say when it's going to happen, but they feel that it's pretty soon, because that's all he talks about. They're telling the truth because they risk punishment if one of Bradley's soldiers finds out they are talking to my father. They're risking it because they don't want to see anything happen to Carter."

"You're saying that Bradley will kill his own son so that they can spend eternity together?" Malik nodded and this time Riley did wail, a loud, soul-tearing sound. "What has he turned into?" she muttered to herself.

"That's why I want you all here with me. You guys will be safe. The house is impenetrable for demons."

"Oh my God!" Riley cried. "This can't be happening. It just can't be happening. He would kill his son? His own son?" she asked, still dazed by the thought.

"It looks that way. That's why we need to get Carter and Brie to safety."

"What about Brie?" Riley asked and Malik's heart ached at seeing the anguish and terror in her eyes.

He answered her truthfully. "He doesn't want Brie because she's a girl and she's too young. But he might do it to spite you. If everything you told me about him is true, and if everything I heard about him is true, I wouldn't put it past him."

"I've got to get my babies. How could you waste time by telling me your history when my kids are in trouble?" Riley shot up and lurched forward. Her legs suddenly went wobbly.

Malik wrapped his arms around her. "Calm down, baby, calm down. It'll be okay," he said soothingly.

"How can it be okay?" she sobbed against his chest. "My dead husband is taking my son to hang out with demons and he might kill my baby girl. How can any of this be okay?"

"We have spirits keeping an eye on Bradley and we have a paladin watching your house."

Riley pulled away and looked Malik in the eyes. "Really?"

"Really," he reassured her.

"Okay, let's go then," Riley said calmly while wiping away her tears.

"I'll drive," Malik announced before they left his house.

Thirty minutes later they were at her front door and after saluting Malik the paladin drove away. They rushed into the house as though they were being chased by the devil. Seeing the living room empty, they ran toward the kitchen where they found Tamia, sitting at the table reading a magazine. "Where are the children?" Riley gasped.

Tamia dropped the magazine. "Upstairs, asleep. What's wrong?"

Riley and Malik hurried past her. "I'll tell you as soon as I get the kids," she called over her shoulder as she made her way to the stairs, Malik following closely behind. They got to Brie's room first. Riley's heart slowed a bit when she saw her daughter in her crib playing with a stuffed animal. She picked her up and held her close to her heart. "Oh, baby, I'm so glad you're okay."

Brie stayed in her arms as she and Malik moved on to Carter's room. Riley heard his soft snores and her eyes immediately went to Malik's. She practically threw Brie into his arms as she leaped across the room to get to her son.

"Wake up!" she shrieked as she grabbed his shoulders and began shaking him. "Carter! Wake up! Momma needs you." He was so limp that it felt like she was shaking a bath towel instead of her son. "Carter Bradley Tyson, wake up now!" she ordered. Carter's eyelids didn't flicker.

"Ca Ca!" Brie shouted.

"Does he take us when we're asleep? Is he that much of a coward?" a panicked Riley asked, remembering how Bradley had gotten to her when she had fallen asleep.

"No, it just seems like it. The demons catch people right before they go to sleep, when you're very relaxed and defenseless."

Tamia burst into the room. "What's going on?"

Malik answered. "We're trying to wake Carter. We're afraid Bradley's trying to get to him." Riley began to cry hysterically. "Move, let me try." He passed Brie off to Tamia and was now by Riley's side.

"I'll do it." She shoved Malik away and vigorously shook Carter. She couldn't rouse him.

"Oh no!" Tamia uttered as she watched her nephew being shaken as though he were a dirty dishrag.

"Stop it!" Malik demanded. "You're going to hurt him." Nudging Riley away, he grabbed Carter's hands and gripped them tightly.

Carter's eyes popped open and he stared blankly at Riley.

"Carter?" Riley ventured. "Are you okay, baby?"

"Give him a minute."

"How did you wake him up by just touching him? What did you do?" she asked Malik.

Carter blinked his mother into focus. "I saw Daddy. We were flying through the air like birds. It was so much fun. Then I heard Mommy calling me and I told Daddy that I had to go and he got mad. He said he wasn't, but I could tell that he was. He turned really red and did loopety loops in the sky. He told me to ignore you. And I told him I couldn't. You kept calling me and I started flying to your voice. I kept flying and flying, then I was back home with you."

"Bradley was there." Riley let out a low moan. "He was trying to take him to his side."

Tamia sidled up next to her sister. "He's trying to kill his own son?" she whispered in Riley's ear. Riley nodded while keeping an eye on Malik and Carter. "That bastard!" Tamia hissed in her sister's ear. Tamia kissed Brie softly on the cheek.

"Mommy!" Carter whimpered, suddenly scared. "Is Daddy trying to kill me?"

Riley scooped him into her arms. "Oh, baby!" she crooned as she hugged him against her.

"We'd better get going," Malik announced. "We have friends on the other side keeping Bradley busy, but as soon as that skirmish ends, he's going to come back for his son," he said to Riley. "We've got to get to my house to prevent that from happening."

Riley jumped up. "I have to pack some things for the kids," she said as she moved toward Carter's closet.

"There's no time for that," Malik said. "We'll worry about all that when we get to my place. Right now, Bradley is pissed as hell and he won't stop until he gets his son. Let's get out of here. Now!" he ordered and everyone scampered after him.

Downstairs, Tamia snatched up her purse and shoes. "I'm coming with y'all."

"Of course you are," Riley said. It was a given that her sister would come with her; she wouldn't have it any other way.

"I'm driving," Malik announced.

"But-but-but," Tamia stuttered as she gazed longingly at her Maserati.

"We're taking one car," Malik said firmly. "That way I don't have to worry about you following me and the risk of losing you if Bradley gets away. This way, I'll be able to protect you all."

"Come on, girl, it'll be here when you get back."

They all piled into Riley's SUV and Malik slid behind the steering wheel. Tamia barely had Brie secured in her car seat before he floored it. As soon as they made it onto the interstate, Malik kicked it up a notch, to over ninety miles per hour.

"Do you really think he'll come after us?" Riley asked quietly.

She sat in the backseat with her arms wrapped around Carter. She hadn't let go of him since he had woken.

Malik wanted to lie but decided against it. She needed to know the truth so that she could be prepared. "Oh yeah, as fast as a fading blonde fighting over the last bottle of peroxide." No one said a word. "I need to make a call." Malik quietly stated his father's name; the phone rang only once before it was picked up on the other end. While torpedoing down the interstate, Malik shot instructions into the phone. "Everything will be set up for you all when you get to my place," he announced after disconnecting the phone.

They were almost to Malik's house when it happened. Bradley and two of his soldiers materialized in the SUV.

Riley looked up to find Bradley leering down at her. She blinked, then glanced upward a second time; Bradley winked. Her eyes stretched open as she shrank against the leather seat. "Malik!" she shrieked. "Malik!"

"What are you doing, Ri Ri? Why don't you get it? You can't get away from me. Ever," he taunted.

As if on cue, his soldiers immediately zeroed in on Riley and Carter. One tried to wrench her arms from around him while the other struggled to snatch him from his booster seat.

Carter's eyes snapped open. "Mommy! What's happening!"

"Oh my God!" Tamia muttered, paralyzed with fear.

The car swerved but Malik quickly regained control. He swore as he alternated his gaze from the backseat to the road.

For the second time in one day, Riley was battling for her son's life.

"Leave him alone! Leave my fucking son alone!" Eyes narrowed with determination, her arms tightened around Carter.

"Oh, he's mine, believe that!" Bradley announced. His presence permeated the car, filling it with a putrid, nauseating smell. "I got this," he said arrogantly. With a wave of his hand the two spirits blew away, leaving Riley and Bradley to fight it out. "You're gonna lose and I'm gonna win," he gloated as he wrapped his hands around his son's neck. "Come to your daddy."

"Malik!" Riley screamed as she felt her grip loosening on Carter.

Malik swerved and stopped the car on a hairpin-thin shoulder alongside the interstate. He turned to Bradley. "Stop fucking with women and children and fight a real man!" he taunted. Before Bradley could reply he shot out his hand and a ray of electrifying blue exploded, hitting Bradley squarely in the chest. Bradley's face distorted in pain as his grip loosened on his son's neck. Sparks flew off him as he shifted from solid to vapors and back again, until he finally dimmed away, leaving the car smelling like fried spoiled meat.

Riley hugged her son tightly to her. She sobbed against his head. "This is getting to be too much. I'm so glad you're okay. Tell me you're okay?" She glanced at his neck then closed her eyes and gave a silent thanks when she didn't see any finger marks. She peeked over to Brie, who was safely asleep in her car seat.

"Why is Daddy trying to hurt me?" Carter asked, bewildered. "I thought he loved me."

"He loves you, just a little too much."

"Oh, okay." Moments later he drifted off to sleep while Riley clung to him and anxiously watched him until he fell into a deep sleep and was out of Bradley's reach.

"Is Bradley dead?" a terrified Tamia asked Malik. She'd spent the duration of the fight squeezed against the passenger-side door.

"I wish. Just a little stunned. He'll go back and reenergize. He'll be back," Malik promised, his voice grim. "But by the time he's ready, we'll be at my house." He eased back into the flow of traffic, going even faster than he had been going previously. Tamia glanced at the speedometer; ninety miles seemed like a snail's pace.

"Is he going to send some more ghosts in his place?" Tamia asked fearfully.

"He might. He's just arrogant enough to do something like that. But we're almost at my house. This is my exit." He zoomed off the interstate and they all held their breath until they got to his house. As soon as they turned into the curving driveway, the garage door opened. "My father is waiting for us," Malik said, answering Riley and Tamia's unspoken question. "As soon as we get into the garage, we're safe. We're trying to get protection expanded to the grounds, but right now it's just the house." Just as they rolled into the garage and the door closed after them, Riley and Tamia let out a loud sigh. Malik's father and grandfather sauntered over to the SUV and walked quickly to the driver's side; Malik stepped out and joined them. They spoke with Malik in hushed tones.

A couple of minutes later the gentlemen opened the doors. Riley could immediately tell that they were Davenports. They both were almond colored and had the family's vibrant blue eyes.

Tamia gratefully took Malik's father's proffered hand. Quick introductions were made before she followed him into the house along with Malik's grandfather.

Malik pulled Brie's car seat out while Riley worked a sleeping Carter free from his booster seat. "Thanks," Riley offered and Malik wasn't sure if she was thanking him for saving Carter or carrying her daughter.

"You're welcome," he murmured. They walked silently into the house.

"I think I'd better put them to bed," Riley said. It had been an incredibly long, emotionally wrenching day. "And I'll be right behind them."

"Let me show you where they'll be sleeping. Is it okay if they share a room?"

"I think that they'd prefer it. In case either one of them wakes up in the middle of the night they'll see each other. And I'll sleep in the same room they're in," she hurriedly tacked on.

You can't keep running from me, Malik thought. "Of course," he said instead.

Malik paced outside the bedroom while Riley put the kids to bed. He would have loved to help, but he knew that they needed private time. He paused outside the door while she prayed with them and for them. Her voice, which had started off soft, ended with such passion that he knew God had heard her.

As soon as Riley stepped into the hallway, Malik grabbed her hand and pulled her to him. "Are you okay?" She nodded. "You're sure? You've been through a lot today."

"I feel okay," she answered truthfully. "I guess it'll all hit me later."

"You've been through so much, and I want to help you in any way I can. I really do."

"I know, and I appreciate it. You're doing so much already, a simple thank-you isn't enough. Now tell me—what did your father tell you? I know he's been talking to his contacts about Bradley."

Malik grabbed her hand and began walking. "Come on."

"Where are we going?"

"To my bedroom," Malik answered. Riley stopped and dug her feet into the carpet like a stubborn mule.

"Uh-uh. You have over thirty rooms in your house and the only quiet one is your bedroom?"

"What's wrong with you? You've been in my bedroom before."

"Yes, and remember what happened? I almost ended up in your bed," Riley reminded him.

Malik grinned. "You'll be okay; I desire you, but I don't want to take advantage of you. You're too vulnerable right now. Here we are." He nodded at the door right in front of them.

Riley reluctantly followed him into his bedroom.

Malik pointed to a plush love seat in a cozy nook. Riley gratefully sank into it. "Would you like something to drink?"

"Not now; maybe later. Tell me what your father said."

Malik settled next to Riley. "Bradley's been hurt. How badly we don't know. He went into seclusion, so no one knows how badly off he really is."

"That's a good thing, right?"

"I wish. Now he's really pissed. His pride is bruised and he's hurt. And not only does he want revenge, he wants both of us dead and he wants his son, preferably in that order."

"How did it get to this point?" she asked. "Why does he hate me so much? I didn't do a damn thing to him." Suddenly the day's events hit her like a bag of wet sand and she began to shake uncontrollably. "Why is he doing this to us?" she stuttered.

"He's an evil monster." Malik knew that tears weren't far behind. His theory was proved correct a minute later when she began sobbing.

"There's no place for me to hide from him. He'll always be able to get to me if he wants."

"He can't get to you or the kids here," Malik reminded her.

"Yeah, but you guys can't kill him, so you're useless," she

muttered, missing the hurt that dimmed Malik's blue eyes. He knew the words were uttered out of fear and weren't intentional, so he ignored them. "You'll have to be our personal bodyguard. I can't stay in this house forever."

"That's not so bad, is it?" Malik cajoled.

The sweet tone of Malik's voice snapped Riley out of her rant. "It's not. I'm sorry," she said almost sheepishly. "I just feel like I'm one scream away from being put in the loony bin. I'm so on edge, I don't know what to do."

Malik tenderly stroked her face. "Your reaction is totally understandable. You're handling yourself quite well considering what's happened. I've known some women who really did snap under the pressure, so you're doing terrifically."

"What kind of man wants to kill his son just for revenge? What kind of man is that? A horrible one, that's what! I'm not dealing with this well," she admitted quietly. "I feel like I'm two seconds away from losing it."

chapter FOURTEEN

Twenty minutes later, Riley pushed open the door to Tamia's bedroom and found her sister sitting on one of the double beds that filled the room. "What the hell is Malik?" Tamia asked.

Riley eyed her sister while contemplating how much to tell her. *Well, she did see Malik use his rays to injure Bradley.* "He's a warrior," she revealed. "He annihilates ghosts. He blasts them to smithereens. And he's a prince."

"Dang! I need to get me one. Here I am sleeping on the geek of the week and you got a prince. You were always the smart one. Not only did you get a fine man, but a rich one too." Tamia guesstimated that Malik's mansion had cost over three million dollars. The guest rooms were impeccably furnished with expensive furniture and exquisite accessories. And the few bedrooms that she got a chance to see reminded her of a high-end spa.

"He does pretty well for himself," Riley said quietly.

"On a principal's salary?"

"Vice principal," Riley corrected her. "But most of his money is inherited," she said simply, not explaining that Malik was over a hundred years old, and his father's and grandfather's ages were unbelievable.

Tamia sighed. "Today was so crazy. It felt like a dream, hell, it still feels like a dream. But I guess you're used to it," she said, trying to joke.

"I don't think I'll ever get used to it. My life has been turned upside down by some crazy, stalking demon who's trying to kill me and my son. It's not like I can go to the police and report it."

"You have something better," Tamia said softly. "You have Malik, his family, and his paladins. They're way better than the APD."

Riley hugged her sister. "You're right, girl. Thanks." She stood up to go. "It's time for me to go to bed. Lord, it's been a long day."

"Are you gonna slip down to Malik's room?" Tamia teased.

"No, I'm going to sleep in the kids' room. I won't be able to rest if I'm too far away from them."

"But Malik said that they're safe here," Tamia said as her eyes nervously began darting around the room, trying to inspect every crevice.

"Oh, they are. It's a mommy thang. You'll understand when you have kids." They grinned at each other. "Sweet dreams, I'll see you tomorrow." She turned toward the door.

"Thanks, girl," Tamia whispered.

Riley stopped and looked at her sister. She looked tired, as though she had been fighting sleep for weeks. "For what?"

"For saving my life," she answered. "You know Bradley would come after me in a minute, just to hurt you. I'm glad I was at your house."

"It didn't matter. I would've tracked you down and brought you here. I won't ever let anything happen to you," Riley said firmly. "I love you as much as I love my kids. Not one of you was going to be left behind."

"Thanks again."

"You're welcome. Go to sleep. Tomorrow we need to talk about what to do with your job."

"There's nothing to talk about; as long as there's a laptop around, which I'm sure there is, I can work."

"Great! You're lucky that you're a freelance writer. You can work anywhere."

"I bet this would make a great story," Tamia drawled.

"Don't you dare!"

Tamia giggled. "Never in a million years. Besides, no one would believe me. G'night."

"Okay, sweetie."

Riley stepped out, closed the door behind her, and ambled three doors down to the children's room. They were already asleep, which didn't surprise her. It had been an emotionally draining day for Carter, and Brie slept all the time. Malik's helpers had set up a crib for Brie alongside the king-size bed where Carter slept. "I guess we're gonna be bunkmates," she whispered to the sleeping Carter. She kissed them both before undressing. Fortunately, a silk negligee was set out on a chair for her.

After a quick shower, Riley dressed in the negligee and sat on the chaise lounge. Even though it was after midnight, she was too keyed up to sleep. She turned on the TV and found *Good Times*. "How could you do this, Bradley? So you hate me so fucking much that you tried to kill our son? You're a fucking coward!" she hissed. The possibility of Bradley even hearing her was nil, but it made her feel better saying it.

A few minutes after she'd dozed off, a knock on the door woke her. She jumped up, startled by the noise, and it took her a second to realize what it was. "Calm down, girl," she said to herself. Riley swung her legs off the chaise and padded to the door. She swung it open and found Malik standing on the other side, wearing nothing but boxer's. Riley inhaled sharply; he was gorgeous. Bradley went to the gym and took care of his body, but he didn't compare with Malik. Malik's body was chiseled to perfection.

"Don't you ever wear clothes?" Riley blurted out, then blushed.

"Not when I'm trying to seduce a woman," he answered, then studied her to gauge her reaction.

"Malik," Riley faltered, at a loss for words.

Malik grabbed her hand and pulled her into the hallway. Riley closed the door after herself. "I want you, Riley. I want to lick, suck, and kiss every inch of you."

"Malik!"

"That's right, keep saying it. I'm going to have you screaming it out all night long." Blood pounded in Riley's ears and desire made her legs weak; she leaned against the door frame. "Look at how much I want you." He motioned toward his underwear. *Oh my!* She licked her lips as her eyes rose to meet his.

Malik reached out and boldly cupped a breast. He leaned down and tenderly traced her nipple with his tongue. Riley shivered with desire. Pleased with her reaction, he locked gazes with her. "So, how long are you going to make me wait?"

chapter FIFTEEN

Riley, Tamia, Malik, his father, Carrington, and grandfather, Bayard, sat around the dining room table. The children played quietly on the other side of the room. "We need to figure out what to do with Riley and Tamia and plan our strategy," Malik announced. "Right now, they can't leave the house."

"I'm stuck here, forever?" Riley protested.

"We're not saying that you can't go out, just that you can't go out without Malik, Carrington, or myself," Bayard said sensibly.

"How am I supposed to work? I can't have you guys lurking around all day."

"I granted you a leave of absence."

"You what!" Riley exploded. In one day, her son was almost killed, she was attacked by demons and almost killed, and now her job was being taken away from her. It was too much! She stood up, made a fist, and banged it on the table. "Who told you to do that? Certainly not me." She turned to Tamia. "Did you tell him to?"

Her sister smothered a giggle. She loved this, as Riley rarely shouted. "No I didn't, and he was wrong for doing it," she said, egging her on.

"He *was* wrong. I'm going to call Principal Wolaski. I bet she'd like to know how the vice principal is abusing his power." She whipped out her cell phone, glared at Malik, then dialed the principal's home telephone number.

"If it helps, I'm taking a leave of absence too."

"Won't that seem weird?" Tamia asked and Malik shook his head.

"Not at all. I've been talking about taking a sabbatical for a while now. I highly doubt that she'll connect us. It's not unusual for a school to have two or more personnel out on leave at the same time." Malik turned his attention back to Riley. "What are you going to tell her?" he asked lazily.

"That you gave me a leave of absence without my knowledge."

"And she's going to ask you why I did it. What's going to be your response?"

"So that my dead husband won't—" Malik simply grinned. "Shit!" She realized how ludicrous the truth sounded. She immediately clicked off her phone and tossed it on the table. It rang. Without looking, Riley knew that it was her boss. Glaring at Malik she picked it up.

"Hi, Pearl. Yes, I did call, but when I realized how stupid it was for me to do so, I hung up. I didn't mean to bother you." Riley made another fist and shook it at Malik. His father and grandfather watched with amusement. "I was just calling to tell you that I was taking a leave of absence. Then I remembered that Malik mentioned he was going to personally hand-deliver the form to you. I realized that I needed to take a break from work. I guess I'm not over my husband's death like I thought I was. Thanks for being so understanding. Yes, I will keep in touch. Bye-bye."

The group erupted with laughter. She turned to Malik. "Don't think that you're out of trouble, because you're not," she scolded before flopping into her seat.

Malik leaned over. "What are you going to do, spank me?" he whispered.

"You wish," she retorted under her breath but she blushed at the idea. Malik winked at her.

"I can hang out for a minute," Tamia announced. Her job as a freelance writer allowed her to work anywhere in the world as long as there was an internet connection. And she could tell by Malik's house that connecting to the worldwide Web wouldn't be a problem. "Just give me the mealtimes and I'll be cool." Riley didn't know whether to laugh or cry. Her sister could find the best in any situation.

"Now that's settled," Carrington said. "Let's focus on something a hell of a lot more serious, our friend Bradley," he said somberly. "Bradley is very powerful. And according to our contacts, he's getting stronger every day."

Malik nodded. "I know, I gave him almost everything I had during the car attack and all I did was injure him. And I think that even if I had given him one hundred percent, the results would've been the same."

"How did you kill your wife's murderer?" Riley asked and four pairs of eyes swiveled in her direction. "Oh, I'm sorry, I didn't mean . . . I just thought if Malik could do the same thing, then . . . ," she said, stumbling over her words more than a drunk rapper.

Malik placed his hand over hers and the mood lightened. "It's okay, that's a legitimate question. Maluxer, her killer, wasn't as strong as Bradley. Besides, that was over a hundred years ago. I was younger and Exor wasn't in charge. He was only a minion serving Lucifer."

"Wife? You're over one hundred years old?" Tamia asked, her eyes rounded with fear.

"It's okay T., I'll tell you everything."

"I want to know now," Tamia said stubbornly. "How can I help if I know only half the story?"

"Hush! I'll tell you later. I promise," Riley insisted. "We don't have time to catch you up."

"You'd better," Tamia threatened.

Malik squeezed Riley's hand, a movement that his father didn't miss. He smiled at Bayard, and they gave each other imperceptible nods of approval. They liked Riley, and she was the first woman Malik had been interested in since his wife was killed. The bloodline will continue, their gaze said.

"You can always go to Ulgani to train," his father offered.

Malik considered the suggestion; the same thought had crossed his mind. "That's an option," he said slowly. "But there's no guarantee that my powers will get stronger. And we don't have time for that. If we don't kill him, we have to at least hurt him so badly that we'll put him out of commission."

Riley dispassionately listened to the conversation; the thing they were discussing was no longer her husband, but an evil entity that needed to be destroyed.

"It doesn't seem right that our weapons didn't keep up with the times," his father said. "We are so ill prepared," he said, chastising himself.

"Naive, that's what we are," Bayard chimed in.

"We couldn't have foreseen this thing," Malik responded. "He came from out of nowhere and has strength that no one has seen before. We need to destroy his power source."

Carrington and Bayard exchanged glances. "It's one thing to destroy Exor's general but to obliterate the source of all evil is another story; it's impossible," Carrington scoffed.

"Maybe we can implode him," Malik blurted out. "Get him from the inside and make him collapse in on himself."

Murmurs went up, causing Carter and Brie to stop playing and fix the adults with a stare. "Hey, boobie," Riley called to Carter. "Why don't you and Brie go to the kitchen and ask Tao for some mashed bananas for your sister and get some cookies for yourself."

Malik squeezed Riley's thigh, causing a rush of heat to her pussy.

Carter grinned; he loved the cookies that were bigger than his hands and full of raisins, nuts, and chocolate chips. "Okay, Mommy."

"I'll call Cecil," Malik said before punching in a couple of numbers on the intercom and instructing the butler to come to the dining room to pick up the kids.

As soon as the children were out of the room, the noise level increased considerably. "Blow that motherfucker up into a million little pieces . . . that's whassup!" Tamia said.

"But how? How can we do it?" Carrington wondered.

"This is a unique situation, our traditional methods aren't suitable," Bayard said.

"And we don't have any new ideas," Carrington finished for him.

"That's why we're here," Malik said, frustrated.

"We need to get to his power source," Bayard said.

"Exor?" Tamia asked.

Malik shook his head. "Bradley." He pointed to his chest. "We have a heart, but Exor has granted a few evil spirits like Bradley a nucleus. And it's almost like a heart; that's his power source. Destroy that, we destroy Bradley."

"So we need to destroy his nucleus. If it serves a role similar to that of a heart—"

"It's not a heart," Malik quickly corrected him, "it's similar and it lasts for eternity."

"Yes, but like everything else, it's got to have a weakness. Nothing is indestructible. We can destroy him, and we will," Bayard vowed.

Carrington fixed his son with a hard gaze. "You realize what this means, don't you?"

"What?" Tamia and Riley asked at the same time.

"First of all you've got to be in tip-top condition," Bayard said to his son and Riley blushed. An image of Malik's towel-clad body popped into her head. She sneaked a peek at him out of the corner of her eye only to find him looking at her. Her heart sped up as their gazes locked and he subtly blew her a kiss. Riley didn't know whether to graze her lips or hips against his mouth.

Malik grinned at her indecision. She inched closer, entranced by his delicious mouth. His father cleared his throat, startling Riley, and she jerked back. "Are you paying attention?" he asked Malik.

"Yes, sir," he drawled.

"You need to train," his father continued. "Since you don't want to go to Ulgani, where would you like to go?"

Malik took a minute to consider his father's statement. "I know just the place to go where I can get a mega workout," he announced.

Riley sat on the edge of her double bed and Tamia sat on one exactly like it across from her. After Carter told her that he was a big boy and didn't need her to sleep in his and Brie's bedroom, she'd moved into Tamia's room. She knew that her children would be fine and that there wasn't a safer place in the world for them to be.

"So why didn't you tell me about Malik's history?" Tamia asked, still stung by not being included.

"Okay, so how would you have taken this? I'm having sex with my dead husband, but it's not necrophilia because he's a ghost. And the guy I'm interested in is not only a prince, but a demon warrior; he's also over a hundred years old and is a widower. How would you have taken that?" Riley asked.

"Well, you already told me a lot about Malik, and I knew about Bradley, so that wasn't news."

"But you *almost* freaked out when you found out about it."

"Who wouldn't? I saw my sister floating around like a piece of paper and humping the air. Who wouldn't be creeped out by that? You should've been concerned if I wasn't alarmed by the whole ghost-lover thing." She inhaled deeply, then continued. "After the whole Bradley thing, I would've understood."

Riley blinked with surprise. "You would have? You wouldn't have thought of me as some type of freak magnet?"

"Well, yeah," Tamia drawled and they both laughed. "But you're my sis and I'll always love you and have your back no matter how crazy things get."

"Thanks, girl."

"So give me the scoop on Malik's dead wife and how he killed her murderer," she asked as she moved into a more comfortable position.

"Would you like some popcorn?" Riley asked dryly.

"I would love some. His story sounds like a blockbuster," Tamia quipped.

Riley got up from her bed then plopped down next to her sister and grinned. "You know, this feels familiar."

Tamia returned her sister's smile. "Yeah, like when we were

teenagers. When I used to run into your room and sit on your bed and we'd talk for hours and then we'd fall asleep together."

"And Mommy would wake us up the next morning. Hi, Mommy, and thanks again," Riley said.

"Hi, Mommy!" Tamia said, and she and Riley grew teary eyed. "Tell me, tell me everything," she encouraged brightly as she tried to lighten the mood.

"Okay, hold on to your thong, 'cause it's a long story." Thirty minutes later Tamia's mouth had dropped open with shock.

"So do you think he's still in love with his wife?"

"His *deceased* wife," Riley corrected her. "And no, I don't think he is. It's been, like, seventy years."

"I don't think he is either. I could tell by the way he mentioned her. It was more in an old-friend kind of way and not an I'm still dreaming of her every night."

"You think?"

"I know," Tamia said firmly. They were silent, then, "Why don't you go over to his room? I could tell by the way he was looking at you that he wants to get into your panties."

"I want him to chase me," Riley said primly.

Tamia rolled her eyes. "Damn, girl, how much chasing do you want the man to do? He came to your bedroom door and told you that he wanted to lick and suck you. And you turned him down. You know how he feels, and neither one of you is a child."

"I know that," Riley said, bristling with irritation. "I'm just used to a man pursuing and courting me."

"That's fine. I understand all that. But both of you know what's up. And Malik is cool, he's experienced many things that neither of us will in twenty lifetimes, and he's seen a lot more. So he knows a slut when he sees one. And I can't see him as just wanting to hook up with you. He's really digging you and I don't think that he'll look at you any differently if you approach him."

"I don't know." Riley hesitated as an image of Malik's body popped into her head.

"You know you want to. Look at you, you've already got one foot out the door," she teased.

Riley scrunched up her nose. "You think he really won't mind?"

"I know so. Just go!"

"Okay, I will," she decided. She pushed herself off the bed and padded toward the door.

"Wait, you wearing that?" Tamia pointed to Riley's outfit, a pair of baggy sweat pants and an even baggier sweatshirt.

"Sure, what else should I wear? It wasn't like I was planning a seduction," she retorted.

"Big sis, big sis," Tamia tsked. "When will you ever learn." She got up from the bed and scurried over to the dresser. Riley impatiently tapped her foot as Tamia opened a drawer and pulled out something black and sheer. "Here you go," she said, surrendering the frothy outfit.

"How the hell did you find the time to get this?" she asked. The outfit was sexy. She doubted that the see-through black baby doll with matching G-string was big enough to fit her. It was just a smidgen bigger than a cocktail napkin.

"I had it in my purse," Tamia answered nonchalantly.

"Who the hell carries lingerie around in her purse?"

"Me!" Tamia quipped. "You never know when you might need it. And it's clean, I've never worn it, the tags are still on it. Put it on!" Riley hesitated. "Now!"

She stomped to the bathroom and took her time changing.

"There are some women who carry an extra tube of lipstick in their purses, but I have a sister who carries a spare piece of lingerie around," she muttered as she peeled off her sweatshirt. "What are you doing, Riley?" she asked herself as she kicked off her sweatpants and cotton undies. She took a deep breath before she slipped on the handkerchief-size G-string then the slightly larger baby doll. It does look nice . . . no *hot*, she decided while admiring her reflection in the mirror. The wispy black material hugged her skin in all the right places.

"Come on out!"

Riley shyly scurried out of the bathroom.

"Now you're ready to get your man," Tamia decided.

"I feel so nasty."

"Good, that means my job here is done. Now go!"

"Okay. Wish me luck," Riley called over her shoulder as she opened the door and stepped into the hallway. Tamia shouted her encouragement before Riley closed the door.

Riley tiptoed down the hall to Malik's room; she giggled nervously to herself. "I feel like a fifteen-year-old, sneaking into my boyfriend's room." All too soon she got to Malik's door and a million butterflies fluttered in her stomach. Taking a deep breath, she knocked softly. When she didn't get a response, she knocked harder, but still no response. After waiting a couple of minutes, she turned to leave. The door opened. Malik stood in the door frame, wearing a towel. Water sparkled on his skin. Riley's mouth went dry. He let out a slow whistle.

"Don't you ever wear clothes?" she joked, her voice shaky with desire.

"Do you want me to?" Malik challenged. Riley shook her head no and Malik grinned. He opened the door wider and she stepped inside. He closed the door firmly after her.

chapter SIXTEEN

"You look good," Malik said. "You brought this with you?" he asked as he lifted the hem of the silky top.

"It's Tamia's," she admitted. Malik cocked an eyebrow. "Well, you know how she is," she replied and he chuckled.

"Do you know how long I've been fantasizing about having you?" Malik asked. Riley remained silent, knowing that Malik wasn't expecting an answer. "For a long time, you blew me away. The first time you walked into my office. You were so refined, so classy and beautiful. My dick got so hard that I couldn't leave my desk for an hour."

"I didn't know," Riley replied softly.

"You had a brother taking cold showers . . . daily. And it's finally going to end."

Riley gasped as Malik scooped her up and lovingly stroked her face. "I hope that I won't disappoint you," he said while looking into her eyes. "It's been a while since I've been with anyone," he admitted.

"That's okay. Bradley was my only partner for the last six years."

"Well, I haven't been with a woman in almost a hundred years."

Riley mouthed a surprised, "What!"

Malik grinned; she was taking it better than he had thought. *Another reason why I love her.* "I don't believe in meaningless sex. I know that it's a hard concept for a lot of women to understand." His grip tightened. "So do you still want me?"

Unshed tears brightened Riley's eyes. "I do," she said and did something that she never would have imagined herself doing and something that certainly would've made Tamia proud. She reached behind him and tugged at the towel; it fell soundlessly to the floor. "I really do," she said.

Malik carried her to the bed and gently put her down. The satin comforter cooled her hot skin.

Riley raised her arms over her head, posing for him, basking in the love and admiration that filled his eyes as his gaze ate her up.

He brought his hands together as though praying and raised them to the heavens. "Thank you," he replied reverently, and he repeated it until tears of joy coursed down his and Riley's faces.

He brushed his cheek against hers, causing their tears to intermingle. He finally moved away and grinned sheepishly at her. "I'm sorry, I couldn't help myself. You're so beautiful and I'm so grateful that you're finally here that I had to thank God." Tears continued to run down her face. "I told you why I was bawling like a baby; why are you?" Malik asked.

Riley tried to stop her tears. Malik lovingly cradled her as he patiently waited for her to calm down. A couple of minutes later the tears had stopped and Riley lay quietly next to him; it was another couple of minutes before she opened up. "I have never ever in my life had a man react to me the way you just did. Never ever," she admitted, feeling ashamed of the confession, as though it was a reflection of her worth as a woman.

"You should have men dropping at your feet."

"Obviously they haven't gotten the memo," Riley joked. "I was in love with Bradley. I put up with his shit . . . because I loved him and I didn't want the kids to grow up without a father. But I didn't really have a clue about love until I met you." She rested her forehead against his before grazing his lips with hers. Malik moaned softly as her mouth glided over his.

He reluctantly pulled back. "You did what you felt was right; there's nothing wrong with flowing with nature. It's better to go with the flow than against it."

"But I feel so stupid," Riley protested.

"Look in my eyes," Malik demanded and Riley grudgingly did so. "Do you see anything, I mean *anything*, that says you're stupid?" Riley shyly studied his eyes. And all the love, admiration, and desire that had lit them before her confession shone even brighter now. She shook her head. "I always say what I mean." He swiped at his face; his tears had dried, leaving behind a thin layer of salt. "This is beginning to itch," he said. "I'll be right back." He pushed himself off the bed and strolled to his bathroom and returned with a damp washcloth and handed her the soft material.

"You do it," Riley said.

"Gladly." Riley shyly met his eyes as he wiped away her dried tears. Malik tossed the cloth to the floor then cupped Riley's face before leaning down and gently swiping her lips with his. He pulled back and looked in her eyes. Riley nodded. Malik groaned before hungrily kissing her. Riley's arms wrapped around his waist, his erection pressed against her.

Malik sat back and studied her. "You're beautiful," he said, causing Riley to blush.

Their gazes didn't waver when he slipped his finger under the spaghetti-thin strap and slid it down. Their gaze remained strong even when he did the same to the other one. But when he pushed the baby doll down and it floated around her waist, exposing her breasts, she shyly averted her eyes, suddenly feeling like a virgin. "Why the modesty?" Malik asked. "I've seen you naked before."

"I know, but we weren't about to make love. And this will be our first time actually doing it."

Malik understood. Even though today's trend was for men and women to hook up, any notion of romance thrown out the window, there were still women who wanted the intimacy of love-making. "Hopefully not our last," Malik answered as he casually lifted Riley and removed the G-string. He threw them and they fell next to the damp washcloth. "You don't have to do this. We can just watch TV," he offered.

"Yeah, right, and my G-string was blocking my view? I guess with it off, I can see better?"

Malik had the nerve to look embarrassed.

Riley stroked his face. "I want to and I want you." And to prove that she meant it, she caressed Malik's penis, causing it to pulse in her hand.

"Stop it!" he ordered gruffly. "Keep doing that and you'll have me making such a mess in your hand that you'd think this was my first time."

Riley giggled, enjoying her power over Malik. He leaned over and rained kisses on her neck. Inching up, he tenderly sucked on her earlobe, then rimmed her ear with the tip of his tongue. Riley sighed; this was lovemaking. Malik stopped kissing her ear and refocused on her lips.

He kissed her slowly, savoring every bit. Riley upped the intensity and enthusiastically devoured him while Malik's hands explored her body. Malik nuzzled her neck before he cupped a breast and brushed his tongue over a nipple. Riley moaned softly. Her back arched and she fisted her hand in his hair when he began sucking it. Her clit throbbed.

He nudged her gently onto her back and she lay proudly before him.

"You're extraordinary," Malik breathed. Starting at her stomach he leisurely kissed his way down to her mound. He teasingly avoided kissing it, instead focusing on the tender spots on the inside of her thighs.

"Stop torturing me," Riley said, frustrated.

"I'm just making sure no part is overlooked," Malik answered, but he did as she requested. The moment Riley felt his tongue on her clit, her legs dropped open and she raised her hips to his mouth. Malik languidly moved over her slit. Riley groaned loudly as her hips begged him not to stop.

Suddenly Malik slid his finger into her slit; Riley let out a strangled cry. With his finger slick with her juices, it slid in and out of her with ease. Riley palmed his head, urging him to continue. She began panting and calling his name; Malik could tell that she was close to the edge. He was right, Riley screamed as a rush of passion overtook her. She continued to tremble even when her orgasm abated.

Malik lovingly parted her legs and slowly eased his way into her hotness. Although he could've easily slipped right in because she was still wet, he wanted to savor it. He slowly moved in and out, his leisurely strokes had a second orgasm building. They locked eyes and Riley noticed that Malik's eyes had changed to the color of molten silver. She shuddered with desire.

Her eyes widened and her mouth stretched wide with surprise. "What happened?" she gasped.

Malik grinned. "I supersized it."

"You can make your penis bigger?" she asked, amazed.

Malik nodded. "Just another perk of being a demon slayer. How does this feel?"

"What?"

Malik showed her instead of answering. His cock doubled in size, then shrank to its original size. He kept doing it until tears of ecstasy rolled down Riley's cheeks. Her second orgasm rolled through her, knocking the breath out of her.

Malik gazed in her eyes as he increased his thrusts, sliding in and out of her wetness, her pussy walls still convulsing from her second orgasm. "You feel so good, babe. Did I make you feel good?"

Riley gave him a satisfied smile. "Very!"

"That's all I needed to hear," he said before swiveling his hips and focusing on his own pleasure. His eyes changed from silver to electric blue, back to silver as his orgasm rocked him. He gasped for breath while exploding inside Riley; she clung to him, feeling his penis pulse inside her. When it subsided, Malik fell on top of her, his breathing labored. Riley allowed him to catch his breath before nudging him. "Oh, so that's how you are, use me then push me away," he joked before rolling off her and onto his back.

"Hey, your job is done . . . for now. I'll let you know when I need you again," she teased, "so be ready."

Malik pulled her against him and kissed her forehead. "Oh, really?" he murmured.

"Really," she replied smugly and when Malik pinched her butt, she giggled softly. Then she stiffened as though suddenly remembering something.

"What's wrong?" Malik asked.

"I feel like I'm cheating on Bradley. I don't understand it, it's not like I'm still in love with him."

"I don't think it's love, I think you're mistaking fear for love."

Riley snuggled against him. "You think?"

Malik nodded then pulled Riley on top of him, gently cupping her behind. "I know," he answered. "What would happen if Bradley were to show up again? What would happen if he walked through that door and said that he had changed, apologized for every bad thing he had done to you; would you take him back?"

"Hell no!" Riley retorted.

"Why not? The man has apologized for every atrocity he had done to you, he's made himself vulnerable for you. Doesn't that make you fall in love with him all over again?"

"Hell no!" she repeated. "He's an—" she sputtered, too angry to find any adjectives horrendous enough to describe her ex-husband.

"Do you still think you're in love with him?" he asked as he feathered his fingers over her ass. Riley trembled.

"He has been such a huge part of my life and now we're looking for ways to destroy him. I can't get rid of him. Most people can go on after their spouse dies, but not me. We have to kill him again," Riley said sadly.

"That doesn't make it love. You're just being very aware of someone, or in this case *something*. Don't confuse the two."

Riley sighed. "You're right." She peeked over at him. "I just realized something."

"What's that?"

"You didn't use any protection."

"I don't wear condoms." Riley opened her mouth to protest, but Malik quickly quieted her. "Remember, I haven't been with anyone for nearly a hundred years and that was before AIDS and

I don't have syphilis or any other STD. So that's why I don't wear condoms."

"I'm not taking anything. I stopped after Bradley died." She was quiet, then, "I guess I can check with Tamia, I bet she would have some. She had a negligee." Riley pulled out of Malik's arms. He tugged her back.

"Was making love to me without a condom so bad?"

"I don't want to get pregnant and become a statistic."

"You became a statistic the moment you were born, sweetheart. Would you mind *becoming* my lady?" he asked.

"What does that mean, exactly?" Riley asked.

"It means exactly what it sounds like," he drawled.

"Does it come with a ring?" she asked nonchalantly. *Where the hell did that come from? Do you even love this man?*

"It can."

"I'm not rushing anything," Riley quickly added, suddenly panicking.

"You're not rushing me. I told you how I felt about you. And I've been feeling that way for a long time. I'm just giving you your space."

Riley poked him gently in the chest. "Oh, I can see that," she joked.

"You can always walk away," Malik whispered as he kneaded Riley's behind.

"And miss this?" she asked as she slowly ground her hips against his, the topic of their relationship forgotten.

The next morning Riley woke up to a warm wisp of air on her cheek; her lips turned up into a smile and she sighed. A second later her eyes flew open and she let out a strangled breath. She began thrashing in the bed, her arms and legs flailing as though she was drowning. "Leave me alone! Just leave me alone!"

"It's me, Riley . . . Malik. Stop it!" Riley continued to fight him, his voice unable to penetrate her nightmare. Malik pressed her hands into the mattress, instantly subduing her. He glanced down just as she looked up.

"Malik, I'm so sorry," Riley said between sobs. "I thought you were Bradley. I thought he was coming back for me."

"It was my fault, I shouldn't've wakened you like that. Believe it or not, I was trying *not* to scare you. I wanted to give you this." He handed Riley a small jewelry box.

Riley took the box and opened it. "You're so—" The words froze in her mouth when she saw the contents.

Malik chuckled as he pried the box out of her hand, pulled himself up, and got down on bended knee. "I've gotten your father's permission and all I need is your answer. Will you marry me?" He slid the ring on her finger.

"This is so beautiful," she said, focusing her gaze on the ring, which was a round diamond in a platinum setting.

"The stone is from my mom's ring. I had it reset."

"Your mom's?" she asked. Bradley had given her a wedding ring that he had gotten from some man on the corner. He had admitted to her during an argument that he had paid only one hundred dollars for it. "This is so sweet, so thoughtful, so—so—so—" She stopped, at a loss for words.

"Amazing?" Malik asked softly.

"Yeah, amazing."

Riley looked up at Malik with tears in her eyes. "This is too quick, it's way too soon."

"You might think so, but I've been in love with you since the first time I saw you, and that was six years ago. In my book, I'm way behind. And I want to spend the rest of our lives playing catch up."

Riley gazed at the ring instead of looking Malik in the eyes. "Malik, you know I care about you," she said haltingly, "but I'm not in love with you."

Malik chuckled. "I know."

Riley's head snapped up. "You know?" she asked and Malik nodded. "Why are you proposing?"

"Because I'm in love with you," he said softly. "And I know the best you can offer me right now is your friendship and your body, and I'm okay with that. And you know that I'm very patient."

She took the ring off and handed it to Malik. "I can't accept this."

Malik took it and put it back on her finger. "Keep it, it's yours. I brought it for you. Besides, I plan on making you so crazy in love with me that I'll be the first thing on your mind when you wake up and the last thing when you go to bed."

"Oh really? You think so?"

"I know so. Be prepared; you have just met the love of your life," he said confidently.

chapter SEVENTEEN

Later that morning Riley was cleaning the children's suite. Normally she'd have Carter clean up his own mess, but straightening up his room kept her from thinking about why they were there. And having Tamia in the suite helped a lot as well. They had just finished eating a light brunch and the children were playing nearby.

Their suite looked like a toy store. Malik had treats delivered for them to play with: Barbies, G.I. Joes, trucks, half a dozen stuffed Elmos, and myriad other toys covered the floor. The latest video game console and a dozen games still lay unopened on the floor. It was Christmas in October and Carter was loving it.

Riley glanced over at her children. She hadn't seen them this happy in such a long time and she knew Malik was responsible for it. His patience and kindness made it easy for the kids to feel so comfortable and to love him in such a short time.

"Your life is just like a freakin' fairy tale." Tamia faked a pout and Riley laughed.

"How?"

"So now you're going blind? It's right in front of you," Tamia retorted. "You were married to an ogre—"

Riley shot a look toward her children.

"Okay, married to a man who was kil—I mean died, and a handsome prince not only saves you but asks you to marry him and puts you up in his very own castle. If that's not a Grimm's fairy tale, I don't know what is."

"I guess you're right." She paused. "I like Malik and I respect him, but I'm not in love with him yet."

"What's not to love? You have everything."

"I didn't say that I didn't love him," Riley asserted, correcting her sister, "I'm not in love with him. And I want to be in love with him. It's just so messed up."

"Why do you say that?"

"There was a time when I thought Bradley was a king; I thought he was so strong and so smart. It took me a long time to realize that he was really controlling and manipulative," she whispered, not wanting the kids to hear.

"You have the real thing this time, girl. Malik is a good man. So don't worry, he won't do anything to hurt you," she said confidently.

"My head knows it, but I've got to make sure my heart knows it too," she said glumly.

"So where's the ring?" Riley stuck out her finger and Tamia covered her eyes. "I'm blind, take it away," she joked.

"You're silly, girl."

Tamia laughed then removed her hands to admire the ring. "He did well. It's simple but very classic."

"It is." She paused, then, "Look at what happened the last time I got a ring."

Tamia wanted to shake some sense into her sister. "Would you stop comparing the two? To be honest, the only things those two have in common is that they're both men and they both have dicks. That's it. They have nothing else in common, *nothing*."

Riley broke into a laugh, glad that the kids had moved to the far side of the room. Sometimes her sister's mouth was worse than Chris Rock's during his stand-up routine. "Okay, I'll stop."

Carter trotted over to his mother and aunt. "I saw Daddy last night," he announced nonchalantly and Riley nearly fell over in shock.

"What!" she shrieked, poised to run to the intercom to call Malik.

"Yeah, I dreamed about him. This was the nice Daddy. We played and flew all around, just like we used to."

Riley dropped to her knees and grabbed Carter's hands. "Where did you see him? Did he take you anywhere? Did you see any of his friends? Tell me!"

"I—I—I," Carter stuttered, his little face scrunched with fear.

"Answer me, Carter. Did he come into your bedroom? Where did you see him?" Riley asked, her voice near hysteria, her grip tightening.

"Mommy, stop, you're hurting me!" Carter shouted.

"Oh, baby, I'm so sorry," she babbled as she dropped his hands.

"What's wrong, Mommy? Don't you want me to talk to Daddy?"

She caught her sister's gaze and forced herself to calm down. "It's okay for you to talk to your father. You didn't do anything wrong," she said, trying to reassure him. She sat down on the carpet and gently pulled Carter next to her. "Tell me what happened." She tucked her shaking hands under her legs.

"I saw him last night," Carter began.

"Did he come into your room?" she asked calmly. Carter shook his head. "Where did you see him, then?"

"While I was sleeping. I dreamed about him."

"Are you sure it was a dream?"

"I am," Carter said as confidently as any four-year-old boy can.

"How do you know? Maybe it really happened and you thought you had dreamed it."

Carter vehemently shook his head. "It was a dream. I know it was a dream because this time he didn't give me anything. Every time we went flying I knew it was real because he always gave me a gift."

Riley blinked; this was news to her. She didn't know that Bradley had given Carter anything. "What did your father give you the last time you saw him?"

"You wanna see it?" Riley nodded. "Okay, it's in my dresser, I'll be right back."

"What could Bradley have given him?" Riley asked Tamia.

"It's hard to tell with Bradley. It could be anything from a gold coin to a dead dog. I just don't know," Tamia said with a shrug.

"A gold coin would be nice. But we'll know soon." A couple of minutes later, Carter propelled himself in his mother's direction and stopped on a dime in front of her. He reached his hand into his pocket and pulled out a handful of items. He thrust them at her. White balls the size of Chiclets fell into her hands.

"What are these?" she asked.

"Skulls. Daddy says they're the skulls of people who were mean to him."

"That's silly," Riley scoffed. But she couldn't resist the urge to study one. She picked it up and turned it around in her fingers as she scrutinized it. Her mouth widened in shock as the objects fell from her hands. She shrieked and shrieked until Malik, Carrington, and Bayard burst through the door.

"What's wrong?" Malik asked as he immediately rushed to Riley's side. Carter, who had run over to Tamia, clutched her legs as though they were his lifeline.

Eyes wide with terror, she pointed to the items on the floor. "They're skulls, he gave my baby skulls," Riley gasped out between sobs.

chapter EIGHTEEN

A couple of days later Malik burst into the children's suite, interrupting Riley and Carter's homeschooling session. Riley frowned at him. Carter had just mastered writing the letter *E*.

"I think I found it!"

"What?" she asked.

"A way to destroy—" He shot a look toward Carter, who was looking at him with interest. "Um, Carter, I think Tao has some cookies for you."

"He does?" Carter shot up. "May I, Mom?"

Riley laughed. "Sure." She watched him race out of the room. "I think he's gained five pounds since we've been here."

"I wouldn't worry. He'll work it off faster than either of us would," Malik joked. Then his excitement returned tenfold. "I found a way to destroy Bradley!"

Riley's heart jumped with excitement. "What? How?"

Malik rushed to her and enveloped her in a bear hug. Riley laughed at his excitement. He unraveled his arms from around her, and pulled her toward Carter's bed. "Come on, let me tell you," he said excitedly, his blue eyes blazing. Riley settled next to him.

"So what did you find?"

"I found something that will give me enough strength to destroy Bradley."

"Tell me!"

"I found it in Kimball's journal. He's my great-great-great-great-grandfather," he hurriedly explained before she could ask. "Something told me to look there. He kept meticulous records of everything. Even the regimen he followed to prepare for battles. He used this secret ingredient to increase his power. He wrote that after a week of drinking it, he had the power of ten demon warriors."

"What is it?" Riley asked impatiently.

"A liquid extract made from bull testicles."

"What?" Riley almost fell off the bed in shock.

"Yeah, that's Kimball's secret ingredient. Amazing, isn't it?"

Riley squeezed his hand. "It sounds weird, but if it's going to work . . ." Her voice trailed off.

"It'll work, babe. Kimball's strength is legendary. Unfortunately, he was killed in the prime of his life. It happened while breaking in a wild horse; it got the best of him and threw him, breaking his neck. He died on the spot."

"How horrible," Riley said, then gently asked, "So you think you'll be able to destroy Bradley's nucleus?"

"I will destroy it!" he spat out.

Riley looked at the determination on his face and knew that he would. "I guess this will take the place of your training." Malik nodded. "So, how are you going to get the extract? And how much do you have to take?" she asked, still a little repulsed by the whole thing, but hoping it would work.

"I won't take the real stuff. Dr. Imes, the leader of our personal security team, is creating a synthetic version of it. It should be here tomorrow."

"That's wonderful; how soon before you begin to notice a difference?"

"I'll have to drink three ounces of it three times a day for three days. On the fourth day, I should be ready for my battle."

Riley looked at Malik worriedly. "I hope this works."

"It will," Malik said confidently.

Riley and Tamia stood on a balcony overlooking the back of the house. It was the day of the fight. Malik stood bare chested, while Bayard and Carrington stood a little ways away.

Riley grabbed her sister's hand. "I don't know if I can watch this," she murmured.

"Malik will squash that monster like a bug."

"I know he will," Riley said, thinking back to the last four days. Malik's strength increased after every dose of liquid bull testicle extract. Every day his biceps seemed to grow an inch. And now they were glistening in the sun. "I'm glad that the kids are down for their nap. I would hate for them to see something like this."

"How do they know if Bradley is even going to show up?"

"He will. Carrington sent a message to him."

"That's it?"

"That's all it took," Riley answered.

Tamia glanced upward worriedly. "So did they lower the shield?"

Riley shook her head. "They wouldn't dare. They're standing beyond it. So we're safe."

"Good. Oh, look, he's here!"

Bradley had suddenly materialized in front of Malik. Hovering behind him were four of his soldiers.

Riley leaned forward, pressing her hips against the railing. "I wish I could hear what they're saying," she murmured while she death-gripped the handrail.

Tamia mirrored her sister. Her gaze bounced from Malik to Bradley. "I don't think you need to hear. Oh my God!" Malik had shot his hand out toward Bradley, hitting him directly in the chest with a red ray. Bradley stumbled back.

Riley froze with fear. "Dear God, please protect Malik." The battle had started. "I have to get closer and I want to be near Malik." She turned away from the handrail.

"What are you doing? He won't be able to concentrate if he knows you're close by," Tamia said. "You need to stay right here."

"I can't. I need to be near him, just in case—" She gulped, unable to finish.

"He'll make it. He's strong and he's a warrior. Come on." Tamia led her sister back to the railing. "Look, he's kicking Bradley's ass."

Riley glanced down. Tamia was right, Bradley's left hand was gone. "Destroy him!" Riley hissed angrily. Bradley's head shot up, his eyes immediately locking on her. Riley stumbled from the railing, her face gray with shock. "He heard me," she whispered, "how did he hear me?"

Bradley let out a deafening roar before zooming upward then torpedoing down toward Malik. Malik jutted his hands up and braced himself for Bradley's impact. He didn't have long to wait. Bradley crashed into him, nearly knocking him to his feet. With his arms high above his head, Malik held him off, his biceps bulging with the effort.

Rings of red, blue, and purple swirled around the pair. Bradley had turned into a churning mass. Riley held her breath as Malik's arms slowly crept down until they were inches from his head. Bayard stood poised to intervene. Carrington angrily eyed Bradley's soldiers, eagerly circling, ready to jump into the fray.

Riley's heart pumped in her chest and she moaned. "Oh my God! If Bradley gets any lower, he's going to suffocate him." She closed her eyes then took a shaky breath. A second later, she looked down to find Bradley even closer to Malik's head. The blood drained from her face and she swayed slightly. Her grip on the railing tightened. "Push, baby, push!" she said weakly. Riley cleared her throat, then yelled it.

Riley clutched Tamia's arm. "Look!" she said excitedly. "He's doing it!" Malik's arms were creeping upward, pushing Bradley away from him. Bradley had turned into an ugly mound of black.

Suddenly one of Bradley's soldiers zoomed toward Malik. "Get him," Tamia yelled while jumping up and down. Bayard shot out his hand and a blue ray bulleted out, hitting the demon. He disintegrated instantly.

"You almost got him," Riley whispered. Malik's hands were now over his head, his body trembling under the weight of Bradley. "Kill him!" Riley yelled.

Malik pulled back his arms as though about to throw a giant ball, then let loose, shooting Bradley into the sky. He jutted both hands out, and red, green, and blue rays blasted, one after another assaulting Bradley. Once the attack ended, the sky was clear and Bradley and his soldiers were gone.

Riley turned to Tamia. "Where did he go? Did Malik kill him?"

chapter NINETEEN

"*I can't believe* Malik didn't destroy Bradley," Riley said sadly. Her anger long gone, she now lingered on the fringes of the blues. They were seated in the high-tech conference room, waiting for the others. "He was so close."

"He had him. If his soldiers hadn't snatched him away, Malik would've finished him off."

"I don't want to sound ungrateful, but we're locked inside this beautiful place and all I want to do is leave." Riley looked longingly out the window.

"So what's this meeting about?" Tamia asked.

"How am I supposed to know? I don't know everything that happens in this house."

Tamia rolled her eyes. "Yeah, right. You're sleeping with Malik; he knows everything."

"Yes, I'm sleeping with Malik. Just because we share the same bed doesn't mean I'm privy to everything that goes on," Riley protested. "He mentioned something about having a reconnaissance meeting with some of the head paladins to talk about what happened yesterday."

"Aha, I knew your ass would know. You two do more pillow

talking than the Obamas," she joked, then the topic of the meeting sank in. "How are you feeling? They're going to be talking about hunting and destroying your former husband, do you think you're going to be able to handle it?"

"The man tried to kill me and his son. Any ounce of feeling that I had for him is gone. Weren't you there yesterday? I wasn't cheering for him. I was on team Malik," she said, then smiled. "I can't believe I'm engaged to him. I didn't look at him like that."

"Of course not, you were being the dutiful wife and keeping your eyes on your sorry husband," Tamia retorted.

"True, and that's the way it should be. Did you see the two dozen roses Malik had delivered to me?"

"I did and they're beautiful."

"He's so sweet, he's always doing little things like that. He's making it easy for me to fall in love with him," Riley said softly.

"And he's rich," Tamia quipped. She still wasn't used to the opulence of Malik's house. Every settee, leather-bound book and electronic gadget screamed wealth. "I bet he has more money than Bill Gates."

"I guess," Riley responded nonchalantly. She'd stopped noticing Malik's wealth; he wore it like he wore his clothing, casually and unpretentiously.

The door opened and a tall brother the color of a toasted marshmallow, with piercing blue eyes strolled into the room. "Who's that?" Tamia hissed into her sister's ear.

"I don't know. I know just as many people as you do, which is three—Malik, Carrington, and Bayard. Check out those blue eyes, he's got to be a Davenport."

"He's gorgeous," Tamia observed.

"Are you talking about me behind my back?"

Riley and Tamia jumped. Riley turned around to find Malik grinning at her. He had entered the room through a secret door. "Umm, yeah," she stuttered and Malik laughed at her discomfort.

He pulled her into his arms and hugged her. "Hey, it's okay to look, it's when you start touching that you're going to get into trouble."

She relaxed at his teasing tone. "What are you gonna do . . . spank me?" she drawled, using his line.

"Oh yeah." He leaned down and nibbled on Riley's lips; she giggled.

Tamia stood up and shot a sexy smile at the blue-eyed man. "You guys make me sick."

Malik looked up long enough to catch his future sister-in-law before she walked off. "I know where you're going, and be careful, my cousin, Dominic has a reputation."

Tamia snorted. "I'd be worried if he didn't."

Malik raised an eyebrow at his fiancée. "Yes, she's serious," Riley confirmed. "I think you should be warning Dominic. I don't think Tamia is the one who's going to get hurt."

"Damn, so Tamia got it like that?"

"My sister and I *got it like that*; haven't you noticed?" Riley teased.

Before Malik could say anything, Carrington and Bayard strolled into the room followed by five other people. Dominic and Tamia quickly jumped apart and sat side by side at the table.

Once everyone was settled, Bayard addressed them. "I'm glad that you all were able to get here on such short notice. I know some of you had a long way to come. Before we get down to business, why don't you all introduce yourselves to our guests, one of whom is Riley, Malik's fiancée."

A lady almost as tall as Bayard and the color of heavily peppered rice stood up. She looked like she could break the conference table in half with her hands. "I am Valencia," she announced in a surprisingly soft voice, then returned to her seat. Dominic was next, and he quickly introduced himself. After him was an eggplant-colored man of average height and weight. His startlingly diluted brown eyes locked on Riley, causing a chill to run up her spine. She squeezed Malik's hand. "I'm Taurus," he stated, not bothering to stand. A small, wispy lady stood up. Matchstick-size arms and legs peeked out from underneath an oversize sweater and skirt. "I'm Peony," she squeaked before daintily sitting down. She reminded Riley of a doll.

Last were twin sisters, Arletta and Loretta, who Riley learned were from Malik's country.

"Let's get started," Bayard announced. "What are you hearing?"

Dominic nodded toward his cousin. "You hurt him, very badly. He was hovering near total obliteration. But Exor was able to restore him."

Malik slammed his fist on the table. His blue eyes flashed hotly. "Damn! I was hoping that we'd have more time to regroup. What else is going on?" he asked Dominic.

"Bradley is building his army and he's already close to a million strong," Dominic stated.

"He's aggressive," Carrington said.

"There have to be over one hundred thousand of his soldiers circling your house and waiting on your lawn. It felt like I just finished swimming through a sea of filth," Arletta said with a shudder.

"There are over a hundred thousand demons outside this house?" Tamia asked, her voice quavering. "Right outside?" Images of demons sliding under the doors and slipping through the cracks in the windows filled her head.

"They can't get in here," Carrington reassured her. "This house is impenetrable."

"What stops them from coming in through the doors or windows?"

"There's the barrier, remember? It's just like the invisible fences for dogs; we have an invisible fence for demons," he said, using a concept that she could understand. "Believe me, they can't get past it."

"What happens if they do?" Tamia asked, her voice rising in panic.

"They won't," Malik calmly reassured her. "Bradley didn't get in yesterday, did he?" Tamia shook her head.

"We'll talk about it later," Riley said quietly to her sister.

Taurus lasered Riley with his gaze. "He's after your parents," he said abruptly.

Riley gasped. *He's after Mommy and Daddy too?*

"Don't you know how to talk to people? You don't blurt out things like that." Malik hated dealing with him, but he was one of the best mediums in the world. He knew all of the spirits that had gone bad and all the goings-on of Lavastar, but he had as much sensitivity as a garbage can.

"I didn't realize we were dealing with children," Taurus retorted.

"How close is he to them?" Carrington calmly asked.

"Not close at all. They're in heaven. And you know that there's no way for him to get into it."

"Why didn't you just say so?" Malik barked. "Why get everybody unnecessarily upset?"

"But as soon as they step out—"

"They know that," he snapped before turning to Peony. "Get

word to them that they are to stay where they are and not leave," he instructed.

"Consider it done," she said, looking at Riley and Tamia. "They'll be fine as long as they stay put."

Riley got up and Tamia followed. They went over to the mini-refrigerator. Tamia noticed that her sister's hands were shaking.

"Do you think they're telling the truth?" Tamia asked.

"I do. They don't have a reason to lie. And I feel better because Peony is going to remind them. The whole thing just shook me up, you know?"

"Yeah. This whole experience is just flip-flopping from surreal to incredible. And I'm just waiting for things to return to normal."

"I don't think that's going to happen for a *loooong* time. But I know what would give you some normalcy."

"What?"

Riley nodded at Dominic, who couldn't keep his eyes off Tamia. Before learning about their parents' imminent danger, Riley could see Tamia vibrating with desire for Dominic.

"I would feel bad about chasing a man while Mommy and Daddy are in trouble."

"They're fine and they will continue to be fine. I hate to say this, but you need the release. I think you're about to burst."

"You sure you'd be okay with this?"

"Sure. Malik and I aren't playing checkers in his room. So why should I deny you?"

"That's why I love you."

Malik could sense Riley's calmness as she slid back into her chair. You okay? his eyes asked and she smiled in response. Tamia returned to her chair and Riley's smile grew wider as Dominic rested his arm on the back of her sister's chair.

"Is Exor trying to make Bradley stronger than he is or make him his equal?" Carrington asked, his brow furrowed.

"He's not stupid. The power he's trying to give Bradley is only about a tenth of his. He wants a strong general to lead his army."

"I thought it was Bradley's army?" Riley interjected.

"Technically it is. But since Exor owns Bradley's soul, it's his army, and he needs a strong person in charge. And Bradley is quickly moving up to be his number one guy. He's ruthless and cruel. Just what Exor likes."

"Why Bradley?" Riley blurted out. "Why did he pick Bradley?"

"Good question," Bayard answered. "You want to answer that?" he asked his grandson.

"You sure you want to hear it?" Riley nodded. "We found out that Exor's been eyeing Bradley for years. Bradley was seven years old when he popped up on Exor's radar, when he used to torture and kill puppies." Riley gasped. "Yeah, then after that he stole money from his friends and family and did it all while wearing a smile. Everyone was duped."

"Oh my God!" Riley gasped.

"And he hurt innocent people." He and Riley locked eyes and she knew he was talking about Bradley beating her. "Exor saw the meanness in Bradley and throughout the years stoked it like a fire until it flared up into pure evilness. So it wasn't very hard to see why he ended up where he did," Malik finished. The room was silent.

"Does anyone have anything more to add?" Bayard asked, his face grim.

"Bradley should be up to full capacity in about a month," Valencia added.

"Thank you," Bayard said.

"Any one of you is welcome to stay here, if you want," Carrington offered the group of mediums.

Each of the mediums shook his or her head. They wore the very valuable badge of being able to communicate with both sides and being able to serve as each side's mouthpiece if needed. No matter how angry the spirits got, they wouldn't bother them. They were safe, at least for now.

"Well, help yourself to some food." As if on cue, Tao entered with three other employees behind him, each pushing a cart of food. In less than ten minutes the carts were unloaded and the sideboard was filled with finger sandwiches, fresh seafood and fruit, delicate desserts, and bottles of wine.

Malik eased Riley into a corner of the room and pulled her into his arms. She leaned into him and groaned softly. "You must've read my mind, this is exactly what I needed. You feel so good."

"I know, I could see it in your eyes." They were silent for a moment as they both enjoyed being in each other's arms. Malik spoke first. "I want you to know that your parents are safe."

Riley pulled back and looked into his eyes. "I know," she said, thinking about how he'd ordered Peony to tell her parents to stay where they were. "I believe you."

Malik crushed his lips against hers, her mouth parted slightly, inviting his tongue in. Everyone evaporated as Riley moaned softly and sucked on his tongue.

"Can't keep your hands off each other, huh?" Carrington teased. Malik and Riley jumped apart like two teenagers caught necking. "I don't blame you," he continued. "She's a beautiful lady; unfortunately, you saw her first. Have fun," he said before walking off.

Riley ran a hand over her mouth. "That was embarrassing."

"Please," Malik said with a laugh as he wrapped his arm around

Riley's waist, pulling her to him. "He's a pure romantic and he's right, I can't keep my hands off you." He had bent down to kiss her when something over his shoulder caught her eye. She lightly pushed him away.

"I have to see this."

Malik sighed and followed her gaze. Standing a few feet from them were Tamia and Dominic. "What's so fascinating about them?"

Riley giggled. "I just love seeing my sis in action, she is so smooth." Acting as though she was watching her favorite TV show, she couldn't take her eyes off her sister. She watched as Tamia leaned in and casually touched Dominic, nonchalantly running her hands over his muscled arms. Everything he said was extraordinarily funny or interesting and she modified her expressions accordingly. Either her brow was pinched in concentration or she was grinning seductively.

"Are you that manipulative?" Malik breathed in her ear.

"She's not being *manipulative*, she's just letting him know that she's interested and available. It's an age-old two-step that every man and woman do."

"We didn't do it."

"No, because we started a new one. Kill a demon, get the girl," she joked.

"Cool, be sure to send the message to *Cosmopolitan*. I can just see the headline now: TEN WAYS TO SLAY YOUR DEMON WARRIOR." Riley raised her eyebrows. "I don't read that stuff; it's staring you right in the face at the checkout line, and what else am I supposed to look at while I'm waiting to pay?" Malik asked.

"Yeah, right," she quipped before turning her attention back to her sister. "Oh look, it worked. I missed the deal sealer," she said, a little disappointed. Tamia and Dominic were headed their way.

Tamia grinned crookedly at her sister. "Ummm, don't come to the room tonight or tomorrow or—"

"Damn, girl, just hang a thong on your doorknob when you're free. And make sure you air the room out."

"Will do," Tamia said as she followed Dominic out.

"I think that's our cue to finish what we started," Malik said.

Riley caressed his face. "I agree. Let's go to your room."

chapter TWENTY

Later that night after the kids had been tucked in and read to, Riley and Malik strolled to his suite.

"You're going to make a great daddy." Riley beamed as she complimented him. "You're so good with them." She loved watching him interact with them.

Malik grinned sheepishly. "It isn't too hard, they're great kids."

"Well, you're a great guy," Riley whispered as they entered his bedroom. As soon as the door closed, Riley nudged him, forcing his back against the door. She Velcroed herself against him, pressing her body to his. She giggled at the look of surprise that flitted across his face. "What's wrong?" she asked as she gently cupped his behind.

"I didn't know that you like being in control," he said, then jerked when she gave him a playful pinch.

"It's not a control thing, I'm just taking what I want. You know us Stewart girls," she drawled.

"I feel so objectified," Malik mocked.

"You're a gorgeous object," Riley said as she drew Malik's lips toward hers. Where Bradley was pretty, with his light eyes and chiseled cheekbones, Malik was all man, from his almond-colored skin to his muscled arms, flat stomach, and piercing blue eyes.

She unbuttoned his shirt and slid it off his shoulders. His pants quickly followed. "What are you doing?"

"This." Riley smiled seductively as she lightly ran her fingernails over his smooth chest. "You're so hot," she whispered.

"I think I'm going to love this," Malik said with a grin.

"I think you're right." Riley teasingly grazed her hand over his nipples, causing them to harden. She smiled up at Malik before she pulled off her clothes. He grew hard as Riley stood in front of him, her hands on her lips. Malik grabbed her hand and pulled her toward the bed. Riley shrugged out of his grasp. "Let me take care of you."

Riley stepped behind him.

"What are you doing?"

"Hush," Riley said then looped her arms around Malik's waist. He moaned loudly when she pressed her breasts against his back.

"I guess you know what you're doing."

Riley giggled. "And you'd better remember that." She lovingly kissed his back as her hands slowly explored his chest. They ran over his muscled pecs and his hard nipples. Riley's hands inched lower; the farther south they went, the more labored Malik's breathing became.

He inhaled sharply when she wrapped her hand around his cock. She squeezed softly and Malik shuddered with desire. Riley tenderly kissed his back as her hand moved up and down his shaft.

"Turn around so that I can kiss you!" Malik begged.

"This is all for you. So just enjoy it." Riley kept her hand on his penis as she stepped in front of him. Malik bent down to kiss her, but Riley drew back. "Uh-uh. I'm about to put my lips somewhere else." She dropped to her knees and slowly took him into her mouth. Malik whimpered as Riley's warm lips wrapped around his dick.

He lightly pressed her head as he leisurely pumped in and out of her mouth. Riley's hands swept over his taut globes while he continued his deliberate movements.

"Hey," Malik called and Riley peeked up at him. And the next thing she knew Malik was lying on his back on his bed and she was straddling him.

"Don't be pulling any of those demon-slayer moves on me," Riley protested.

"I wanted to feel you. Every inch of you," Malik said before grabbing her waist and thrusting into her. Riley groaned loudly as she rode his cock. "You feel so good."

Lost in ecstasy, Riley grunted in response. Malik slapped her behind, and Riley squealed. "Do that again!" He did and Riley nearly swooned with pleasure. Sweat glistened on both bodies as they rocked together. "Spank me again!" Riley demanded; Malik slapped her bottom and she shuddered as her orgasm washed over her. Her moist folds clutched his dick and Malik exploded.

Exhausted, Riley fell on top of Malik. Their labored breathing filled the room. "So?" he said.

"So what?" Riley laughed. "Is this a fill-in-the-blanks type of game?"

Malik grinned, but his question was hardly funny. "Are you in love with me yet?"

Riley cupped his face in her hands and looked in his eyes. "I might be. And if I am, I'm too scared to admit it to myself," she said. "I don't want to make another mistake."

"Loving someone is never a mistake."

"I'll remember that," Riley said. She pulled away from Malik, slipped on a sweater, padded over to the balcony, and swung open the French doors. "It's so nice." She inhaled the cold October air.

Malik stepped behind her, coiled his arms around her waist and pulled her against him. "I know, it's one of my favorite places to relax."

"And it's so beautiful. There are fireflies swarming the yard. But it's October, aren't they supposed to be dead by now?" Riley felt Malik tense against her. "What's wrong?"

"Those aren't fireflies, those are Bradley's soldiers." As soon as he said it, hundreds of spirits made themselves visible to her one at a time. Bile rose in her throat as she gazed up and around; over a hundred pairs of red eyes glared at her.

Riley watched in fascination as they methodically assembled into a football-field-wide line, but it quickly changed to terror when they zoomed toward them at warp speed. "Oh no!" Horrified, Riley jumped back. They hit the barrier with such fury that the room vibrated. The demons were smeared across the shield in a giant congealed mass.

"They can't get in," Malik calmly reassured her. "The invisible force field is blocking them."

Riley leaned into him and tried to force her beating heart to slow down. "I see that, but they are so close. I thought you said it electrocuted them."

"It does; just wait and you'll see fireworks."

Seconds later it looked like a Fourth of July fireworks celebration, every color imaginable and some that she had never seen exploding into dozens of rainbows.

Riley's fear turned to wonderment. "I hate to say this, but it's beautiful," she murmured.

"It is. But the sad thing is that there are just as many soldiers waiting to replace them," Malik said, his voice somber. Riley watched as more swarmed the invisible field and were instantly electrocuted. She and Malik spent the next five minutes watching the scene replay itself. "Ready to go back in?" Malik asked, bored with this. He had killed hundreds of demons and had seen just as many of them destroy themselves.

Riley nodded, then glanced at the blob in front of them. Her eyes bulged and she stumbled backward.

Malik caught her before she fell. "What's wrong?"

"I saw my cousin Rayshaun. He and his twin brother, Keyshaun, were murdered four years ago. I can't believe it, a family member is part of Bradley's army. My own family is trying to kill me," she muttered, dazed.

chapter TWENTY - ONE

Riley and Malik sat on the edge of the indoor pond. Carter frolicked in the water and Brie slept peacefully in her bassinet. "This is so amazing," Riley gushed as she looked around the room. Instead of the traditional rectangular swimming pool, there were two seven-foot-deep ponds and one wading pool surrounded by palm trees, sand, and fiery-colored flowers. Against one wall was a ten-foot-high waterfall with cascading water. "I can't believe you did this."

Malik nibbled on her ear, causing Riley to giggle. "I like the water, but I didn't want the traditional swimming pool, they are so boring. And since I'm not trying out for the Olympics, I didn't need anything that big. I just wanted a place where I could come down and unwind when I wanted to."

"You achieved it. This is so peaceful; I haven't seen anything like this since—" She abruptly stopped talking.

"Since when?" Instead of responding, Riley glanced across the ponds; she could've sworn she had seen a bird flit between the trees. "Since when?" Malik persisted.

"Since Bradley . . . when he took me to his world, to Lavastar," she muttered softly.

Malik's heart hurt for her. "Do you want to talk about it?" He'd always felt he had never gotten the full story on what had happened with Bradley.

Riley shook her head. "There isn't anything to talk about. He fooled me into thinking that he really loved me and that he had changed. Nothing more, nothing less," she said nonchalantly, then slid into the wading pool. The warm water massaged her skin. "This is delicious."

"Mommy! Swim over here. I got to show you something."

Riley grinned. "Here I come," she said as she leisurely walked over to her son. "So what do you want to show me?"

Carter looked sheepishly at her. "Nothing, I just wanted you by me."

"Aw, baby." She pulled Carter into her arms and hugged him tightly. "You don't ever have to make something up to get me to see you, all you have to do is to call me and I'll be right there." She looked down into his eyes. "Okay?"

"Okay," Carter muttered, then, "I didn't want to bother you."

"You're *never ever* bothering me. And I always have time for you. Okay, baby?"

"Okay. When is Daddy coming back?" he squeaked and Malik, who was wading toward them, stopped to hear Riley's response.

Damn you, Bradley. "He's not. Remember? I told you that the angels came for him." *God forgive me.*

"When will they bring him back? I miss him," Carter said, and angrily splashed the water.

"They won't," Riley said softly. "But Malik is here. Don't you like Malik?"

Carter nodded his head. "But I still want Daddy," he insisted.

"You'll—"

"Hey, catch!" Malik yelled; he had lobbed a huge beach ball at Carter. As soon as it hit the water, Carter happily chased it, his question forgotten.

"Thank goodness for the forgetfulness of children." She paddled over to the edge of the pond and pushed herself out. She hurried over to a wet bar where there was a bottle of milk waiting to be microwaved for Brie. As soon as that was done, Riley picked up her baby and fed her. "You're such a good baby and thank goodness you won't be asking about your crazy daddy." By the time Brie had finished her bottle, Riley had changed her and placed her in her bouncy seat. Malik had gotten out of the water.

Riley and Malik each slid into their chaise lounges. Drained, Riley leaned back.

"You could've handled that better."

"What?"

"I think you're sugarcoating the situation for him. He should know the truth about his father."

Riley shot up. "How can you say that? He's way too young to understand the truth. That is the stupidest thing I've ever heard."

"I think he should know the truth."

Riley stared at Malik. "I don't know what's wrong with you and I refuse to continue this conversation any longer." She gingerly picked up Brie before calling Carter. After Carter toweled off, they hurried to their room.

Thirty minutes later, after cooling off from her Spat with Malik, Riley walked into one of the family rooms and stopped short. Sitting in front of the fireplace was Bayard, staring into the fire as though it held a secret and listening to Mozart. "Oops, I'm sorry. I was looking for a quiet place to read." She held up a Maya Angelou novel. She had found that the family had an extensive book collection ranging from the classics to many recent *New York Times* bestsellers.

"You're not bothering me. Come in." He picked up a remote and aimed it at an expensive sound system; the volume went down.

Riley made her way into the room and sat on an overstuffed settee. She set the book aside.

"Please read," Bayard encouraged her. "I know how hard it is for you to be cooped up in the house. And a good story helps you to escape."

Riley smiled. "This *house* is bigger than the size of Rhode Island and I don't have cabin fever. I love it here."

Bayard's blue eyes studied her. "So you're telling me that you don't want to feel the grass on your toes or shop in a mall or eat in a restaurant?"

"I can deal with this, especially if it's saving my and my family's lives."

"You're sure? What about your students? I bet you miss them. It's human nature to want freedom," he said and she flinched, which his sharp eyes didn't miss. "We're humans regardless of what you think," he said sharply.

Riley quickly apologized. "I know that."

"I didn't mean to snap at you, but it's something that we've had to deal with for a long time. One time my father and I were run out of town when people realized we weren't aging."

"You were run out of town?" Riley asked; she couldn't imagine that happening.

Bayard nodded. "It happened centuries ago. There were hundreds of them, practically the whole town came after us with torches. They thought we were possessed by the devil."

"How did you get away?" Riley asked breathlessly.

"One of my father's friends owed him a favor. He owned a fleet of ships, so he sold one to us, dirt cheap, and we sailed to Europe, where we lived for a while."

"Did this happen in Ulgani? Did your own people chase you out? You're the king."

Bayard smiled and shook his head. "The city I was referring to was a small one in Africa. I was foolish, I didn't think of the consequences of staying in one place for any length of time. I was still young and naive. My country loved and adored us even back then; they knew what we were and they embraced us. We are revered."

"Well, why not just live there? It seems like the perfect place."

Bayard laughed. "It is perfect, but can you imagine living in the same place for centuries? No matter how idyllic it is, it can get very boring."

"So who's in charge now? You are the king of Ulgani, right?"

"I'm still very much in charge. I fly home several times a year."

"Do you think you'd ever get run out of a city again?" she asked; the Davenport family history intrigued her.

"We got smart; back then we moved every fifteen years or so. Once our neighbors started to show their age, we knew it was time to move."

"That's smart," she said softly before changing the subject. "I want to know how long this battle that Bradley and I are having is going to last." Even though she was involved in the meetings, she had a feeling that they weren't telling her everything. They watched their words more carefully than a presidential candidate.

Bayard chuckled. "I'm not a psychic. I have every confidence that my grandson will find a way to destroy him. As far as how and when, it's anybody's guess," he said with a shrug. "But everyone knows how tirelessly he's working on it. He loves you and your children and he doesn't want to see any of you hurt."

"Oh, I know. I just thought—"

"That he told me something he hasn't told you?" he asked gently and Riley nodded. "I don't think so. He's a warrior by nature so he might be keeping some things to himself that he isn't telling either of us. Warriors are like that. They never divulge their entire plan, for security reasons."

"But he can tell me!" Riley protested.

"And he might not be so forthcoming with information after what happened with the liquid bull testicle extract. He wouldn't want to get your hopes up only to have them crushed."

"I see," Riley said quietly. "So I just have to wait and see what Malik comes up with?"

Bayard nodded. "That about sums it up."

Riley groaned. "I don't know if I can."

chapter TWENTY-TWO

Riley felt free; she wanted to stick her head out of the window and have the wind blow in her face, but it was late November and a little chilly out. Thanksgiving sneaked in and out like a robber, stealing their time and reminding them of how long they'd been cooped up.

When Malik told her to get dressed for an evening out, she'd thought he was joking. What he didn't tell her until the last minute was that Dr. Imes had devised a mobile force field that would protect their vehicle. His Bentley was just as secure as his house.

According to Dominic, he had gotten word from his contacts that Bradley had been given strict orders from Exor to focus on the task of building his army, which gave them a temporary reprieve.

"This is so nice," Riley said, her voice giddy. She didn't realize how much she'd missed being out.

Malik took one hand off the steering wheel and caressed her thigh. "I'm glad," he answered; he hadn't seen her this happy in a long time.

He drove quietly, letting her relish her freedom. He felt her sizzling with excitement, her energy filling the car.

"Where are we going anyway?" The only thing he had told her

was to dress for an evening out. She and Tamia had pored over tons of clothes that the paladins had dropped off. After much coaxing and some arguing, Tamia had convinced her to wear a form-fitting, cleavage-and-shoulder-exposing cashmere sweater, a pair of skinny jeans, and strappy heels. She had felt like she should be walking the streets, but when she saw the look of lust on Malik's face, she worked it.

"Where the desperate people hang out," he teased.

Riley wrinkled her brow. "The racetrack?" she asked, thinking back to when he had told her that was where he had gone to train to fight ghosts.

"Nope."

Riley thought for a second before responding. "A strip club?"

"Nope. Good guess though. There are some Inhibitors lingering around to temporarily possess the bodies of some of the dancers but for the most part everybody there is not desperate. I mean, most of the men are seeing some T and A and getting a little something on the side, and the women are making a shitload of money. It's a win-win situation."

Riley didn't agree with that, but she kept her thoughts to herself. "Where then?" The Atlanta skyline came into view and Riley giggled with excitement, temporarily forgetting about finding out their destination. She was just so glad to be out.

"A poker tournament," Malik announced.

"Huh?"

"Yeah, it's the new racetrack. There are so many desperate people there, losing money, homes, and cars that it's the best place to go to hone my skills."

"A poker tournament?" she repeated; she knew as much about poker as she knew about sexy dressing. "Besides, I thought this was supposed to be a romantic evening out."

"It is," Malik reassured her. "We're going to have a romantic dinner. Then, if you want, we'll listen to jazz. After that we'll go to the tournament; by the time we get there, the desperation level should be pretty high."

"I can't wait," Riley said. This time she reached out and stroked his thigh and her hand went dangerously higher.

"Keep moving that hand," Malik said, "and we might end up having an accident."

"I just feel so free and so horny," she admitted. "I want to do something naughty."

"Not at ninety miles an hour you don't," Malik said. "Can you wait until we get home?" Riley shook her head.

"I can't, can you pull over?"

Malik glanced in the rearview mirror and then at the stretch of highway in front of them. "Where am I supposed to stop? The shoulder is closed; besides, we're only about twenty minutes from the restaurant."

"I want to feel you inside me so much. Since you don't want to do anything, I guess I have to do it myself." Riley reached to the side of the seat, released the knob, and the seat slowly reclined. She shot him a mischievous look as she unzipped her jeans.

"Are you sure you don't want to?" she asked as she pushed her jeans down to her knees. "You can still change your mind."

"What are you doing?" Malik asked. The car veered into the next lane when Riley splayed her legs open and began stroking herself. Horns blared; Malik regained control of the car and got it into its correct lane.

"Doing me," she whispered through softly parted lips as she continued to caress herself.

Malik gripped the steering wheel. "Baby, stop, you're torturing me," he pleaded as his dick throbbed.

"I don't think I can." And to prove it, she slid her thong to the side, giving her better access to her pussy. "I wish this was your finger," she said as she leisurely explored her moist folds.

"I wish it was my tongue!" Malik slowed down from ninety miles an hour to sixty. He couldn't take his eyes off his fiancée.

"Why, you wanna taste me?" Riley teased.

"I do, but I can't."

"Sure you can." And before Malik could ask her how, she'd kicked off her jeans, whipped off her thong, and was waving the dainty material in his face. "See? Taste me!" she ordered.

"I'm not going to put your drawers in my mouth."

"They're not *drawers*, they're La Perla and at a hundred dollars a pair, I wouldn't call them *drawers*. So taste me."

"Riley," he protested, but weakly.

"Just tongue them then."

Malik shot her a glance. "You're lucky I love you."

"Yeah, right. You want to taste me," Riley taunted. "Don't use the *L* word as an excuse."

Malik gulped. "You're right." Malik stuck out his tongue and ran it over the crotch of her thong.

As soon as Malik was done, she tossed her panties over her shoulder, into the backseat. "I'm pretending that you're licking me." Riley groaned before returning to her position, splaying her legs open and slowly inserting her finger.

Malik reached down and adjusted himself. His loose-fitting pants were beginning to feel too small. "You know, you need to stop, you're going to make me come all over myself and ruin my pants," he chastised, but not too harshly. Fortunately their exit was coming up. Malik smoothly changed lanes and followed the signs.

The first thing Malik saw as he exited the interstate was a Publix grocery store. He turned into the parking lot and navigated his car just far enough away from the crowd for privacy but not so far that security would feel compelled to investigate. "So you couldn't wait?" Malik kept his eyes leveled on her as he stripped down to his underwear in record time. Riley had stopped her self-pleasuring and locked her eyes on his penis. "Keep doing you," Malik ordered. "And I'll do me."

He leaned back and grasped his cock. No lubricant was needed, he was already slick with his own juices. He moaned as he stroked his penis.

"Supersize it for me, baby!"

Who is this lady? Malik wondered; he loved her and wished she'd come out to play more often. Malik shot her a grin as his cock lengthened three inches and widened an inch at his command. "Babe, I'm about to bust. Help me out."

Malik adjusted the seat so that he lay flat. Straddling Malik she gingerly eased herself onto his penis, pausing every couple of seconds.

"Hurry up," Malik begged. "I don't know how much longer I can last."

Riley gritted her teeth. "I'm trying. Maybe you can make it smaller."

Malik trembled. "I don't think I can. I can't concentrate. There's only one way that'll go down. If you can't handle it, then I'll do it myself," he offered.

"No, I'll do it. It might take a minute."

"Riley!"

She suddenly got an idea. "Hold on." Before Malik could protest she reached behind her for her purse, rifled through it, and pulled out a small tube.

"What's that?"

"Lube."

"What?"

"Tamia gave it to me."

"I should've known," Malik said wryly.

Riley squirted the clear gel into her hand then tenderly massaged Malik's cock, coating it with the slippery goo. Malik's pelvis moved with her hand movements.

"Perfect! I knew that this would work." Riley tossed the tube over her shoulder then straddled Malik again. She cautiously placed the tip of Malik's penis at her opening. She slowly eased herself onto him and he slipped into her. Riley gasped with pleasure.

"Just ride me slow, baby," Malik said between moans. "Take your time."

"I am," Riley said, stroking his face as she savored the feeling of him inside her. He filled every inch of her.

"Put your hips into it!" Malik ordered. Impatient, he grabbed her waist and began moving her, Riley's screams filling the car. She began trembling and Malik knew that she was about to come; her pussy desperately grabbed his dick, begging it not to leave. "I'm with you, baby, let it go." Riley screamed as her orgasm ripped through her. As soon as she was done, Malik let himself go. Exhausted, Riley fell against him.

"I think I need to make sure you get out more." Malik grinned as he held her against him.

Riley reorganized her clothes; with the exception of a little wrinkling, she still looked hot. "I don't have my panties."

"And?" Malik cocked an eyebrow at her.

"I can't go out without my panties," Riley protested, suddenly shy.

Malik burst out laughing. "So now you're back to Ms. Prim and

Proper. Two minutes ago you were finger-fucking yourself and making me eat your thong. Don't act bashful now that you're going commando."

"Okay," she acquiesced. Ten minutes later, at the restaurant, she stepped out of the car feeling powerful and sexy as the soft denim rubbed against her clit.

Once outside the door to the club, Riley hung back, her earlier bravado gone. Dinner and the jazz show had gone well. Three hours ago, she and Malik were normal people and demons didn't exist.

"Whassup?" Malik asked.

"I don't know if I can do this. I'm not sure if I can be that close to demons. They can hurt me."

"The ones that are here aren't part of Bradley's army. I've already checked, so you're fine. Besides, baby, I'm here to protect you," Bradley reassured her as he nuzzled her neck. She stood against him, stiffly. Malik stepped back so that he could look in her eyes. "You're safe, trust me. But if you don't want to go in, that's okay. I can do it another time. I'll just bring my dad or Bayard."

"I'm sorry, but it sounded like fun when you suggested we go out. I felt like I was released from prison and the ride over was mind blowing but now . . ." Her face tightened with anguish.

Malik grabbed her hand and started walking toward the car. "Come on, I'm taking you to a drive-in; I don't want to put you through this. I can do it another time."

Riley stopped. She absentmindedly glanced at a couple, a man and a woman, two cars down. She could tell by their body language that they were arguing. *They probably fight about normal things. Not whether to go demon slaying.* Tears threatened to fall and she squeezed her eyes shut trying to keep them from sliding down her face. She was unsuccessful, as one escaped and rolled down her cheek; Malik thumbed it away. "We have to do this . . . *you* have to do this."

"No, *you* don't, and I don't have to either," he said softly. "We can continue walking, get in the car, and go wherever you want and forget about tonight."

"But I won't be able to forget about it. I'll always think about the time I freaked out and prevented you from training. No, I can't do it." She straightened her back and squared her shoulders. "Come on." She grabbed Malik's hand and pulled him toward the club.

Malik and Riley breezed by the front-door host. "Paladin?" Riley asked. Malik nodded. "Are they here?" Riley asked as soon as they got inside.

Malik's lips twitched. "They're here, about fifty or so. A lot of them flew off when I walked in."

Riley glanced around. A thick veil of smoke hovered near the ceiling; people dressed as though they were trying to find their next fuck buddy stood in clusters eyeing each other. "Come on, let's go where the action is."

They cut their way through the room, nosing toward the back. The space opened to a large room filled with a sea of tables. Every seat was taken by poker players. Riley looked at the table closest to her; most of the players wore the bored expressions of experienced gamblers, but there was one Riley knew wasn't doing very well. He looked like he was on the verge of losing his shirt, his car, and his house. Riley discreetly nodded toward him. "He doesn't look too good," she said.

"Good eye. Demons are circling him as though he's a piece of meat. Oh!"

"What?"

"Four Inhibitors are fighting over who's going to take over his body."

"I wish I could see," Riley said.

"Well, you'll get to see the winner. I think there's a winner, right now."

Suddenly the man jerked up like a puppet on strings and a dopey smile crossed his face. His eyes glazed over and he dumbly threw out chip after chip, making one bad decision after another. Riley jutted out her chin at the other players at the table. "Isn't someone going to stop him? He's going to lose everything." His pile of chips was shrinking with every hand.

"Why would they say something? That's somebody's mortgage right there, or car payment. Why chance it? All they think is that he's playing recklessly."

"How long will this go on?" Riley asked, sick to her stomach. *The Inhibitors are really demented*, she thought.

"Until he loses everything. The spirit will have him go to an ATM, empty his accounts, and force him to make dumb mistakes and ultimately lose all his money."

"But why him? Why this man?"

"He's the weakest of the bunch. These spirits prey on weak people. That's how they get their strength."

Riley shook her head. "This is so sad," she muttered; just then the man turned to her and their gazes locked. His eyes flashed red and he grinned maniacally at her; Riley stumbled back.

"You okay?"

"No, it looked at me, and I don't know," Riley stuttered. "It was as if it was taunting me."

Before she could say another word, Malik turned to the man

and held out his arm, the lights flickered, and sparks fell on the other patrons. People jumped up and raced toward the door. The man bounced against the chair before slumping over the table. The spirit torpedoed from his body and shot into the air.

"Is he going to be all right?"

"Yeah, he's just stunned. The shock of the spirit leaving his body so quickly confused him. And it didn't hurt that I blasted him a little."

Riley glanced around the room. "Is it gone?"

Malik nodded. "For now."

A statuesque woman with long, curly black hair and an olive complexion stalked into the room; she took one look at Malik and stopped. "I should have known it was you. Malik Davenport, what the fuck are you doing here?"

chapter TWENTY - THREE

Malik laughed. "Shervita, you're working here? I didn't know," he said.

"Of course you didn't, you just randomly chose my club to destroy."

"I didn't, really," Malik answered. "Hey, this is my fiancée, Riley," he added in an attempt to divert attention from himself.

Shervita's only reaction was a raised eyebrow. "Really? So you caught him. You must have a magic pill, because I've been after this man for the last ten years and he's never looked my way."

Riley didn't know whether to show off her engagement ring or offer her apologies, but common sense told her to keep silent.

"She's a paladin," Malik explained.

"Your *most loyal* paladin," Shervita added. With her hips swaying she sauntered next to Malik and casually stroked his arm. "I see you took my advice and put some oomph into your workout. You're all nice and hard. I like."

Malik stepped out of her reach. "Ah, yeah, thanks for the tip. I appreciate it."

Riley eyed her fiancé and Shervita. They looked like more than just colleagues; there was more sexual tension floating between them than two teenagers on prom night. Riley's hands curled into fists, she could feel her nails cutting into her skin.

"I can think of a few exercises we can do together," Shervita teased, her voice low and throaty. The man was now stirring and people were returning to their tables. She jutted out her chin toward a red door. "We'll have more privacy in my office. Come on." Grabbing Malik's arm she tugged him.

Riley seized Malik's other hand. "I want to talk to you."

Shervita yanked his hand. "Come on," she persisted. "It's getting *really* crowded."

"Hold on. I'm starting to feel like the last turkey wing at a Thanksgiving dinner," he joked as he firmly disengaged both hands from his fiancée and paladin. "Give me a minute," he said to Shervita, who pouted like a two-year-old who'd had her favorite Dora the Explorer DVD taken away. "What's wrong?" he asked Riley as soon as they were a safe distance away.

She rolled her eyes in Shervita's direction. "I don't like her."

Malik chuckled. "Jealous?"

"No!" she insisted, but a sliver of insecurity, which she hadn't felt since Bradley, sliced through her.

"Yeah you are," Malik teased.

Riley forced herself to ask him something that had been bothering her as soon as Shervita and Malik looked at each other. "Do you like her?" she asked quietly.

"As a friend. I haven't seen her in years. I honestly didn't know she was managing this club. Dominic told me that this was a safe place, otherwise I wouldn't have come. You believe me?" he asked, his voice soft and dripping with honey. He nuzzled his nose against hers, causing Riley to giggle.

"I believe you," she decided; the sliver of insecurity vanished and was replaced with a burst of love.

"I love you. Listen, if I was interested in her, I would've had her. But Shervita can cut a man's balls off and fry 'em up and eat 'em without batting an eyelash. She's too hard for me. I like you, you're a real woman."

"A wimp?"

"No, a real woman. You're a lady. And that's what I love about you. You're soft, sexy, and feminine." Riley blushed at his words. "Look at her," Malik glanced over at Shervita, who had her finger in a man's face and was berating him in front of his friends. "She's about to cut off his balls and make soup out of them. I don't want that."

"I bet she'd be good in bed," Riley muttered.

"Why? Because she's passionate?" Riley nodded. "Trust me, I don't want to fuck, I want to make love. If I'm ever looking for a wrestling partner, I'll call her, but otherwise I'll stick with you."

"You'll stick with me?" Riley said, feigning indignation.

"Yep, you're stuck with me for life," Malik said. "Come on, let's do what we came here to do."

"What about Shervita?" Riley looked over her shoulder as she and Malik walked in the opposite direction.

"She'll be okay. She's used to me running away from her."

"So demons don't scare you but Shervita does?" she teased.

Malik shrugged. "I can't explain it either. Here we go." They walked into a small room with about ten tables, each filled. "These are the big-money games."

"Are they here?" She stared at the ceiling.

"Yeah, they're swarming over the ceiling and walls." An image of the soldiers chasing her in Lavastar popped into her head and her eyes widened with fear. She unconsciously hugged herself as she inched toward the door. "You okay?"

A wave of nausea rumbled in her stomach. She closed her eyes and prayed for it to go away. She nodded, afraid that if she opened her mouth, Malik would get a nasty present.

"We can go. It's okay if you want to, believe me," he insisted. But Riley could see him flexing his hands then his arms.

"I'll stay," she muttered before squeezing his hand. "Did any of them leave?"

"None, these are bold demons."

"Do they know who you are?"

"Of course. But they think they can take me."

"How are you going to do this? You can't destroy them in front of all these people. That other man was okay. But if there are as many as you said there are, I don't see how it's possible. You're going to burn down the club."

"It's easy. I'm going to get them in a secluded spot."

The sliver of insecurity returned. "Shervita's office?" she heard herself say.

Malik shot her a look, but shook his head. "The bathroom. It's private; the last thing these men are thinking about is using the toilet."

"Aren't the demons more interested in possessing their victims?"

"Yeah, but killing me would be a major coup."

"So you're going to use yourself as bait?"

"I've done it before. But you're going to have to wait out here while I do it."

"I don't like this. I really don't," Riley confessed as she leaned against the wall for support. She knew that if she didn't, she'd fall over in shock. "Anything could happen to you."

"What about this? If I'm not back in half an hour, break down the door and pull me out," he said, then laughed at the look of horror on her face.

"Asshole!" she yelled before punching him in the chest. "You think this is just a joke, don't you? Well, it's not, it's very, very real."

Malik pulled her against him. "I'm sorry; I know that I got this. They aren't as bad as they think they are." He warily looked at his opponents. "I'd better do something, they're getting restless." With his arm coiled around her waist, he walked her toward an empty table. "Sit here. I'll be right back."

"Malik!" she protested.

"Sit!"

Riley plopped into the chair. "Be careful."

Malik bent down and kissed the top of her head. "I will. I promise."

Riley watched him march away. A shout and chairs thudding against the floor pulled her attention away from her fiancé. A man wearing a maniacal grin overturned a table and was on his knees scooping up the fallen chips. A bouncer stalked over and escorted him out of the club. "Obviously all the Inhibitors aren't in the bathroom," she muttered and gripped the edge of the chair. Watching a demon possess a human was scarier by herself than when she had Malik with her.

"I've got to see what's going on." Riley stood up and carved her way through the maze of tables. At the bathroom door she took a deep breath before pulling it open. A demon shot out, almost pushing her to her knees. She clung to the door handle as she fought to pull herself upright. As soon as she secured a spot at the door, she looked inside and gasped with fear.

Malik was moving around as though performing an intricate dance routine. The fluorescent lights were flickering ominously and the dust from the spirits that Malik had destroyed was floating around like neon confetti. Under different circumstances, Riley would have appreciated the beauty of it all.

Malik's name stuck in her throat; she didn't want to distract him. He looked in her direction, shocked to see her, then stumbled. Riley shouted his name.

"I'm okay," he quickly reassured her as he brought his hands together and aimed them at a spot over his head. A sound so loud and piercing erupted that Riley had to cover her ears. Seconds later an outline of a ghost appeared before it slowly disintegrated. "Go sit down!" he ordered.

"I want to watch," Riley pleaded, then screamed when Malik suddenly jerked. He fell to the tiled floor and began flopping around like a fish caught in a net. "What's wrong?" she screamed. "What's wrong?" She stepped into the room, but Malik found the strength to wave her away.

"Get out. They're trying to possess me. Leave," he demanded. Riley hesitated; she didn't want to leave him, but she wanted to be somewhere safe. "Now!" Malik ordered and Riley backed out of the bathroom and fell into the nearest seat.

She dropped her head into her hands. "I hope he's all right. Oh, God, please make sure he'll be okay. I'm in love with him. Please." She continued to pray and plead for Malik's safe return. Ten minutes later she couldn't take not knowing what was going on with her fiancé any longer.

On wobbly legs she inched toward the men's room and said a prayer before putting her hand on the doorknob. Before she pulled, the door flew open, and she jumped back, just barely avoiding a collision of the door and her face. She looked up and into her fiancé's eyes.

"I thought I told you to sit down," he growled.

Riley jumped into his arms and hugged him tightly, tears of joy streaming down her face. "You're okay. You're okay," she chanted.

Malik smoothed her hair. "Were you worried?" he asked with a chuckle.

"I was," she said honestly. "Especially when they were trying to take over your body; I didn't know what to do. I was going to get Shervita," Riley admitted.

Malik snorted. "She would've caused more drama." Suddenly his legs went limp and he fell against Riley. She almost collapsed to the floor. "Oh shit! I guess I'm a lot more tired than I thought. Let's sit down."

Riley looked around. The closest table was about ten feet away and she told him so. "Do you think you can make it?"

Malik gritted his teeth. "I guess I have to." No one offered to help Riley get Malik to the table; the hunger for money overruled etiquette. By the time they got to the table, the ten feet felt like a hundred yards to Malik.

Riley flagged down a waitress and ordered drinks, a beer for Malik and wine for her. "Feeling better?" she asked as she finally took a look at her fiancé. His clothes looked like he had walked through rings of fire. They were singed and smelly, and multicolored powder dusted his shirt and pants. She caressed his cheek.

Malik nodded. "A lot better. Thanks, baby." He grazed her lips with his. "I'm glad you were here."

"Tell me what happened after I left," Riley asked as soon as the waitress deposited their drinks on the table and sauntered off.

Malik gulped down his cold beer. "It was crazy. They all swarmed on me like I'd just lost my last penny playing the lottery. I mean, damn, they were trying to possess me any way they could."

"What did you do?" Riley asked, caught up in his story.

"I fought." He stretched out his hands. "Pop! Pop! Pop! I got them all," he said, sounding a little like a seven-year-old who'd just finished playing cops and robbers. His eyes had changed to a silvery gray, his skin was glowing, and nervous energy was coming off him in waves.

Despite herself, Riley smiled. He looked so cute. "But how did you get away? When I walked in they almost had you. They almost possessed you."

"I got a burst of adrenaline and I amped up my powers. So I was able to prevent them from doing anything. But man, they were trying."

"I don't know what I would have done if anything had happened to you."

Malik looked in her eyes lovingly. "I wouldn't have let anything happen to me. I'm here to stay. But it was great training though." He grinned at her. "A couple more training sessions like that and I'll be good to go."

Riley rolled her eyes. "Yeah, we'll see about that."

His cell phone rang; he yanked it out of his pocket and clicked it open. Riley watched as his expression changed from wariness to disbelief to fear. He clicked the phone off. "Oh shit!" His tiredness forgotten, he grabbed Riley's hand and raced toward the door, using a burst of adrenaline that hadn't been there ten minutes before.

Riley's blood ran cold. "What's wrong?"

"That was Dominic. His contacts told him that Bradley knew we were here and would show up as soon as he finished some business. Which means he could show up any second."

"Oh my God! Can't you take him? You did it before."

"I did, but after all my practicing, my power isn't at a hundred percent. And he's even stronger than he was the last time we fought. I think I might be okay, but I don't want to chance it. We've got to get to the car," Bradley said as he raced through the club mowing down people. "It's the only safe place."

chapter TWENTY-FOUR

Halfway through the club, Shervita jumped in front of them, blocking their exit. Malik nimbly skirted her, pulling Riley along. "What's wrong?" she asked, on their heels.

"We've got to go. Bradley is on his way!" he yelled over his shoulder.

"Do you want me to do anything?" Shervita asked.

"We're cool!" Malik assured her. They burst through the club doors and out into the cold night air.

Shervita strolled over to the bar for a drink. "Be safe," she whispered as they sprinted into the darkness. She had heard about Bradley and knew how evil he was.

Malik's hand didn't pause as he reached into his pocket for his remote control and unlocked the door. "Keep running!" he yelled, wishing he could roll her into a ball and toss her into the car. Instead he wrapped his arms around her waist, hoisted her up as though she were an oversize box, and dashed to the car.

Riley swallowed a protest and clenched her teeth. With every step, it felt as though her insides were being shaken.

Malik snatched open the driver's-side door and tossed Riley in, then dove in after her. As soon as he slammed the door shut, the car shot up five feet then slammed down, Riley and Malik hit their heads against the roof, bouncing around like two rag dolls. Riley screamed and Malik grunted softly. He had been through worse. Then it became quiet. "Bradley," Riley whispered.

Malik fumbled for his keys, which had fallen out of his hand when the car jumped; he glanced over at Riley, who looked like she had just come face-to-face with Exor. "It's okay, baby, he's just trying to scare us. There's no way in hell that he can get into the car," he said firmly. Malik found his keys, scooped them up, started the car, and drove out of the parking lot.

Riley scooted over to Malik and clung to him. He wrapped an arm around her shoulders and silently thanked his father again for suggesting that he get tinted windows. They were dark enough that no one could see in. "Do you think he's going to follow us home?" Riley asked fearfully, peering out into the night.

"He's pissed enough and just arrogant enough to do it. But let's hope that he gets bored and moves on." Riley looked unconvinced. "We'll be home in half an hour." Riley liked how that sounded. She snuggled so close to Malik that she was almost sitting on his lap.

While keeping his eyes glued to the road, Malik lovingly kissed the top of her head. He knew that Bradley could reappear at any moment and cause all kinds of destruction. It wasn't unheard of for a demon of his strength to take control of unsuspecting drivers, causing a five-, ten-, or even twenty-car pileup.

Nor was it unusual to have boulders or trees thrown in the car's path. "Thank God for a clear night," Malik murmured. Rain, fog, or even the occasional snow would've hampered his visibility. "I need every bit of help I can get," he muttered.

Soft snores filled the car, and he realized why his fiancée was so quiet. His full lips turned up into a grin as Riley rested her head in his lap. "How can you be asleep? You were scared silly but now you're asleep, go figure. This is one of the few times that you're going to be able to stick your head in my lap without having to do anything," he joked.

Malik glanced in his rearview mirror. A fiery red Ferrari 599 was bulleting toward him, zigzagging in and out of traffic like a knife slicing through skin. "Round two," Malik muttered. His hands tightened on the wheel and with the precision of a race-car driver, he cut through the traffic in front of him, widening the distance between them and the Ferrari. "I doubt my lead is going to last long."

For four miles Malik snaked through the heavy traffic on the interstate. The Ferrari stayed a couple of cars behind him, keeping Malik in its sights. "He's just playing with me." As soon as he said it, the Ferrari ate up the road, closing the gap between them.

It zoomed up next to his Bentley and the driver leaned on the horn, demanding Malik's attention. Riley slept on blissfully. Malik powered the window down just as the Ferrari's windows inched down, Lil Wayne's latest song blared at him. The driver stiffly turned his head toward him, as though he was unused to moving it. Shock jolted through Malik. "You didn't have to do that," he said sadly. By the man's rigid movements, he instantly knew that Bradley had killed him. The man's blond hair was matted with blood and his left arm dangled at his side, but the giveaway was the blood-red eyes that glared at him. Bradley jauntily waved the man's lifeless arm at Malik.

Malik squinted past Bradley's host. Huddled against the car seat was a lady. Tears were streaming down her face, her hand was clamped over her mouth, and her body was shaking with fear. Malik wanted to kill Bradley. He hated innocent casualties.

"You fucking bastard! You think you're the king of hell, but by the time I'm done with you, you're going to be nothing but a pile of shit!"

The host's mouth turned into a crooked maniacal smile as Bradley sharply turned the wheel to the left, metal clashing against metal. Riley was jolted awake.

"What's going on?" she asked sleepily. Bradley hit the car a second time, almost knocking Riley to the floor. "Is he back?" Their peace hadn't lasted long.

"He is, and I want you to stay down."

"Is that smart? Maybe I should put on my seat belt."

Riley watched as Malik slowly weighed the pros and cons. "Okay, put on your seat belt," he said, acquiescing. "But when you sit up I don't want you to look at him. Do you understand?" Riley nodded. "Tell me that you understand!" Malik demanded.

"I understand," Riley said irritably. She righted herself and reached for the harness. Just as she clicked it in place Bradley banged into them again, and Riley looked over automatically. She blinked, then blinked again, then blinked a third time before letting out a bone-chilling howl. "Is that man dead?" she asked, stunned.

"I told you not to look," Malik growled as he expertly managed the car. "Yeah, Bradley took over his body and his soul."

"So he took the man's soul and now he's using his body to kill us?"

"That's right," Malik answered succinctly.

"Oh my God!" she whimpered. She peeked over at the car again and the host gallantly gave her a half wink, all it could manage since its eyelid was getting rigid. Riley drew herself away from the window. "Did I see a lady in the car?"

"Yeah," Malik answered as he focused on the road.

"Do you think he's going to hurt her?"

"What do you think? I don't like it, trust me, baby, I don't. But this is a war and Bradley and his demon army could care less about who's killed. To them, humans are just little ants waiting to be squashed."

Malik saw an eighteen-wheeler in front of them. "We may have just gotten a lucky break."

Before Riley could reply, he pressed down on the gas and sped up, leaving the Ferrari behind. Bradley grinned and tapped the gas.

Riley watched the speedometer as it went higher. She pressed her hands against the dashboard, but she kept her mouth closed; she trusted Malik. They were getting closer to the tractor trailer. "If this works, it'll buy us some time." Malik zoomed up behind the truck, so close that Riley could read its bumper sticker. At the very last minute, Malik cut over to the left lane. Bradley, who was going too fast and was focused on getting Malik and Riley, zipped right and slid under the tractor trailer.

Riley snatched off her seat belt and looked over her shoulder; Malik watched the scene from his rearview mirror. There was an earth-shattering explosion and the tractor trailer turned into a rolling ball of fire.

Riley turned terror-filled eyes to Malik. "Is he dead?"

"I doubt it. I'm sure he pulled out just in time."

"And the lady?" she croaked, already knowing the answer, but having to ask it anyway. Malik squeezed her hand.

They were about ten minutes from his home. "I need to call home, just to make sure everything will be set when we get there." Malik pulled his cell phone out and flipped it open.

He barked out Bayard's name and the phone automatically dialed his number. Halfway through the first ring, Bayard answered. Malik quickly explained the situation before he spat out instructions then clicked off.

The rest of the ride home was spent in silence. Malik roared across the pristine lawn, his tires chewing it up as though they were hungry, and braked to a stop at the front door. As soon as Tamia heard his car, she flung the door open. She stared at the car, unable to see its occupants because of the tinted windows.

Malik faced Riley and grabbed her hands. "You have a vulnerable spot. It's only five steps to the door. Everything after that is protected by the barrier. I've got the car as close as I can to the door and I'm going to need you to dive for it."

Bradley materialized on the hood of the car, right in front of the steering wheel. Crouching, he watched them closely through his blood-red eyes, occasionally blinking. They locked gazes and he winked at her; she shrank against the car seat and he laughed.

"You're going to have to do this," Malik said.

"What about you?" Riley asked.

"I'll be okay. Dad and Bayard are coming out. The three of us can hold him off long enough to get in the house. Give me a kiss."

Riley ignored Bradley as she leaned in to kiss her fiancé. She couldn't resist opening one eye to peek at Bradley. He had materialized into a recognizable form and had cocked his head, studying them as though they were foreign objects. He gave her the thumbs-up sign and Riley shuddered then clamped her eyes shut. A moment later she tentatively reopened them.

Malik cupped her face and looked in her eyes. "This is probably one of the hardest things you have ever done. Are you listening to me?"

Riley couldn't resist looking to see if Bradley was still at the front window. He had moved to the driver's-side door and was staring intently at her. "I need you to focus!" Malik ordered, forcing Riley's attention back to him. Pulling her attention away from Bradley, she looked into Malik's intense blue eyes. "I'm going to open the door; I'm going to open and close it so fast that if you're too slow, you're going to lose a leg. Do you understand?" Riley sluggishly nodded, as though her head was moving through a vat of honey. He tapped his thumb lightly against her cheek. "I need you to pay attention. Do you understand? I want you to say yes or no."

Riley blinked, clearing her head. "I understand. I mean yes, I mean I hear you," she stuttered.

"Good, you're back with me." Although Malik couldn't see Bradley, he knew that he was behind him, he could feel him. "I love you and I won't let anything bad happen to you. You know that, right?" Malik asked, his voice earnest.

Riley kissed the palm of his hand. A sense of peace fell over her, calming her. "I love you too, babe. And I trust you with my life. Tell me again what you want me to do."

Malik smiled at the steely determination burning in her eyes; he knew then that it was going to be okay. "Ah, that's my girl." He slowly repeated his instructions.

"I'm okay, I'm going to do it. I can do it. Carter and Brie need their mom." She jutted out her chin at Bradley then gave him the finger. "Fuck off!" Bradley recoiled at the hate on her face. Seconds later, wearing a leer that would make the devil squirm, he calmly slithered over the car, patiently waiting for the door to open.

Riley glanced at her sister, nervously waiting for her. At her side was Dominic.

"You ready?"

She exhaled a soft breath of air. "I am."

"On three, I want you to run for your life."

"Got it."

She crouched beside the door, her hand on the handle, ready to leap out as soon as she got the okay.

Malik slowly began to count. "One, two, three!"

On three, Malik pushed the door open and Riley jumped out and raced toward the house. She heard the car door slam behind her. Tearing across the grass, she rapidly counted her steps: one, two, I'm almost there.

Tamia's and Dominic's shouts coincided with her counting.

A band of heat coiled around Riley's ankle. "Oh no, he got me!" The last thing she remembered was Malik yelling at her to run faster.

chapter TWENTY-FIVE

Riley hobbled into Malik's home office. Dozens of leather-bound books were strewn across his desk. He was so preoccupied that he didn't look up when she came in. Instead, he turned a book page that was as thin as an onion skin.

Riley gingerly sat down on the leather couch. "So what's next?" she asked. Last night had scared the hell out of her. Bradley had gotten so close. She unconsciously rubbed her knees; three-inch-thick gauze covered each. Both knees had been almost shredded after Bradley had grabbed each ankle and dragged her across the stone walkway. He had her dangling in the air, ready to make his escape, when Malik, Carrington, and Bayard combined forces. With the precision of sharpshooters, they jutted out their arms, shooting their lasers at his hand. They had sliced through it like scissors cutting silk and she had dropped two feet onto the concrete. In an adrenaline-fueled move, she had jumped up and raced in the front door, Bradley's angry howl close behind her.

Malik looked up from his book long enough to say, "That's what I'm trying to figure out, babe. Some of these books are centuries old, but I'm not finding anything." He angrily closed that book and immediately scooped up another one.

"Have you guys considered combining forces . . . just like you did last night?"

"We did, we talked about it after the incident," he answered and Riley shot him a look of surprise. He'd been beside her when she drifted off to sleep and when she had woken up. "While you were sleeping," he quickly explained.

"I didn't realize I was sleeping that deeply. That drink your father gave me knocked me right out." Carrington had given her one of his herbal concoctions that reduced the pain and allowed her to sleep peacefully.

"You were out," Malik said teasingly. He closed the book and patted his leg. Riley struggled to get up. "Sit!" Malik ordered. "I'll come over there." He moved to the couch and pulled Riley to him. "I'm sorry I've been so distracted."

Riley stroked his leg. "That's okay. I understand."

Malik kissed the top of her head. "How're your knees? It looked like it's hard for you to walk," he said, his eyes darkened to a sapphire blue.

Under the gauze her injured knees were slippery squares and they reminded her of raw filleted fish. "You weren't even looking at me," Riley mumbled.

"I noticed when you limped in. I see *everything*, even if you don't think I do."

"Okay all-seeing one," Riley joked. "They still hurt, but not as much as last night. At least I can hobble around."

She thought about the night before, when Malik had had to carry her through the house after she had skidded in the front door. And how he'd had to scissor her jeans off, and she'd fainted after seeing her knees looking like raw ground beef.

"Whatever your father gave me worked."

"Oh yeah. He's good. Back in the day, people would come from miles away just for his special drink."

"I believe it," Riley said. "But back to my original question. Will it work if you guys triple-team Bradley?"

"Maybe, maybe not. But I want to do it myself," he said fiercely. "This is *my* fight!"

"I know, baby. But what about Glazier, can't he help? Dominic says that he's as strong as Bayard. Just imagine the four of you teaming up on Bradley, I bet you all could demolish him."

Malik narrowed his eyes at her; he'd never mentioned his uncle to her. "What do you know about Glazier? And why are you and Dominic talking about him?" he snapped.

Riley blinked at his sudden anger. "We were just talking about different options and his name came up. He sounds powerful, and he could be the missing link in helping to destroy Bradley," she said enthusiastically.

"I don't want to use him," Malik said dismissively and Riley could feel his body stiffen.

"But why not?" Riley pleaded. "Why don't you want to contact him?"

"I just don't." Malik shifted away.

"But he might be able to save Carter and give me my life back. With Bradley gone, the other demons won't have him to tell them what to do and they'll focus on someone else."

"I can do it without his help," Malik said stubbornly.

"I bet your father and grandfather don't feel the same way. I'm going to ask them if we can contact Glazier."

"Leave them out of it! I can do it without his help," he repeated.

"Well you haven't done it yet!" Riley yelled. "He's still lurking, waiting for an opportunity to kill me and his son. I can't believe you're being so heartless. I just can't believe it."

"Come here." Malik grabbed her hand and Riley snatched it away. She pushed herself up and limped to his desk, where she leaned against it precariously.

"No. You don't love me!" she shouted.

"Of course I do. Why would you say something like that?"

"Because if you did, you wouldn't be so stubborn. You'd want to make sure that I'm safe."

Malik's eyes glittered an icy blue. He gestured toward the room. "What do you think this is, a shack in the woods? It's one of the safest places in the world, in *either* world. If I didn't care about you, I wouldn't have invited you to stay with me," he answered calmly.

"It's more like a prison. The children haven't seen the sun in weeks. I'm afraid they're going to get rickets."

"Now you're just being silly. You know that they have several balconies they can play on. And they have one specially for them with a swing set, a jungle gym, a sandbox, a wading pool, and a bunch of other stuff. I doubt that their bones will be breaking anytime soon."

"All this can end if you just call him!"

"There's no guarantee that he'll be able to do anything. So if he comes, it could be a waste of his time."

"How can trying to kill a demon worse than the devil be a waste of time? Tell me that!" Riley seethed.

"I'm going to do it!" Malik yelled, mirroring her tone. "Just give me some time. I'll destroy Bradley."

"Is this some macho thing, that you have to do it yourself!" Riley screamed. "Because if it is, it sucks. It really sucks, Malik."

"I don't want him to come because—"

"Because what!"

"Just because."

Riley returned to the couch. "Can you please think about it?" she asked plaintively. "At least for the kids. Don't think about you, your uncle, or anybody else, just the kids. Can you do that?" she begged gently.

Malik averted his gaze. "I don't think so."

"Fuck you!" Riley screamed as she struggled off the couch and hobbled to the door. Malik ached to help her, but he knew that she'd push him away.

"We can consider Glazier as a backup plan," he said to the empty room.

chapter TWENTY - SIX

Riley's gaze flitted over each person sitting at the table. The top paladins were there and she wanted to scream, "Why can't you all help me?" So far their meetings had proved to be a summary of Bradley's activities. Nothing concrete on how to destroy him had been resolved.

She was sitting next to Malik, but she ignored him during the meeting and scrunched herself so tightly in her seat to avoid touching him that her bones hurt.

Carrington and Bayard exchanged concerned glances. The coolness between the two had been going on longer than they would like, and it was distracting Malik from his goal, destroying Bradley.

"Did he tell you what's going on?" Bayard whispered to his son.

Carrington shook his head. "I didn't hear it from him personally, but Tamia told Dominic who told me."

Bayard stifled a chuckle. "Now you're sounding like you're in grade school."

Carrington grinned at his father. "With the way those four are acting," he said, nodding toward, Riley, Malik, Tamia, and Dominic, "I feel like I'm in charge of teenagers. They sneak into each other's rooms at night, as though we didn't know."

"As long as everybody's happy," Bayard said affably. "So what happened between them?" he asked, getting back to his question.

"She wants him to call Glazier and he doesn't want to," Carrington answered succinctly.

Bayard drew back in surprise. "You know he can't do that. Glazier's never to set foot in my house," he hissed. "He made his choice centuries ago about where his loyalties lie."

Carrington held up a hand. "I know, Bayard, don't shoot the messenger."

Bayard turned his attention back to the meeting, dismissing thoughts of his grandson.

Two hours later they weren't any closer to a solution. Frustrated, Bayard abruptly ended the meeting. Riley shoved away from the table, grabbed her crutches, and pointedly ignored Malik as she limped toward the door.

Malik shot up out of his seat and turned to follow Riley but Bayard stopped him.

"You were a little distracted today. Want to talk about it?"

Malik shot a glance over his grandfather's shoulder and watched helplessly as Riley made her way closer to the door. "I'm focused. There's nothing for you to worry about," he replied absentmindedly, not taking his eyes off Riley. She was almost out of the room; he swore to himself softly.

Bayard followed his grandson's gaze. "I see that you have something in your sights on which you are quite focused. Go," Bayard commanded, grudgingly dismissing his grandson. "We'll talk later."

Malik didn't catch up with Riley until she was halfway down the hall. "Let's talk," he said as soon as he was by her side.

"Let's not!" Riley shot back.

"I've been very patient with you. I've given you your space and time for you to cool down. Come on now." He grabbed her arm and snatched her toward him; Riley instantly stiffened and her eyes widened with terror as flashbacks of Bradley's abuse paralyzed her.

"What are you doing?" she shrieked before pulling her arm free. Ripples of fear shot through her, causing her body to break out in little tremors.

Startled, Malik stepped back and immediately saw the trembling. "I'm sorry, baby. I wasn't going to do anything, I only want to talk to you."

"You could've talked to me without grabbing me like you were going to beat me senseless," she said, her voice shaky. She turned on her heel and walked with difficulty down the hall. Malik hurried after her.

"Riley, that's not what I meant to do. You know me. You know that I didn't mean that. I love you, talk to me," he pleaded.

Something in his voice made her pause and she glanced back at him. "You've got two minutes. Come on," she ordered and pushed open the door closest to them. She froze on the threshold. She had pushed open the door to a guest bedroom. She glanced back at Malik, who was struggling not to grin. *Nothing's going to happen.* "Come on!"

Malik followed her then closed the door before sitting on the edge of the bed. Riley set her crutches on the floor before she sat on the opposite side of the bed.

"So what do you want to talk about?"

"I miss you," Malik stated and Riley gulped. She missed him too. She missed lying next to him at night, she missed waking up in the middle of the night, reaching over, touching his hard body and knowing that he was there. She missed talking with him and laughing so hard at something he had said that her stomach ached.

"Whatever," she said nonchalantly then rolled her eyes.

"Can't you at least talk to me?"

"You're the one who manhandled me, requesting that we talk, so *you* talk."

Malik narrowed his eyes and they deepened to a dangerous indigo. "I just wanted you to know that I'm doing everything to keep you safe."

"Not everything!" Riley shot back.

"I am," Malik shouted.

"If you were, I'd be out of here already."

Malik bulleted over to her side; he had moved so fast, she didn't have time to jump up. His body pressed against hers. "And miss this?" he said softly before cupping the back of her head and brushing his lips against her cheek. Riley breathed softly as she went limp.

"This isn't going to make me change my mind," she protested breathlessly, but she didn't pull away.

"Would this?" he whispered in her ear as his hands leisurely roamed over her body before sliding under her blouse and skimming her silky skin.

"No," she squeaked and Malik's hands traveled languorously to her thighs, where with his fingertips he traced his name on the insides. "What are you doing, casting a spell over me?" Riley asked as her eyes closed and her legs spread open.

"I don't need magic to get you to make love to me, just good old-fashioned skill."

"How do you know that I'm going to make love to you?"

"Because of this." Malik ran his thumb over her panties. "You're sopping wet. Magic can't do this."

"I'm so not liking this," Riley said with a groan.

"Do you think you'd like this?" Malik slid her thong aside and slid his finger into her wetness; Riley shrieked before falling onto her back. He slowly moved his finger in and out of her. "I think you do, see how wet you are?" he casually asked as he held up his finger for her to see. It was slick with her juice. "Let's see if you still taste good."

"Malik," Riley gently pleaded, "I don't think this is a good idea. I thought you wanted to talk."

"Oh, I do, and we will," he answered as he pulled off Riley's shoes and socks.

"Can't we talk without getting undressed?" she squeaked as he slid her thong over her thighs and onto the floor.

"We can," he answered agreeably, "but that wouldn't be much fun." He quickly shrugged out of his clothes. He dropped down to the floor in front of the bed. "Come closer!" he ordered and Riley scooted toward the edge of the bed. "Drape your legs over my shoulders."

With some assistance from Malik, Riley did as he instructed; soon her legs were hugging his shoulders. "I can't see you, this skirt is blocking my view."

"Would you like me to take it off?" he asked politely.

"Please," she replied primly.

After a couple of minutes the skirt was removed and Riley's legs were again on Malik's shoulders. Her sex wafted up to him; he inhaled deeply and licked his lips with anticipation. "Can you see now?" Malik teased.

Riley averted her eyes. "I guess."

Malik chuckled. He dipped his head in response and gently probed her moist folds with his tongue. Riley jerked her hips. Malik delicately nibbled on her clit, causing Riley to whimper.

"You're going to make me come."

"Oh, I don't want you to come. I just want you nice and wet."

"You got your wish. I'm soaking wet."

"I know. You're perfect for this." He stood up, placed the heels of Riley's feet against his chest, and slowly slid his dick inside her. Tears of ecstasy sprang into Riley's eyes as her hips languorously moved with his.

"Oh, Malik," she groaned.

Malik glanced down and saw the tears, and he hesitated. He didn't know if they were from pain. "Why are you crying, babe?"

"Because," Riley stuttered, looking into Malik's eyes, which seemed to be glowing. "Because you feel *soooo* good. Aw, God!"

Malik grinned; this was a first for him. He had never made a woman cry during lovemaking before. He picked up his pace just a little. "You feel good. Baby?"

"Yeah?" Riley managed between moans.

"How are your knees?"

"Okay."

Malik grunted. "Okay? Let's change positions." He eased himself out then pulled Riley up. He sat on the edge of the bed then drew her between his legs. "I want you to sit on me." Riley turned away from him and was about to slide on him when he stopped her. "Face me." Riley followed his instructions. And without saying a word, Malik grabbed her by her thighs, lifted her, and maneuvered her onto him. "Is this better?" Malik whispered in her ear.

Riley nodded, her legs comfortably stretched out on the bed. They slowly rocked together. "I like this."

"Do you like this?" Malik palmed her behind and slowly guided her up and down on his cock. Riley groaned as she grabbed his neck for support. Their warm bodies rubbed against each other.

"I do."

Malik kneaded her bottom as he continued moving in her. Riley whimpered softly as he slid in and out of her.

"Would it hurt your legs if I go a little faster?" Malik asked.

"I don't think so. I'll tell you if it hurts."

"Okay, baby." His grip tightened on her butt as the speed increased; Riley moaned. "You're getting slippery, baby."

"Your dick feels so good."

"Your pussy feels even better," Malik said before catching Riley's lips with his and hungrily kissing her. Riley's breathing quickened and Malik felt her shudder, her moist walls spasming against his dick. This was the green light for his release. He groaned loudly as he let himself go.

Malik gently lifted Riley and placed her on the bed. "I'll be right back. Let me get something to wipe you with." Malik slid off the bed and swaggered to the bathroom.

"Ah, the ass of a prince," Riley whispered to herself. "That's what should be on the family crest."

Moments later Malik returned with a small basin of water and a cloth. He tenderly wiped her face then swiped the cloth across her breasts. He grinned when her nipples hardened. Dipping the cloth in the liquid he pulled it out and held it over her crotch, letting the warm water drizzle over her pussy.

"If you keep doing things like that, we're going to have to do it again."

"Just let me know. I'm ready."

Riley glanced at him; he was right, his aroused penis was pointed right at her. Smiling seductively Riley reached out and grabbed him.

Hours later, Riley slid out of bed and quietly dressed; she

glanced over her shoulder at the sleeping Malik. "I love you, and you give good dick, but do you love me and my kids enough to protect us?"

She grabbed her crutches, limped out, and closed the door firmly behind her.

chapter TWENTY-SEVEN

Riley stared at the door. What had started off as polite taps had turned into I'm-going-to-break-down-the-door bangs.

"What are you gonna do?" Tamia asked calmly. This was the third night in a row that Malik had come to their bedroom attempting to talk to Riley. During the day, he and Riley talked about as much as feuding gang members.

Riley had moved into an empty bedroom and insisted that Tamia join her, for solidarity purposes.

"Let him knock until his hands are bloody stumps," she said nonchalantly before turning onto her stomach and pulling the covers over her head.

"Since when did you get so mean?" Tamia asked before returning to her laptop.

"I'm tired of talking with nobody listening," Riley answered sadly, her voice muffled.

"Malik listens to you. You're—" Tamia looked up from her laptop and glanced at the lump on the bed. "Take off the covers," she ordered. "I want to see your face." Riley slowly lowered the blankets and peeked over at her sister. "This is about Bradley, isn't it?"

Riley nodded. "He never listened to me. My opinion never counted. Bradley thought I had shit for brains."

"We know that isn't true, don't we?" Tamia asked quietly. "I don't know how many times I have to tell you, Malik is not like Bradley. *They are not alike.*"

"I know that. I really do. But then Malik will say something and I get a Bradley flashback. And I remember how stupid Bradley made me feel."

"Riley," Malik hissed, his voice slicing through the door.

"Malik's not like that," Tamia said for what seemed like the millionth time. "I don't want to sound cruel, but I need to concentrate. I want to get this assignment done before Dominic stops by tonight."

"Oh!" Riley said, making the one word sound like an accusation. They were sisters and she had expected solidarity from Tamia even if it meant abstinence.

"Hey, I'm with you a hundred percent, and in another half hour, I'll still be with you a hundred percent, just in spirit." Riley grimaced. "Oops, I'm sorry, bad choice of words. But you know what I meant."

"Open the door!"

"I know what you meant. I just wish you could stay. I love your company," Riley said while ignoring Malik.

Tamia laughed. "I thought you'd be tired of me by now. We haven't spent this much time together since we shared a bedroom when we were teenagers."

"I—"

"Riley, open this door!" Malik ordered.

"You're beginning to sound like a scratched CD," Riley taunted.

"Why doesn't he just use his key to unlock the door?"

"I bet it has something to do with his code of honor," Riley answered with a roll of her eyes.

Tamia slammed her laptop shut and turned to her sister, giving her her undivided attention. "Would you give Malik a break? He's a good man, and so far he's protected you better than the FBI. He has more informants than the CIA and more money than the city of Atlanta."

"Riley?" Malik yelled.

Riley snorted. "He isn't doing *everything*. He could call his uncle and that would put an end to all this."

"Obviously there are some issues there. And how do you know that his uncle will save the day? He might not be the savior you've built him up to be." Riley glared at Tamia. "Hey, I'm only saying."

"Whatever."

"Just stop being unrealistic, the man is battling demons. I've never been in this situation before and as far as I know you haven't either. This is a whole new terrain for us. Scary, but new."

Riley stubbornly crossed her arms over her chest. "So?"

"So. We aren't experts, he is. Let him do what he does. And even more important, trust him." Tamia tucked her laptop into its bag and swung it, along with her purse, over her shoulder. "Trust him, sis," she repeated before stepping into the hall. She left the door wide open. "Here's your invite, have at it," she drawled to Malik before she sauntered away.

"The invitation has to come from me!" Riley yelled just as Malik stepped in.

"It's an invite, doesn't matter who issues it," Malik responded and Riley snorted. "Can we talk about this . . . calmly?" he tacked on as if doing so would make it happen.

Riley dared to look in his eyes. She quickly glanced away but not before seeing his anguish. She grabbed Malik's hand. "Make me understand. All I see is someone who isn't doing everything he can to save me or my family. Am I wrong?" she asked softly.

Malik pulled his hands out of hers and curled his into fists. "You're so off the mark that it's not even funny. You know that I would die for you. I consider all of you Davenports and I wouldn't let anything or anybody harm any of you."

"But why won't you call him?" Riley asked softly.

"He used to be a soldier for Exor," Malik admitted.

Riley blinked. "I thought only people on the other side could work for him."

"Doesn't matter. You don't have to be an angel to do God's work, do you?" Riley shook her head. "I never met him. Dad and Bayard kept him away from me as he was too dangerous to have around. He was a walking bull's-eye for demons who were trying retaliation against Exor. Just being seen with him was dangerous. We could've been overpowered by thousands of Exor's soldiers."

Riley began crying. Her only hope of destroying Bradley and living a normal life was gone. "I'm sorry," she mumbled between sobs, "I should have trusted you."

Malik pulled her against him and she buried her face in his chest. "I know," Malik murmured while silently cursing Dominic for even mentioning Glazier. If he hadn't said anything, all of this would've been avoided. "Besides, you have three men who are on point and will always take care of you and your family. You don't have anything to worry about. I can't stress that enough."

"I know." Riley looked up at him through tear-soaked eyes. "I should have trusted you."

"Don't be so hard on yourself. You saw a little glimmer of

hope and you snatched it. Any mother, oh hell, any sane person would've done the same thing," he said soothingly.

She sniffled, then asked, "You think?"

"I know so. Babe?"

"Yeah?"

"Can you do a couple of favors for me?"

"Sure. What?"

"Believe in me, I won't steer you wrong. I've been on this earth for a long time and I've seen so much, more than some people see in ten lifetimes, so trust me. I know what I'm talking about at least ninety-nine percent of the time."

"What about the other one percent?" Riley teased.

"I was just trying to be humble. I'm always on point," he replied.

"You're silly," Riley said with a laugh. "What's the second favor?"

"Don't cut me off, babe. I missed you."

"You missed the sex?"

"I missed the sex," Malik agreed, "but I missed *you* more. I missed having you around. I missed having you snuggling in bed with me. I missed not having you near when I played with the kids. I missed talking to you in the middle of the night. I missed *you*, babe."

Riley reached up and traced his lips with her finger. "I missed you too." She pulled his face toward her for a kiss. Their lips met and they kissed as though they hadn't seen each other in years instead of just days.

Suddenly, Malik broke away and stared into her eyes. "So you see, if I were to invite him to our house, we'd be welcoming the very evil we're trying to destroy, and you don't want that, do you?"

chapter TWENTY-EIGHT

Riley sat on Malik's balcony. She sighed loudly.

"What's wrong, baby?" Malik slipped his arms around her waist, pulling her close to him. She giggled.

"I didn't hear you come in." Riley turned around so that she could face him. She never tired of looking in his eyes. Riley was filled with so much joy and love that her heart swelled. It was hard to believe that this was the man who destroyed demons. Riley seductively ran her fingers up his back.

Malik cupped her face in his hands and thoroughly kissed her. "I couldn't resist. They looked so delicious."

"You may have a taste whenever you want." Riley grinned as she leaned into him. She let out a happy sigh.

"There's that sigh again," Malik observed.

"This was a happy one."

"And the first one wasn't?"

"No," Riley admitted. "I'm just so bored, I wish I could go out. I wish the kids could run around the yard. It's so beautiful."

"I know, babe, I know," Malik said, his eyes flashing dangerously. "It's going to happen . . . soon. My baby's going to get out and enjoy the city, and the kids will be able to play outside."

"I know you're doing everything in your power to annihilate Bradley." Riley stroked Malik's face and the dangerous glint in his eyes sharpened to desire.

Malik pushed her blouse over her shoulders, exposing her cantaloupe-size breasts. "I bow to the goddess of beautiful titties," he said.

Suddenly his bedroom door flew open and Carter rocketed in. Malik hopped up and Riley hastily adjusted her clothing. "Hey, guys. What are we having for lunch? Tao told me to ask," he said breathlessly, as though he had run from the kitchen and straight to their room.

"Let's have a picnic," Riley decided. "It's beautiful out." Even though it was early December, it was a balmy eighty-five-degree day. Warm enough for them to sit out on the balcony and enjoy the weather.

"Cool, I'll tell Tao." Carter whirled on his heel and was about to make a return trip to the kitchen when Malik placed a hand on his shoulder, stopping him.

"You're going to wear yourself out, little warrior. Use the intercom."

Carter smiled sheepishly. He adored the unconditional love he received from Malik, which was very different from the sometime attention he used to get from Bradley. "Okay." He sauntered over to the intercom and buzzed the kitchen. "We would like a picnic," he announced.

Tao chuckled. "And what would you like for your picnic?"

Indecision flashed across Carter's young face. "Tell him you want hot dogs, chips, soda, and brownies," Riley called, smothering a laugh. Carter was so adorable.

Malik hugged Riley and they shared a lingering look, which

promised that they would pick up where they left off later in the evening. An oblivious Carter ordered his food.

"Buzz your auntie and tell her to bring Brie and come to Malik's suite." Carter happily did as he was told. Thirty minutes later they were all sitting on a blanket on Malik's balcony stuffing their faces with food.

"This is perfect!" Tamia announced. "It's exactly what I needed."

An hour later they all found a bit of space in their stomachs for ice cream.

Riley leaned into Malik's arms and sighed.

"Happy sigh?" Riley nodded. "Great."

"Look, there's Daddy! Hi, Daddy!" Carter screamed excitedly. Hovering in the air over the balcony was Bradley.

Riley sprang out of Malik's arms and raced toward the banister. "Get away from here! Get the fuck away from here!" she yelled hysterically. Carter and Brie started crying at the sight of their mother yelling.

"Get them out of here," Malik ordered Tamia. She grabbed Brie and firmly gripped Carter's shoulder before pointing him toward the door.

"I don't want to go, I want my daddy!" Carter screamed. "I want my daddy!"

Bradley grinned as he watched the scene. He gave Carter a thumbs-up. Carter broke out of Tamia's grip and zoomed toward his father.

"Carter! No!" Riley yelled. "Come back."

Carter tried to scale the banister, but Malik snatched him up by the waist and carried him, kicking and screaming, from the balcony.

"Do you need me to stay?" Tamia asked, looking fearfully toward Bradley. He motioned to Tamia to come closer. "Aw, hell naw, are you crazy?" She buried Brie's face in her chest. Bradley winked.

Riley turned to her sister and shooed her away. "Just ignore him. Take Brie to her room."

Just then Tamia's mouth gaped open, her face frozen in horror, and she nearly dropped Brie.

"Go!" Riley ordered before giving her sister a nudge; it was like trying to move a boulder; Tamia was glued to the floor. "What's wrong?" Tremors took control of Tamia's body. Brie rattled in her arms like a rag doll. Riley snatched her child from Tamia. "What's *wrong* with you?" Tamia lifted a shaky finger and pointed over Riley's shoulder.

Riley turned around and what she saw almost made her drop Brie. "Oh my God!" she screamed just as Malik returned to the room.

Bradley was racing back and forth in front of the balcony while dragging Tamia and Riley's father's spirit. Bradley's arm was looped around his neck while he pulled him as though he were a fish.

"Daddy!" Riley screamed as she ran toward the balcony. Her father waved at her, motioning her back. "No!" Brie began wailing and for a sliver of a minute, Riley's father's lips curled into a smile.

"Take Brie and get out of here!" Malik barked at Tamia, who stood frozen. "Now!" he roared. Tamia blinked herself out of her daze and kept her eyes glued on Brie while inching toward her sister and plucking her niece from Riley's arms. She raced toward the door. Once there, she stopped to look at her father. She knew in her heart that this would truly be the last time she'd ever see him. She blew him a kiss. "Bye, Daddy," she whispered tearfully before racing out of the room.

"I want my son!" Bradley yelled and Malik's eyes widened. Bradley chortled at Malik's expression. "That's right, you can hear me. Pretty soon my voice won't be the only thing that will be able to get through your thin barrier," he mocked.

"You're not getting Carter, you will never get him!" Riley yelled.

"You're sure about that?" Bradley teased and Riley could see a small piece of the old Bradley . . . the charming Bradley who had courted her.

"Yes!" Malik interjected forcibly as he pulled Riley away. "You will never get Carter, he's my son now. You weren't man enough to take care of him while you were here, so what makes you think you can take care of him on the other side? You're not a man, you're an animal," Malik spat out.

Bradley made a big show of stroking his chin, but all he was doing was fanning air. "So he's your son now?" Bradley asked slowly. "And I never took care of him? And I'll never have him?" he asked. "What about if I do this?" His hand transformed into a dagger and he sliced off Riley's father's right arm.

Her father and Riley simultaneously let out a roar. She turned anguished eyes to Malik. "Make him stop," she begged, "please make him stop."

Malik's heart clenched at his fiancée's cry and the man who would've been his father-in-law. He knew that he had to distract Bradley. "How are you doing this? I didn't realize that you could slice each other up like animals."

Bradley tilted his head and studied Malik. He decided to humor him. "Everybody can't do it. Only a few of us can. Exor can, as well as a handful of other people. But I'm almost as strong as Exor." He tightened his grip on Riley's father and the old man thrashed, his feet dangling in the air.

"Stop it!" Riley yelled, stretching the cords in her throat.

"So if you're so strong, why can't you break through the barrier?" Malik taunted.

Bradley smiled. "Oh, I'm gonna get through, believe me." He leaned in closer, as though he was about to share a secret with his best friend. "I want to tell you something and I don't want you to be alarmed, but"—he paused dramatically and whispered—"your barrier has been penetrated; I did it. Right now there are millions of little pricks in it. All I need to do is connect several of those teeny-tiny holes to make one big one. Then I'm in like Flynn."

Malik stalked to the edge of the balcony and studied the barrier. Bradley was right. There were minuscule holes throughout the barrier. A chill went through him. "How did I miss this?" he muttered.

"So he can really get in?" Riley asked. Her heart thudded against her chest. "He can get me?"

"Oh, yes, beautiful, I can get you. And I can get my son. Speaking of whom, my son for your father."

Riley's father shook his head. And Riley heard a weak no.

She caught her father's eye. "You're not getting him!"

Bradley shook his head. "Why must you delay the inevitable?" He callously sliced off his prisoner's left arm and right leg.

"You're not getting him!" Malik shouted. Riley trembled against him. Her perfect day had ended and now she was about to lose her father again.

"I wonder how many soldiers it'll take to break through," he asked, toying with them. Just then hundreds of spirits pushed themselves against the barrier and seconds later they were all electrocuted. "See, they're all here watching the show. And they're loving it."

Riley turned away and pressed her face into Malik's chest. She clamped her mouth closed. She was very close to throwing up her lunch.

"You're not getting him, so leave!"

"Indeed I will," Bradley said. He locked gazes with Riley, grinned sardonically, and stuck his dagger arm into her father's chest. Her father let out an anguished wail, the sky filled with pink dust, and then he was gone.

Riley tried to wrench herself from Malik's arms but he held her tightly. "Daddy!"

"Oh, you'll learn not to fuck with me!" Bradley spat out before disappearing.

"It's like losing him all over again," she sobbed in Malik's arms. "He killed his spirit. He's really dead now." Suddenly she went mute, her mouth gaping open and closed as she stared blankly at Malik.

"Riley!" He cupped her face to calm her but she jerked away so fast it looked like an invisible force had pulled her back. "Come on, baby!" Malik coaxed. He had seen this happen only one other time in his life. The lady had a nervous breakdown, and unfortunately she never recovered.

Riley was still as her eyes lasered in on a spot on the wall. "Riley?" Malik quickly snapped his fingers in front of her eyes. She didn't blink. He clapped his hands and she didn't even flinch. "It's okay, come back. We'll fight this together," Malik pleaded, his voice filled with anguish. But it was like talking to a brick wall.

He used the intercom to contact his father and grandfather and they rushed into the room. "I'm surprised this hasn't happened to her sooner. But she's a strong lady. Unfortunately, this was her breaking point," Carrington said to Malik.

"She is strong," Malik agreed as he lovingly stroked Riley's cheek. "But she wouldn't agree."

"She'd be wrong," Bayard said gruffly. He loved and admired Riley's wit, intellect, and warmth and hated to see her spirit broken.

"What can I do to help her?" Malik asked.

"Just give her time to come back to you. And be sure to bring her kids in to visit her. And always, I mean always, let her know how much you love and miss her," Carrington ordered.

"I will, Dad."

For a few minutes, the trio quietly observed Riley, each silently willing her to snap out of it. Malik reluctantly broke the silence. "I'd better change her clothes and wash her."

His father and grandfather headed out of the room. "We'll be back later tonight to visit her," Bayard said.

"She'll be okay," Carrington offered.

"Thanks, Dad."

Malik filled his oversize tub with warm water. He undressed Riley while she stayed as stiff as a life-size Barbie doll. "I kinda like the demure, silent lady," Malik joked as he carried her and placed her in the water. "There isn't any back-talking." He laughed at his own joke, while Riley stared blankly ahead. Mannequin still, Malik was afraid she'd topple over and drown.

He tenderly washed her hair, the wet tresses reaching past her shoulders. "Whoa! You look hot with your hair down. You should wear it this way more often."

An image of the first time he'd bathed Riley flitted through his mind as he caressed her back with a soap-covered washcloth. "We'll get there again," he promised.

Riley didn't blink while the water cascaded over her body, nor did she acknowledge Malik's gentle voice or movements. When he finished bathing her, he lifted her out of the water, wrapped her in a bath towel, and placed her on the bed, where he dried her off and rubbed lotion on her body.

For the next several days, Malik fed, bathed, and nursed Riley while her spirit lay frozen within her. Carter, Brie, and Tamia were all glued to her side and only left her to eat and sleep. Carrington and Bayard kept their promise and visited as often as they could. Most of their time was spent on conferring about ways to destroy Bradley.

On the fourth night, Riley's eyes snapped open. She looked directly into Malik's eyes. "Kill the motherfucker!" she barked.

chapter TWENTY - NINE

"Hey," R*iley* w*hispered.* Malik, who was sitting next to her bed reading a book, thought he had imagined the sound. "Malik."

The book slipped from his hands. "Riley?"

"Malik?" she croaked, her throat feeling as if she had swallowed a whole package of sandpaper.

"You're back!" he unabashedly cried as he hugged Riley. He quickly called the family, who rushed into the room. Riley sipped a glass of tepid water while reconnecting with her loved ones.

"How long was I out?" she whispered. Malik and Carrington glanced at each other, unsure whether to tell her the truth.

"A week," Malik answered, opting for the truth. He knew that she would find out. Might as well make it sooner rather than later. "Do you remember what happened?"

Riley's eyes filled with tears, but her voice was strong when she answered. "I do. Has anything happened? Did you destroy him yet?"

Malik chuckled. "You're going to be okay." He gave Bayard an imperceptible nod; taking the hint, Bayard cleared his throat.

"I think it's time for us to leave."

Neither Carter nor Brie wanted to leave their mother, but Tamia promised Carter an ice-cream sundae and Brie was coaxed away with her favorite stuffed animal. As soon as they all left the room, leaving Riley and Malik alone, Riley grabbed his hand.

"Everybody's gone. Tell me what you didn't want the kids to hear."

Malik tenderly caressed her fingers. "I think I got him," he said eagerly, his eyes gleaming triumphantly.

"What? Tell me!"

Malik shook his head. "Not yet. I don't want to say anything until I'm sure that it'll work. It's very tricky and it's all a matter of timing."

"Can't you give me a little hint?" Riley pleaded and Malik shook his head.

"Nope." He leaned down and kissed her softly on her forehead. "All I want you to do is rest."

Riley sighed. "Thanks for taking care of me."

"You'd do the same for me," he answered.

She gave him a shaky smile as she searched his eyes. "Do you think I'm crazy?"

Malik shook his head. "You're normal. I'd think you were crazy if you hadn't reacted the way you did."

"Really?" Surprise laced her question.

"Really. This was a way to take a break from everything. You've been through so much. And you know what?"

"What?"

"You always stayed beautiful," he said before leaning over and kissing her gently.

"This sounds weird, but I remember saying, 'Kill the mother-fucker.' Did I do that?" she asked as soon as the kiss ended.

"Yeah. Now tell me what was happening when you ordered me to kill Bradley."

"I was dreaming about him," she said and Malik frowned. "It was a real dream, he wasn't here."

"Are you sure it was just a dream?" Malik persisted. He hated himself for badgering her in her condition, but he had to know. The last thing he needed was Bradley inside his house. That would be horrendous.

"It was. When I was with him in Lavastar, I was *there*, I was in the moment. But this was a dream, I felt like I was watching everything unfold on TV. Anyway, I dreamed that he had killed my mother and Tamia and was taunting me. He kept saying that he was going to get Carter and that there wasn't anything I could do about it. He made me so mad. That's when I said, 'Kill the motherfucker.'"

"We will," he said and nodded knowingly. "I promise. Now I think you need some rest."

"I've been sleeping forever. I'm okay," she protested.

Malik shook his head; her drooping eyelids told a different story. "Okay, just lie there and rest."

"Whatever," Riley muttered. Three minutes later, she was fast asleep.

"I love you, baby," Malik whispered.

Later that night, Riley huddled in the comforter Malik wrapped around her. He pressed a cup of hot chocolate laced with brandy in her hands. She brought it to her mouth and slowly sipped.

"Consider him dead," Malik said ruthlessly.

"I still can't believe I married that man. He's the epitome of evil." Malik agreed. Riley placed her cup of hot chocolate on the nightstand and grabbed Malik with an urgency that surprised him. "I need you," she said, her voice thick with passion.

"I think you should rest."

"I don't want to rest. I want sex!" She pulled Malik's face toward her and kissed him hard.

"Riley!"

Ignoring him, Riley pulled off her nightgown. "Take off your clothes!" she ordered.

"What?"

"Take them off."

"Okay." Malik slowly removed his clothing while keeping an eye on Riley; he wasn't sure what was going on but he knew that she needed rest. He silently wished his penis to stay soft, but unfortunately, it had a mind of its own.

Riley saw his excitement and pointed to the bed. "Get on your back."

As soon as he was in position, Riley straddled him and his cock slid easily into her hotness. She grunted as she moved her hips back and forth, her breasts rocking in sync with her movements.

"You're going too fast," Malik protested weakly. "If you keep it up, I'm going to come."

With her eyes closed and her head thrown back in abandonment, she ignored him. "Grab my waist!" she demanded and Malik did as he was told. "Now we're going to flip. I want to be on my back."

Malik stopped moving long enough to execute the move with such finesse that it would have made an acrobat jealous. "Now fuck me!" Riley commanded.

Ten minutes later, Malik placed his hands out to ward Riley off. "Whew! I can't believe I'm saying this . . . but stay away. You wore me out." He lay back on the bed, breathing hard. "I don't think I've ever worked that hard."

Riley smiled sheepishly. "I'm sorry. I don't know what came over me."

Malik gently stroked her thigh. "A lot of things, and they're all normal. I think you were upset over losing your father again, mad at Bradley, and just plain sad. And you needed a way to release those feelings."

"I didn't mean to use you."

"Use me, abuse me, sex me whenever you want," Malik said with a laugh.

"I want him obliterated," she stated.

"Do you want to talk about what happened?" Malik asked gently.

"What happened when?" Riley asked, feigning ignorance.

"During your week-long nap," he said lightly. He tenderly stroked her hair. "You came out of it a different person. Talk to me, baby," he coaxed.

"Are you complaining?" she snapped.

Malik pulled back. "Come on now. I'm not the enemy."

"Oh God, I'm so sorry." She grabbed his hand and softly kissed his palm. "I didn't mean to attack you."

"I know, I know."

"I told you about the dream."

"Yes, but there has to be something else. You seem harder, more jaded, more cynical."

"Can you blame me? After everything that has happened to me?" she asked, and before Malik could respond, she continued. "Listen, I guess I needed to feel alive. And fucking you—yes, it was fucking because it wasn't making love—made me feel alive. And you're right, I did need to let off some steam." She looked over at her fiancé and started sobbing. "I'm sorry. I'm just so confused right now."

Malik caressed her hair. "You're normal, sweetie. You're normal." Riley snuggled against him. When she had calmed down, Malik kissed the top of her head. "Let's just relax."

chapter THIRTY

Riley swiped at the tickling sensation that swept across her face. Malik gently feathered his fingers through her hair, causing her to shoot up and bounce off the bed, nearly knocking Malik to the ground. Clenching her hands, Riley viciously boxed the air.

Malik grabbed her hands. "It's just me. It's Malik." Riley continued with her one-person fight. "Riley!" Malik hissed. "Stop it!"

Her hands fell to her sides and she blinked and zeroed in on her fiancé. Her face crumpled when recognition sank in. "Oh my God. I'm sorry. I thought you were Bradley."

Malik pulled her into his arms. "How many times do I have to tell you that this house is impenetrable? Nothing can get in, unless we let it in."

"I know, I'm sorry. I'm tired of my knee-jerk reactions. I just want to live a normal life, I mean as normal as somebody could in our situation."

"No, *I'm* sorry. You'd think that I'd know better by now." He pulled away and guided her toward the bed. "Hold on a sec," he said before reaching down and fishing under it. He stood up with a small gift-wrapped box in his hand. "This is what I was trying to give you."

A calmer Riley blushed. "I'm sorry, I didn't mean to knock it out of your hand."

"Merry Christmas. Open it."

Riley slowly unwrapped the gift, and gaped at the porcelain Tiffany's box. "Malik!" she protested. He was too generous.

"Open it," he coaxed.

Riley pulled off the top and inside was a platinum open-heart pendant with pavé diamonds. She gasped. "It's exquisite."

"That way our hearts will always be touching."

She cupped his face with her hands and tenderly kissed him. "Would you put this on please?"

After a couple of minutes of fumbling with it, Malik finally got it on. Riley glanced down at the heart nestled between her breasts. "I'm sorry, but the gift I got for you isn't as nice as the one you got me."

"This isn't a competition. Whatever you give me is fine."

Riley slipped out of the room and returned a couple of minutes later with a gift. "Here you go. I hope you like it."

"I'm going to love it," Malik reassured her while he unwrapped his gift. "Hey, James Patterson's newest novel. Thanks, babe." He wrapped his arms around her and hugged her tightly.

"And it's autographed."

Malik flipped open the book and read the message. "How did you manage this?"

"Paladins," Riley answered and Malik laughed.

"You're learning. Let's go downstairs. I bet Carter is driving Bayard and Dad crazy."

Standing at the threshold of the living room, Riley giggled. Under a seven-foot Christmas tree and surrounded by a mountain of gifts were Carrington, Bayard, Tamia, Dominic, and Brie. In charge of it all was Carter, who was ordering everyone around. Bayard was assembling his train track, Dominic and Carrington were responsible for putting together his bicycle, and Tamia and Brie munched on cookies and enjoyed the activity.

"Bayard and Carrington are quite agile for men their age."

"Yep!" Malik nodded toward Carter. "And we can see who the true ruler is. Come on." They strolled into the living room where they opened even more gifts, sang carols, and enjoyed a festive brunch.

"I got you," Malik reassured Riley as he guided her out of the elevator. Riley tugged at the silk mask that covered her eyes. "Leave it alone, you'd better not take it off."

"Why do I feel like I'm being led to the lions?" Riley grumbled as she stumbled and Malik grabbed her arm.

"Because you want me to eat you," Malik joked.

Riley heard a swooshing sound. "Ha! Ha!" She wanted to know where Malik was taking her. "How much farther do we have to go? I know your place is huge, but da—!"

"Surprise!" A riot of voices cut her off.

Riley whipped off her mask to find hers and Malik's family and the mediums standing in front of her. Taurus eyed her sourly. Everybody had on formal attire and looked like they were dressed for a New Year's Eve party. Tamia wore a sexy black strapless dress with equally sexy shoes, and Malik's father, grandfather, and Dominic wore black tuxes. Even Carter and Brie were dressed up. Carter sported a tux and Brie looked adorable in a black velvet dress, with white tights and black patent leather shoes.

Lush tropical trees were scattered throughout the room and

hundreds of white lights laced in white gauze covered the ceiling.

She turned to Malik. "Oh, baby! This is so beautiful."

Malik stroked her face, pleased that she liked it. "I know how hard it is being cooped up the way you are. You're a prisoner. And you can't go out until all this stuff with Bradley is settled."

"I don't mind," Riley protested. "It's almost like being on vacation."

"Now you're just being nice," Malik said dryly.

"No I'm not," she softly protested.

"It doesn't matter. I have something that'll make you happy . . . I hope."

"What?" She fingered the Tiffany pendant. "You've already given me a beautiful Christmas gift. I don't want or need anything else."

"Welcome to your wedding," he announced and everybody started clapping. "Merry Christmas."

"My wedding?" echoed a stunned Riley as Tao and his crew rolled in tray after tray of food and, last, a five-tiered wedding cake.

"I want us to be married today," Malik said. "This is my Christmas gift from me to us."

"This is so romantic," Riley said, her eyes glistening with unshed tears. "You got the food, the decorations, and even the cake. And all you guys are dressed up, but I'm not. I don't even have a gown."

Malik grinned. "Do you really think I wouldn't take care of my baby? Tamia."

Tamia sauntered up to her and grabbed her hand. "What's going on?" Riley asked.

"Come with me."

Riley looked worriedly over her shoulder at Brie and Carter. "What about the kids?"

"I've got them!" Malik called after her.

Tamia directed her into a small room. Inside was everything a bride could need: makeup, underwear, veil, and shoes. And hanging on the back of the door was a strapless satin organza wedding gown.

Riley sighed happily as she fingered the material. "I think this is a Vera Wang. Do you know how much this costs?" she asked, awed by the exquisiteness of the dress.

"I can just imagine," Tamia said, businesslike. "Take off your clothes and take a quick shower."

"There's a shower down here?" Tamia rolled her eyes at her sister. "Yeah, right, it's the Davenports, they have everything." Tamia pointed to the bathroom door. "I'll be right back."

"Here, take these." Tamia tossed her sister's underwear to her. "I have some papers for you to sign when you're done!" Tamia called out.

After a quick shower, Riley emerged wearing an ivory-colored thong, a sheer bra, thigh-high stockings, and a garter belt.

"Woo hoo! All you need now is a pair of clear-heeled shoes and you'll be ready to make some money, honey."

Riley stuck her hands on her hips and sashayed over to her wedding gown. "Well, if you got it, flaunt it."

"You got it; you look good, girl, and you're radiant," Tamia said while tearing up.

"Stop it!" Riley gently scolded her sister. "We've been through this before."

"I know," Tamia said with a sniffle, "but I like this one."

"Bitch!" Riley said with a laugh. "You're silly."

Tamia chuckled. "Just telling it like it is, sis. Come on, sit down, let me do your hair and makeup."

"I can do it."

"Yeah, and have yourself looking like a nun trying to play dress up."

"Better than a five-dollar ho," Riley muttered.

"I heard that! Sit down!" Riley reluctantly sat down at the vanity and Tamia draped towels over her.

"You mentioned that you have papers for me to sign."

"Yeah, it's your marriage license and stuff, just do it while I'm doing your hair."

An hour later, with Tamia's help, Riley was transformed into a beautiful, jaw-droppingly, drop-dead gorgeous beaming bride. Riley admired her reflection. Her makeup was flawless and Tamia had gathered her hair up into a sexy topknot. She pulled herself away from the mirror. "We'd better hurry up," she said.

Tamia snorted. "Take your time; that man ain't going anywhere. He loves you so much. Are you having any doubts?"

Riley smiled and shook her head. "Not one."

"I can see that. You're glowing, girl. You're making the right decision. You and Malik are a good couple."

"What about you and Dominic?"

"We're cool. Nothing serious," Tamia answered vaguely.

"Yeah, right."

"Today isn't about me, it's about you," Tamia said, redirecting the conversation. "Let's go."

They strolled out and at Tamia's signal, the wedding march began, filling the room with beautiful music. "Who's playing that?" Riley asked, amazed.

"Carrington, he's a trained pianist."

Riley peeked out. In the short time they had been gone, a white aisle runner had been put down, a dozen white chairs hugged both sides, and red tulips decorated the small area. Tamia handed her a bouquet of tulips and roses. "This is beautiful."

"Ready?"

"You're walking me down the aisle?"

"I am; you know Daddy would want me to."

"I know." She hugged her sister. "Let's go."

They slowly made their way down the aisle to Malik, who had changed into a tuxedo. Dominic stood next to him. Riley and Tamia glided by Bayard, Valencia, Peony, Arletta, Loretta, and Shervita. Riley stumbled at seeing her, and Shervita shot Riley a jaunty wave. "Slut," she muttered.

"She looks like it, but who got the man?"

"I do!" Riley crowed.

"That's right, let's do this, girl," Tamia said as they serenely strolled the rest of the way to Malik.

"You look stunning," Malik whispered.

"Thank you. You look so good in that tux." They grinned at each other. "So, he's performing the ceremony?" She motioned with her eyes toward Taurus, who stood a few feet away.

"He's an ordained minister and he offered to officiate."

Riley shrugged. "Well, as long as he's legit." She reached for his hand and they both eagerly faced Taurus. "Let's get married."

Ten minutes later, Taurus pronounced them Mr. and Mrs. Davenport.

Riley and Malik swayed together to classic Luther Vandross with some of their guests, while the others nibbled on the delicious food Tao had prepared.

Malik smiled down at Riley. "So, any doubts?"

Riley shook her head. "None at all. To be honest, I'm still in a daze. Remarrying was never on my mind, and then I fell in love with you."

"And the rest is history," Malik said softly and kissed the top of her head.

"What a wonderful Christmas gift. I would have been happy with just the pendant."

"It looks beautiful against your skin."

Riley looked up at Malik; his eyes were darkening to a midnight blue and her hands slid down and caressed his bottom. "Do you want to sneak away to my dressing room? It's pretty private and it has a couch."

Malik's lips turned up in a mischievous grin. "Let's go." They were halfway to the room when they were stopped by Bayard and Carrington.

"I just wanted to welcome Riley to the family," Bayard said before hugging her. "And I wanted her to have these." He reached into his pocket and pulled out a pair of diamond stud earrings. "The ladies in our family have worn them for centuries, and I want you to have them."

Riley threw her arms around her grandfather-in-law. "Thank you so much," she said before pulling back and taking the present. She admired the earrings. The diamonds were the size of large grapes.

"Welcome, Riley," Carrington said.

Riley hugged her new father-in-law. "Thanks, Carrington." Suddenly Carter stepped in front of them.

Malik threw his new wife a frustrated look but that didn't stop him from picking up his new stepson.

"So you're really my new daddy?" Carter asked shyly.

Malik hugged him tightly. "I am."

"What's gonna happen to my other daddy? Will he still be my daddy?" he asked and Riley held her breath.

"He will always be your daddy," Malik answered.

"Now I have two daddies," Carter squealed. Malik lifted an

eyebrow at Riley, and she shrugged in response. Malik deftly diverted Carter's attention. He pointed to Riley's wedding band. "Did I do a good job?" he asked Carter.

Carter shook his head. "No!"

"What did I do wrong?"

"I would've given her a different ring. I saw one in a machine that she could stick on her finger and suck on whenever she wanted."

Everybody burst out laughing.

"That's a good idea, baby. Maybe you can buy one for your girlfriend," Riley said.

Carter frowned. "Yuck, I hate girls."

"I'll see how you feel ten years from now," Malik joked. He set Carter down and he ran over to play with his little sister. "I don't think a quickie is in the cards."

"Me either. But we always have tonight."

He and Riley gravitated toward the chairs.

"This is so nice. I can't believe you did all this for me. It's amazing—I mean, *you're* amazing."

"Anything to make my lady happy," Malik said as he grinned at his new wife.

"I'm deliriously happy." She nodded toward Tamia and Dominic. "They look good together. And Tamia looks happy."

"Dominic's a good guy. He'll take care of Tamia."

"I know. The Davenport men know how to take care of their women."

Riley settled in her chair. Carter and Brie played nearby. Malik kissed the tip of her nose. "I'll be right back. I'm about to get us some drinks. We never did toast."

"Get me something sparkly and fruity."

"Damn, you're already becoming bossy. I just put that ring on your finger," Malik joked. "Give me at least a couple of months to enjoy having a wife before you start nagging me."

"I'll give you a month of no nagging, but after that . . . ," Riley teased back.

"I love it." Malik sauntered across the room to the wet bar. And Riley resumed her resting. Suddenly she felt a wisp of air across her face. And she laughed. "You're back already? That was fast." She opened her eyes and the smile slid from her face. "Oh fuck!" Her cousin, Keyshaun, hovered over her. Riley's stomach felt as though someone had tightened a belt around it. Then, as if someone had doused her with ice-cold water, she threw off her fear and faced her cousin.

"What the fuck are you doing here?" she hissed.

Keyshaun had materialized just enough so that he looked as if Riley was staring at him through a pair of sheer panty hose. He raised an eyebrow. "You've gotten quite spunky, haven't you, Miss Thang?" he taunted.

"Do you think I should be cowering in the corner? You didn't scare me when we were teenagers and you don't scare me now!" she shot back.

Keyshaun chuckled. "Oh, look at Miss Thang, you're a little spitfire!" He lazily swished over her, snaking around her body. "You really should be very afraid of me. I'm moving up in Bradley's army. And my cousin-in-law has given me crazy powers. Like this." Keyshaun coiled himself around Riley's torso, causing her to struggle for breath. "This is just one of the powers he gave me. Do you want to see more?" Keyshaun gleefully asked.

Riley shook her head as she frantically grabbed for Keyshaun but only touched her own skin. Keyshaun loosened his grip and

Riley swayed back and forth as she gasped for air. "I'm not going to hurt you just yet. I have a whole house of people to destroy and I want to savor it."

"Like hell you will," Riley spat out. "You were stupid when we were kids and you're stupid now. Just like your brother. He's gone now, and you're going to be soon. You really think Malik is going to let you out of here alive? You must be crazy. Malik!" she called. "There's a demon in here. Keyshaun got through."

"What!" Malik turned away from the bar and Riley's mimosa slipped from his hand; a demon had penetrated the shield. He looked wildly around the room. *How many more had gotten through?*

chapter THIRTY - ONE

Malik immediately sprang into action. "Dad! Bayard!" he roared. "We've got trouble. Dominic, get them out of here." The mediums, along with Shervita, had vacated the room after seeing Keyshaun. Shervita had done it for self-preservation, but the mediums did it because they needed somewhere comfortable to talk with their contacts on the other side.

Tamia, who had been watching the children play, had glanced up and her bowels had cramped at the sight in front of her. Keyshaun idly drifted in the air, as though he had been invited over for a beer and a burger. He and Tamia locked gazes; he gave her a thumbs-up. She grabbed Carter and Brie and held them close.

"Go!" Malik ordered. "Get them out of here," he repeated to Dominic. Dominic quickly rounded up Tamia, Carter, and Brie, but when it came to Riley she stood firm.

"I'm not going anywhere," Riley decided. "They don't scare me anymore and I'm not running."

"Come on, Riley!" Tamia urged. "We've got to go!"

"You go. I'm staying. They're not going to run me out of my house."

"I really think you should come with us," Dominic quietly stated. Riley stubbornly shook her head and Dominic shot a look at

Malik. He would gladly throw her over his shoulder and carry her out if necessary. All he needed was a word from his cousin.

"Go!" Malik ordered. He, Carrington, and Bayard had formed a circle around Keyshaun, who looked amused by them. "I don't have time for your bravado. Get the hell out of here."

"But I want to help!"

"Believe me, we got this. And you'll help me a lot if you and the kids go with Dominic."

At the mention of the kids, Keyshaun slowly scrutinized the small group before he lasered in on Carter. He zipped into the air and bounced down in front of him.

"Get away from him!" Riley screamed as she raced toward her son; never had such a small distance between them seemed so wide. Malik broke from the circle and ran toward his wife.

"I must be slipping, how did I miss this?" Keyshaun said. "I bet Bradley would be very happy if I brought this back to him." He tapped a finger against his chin. "I might even get promoted again." He studied Carter. "Oh yeah, I bet Bradley would just love this. And all the perks I'll receive when I present this little gift to him. You won't believe it."

Carter pressed his face against his mother's leg. Riley scooped him up. Keyshaun orbed himself and playfully bounced in front of him. Carter turned toward the brilliant light, mesmerized by its brightness. "If I get you," Keyshaun started in a singsong voice, "I'll have all the riches I ever imagined, and all the souls."

"Leave now!" Malik ordered. Dominic grabbed Brie and raced toward the door, Tamia, Carter, and Riley close behind.

"So you came here to fight?" Riley heard Malik roar as she made her way across the threshold and out of the room.

"Come on!" Dominic hissed. The group flew down the corridor, following Dominic as though he were their lifeline.

They continued to weave their way through the intersecting halls. Recessed lighting coated the hallways in a warm glow. Hundreds of artifacts and paintings dotted the walls. The group passed dozens of closed doors. Until now, neither Riley nor Tamia had any idea that the lower level was so big. Dominic braked in front of a stone wall. "We're going down some stairs. Get ready," Dominic warned. "You might want to take off your heels," he said to Riley and Tamia. They were quiet as they slipped off their shoes.

"I want my daddy," Carter whined.

Riley's grip tightened just as her stomach clenched. How do you tell your son that his father wants to kill him? "Malik will be with us soon," she said instead. She caught Dominic's eyes and he nodded a confirmation.

"We've got to hurry. We don't know how many might have broken through the barrier," Dominic said. Tamia and Riley watched, transfixed, as he shifted a steering-wheel-size rock, exposing a lighted keypad.

"Wow!" Tamia murmured.

Despite himself, Dominic grinned. He pressed a sequence of numbers into the keypad and a huge boulder the size of a double stainless-steel refrigerator effortlessly slid open. Riley's and Tamia's mouths dropped open with astonishment. "Move it! We're almost there." Dominic stepped into the corridor. As soon as Riley and Tamia hopped in, he repeated his steps on an identical keypad and the boulder swooshed closed. It looked as if they had stepped into a cave. Dominic pulled his key chain out and flicked on a mini flashlight. Light bounced off the dull gray stone walls and was absorbed by the packed-clay floor. A little distance away was a metal spiral staircase.

Riley walked over and peeked down; darkness stared back at her. Nausea rolled up to the back of her throat and she looked around wildly.

Dominic hurried to her side; he had seen that look before. "Step away from the stairs," he instructed and Riley slowly backed up. "Now take a deep breath." Riley breathed deeply. "Slowly," Dominic coached. Moments later Riley's breathing returned to normal. She shot Dominic a sheepish smile.

"Sorry!"

"No prob. Let's do this." He nodded to Riley. "You go first."

Riley blanched as she hung back. "Why do I have to go first? I thought you were leading the way," she said stubbornly.

"Trust me, I am."

"Just go!" Tamia barked. "Besides, what happened to the lady who wanted to kick some demon ass?"

"I'm still here, dammit!" Riley turned, pushed Carter toward Dominic, and almost ran down the stairs.

Dominic winked at Tamia. "Great job!"

"Remind me that you owe me a back rub after all this," Tamia whispered to Dominic before she followed Riley down the stairs.

"I'll give you that and a whole lot more," he promised. "Okay, man, hop on my back and I'll give you a piggyback ride."

"Yeah!" Carter shouted.

With Carter clinging to him and a quiet Brie in his arms, Dominic lumbered after Riley and Tamia.

"Where are we going?" Riley asked, puffing hard.

"The secure block," Dominic called down.

Riley vaguely remembered Malik talking about the secure block and she almost smiled. It was the house's panic room. After circling down for what seemed like miles, she finally hit the ground. The rest of the group quickly joined her. Dominic knelt down so that Carter could slide off.

"Did you see me, Mommy? Mr. Dominic gave me a piggyback ride."

Riley glanced down at her son, her eyes tearing up. "You're such a sweet boy," she murmured as she caressed his face.

Dominic cleared his throat. "Come on, we're almost there." They raced down the hall and stopped at a stainless-steel door. To the right of it was a keypad. "This is it," Dominic announced before punching his password into the miniature keypad. The door swooshed open and they all stepped in. The door automatically closed after them.

"What, no giant-size boulders?" Tamia joked.

Dominic chuckled, knowing that not only was she tired but still a little shell shocked over these events. "Don't be fooled by appearances; that door is made from some of the strongest materials known to man. It's actually stronger than the boulder. And so is this." He jutted out his chin at the door in front of them. Instead of a keypad there was a shiny black square the size of a deck of cards to the right of the door. Dominic breathed on it.

"What the—?" Riley asked.

"The secure block is on the other side and the only way to access it is through my DNA. We were going to use eyeballs or fingerprints or even a tongue to access it. But we decided that each of those pieces can easily be removed," he said in an undertone to Riley. "My DNA is programmed into the system and all it takes is a couple of seconds to verify and the door will—"

Just then the door swung open and the group stumbled inside. As if it knew they were all safely inside, the door rolled closed.

Riley grabbed Brie from Dominic and sank to the nearest thing, a white wicker sofa with print cushions.

"This place is the truth!" Tamia announced. "This is bigger than my townhome."

"It's huge. It spans almost half the mansion," Dominic said.

"Are we safe?" Riley asked warily, the Superwoman in her deflated.

Dominic nodded. "This is the safest place on earth. *Nothing* can penetrate these walls," he asserted. Riley simply nodded. She had heard that line before and hugged Brie to her. Carter sat quietly at her feet.

"Are you sure we're underground? It doesn't feel like it." Tamia glanced around; the place looked more like a page from *Elle Decor* than a hideout. The South Beach-themed space instantly calmed her. Two sets of windows ran from the floor to the ceiling.

"We're twenty feet below the surface," Dominic confirmed. "But we didn't want it to feel like that. We had the decorator hook it up so that it felt homey. It'll be interesting to see how good a job she actually did, since this is the first time we've ever used it."

"Well, I love the windows!" Tamia nodded toward them.

"They're not real. They're made out of a special plastic that a paladin created. Behind it is a white wall where a computer-generated image runs twenty-four seven."

"But it looks so real. It's like I'm really looking outside. It's the same view as the one . . . from Malik's bedroom."

"The woman who did it did a phenomenal job, but trust me, you're looking at a wall. When you get a chance, touch it. One unique feature about the system is that we can set it up to beam shots of the outside in here. So you'll always see the sunset and sunrise, you'll see exactly what's outside."

"How does it work?"

"There are cameras on the house that take pictures of it all and send it in. There's a five-second delay, but of course we don't see it."

"Wow!" was all Riley could say.

Tamia sauntered over to Dominic and whispered in his ear. "You were so calm and in control, it got me hot. How many bedrooms does this place have?"

"Five," Dominic replied.

Tamia didn't raise an eyebrow. She didn't expect anything less from Malik. "Darn it, it looks like there won't be enough beds to go around. I think we're gonna have to share," she drawled.

Dominic winked. "Gladly."

Tamia grinned in response. "Is it okay for me to walk around and check things out?" she asked, knowing that she needed to be patient as Dominic had work to do.

"Sure. I think you're going to be happy."

"Ecstatic is a better word," Tamia teased. "The back scratching, cursing, and panting type of happy." She cupped Dominic's butt before sauntering off.

"I wonder if Malik found any other intruders?" Riley asked Dominic.

"We can find out for you," Dominic answered softly. He felt sorry for Riley; she hadn't signed up for this situation. He scooped up a remote and aimed it at a faux window. In one smooth motion the windows spread wide and the glass slid into the ceiling, exposing a bank of monitors.

Riley laughed. "This place has more gadgets than a James Bond movie set. This is cool," she said, suddenly feeling a little bit more like herself.

"Yeah, this is cool," Carter parroted.

A compartmentalized version of the mansion popped up. Every nook and cranny was shown in living color. Inch-size versions of Malik, Carrington, and Bayard ran on screen after screen.

They silently watched as Malik, Carrington, and Bayard searched the house for demons.

"We need to repair any holes," Riley heard Malik say.

"Are they doing a really thorough search?" Riley asked worriedly.

"They are," Dominic answered, trying to reassure her. "Even though it doesn't look like it. They can sense demons."

"Why didn't they sense Keyshaun? There were three of them in the room, for Pete's sake."

"Because they weren't on alert, and why should they be? They were in their own home," he answered patiently.

"Well, the hairs on the back of their necks should've stood up— or at the very least, they should've gotten an uneasy feeling in the pits of their stomachs. What would have happened if more had gotten in?" she fretted.

"Let's see if they did," he said calmly. He pushed a button on the console. "How's it looking?"

"So far so good. It looks like Keyshaun was the only one. We're checking the whole house." Malik didn't pause as he answered. "We should be done in about five minutes."

"Take care of yourself, baby," Riley whispered.

Malik stopped in midstep and stared into the camera. "I always do," he said plainly.

Riley jumped with surprise. "You heard me?"

"Of course. The mics can pick up a mouse's fart," he replied and Carter giggled.

"He said *fart*," he said around a chuckle.

Riley rolled her eyes. "He sure did. Bad boy!" she jokingly scolded as she wagged her finger at the screen. "It looks like I'm going to have to talk to you about your language."

"I can imagine what type of talking you two plan on doing," Dominic muttered.

Riley and Malik ignored the comment. "I'll see you in a minute," Malik said to Riley.

Riley watched as the three men searched the house, and her eyes widened when they got to Malik's bedroom. "There's a camera in Malik's room?"

"Yeah, but there's a secret code to turn it on and off that only Malik knows."

Riley sighed a breath of relief. She didn't want to become the next Kim Kardashian. "Where are the bedrooms? I want to put the kids to bed." She looked down at her beautiful wedding gown. Fortunately, it only had a couple of smudges. "And change my clothes."

"Down the hall, the first door on the left; the bathroom is connected."

Riley followed his directions, stared around the room, and backtracked to Dominic. "How did he do it?"

Dominic glanced away from the monitors, his mouth turned up in a grin. "The paladins."

"Of course, *the paladins*. Why do I even ask," she muttered to herself as she made her way back to the kids' room. It was one room, but with two distinctly different personalities. Brie's side was all pink. Pink fairies danced across the walls, child-size lamps with pink tutu shades hugged her crib. A frothy pink throw rug lay in front of it. "Oh, this is too cute." Riley hugged Brie before placing her in the crib. She turned to Carter. "Now you."

His side of the room looked like an Atlanta Falcons locker room. Everything was red, black, and white. The white ceiling was in stark contrast to the red- and black-striped walls. An Atlanta Falcons' throw covered his bed.

"I'm going to be a football player," Carter decided as he scooped out one of the half dozen footballs in his toy chest and lobbed it at his mother.

"You can be whatever you want," she said gently. "Just don't let anyone tell you that you can't do something."

"Even you, when you say that I can't have any cookies."

Riley laughed. "That's different. I mean don't let anyone steal your dreams."

"Oh, like Daddy," Carter said.

Riley clenched her hands. "Have you been seeing your daddy again?" she asked lightly.

"No. Just wondered, that's all."

Riley let out a breath of air. "I see; those are different dreams. We'll talk about the difference when you get older. But in the meantime, go to bed."

"Okay, Mommy."

"I'll be in later to check on you."

"Do I have to take a bath?" Carter asked, his little mouth turned into a frown.

Riley pretended to contemplate his question. "No, I'll let you go tonight, but tomorrow you'll have to stay in the bath twice as long."

"Awww, Mom!"

"Love you, sweetie. I'll be back." She was so distracted that she walked out forgetting to find a change of clothing. By the time she returned to the living room, Tamia was back.

"This place is the business," Tamia gushed.

"Yeah, just the perfect shelter from demons," Riley said dryly.

"Did you see everything?" Tamia asked. "There's a fully equipped playground. It has everything, a swing, a jungle gym a—"

"For kids or adults?"

Tamia grinned. "For either, I guess."

Suddenly the door slid open and Carrington, Bayard, and Malik strolled in. Riley raced to Malik and threw herself in his arms.

"Did you fix it? Did you patch the holes?"

chapter THIRTY - TWO

Malik hugged Riley to him. "The fix is temporary; we're going to have to find something permanent."

Carrington sprinted out of the room. "I need to get Dr. Imes on the phone. He's the one who created the original shield. I'm sure he can come up with something stronger," he called over his shoulder before disappearing down the hall.

Malik settled on the couch and Riley crawled into his lap, arranged her wedding gown around her legs, and rested her head against his chest. "How bad was it?"

Malik caught Dominic's eye and struggled with how much to tell her. He kissed the top of her head. "It could've been disastrous, but fortunately it wasn't. I think Keyshaun got lucky. The entry points were so small that he either was looking for them or he accidentally flew into one."

"So you don't think he was followed?" Riley asked worriedly.

"I know for sure that he wasn't."

Riley pulled back and looked up into his eyes. "You sure?"

"I am." They were silent for a minute before Malik gently nudged her. "Why don't you take this thing off and have a shower, and I'll be there in twenty." Riley kissed him softly and was almost up when he reached for her hand and pulled her toward him and whispered in her ear, "See you soon, Mrs. Davenport." His warm breath stroked her cheek.

They gazed lovingly into each other's eyes. "Okay, Mr. Davenport," she said breathlessly before going to their bedroom.

Dominic and Malik looked pointedly at Tamia.

"What? I want to know what happened."

"I'll tell you everything," Dominic reassured her. "Why don't you go into our bedroom and I'll be right in."

"But I want to hear," Tamia pouted.

"I said I'll tell you."

Tamia rolled her eyes and pushed herself off the couch. "Whatever," she flung over her shoulder as she tramped off to her bedroom.

Malik shook his head. "You have your hands full."

"Who you telling?" He laughed. "So what's the next step?" Dominic asked, all business. Which is what Malik admired about him, he could switch from play to business mode faster than a double-talking politician.

"Dad is calling Dr. Imes. You know he created the original shield and adapted one for the car that is twenty times stronger than what's on the house. Dad is going to check to see if he can replace the field around the house with a larger version of the one that's protecting the car."

"So how many did you *really* destroy?"

Malik ran his hand over his face. He hated lying to Riley but he knew that she'd worry if he told her the truth. "We destroyed about twenty."

"Shit! That's bad."

"I can't believe that it happened. I'm glad it was Bradley's soldiers and not Bradley, or worse, Exor."

Dominic nodded in agreement. "We would've been in some serious trouble." Dominic studied his cousin. "I know you don't want to, but—"

"Oh, hell naw!"

"But he can help us," Dominic protested.

"I have something that'll destroy Bradley. I just need to do more fact checking."

"You can still do your thing. I'm not stopping you. But you and I both know that the fix is temporary and that it's about as strong as a baby's diaper. If Bradley and Exor find out—"

"They won't," Malik said stubbornly.

"If Bradley and Exor find out," Dominic continued, his voice firm, "they're going to converge on us like flies to shit and it's going to be over. Just think about it."

"We don't need his help," Malik said and pounded his fist on a tabletop. "I don't think Bayard would appreciate his coming."

"Just think about it," Dominic said. "Besides, I think he might enjoy seeing his brother."

"Yeah, right," Malik spat out, "the same man who partnered with demons. He went against the family for riches."

"We don't know that. You never heard his side of the story," Dominic protested. "And the rumor is about as flimsy as a piece of Victoria's Secret lingerie. I don't believe it." Dominic had met him once, in passing, some years ago in Italy, and he had appeared to be a man of integrity.

Malik stuck his face into Dominic's. "I'm not changing my mind," he said stubbornly. The men stood nose to nose, glaring at each other.

"But he's strong. And he might know of ways to destroy Bradley and Exor. Just think about it." Dominic and Malik broke apart as soon as Carrington strolled into the room.

"Any luck with Dr. Imes?" Malik asked.

Carrington eyed them but didn't comment. "He's working on it for us. He thinks he might have something, but it won't be for a couple of days."

"Is he *crazy*? We don't have that much time."

"He knows that. And he's doing his best. Just go to bed and take care of your wife. She needs you. I'll stay up and watch the monitors."

"No, I'll stay," Dominic half-heartedly offered; Carrington swatted him away.

"Go!"

Malik and Dominic walked out of the room. "Think about it," Dominic murmured.

"Drop it!" Malik barked before turning toward his and Riley's bedroom. Dominic stalked past him, muttering under his breath. Malik stood outside the door and calmed himself down. He swung open the door and stood on the threshold; he loved this bedroom almost as much as his aboveground one. With its soft green and beige coloring it was relaxing.

He heard the shower running and he got excited, his cock hardening. Destroying demons and Dominic were quickly forgotten as he stepped into the bathroom. Riley sat on the built-in shower ledge while letting the water cascade over her naked body.

"You're absolutely stunning," Malik murmured and Riley jumped; she hadn't heard him come in.

"And you slip around like a ghost," she laughed. Malik peeled his now wrinkled and dirty tux off and joined Riley in the shower. She wrapped her arms around his neck and pressed her wet body against his. "Seeing my cousin in the house unnerved me. I had such a false sense of security. I didn't think anything could get in."

Malik's hand roamed over her back as he whispered in her ear,

"We *all* believed we were safe. Hell, I'm mad; he was so close and we didn't even sense him. So everybody's radar was off. And I was supposed to protect you but I didn't."

"I hope you're not blaming yourself for what happened. It wasn't your fault."

"I should've protected you," Malik insisted as his hands coasted over her breasts.

"You did, babe. Keyshaun is destroyed, right?" Malik nodded. "Then you protected me."

Malik gently outlined her ear with his tongue and Riley shivered. "Thanks," he whispered.

"For what?"

"For being the woman you are. You're so strong."

Riley was silent. *Bradley never called me strong.* She straightened her shoulders and sat a little taller.

Malik smiled to himself. He slowly inched Riley back until her heels touched the built-in seat. "Turn around!" he ordered.

"Why? I like sitting here with you, the water running over us."

"There's something else I want to do that I think you'll like. Now turn around."

Something in his voice made Riley turn around and quietly face the tile. A wisp of air caressed her neck and she whipped her head around. Malik jumped back.

"Hey, watch it. You almost gave me a black eye."

"I'm sorry, I thought . . . oh, forget it," she mumbled, embarrassed.

"You thought what?" Malik whispered in her ear. He had eased his way back to her.

"I thought you were Bradley," she said before laughing at herself. "I really need to get a grip."

"You're perfectly normal," Malik told her, for what felt like the millionth time. "First I want you to grab a towel and fold it on the bench, then I want you to hold on to the bar and put one leg on the bench."

"Why do you—" Malik's hard cock grazed her behind. "Oh!" She quickly assumed the position.

"Thanks, babe," Malik said as he slowly inched himself inside her. Riley inhaled softly.

He feels so good! "No, thank *you*," she murmured then pressed her bottom against his dick; his balls brushed against her.

Malik grabbed her waist as he leisurely moved in and out of her. The water glided over their bodies.

She reached down and began stroking her clit. Malik saw what she was doing and pushed her hand away. "Why did you do that?" Riley sputtered.

"'Cause I don't want you to come so fast."

"You're crazy. You're lucky I love you. Are you going to give me a sign telling me when it's okay for me to self-pleasure?"

"I'll do it for you when I think the time is right." Riley shook her head. Malik tenderly nipped her shoulder. "Just enjoy it." Their moans filled the shower. The water turned tepid.

"We're running out of hot water."

"I'll have to get that fixed. Um, would you mind?"

"Go ahead," Riley muttered. Malik gladly increased his pace and a minute later grunted his release. He turned off the water, reached for a towel from the warmer, and quickly dried himself off. Riley grabbed a second one and began drying herself.

"I'll take care of you." He lovingly dried his new wife off before carrying her to the bed and placing her down gently. He stretched out beside her. "Are you happy you married me?"

"I am. I would never have imagined us together. And think

about how much we've been through in such a short time," Riley said with amazement. "But I'm so happy that we're together. I have never been so happy. I don't want it to end. I'm Mrs. Davenport," she said, then giggled.

"I love how you say that." Malik reached down between her legs.

"What are you doing?"

"I told you I was going to take care of you. Besides, do you think I'm so selfish that I'd satisfy myself and not you?"

"I know you're not, babe," Riley said between whimpers. Malik was slowly stroking her soft folds.

"Let me satisfy you." He quickly moved between her legs, nestling his mouth on her pussy. He tenderly ran his tongue in her moistness, electrifying every inch of her body. His tongue outlined her soft labia and she moaned softly. Malik kneaded her behind as his lips slid over her clit. Riley gasped with desire and Malik grinned against her pussy, pleased with himself.

To Riley's dismay, he began kissing the inside of her thighs. "Hey, you're moving in the wrong direction," she protested.

"I'm just saving the best for last," he whispered as he kissed his way back up to her pussy. He lovingly sucked her clit before gliding his tongue over it. Riley began vibrating with ecstasy. He swiped it again and Riley screamed out in passion. "I'll always take care of you," Malik vowed before gathering her in his arms.

Riley was Velcroed to Malik's side when she heard Carter's bone-chilling scream. Wearing just a sheet wrapped around her, she raced down the hall to his room. She found his blankets roped around his body and him struggling against them as he mumbled incoherently.

"Thank God, you're just having a nightmare." She laughed to herself and looked up to find Malik standing at the door.

"Why don't you bring him in the bed with us?"

"You sure? He's a rough sleeper."

"That's cool, the bed is big enough for all of us to have our space. I'll carry him and you get Brie."

A few minutes later they all trooped back down to Malik and Riley's room, where all four of them tumbled into bed. After they were all settled, Riley looked over at Malik. "It seemed like a lifetime ago when we got married, but it was only eight hours."

"This is a peaceful end to a hectic day. Night, babe."

"Night, Daddy," Carter whispered and Malik jumped out of bed.

"Are you in here?" he yelled as he stalked around the room inspecting every inch of it. A terrified Carter huddled against his mother.

"Carter, why did you say good night Daddy?"

"I was saying good night to Malik," he whimpered. "I thought that since you're married now—"

"Oh, sweetie, I'm sorry, we misunderstood." Riley called to Malik. "It's okay, Bradley isn't in here. Carter was calling *you* Daddy."

A sheepish but relieved Malik returned to the bed. "I'm sorry, I guess I overreacted." He rubbed Carter's head. "Hey, man, good night."

"Good night, Daddy," he whispered in response.

chapter THIRTY - THREE

Two days later Malik walked in on Riley mindlessly staring at the computer-generated window. He bent down to kiss her shoulder and she whipped around, her mouth wide with terror.

"I—I—I," she stuttered, looking as though she had come face-to-face with the devil.

Malik pulled his wife into his arms. "It's me, Riley, Malik." He stood back and tilted her face toward his. "See? It's me."

"I'm sorry," she mumbled. "I used to do the same thing in Lavastar. I guess I'm really getting a case of cabin fever," she said shakily.

Malik grabbed her by the shoulders. "I'm going to take you over to that couch and you're going to tell me everything that happened in Lavastar."

Riley nodded then followed him to the couch. As soon as they sat down, she told him every horrific detail. By the time she'd finished, Malik's hands were clenched to his sides and his body was rigid with anger. "Consider him dead." Malik protectively wrapped his arms around Riley and they sat that way until they both felt calm.

"It is kind of cozy down here," Riley offered, attempting to lighten the mood.

Malik grinned. "You lie worse than a cheap rug."

Riley sighed. "You caught me." She gazed into his eyes and he boldly met her stare. Her heart hitched when his eyes darkened to azure. "I've never seen that color before," she murmured. "You're gorgeous."

"You say it like you've never noticed it before," Malik teased.

"Of course I noticed."

Malik bent down and began blowing in her ear. "What else have you noticed?" Heat rushed through Riley.

"That you're driving me crazy. Let's go to *our bed*," she whispered.

"We can't, Carter and Brie are napping in it."

Riley grinned. "Let's forget the bed. What about here?"

Malik snorted. "This thing is barely big enough to hold Carter, we'd probably end up breaking it."

"No we won't, come on," she pleaded. Riley tugged at Malik's shirt and almost had it unbuttoned when Bayard strolled in. Malik groaned and his penis deflated faster than a five-dollar tire.

"How are we coming along with your new tactic?"

"I'm close, very close. Let's talk about it later."

"Great."

Bayard turned away and was about to go when he motioned to Malik.

"I'll be right back, babe," Malik said and joined his grandfather while Riley sat on the couch. She strained her ears to listen and her heart tightened when she heard: "broke through," "destroyed," and "keeping an eye out." *More demons have gotten in!* She gulped deeply, swallowing her scream.

"Is everything okay?" she asked when Malik rejoined her on the couch and Bayard left the room.

"Fine," Malik answered quickly before reaching for her.

Riley pulled away and looked in his eyes, when he averted his gaze, her stomach clenched. "They're still up there, aren't they?"

"No, they—"

"Don't you lie to me, Malik, don't you dare lie to me," she hissed.

Malik sighed. "Okay, you're right, some are still slipping through. The temporary fix isn't worth shit. It's about as flimsy as this material," he said and pointed his finger at the whispery-thin lamp shade.

"So the situation is actually worse than what you told us. You aren't testing the repaired shield, you're keeping us here because you know that it's worthless." Malik nodded; he hated lying to her. "Why not tell us the truth, Malik?" Riley asked heatedly. "We're not some southern hothouse flowers who can't handle the truth."

"I know, I only did it because I was trying to keep your stress level down and alleviate some of your fears. I'm sorry. Will you accept my apology?" Riley childishly rolled her eyes and looked toward the ceiling. Malik gently cupped her chin, forcing her to look in his eyes. "I'm sorry," he whispered.

Riley looked deeply into his blue eyes and saw love and sincerity. Her eyes swelled with tears. "I know you are. I'm just so scared," she admitted and started crying. "I didn't mean to yell at you."

"That's okay," Malik said soothingly while he dabbed at her face with the hem of his shirt.

"What a honeymoon, huh?" Riley sniffled.

Malik ran his thumb over her palm. "As soon as this ends, I'll take you on a trip around the world."

"That'll be nice, but it doesn't have to be around the world. Right now, I'll settle for a trip to Walmart."

"Well, Walmart does have everything," Malik joked.

"I would love anything that has a sense of normality to it. Anything that reminds me of my old life. Not with Bradley," she hurriedly explained, "but when I could come and go whenever I wanted and go wherever I wanted."

"You'll have that life again, I promise."

"Now tell me what you found on your rounds." For the past couple of days, Malik, Bayard, and Carrington had been assigned shifts where their primary duty was to search the upper levels for demons. Their usual response to Riley and Tamia was that the force field was still strong and nothing could penetrate it, making the house demon free.

"I didn't find anything on my earlier round, but I destroyed two of them this morning," Malik answered honestly.

Riley's eyes widened with terror. "How much longer before Bradley gets in?" she asked in a hushed tone.

"First of all, if he gets in, he won't be able to get in here. This area is twenty feet underground and encased in metal. No demons can get through."

"You said that about upstairs," Riley snapped and Malik sighed.

"That's what I believed at the time," he answered patiently. "Unfortunately, I was wrong. I make mistakes."

"And you lie," Riley quipped. She couldn't resist the opportunity to tease.

Malik grinned. "Lady, your mood changes more than Atlanta's weather; first you're crying, then you're scared, then you're pissed, and then you're joking with me, and this all happened in ten minutes."

"I'm a female. What can I say, we're very complex beings."

"I hope you aren't too complex for this," he murmured before nuzzling her neck. Riley lovingly stroked his face. "You know that I'm really sorry for lying to you, don't you?" he whispered in her ear and Riley's heart swelled with love.

"I know." She shifted her face so that their lips touched and they hungrily kissed each other.

"Is your offer still on the table?" Malik asked when they broke for air.

"What?" Riley asked, confused, then understanding she nodded before reclining and pulling Malik on top of her.

He grunted. "Babe, this is way too little." He snaked his arms around her and lifted her up. He sat down and placed her on top of him.

"I can't see you," Riley grumbled as she squirmed on his lap.

"That's okay, you have a lifetime to see me," he said in her ear as he gently kneaded her breasts. Riley rested her back against his chest and he nibbled on her neck. "Take off your clothes," he breathed into her ear.

She pulled away and stood in front of him. Riley unbuttoned her jeans. "I'm not taking off my sweater, just my jeans."

"And thong," Malik drawled as he pulled off his jeans and underwear then tossed them on the floor.

"Right, just in case somebody comes in."

"Nobody is coming in."

"They might."

"They won't."

"Did you stick a do-not-disturb sign on the door?" Riley asked.

"Nope."

"So somebody might come in. The top stays on."

"That's okay, as long as I have access to that beautiful pussy of yours. Let me see it." Riley stood proudly in front of her husband.

Malik ran his tongue over his lips as he reached down and stroked his penis. "You're beautiful, babe, so beautiful. Come here."

Riley sauntered to him and Malik grabbed her by the waist. He turned her around. "You have a sweet ass," he said adoringly before kissing both cheeks. "Come on." Malik positioned Riley over his cock and slowly lowered her down. He slid easily into her hotness.

Just then, Carrington burst through the door. Riley let out a yelp, jumped off Malik, and plopped down on the couch where she sat with her legs crossed. "I'm sorry." He did an about-face and marched out of the room. "Come see me when you're done. Dr. Imes may have solved our problem," he called out.

"Oh my God, how embarrassing was that? I can't imagine what your father thinks about me now."

"That I'm one lucky guy," Malik said as he repositioned Riley in front of him.

"Hey, what are you doing?"

"I'm going to finish what I started. Come on now," Malik softly pleaded. His dick was hard and he needed some relief.

"He said for you to come see him when you were done, and we're done," Riley said stubbornly.

"Right!" Malik said, ignoring her. "So let's finish." He tried to grab Riley but she skirted his reach.

"I'm not doing anything!"

"Why?"

"Because he knows what we're doing."

"He knows that neither one of us is a virgin. Hell, you have two kids. And I'm pretty sure he doesn't believe the stork brought them."

"I know that!" Riley stood up and began putting on her clothes.

Malik bit his lip. "Okay, can you at least give me a blow job?"

Riley rolled her eyes and stomped out of the room. "Men!"

"Riley!" Malik yelled, but either Riley didn't hear him or was ignoring him. "Shit!" he glanced down at his dick. "I guess it's just you and me now."

Thirty minutes later, Malik sauntered into Carrington's library. Bayard, Riley, Dominic, Tamia, and Dr. Imes were already there.

"Thanks for stopping by," Bayard said dryly.

"I didn't realize that we were having a meeting," Malik muttered. "I was researching some techniques." He settled into the empty chair next to Riley.

"For destroying Bradley?" Carrington asked, feigning ignorance.

"Of course. What other type of techniques would I be researching?" Dominic cleared his throat and Tamia laughed. "Hey, whatever happened to the father-and-son sacred bond?"

"Oh, it's there," Carrington replied, "just as strong as ever," he answered, his voice teasing.

Bayard chuckled before turning to Dr. Imes. "Tell everybody what you just told Carrington and me."

"I believe I have solved your problem—"

"Will anything else be able to slip through?" Riley asked.

"No, I can promise you that."

"Is it one hundred percent safe?" Riley pressed.

Dr. Imes smiled benevolently at her. "Nothing has a hundred percent guarantee. But it's very good, exceptional, to say the least. I have—"

"So why use it?" Riley spat out. "If it's not a sure thing, why use it?"

Malik pressed his leg against hers. "Give him a chance," he

whispered so softly that Riley wasn't even sure he had said anything, but she clamped her mouth closed.

Dr. Imes continued. "Like I was saying, I designed a stronger
force field, and an even bigger one. This one will encapsulate
three acres in addition to the house. Now the kids can enjoy the
outdoors."

Tamia let out a squeal of delight. "That's awesome."

"I'm not sure," Malik said. "I don't feel comfortable with this."
Riley smiled smugly. "Why is this so much better?"

Dr. Imes clearly loved talking about his work. With a PhD in
biophysics, and cellular and molecular biology, and a master's in
chemistry, he could talk about this with as much enthusiasm as the
tabloids did about Amy Winehouse's latest antics. "If you recall,
the field we were using was electrical, but this one is plasma."

"What's the difference?" Malik asked. "It seems as if the plasma
would be more vulnerable. I'm picturing a gel-like shell."

"You're partially right," Dr. Imes answered. "It will be a gel-
based field. The gel is made of poloxy, a compound that repels demons. It's synthetic based so we can manufacture as much as you
need, whenever you need it."

"How come you weren't using poloxy in the first place?" Riley
asked angrily and this time Malik didn't say anything. He wanted
to know why as well.

"My colleagues and I were always working on it, trying to perfect it, but we didn't see the rush since we thought what was in
place was adequate. But as we all found out, I was wrong; please
forgive me," he said directly to Riley. "We've been working nonstop
to correct the problem and we finally got the formula right."

"Go on," Malik ordered.

"Sure," Dr. Imes responded easily. "The poloxy gel will be

layered over and under a laser field, so you'll be getting three layers of protection."

"And this is much stronger than even the field that's protecting my car?" Malik asked.

"Much stronger," Dr. Imes reassured him.

"Are you comfortable with this?" Bayard asked the doctor. "I want to make sure that it'll protect my great-grandchildren."

"I'm so sure that we can try it out now. My crew has been setting it up while we were talking."

"You mean go outside?" Riley asked, wide eyed.

Dr. Imes nodded. "That's right. Come on. Let's go outside."

chapter THIRTY-FOUR

Riley reluctantly woke up Carter and Brie, then followed the group down the hall. A little way down, they stopped at an elevator, something Riley had missed when they raced into the secure block.

"Why didn't we use this instead of running and zigzagging down corridors and stairs like we were making a prison break?" Riley asked, her voice sour.

"The stairs were closer," Malik said softly. "Dominic probably saved your life with all that *zigzagging*."

"I know, I'm sorry," she said to Dominic, who stood next to Tamia, who wisely kept her mouth shut.

"Forget about it," Dominic said graciously. The elevator doors swooshed open and the group cruised in. A moment later the doors opened and they stepped into the kitchen.

"This is the fastest way to get outside from the elevator," Malik explained as he crossed the spacious room. Riley was blind to the restaurant-style kitchen. The stainless-steel appliances, granite countertops, two double ovens, and one wood-burning stove were all a blur. On previous trips there, she'd found something to admire.

They braked at a set of white French doors. The Davenport men exchanged glances but neither moved to open them.

Dr. Imes confidently stepped forward. "Since you guys are risking your lives based on my word, I'll go first."

Bayard moved next to him. "No, I am the head of this household, the king of Ulgani. I will go first."

Malik and Dominic shared a look before jumping in front of Dr. Imes. "We'll go first," they said simultaneously.

Bayard smiled proudly at his bloodline.

"Let's do it together," Carrington offered.

On a silent count of three, all the men confidently stepped outside; only Riley and Tamia held back.

Malik, Bayard, and Carrington silently scanned the area, each heightening their demon radar. With the concentration of a drug-sniffing dog, Malik slowly strolled around the perimeter of the house.

Fifteen minutes later, Riley and Tamia were still fearfully peering out the French doors. Neither budged, even when they got the thumbs-up sign from Malik and Dominic.

Tamia had her arms around Carter, forcing him to stand in place; it had been months since he had actually walked on grass.

"Come on, babe," Malik coaxed, "it's okay, look, nothing has happened to us."

Riley gazed past Malik. "It could be a trap. Bradley could be waiting for me to bring Carter out before he and his army strike."

Malik walked over to Riley. "This morning you were talking about how you would like to get out of the house; now you have your chance. Just go with it."

The warm air tickled her face, and she stared longingly outside. *Freedom is just one step away.* "I can't, I just can't," she muttered before turning away. "Come on," she called to her sister. "I don't want Carter out there."

Tamia was about to argue, but decided against it. She didn't trust the new force field any more than she trusted a new contraceptive. Both always ran the risk of some little bugger slipping through.

Riley, Tamia, and the kids hurried to the elevator. Tamia covered her sister's hand with her own. "Are you sure you want to go back down there?"

"I don't, but that's the safest place," she argued. "Don't you agree?"

Tamia leaned against the wall. "You're right, but we've created a mini prison in our big prison. I just hope that our secure space doesn't shrink to the size of a closet."

Riley gave her sister a half smile. "Can you see all of us squashed into a closet?"

"That sounds like fun," Carter said.

Riley looked down into her son's hopeful eyes. "That does sound like fun, but I can think of something that's even more fun, can't you, T.?"

"Yeah!" Tamia grabbed her sister's hand. "Come on, let's reclaim our freedom."

"Yes, come on, Mommy," Carter chimed in. They all raced through the kitchen and toward the doors, bursting outside.

While Tamia flew into Dominic's arms, Riley froze on the lawn and looked up, searching for any sign of Bradley. Malik stepped up behind her. "He's not here. It's safe."

Carter tugged at her hand. "Can I run, Mommy, can I?"

Riley closed her eyes and leaned against Malik. Her husband squeezed her arm and she loosened her grip on Carter's hand. He pulled away and ran off. He was running so fast that it looked like he was flying over the lawn. Riley nuzzled her face against Brie's.

"It's okay, he'll be fine," Malik reassured her for the second time when Riley looked at him helplessly. "Look at how much fun he's having."

Riley followed his gaze and couldn't help but laugh. Carter was running in circles with his arms wide, as though he was an airplane. When he tired of that, he'd spurt forward a couple of yards before racing back to his starting point. "He's really having a good time, he looks so happy . . . so free." They spent fifteen minutes watching Carter reacquaint himself with nature.

"Come on, let me give you a mini tour of the grounds before it gets too dark." He nodded toward Carter. "And grab him, he's been running around so much that I'm afraid he might get sick. Let's give him an opportunity to rest."

Five minutes later they were all sitting on a golf cart ambling across the lawn. They waved to Dominic and Tamia, who were snuggled together on the grass while they gazed into the sky. They saw Bayard, Carrington, and Dr. Imes a little way off, engrossed in conversation.

"I can't show you everything, we don't have time. I just want to give you a little taste of what's yours now."

"Malik!" Riley began to protest. "This isn't mine, it belongs to your family, the Davenports."

"You're a Davenport now," Malik quietly reminded her.

"That's right. I am," Riley said happily.

"Yes you are, so this is yours, Carter's, and Brie's, you're all Davenports now. So hold on—let's get this tour started."

"At least the weather is on our side," Riley commented. It was a balmy seventy degrees.

"Yes, winter in Atlanta. I love it." Malik pointed to his left. "Over there are the tennis courts. And if you look over there, you'll see mounds of dirt. That's going to be the kids' play area. I'm having a full playground installed."

"Malik, that's too much!"

"I don't think it's enough," he quipped before continuing, "and on the other side of all that is a ten-hole golf course."

"Your place—"

"*Our* place."

Riley blushed. "*Our* place is huge. I can't wait to really explore the grounds. It'll probably take all day." Malik made a U-turn and headed back toward the house. "Are you okay back there?" Riley called out to Carter before twisting around in her seat to see him.

She found Carter looking up at the sky and waving. "What are you doing, sweetie?" Riley asked.

Carter pointed up. "Look who's here."

Riley glanced toward the sky. "Oh no! It's Bradley! Hurry up, Malik, get us out of here!"

chapter THIRTY-FIVE

"He's still lurking," Riley spat out.

"You know that he won't give up until he has what he wants, and that's Carter," Malik gently reminded her. "The good thing is that he didn't get in. The shield held."

"Thank God! I don't know what I'd do if he ever got in."

"He's trying to intimidate you. He can't get in and he knows it," Malik explained.

"I know," Riley answered before covering her mouth with her hand, hiding a yawn. Malik gave her thigh a sympathetic squeeze. He knew that the meeting was going on too long, much longer than either of them had anticipated. The clock chimed midnight; so far they had been meeting for six hours. Tao had long since served dinner and taken away the plates. But he had left blocks of cheese, cut fruit, bread, olive oil, and bottles of wine for them to snack on. Tamia snored softly on the couch. Dominic had kept her up late the night before.

The conference room was filled with the usual crew, including Taurus, Valencia, Peony, and the twins.

"I've been working on something and I'm really close. All I need is a couple of things verified," Malik said confidently.

"Is it something Dr. Imes can help you with?" Bayard asked.

Malik shook his head. "It's got to be someone who knows Exor's and Lavastar's history. Because if I'm wrong, I'll destroy us all."

"It's imperative that you get what you need as soon as possible; this has been going on for way too long," Bayard boomed.

The room went silent. Dominic cleared his throat. "I hate to repeat myself, but my sources are telling me that Exor and Bradley are getting ready to make their move," he said. Even though he'd had only a bit of sleep the night before, it didn't show on his face nor did it affect his ability to think clearly. Sex rejuvenated him; he'd take it over an energy drink any day.

Riley nervously jiggled her leg. Bradley was spiraling out of control.

"How close are they? Realistically?" Bayard asked.

Dominic clutched his pen. Only Malik saw the movement and knew his cousin was as frustrated as he was.

"Realistically? Any day, and it could happen without any warning. That's what happened in the Dominican Republic."

Nervous murmurs went up around the table. Two weeks ago, demons had invaded that country. The crime and suicide rates had jumped higher than the unemployment rate. There were stories of thousands of mutilated bodies being found in empty buildings throughout the country, clustered together like empty shells. All the major news networks aired videos of people committing brutal crimes against each other. Only Malik, Bayard, Carrington, and their paladins knew the truth and what was on the horizon for mankind. The unprovoked attacks, the senseless killings, were all caused by demons, and if they didn't intervene, the orderly chaos that is mankind would end.

Riley was scanning a status report showing the United States's growing crime problem when the lights dimmed. An expletive was on the tip of her tongue but an inner voice told her to remain quiet.

Dominic grabbed a remote and aimed it at the wall and the projector screen slid down from the ceiling. "I want to warn you that this is very graphic. I wouldn't advise you to watch it if you have a weak stomach," he said somberly.

Taurus picked up. "Steven Woeber, one of our renegade paladins, filmed this."

Malik leaned in closer. "It's getting late, you can leave if you want. I'll update you later," he whispered.

"I want to stay," Riley replied stubbornly and Malik shrugged before reclining in his chair.

The scene opened with a shot of a busy street in some unnamed city in the Dominican Republic. People were hurrying, on their way to work or running errands. The footage was boring, until it hit the two-minute mark.

A man wielding a machete strolled down the street, then braked to a stop behind an unsuspecting lady. He tapped her on the shoulder, and as she turned around, brought the machete up high and sliced off her head. It rolled on the ground, looking like a defective bowling ball. The lady's hands automatically reached up, but made it only to her shoulders before her body realized that the connection had been severed and dropped to the ground next to its head. The man looked directly into the camera and grinned maniacally before skipping down the street, leaving a trail of blood. In the stunned silence, Dominic flicked off the video and turned on the lights.

Riley felt her dinner coming up and pushed herself away from the table. Malik saw her reaction and rushed for a wastebasket. He got it under her mouth just as her dinner spewed out.

Embarrassed and still a little shaky, she returned to the table. But she had enough strength to straighten her spine and pull back her shoulders, managing to look confident while still feeling a little woozy.

Malik smiled at his wife with admiration; she was a fighter.

"We don't want any more killings, but our first priority is destroying Bradley. Is Exor next?" He surveyed the group, then shrugged. "I don't know, but I would love to stop them all," he said.

"But how?" Riley burst out. "It's like we're a swarm of mosquitoes trying to kill a herd of elephants and all they're doing is swatting us away in annoyance."

Just then Dominic's phone buzzed and all heads turned toward the intrusion, then to Bayard. The number one rule that Bayard strictly enforced was that all electronic devices must be turned off during their meetings, unless otherwise permitted by him. It buzzed a second time and Dominic squirmed in his seat, something he hadn't done since he was three.

"Answer it!" Bayard barked.

Dominic clicked on his phone and hurriedly whispered into it. He got up and moved toward the door. "I'll be right back."

Five minutes later the door swung open and Dominic entered the room and nervously looked around. "I've got someone who will help us," he announced. "Come on," he called over his shoulder.

Bayard sauntered in grinning, as though he was entering a cocktail party and was the guest of honor.

Riley shot a look of surprise toward Bayard's seat, she hadn't seen him get up. She nearly fainted when she saw that Bayard hadn't moved. Her gaze went from Bayard number one to Bayard number two then back again. They looked exactly the same except for the fact that Bayard number two was dressed all in white.

Taurus yawned, Valencia raised an eyebrow, Bayard shot up in his seat, and Carrington reached for his hip as though reaching for a gun.

"Oh no!" Malik squeaked.

Riley looked from Malik to Carrington to Bayard, all of whom looked as though they wanted to spring from their seats and attack Bayard number two.

"Glazier?" Riley whispered.

"Glazier?" Malik murmured.

His uncle sauntered in, followed by an attractive, slim man. "Bayard," Glazier drawled. "You're looking great. I heard you could use my help."

chapter THIRTY - SIX

Bayard shot up from the table. "Get him out of here! Get him the fuck out!" he roared, his voice shaking with rage.

"You're always so dramatic," Glazier drawled as he seemed to float across the room and settle on a couch. His guest sat down beside him. "I know it's late, but is any of your help still on duty?" he asked, then before anyone could answer, he continued. "Because if they are, can you have somebody bring me a drink? I'm a little parched." He turned to his friend. "Oh, by the way, everybody, this is Harland. Would you like something?"

"Maybe a little champagne; that's always good after a long flight."

"Perfect!" Glazier exclaimed. "Champagne for everybody."

For the second time that evening, all eyes turned to Bayard.

"I want you out!" Bayard roared. "Malik! Carrington! Get them out!"

Glazier sniffed. "Don't you at least want to know how I'm doing? We haven't seen each other in ages. The centuries just flew by," he said teasingly. "I think we have a lot of catching up to do."

"I don't have anything to say to you. Nothing!" Bayard said before storming out of the room.

Carrington shot Dominic a pointed look. "I'll talk to you later," he said quietly; he then turned on his heel and raced after his father.

"He'll get over it," Glazier reassured Dominic calmly. "Now where's that champagne?"

"Meeting adjourned!" Malik barked. But no one moved. Malik pressed his lips together. Expectation hung in the air as they all stared at Glazier and Harland as though they were characters from their favorite TV show. "Meeting adjourned," Malik said in a voice so sharp that even Riley flinched. She hadn't heard him use that voice before on a nondemon. Everybody jumped up, as though Malik had shot off a cannon, and scurried out. Ten seconds later, only Malik, Riley, Dominic, Glazier, Harland, and Tamia, who was just waking up, were left.

"Aw, man, did I miss the whole meeting?" Tamia asked sleepily.

"That depends on which meeting you are referring to. I have a feeling that another one is about to start," Glazier answered while scrutinizing his nephews.

"Who's that?" Tamia asked.

"Glazier," Riley muttered; she was just as fascinated by him as everyone else was.

"Oh!" Tamia looked at Glazier, then her boyfriend, then Malik, then back to Glazier. She instinctively kept her mouth shut. Something told her that now wasn't the time for jokes, and so instead she curled up on the couch.

"What are you doing here?" Malik asked.

"Dom asked me to come. He said he needed my help," Glazier answered. "Did he lie?"

"Yes, I mean no," Malik answered, fumbling over his words more than a teenage boy fumbling with his girlfriend's bra. He closed his eyes and took a deep breath. "I mean yes he lied and no we don't need your help."

Dominic opened his mouth to protest, but Malik held up a hand, shutting him down before he could get started. "You may leave now," Malik said regally.

Glazier chuckled. "You are Bayard's grandson. You are definitely a prince. *Where is* that champagne?" he asked, looking around.

Malik clenched his hands. "You're not getting any champagne. We don't want you here. Get out!"

"Why?" Harland asked, and the question froze Malik with its simplicity.

"He doesn't care about us, he never did. He wanted to serve demons instead of destroying them."

"You need to tell them the truth, Glazier," Harland said.

Glazier smirked. "They'll never believe it."

"There's nothing to tell," Malik spat out, and Riley touched him softly on the thigh, trying to calm him, but he ignored her. "He betrayed the Davenports."

"Tell them," Harland persisted. "If you don't, I'm going to walk out of this house and out of your life for good."

The smirk fell from Glazier's face; he knew by the tone of Harland's voice that he was serious.

Glazier winked at Malik. "Fine! I think Bayard and Carrington should be here; I hate repeating myself," he drawled. "And where the hell is that damn champagne!"

Twenty tense minutes later, with Bayard and Carrington in the room and a glass of champagne in his hand, Glazier began his tale.

"It happened in a small town outside Paris, in the countryside. I don't remember the century, but obviously it wasn't a good one for me." He smiled sadly before continuing. "I was fourteen and had just started getting urges, sexual urges."

Bayard rolled his eyes. "Yeah, you and all the other little fourteen-year-old boys." He remembered all the girls chasing his brother. Some were ladylike and subtle about it but some were more brazen about their interest in him. It wasn't unusual for Glazier to find, uninvited, half-naked prepubescent girls in his bed trying to seduce the young prince. Even though they were identical in looks, they were complete opposites when it came to personality. Bayard preferred reading books, learning to run an empire, and riding horses. Glazier, on the other hand, loved to spend his days gambling, racing horses, and drinking himself sick.

"And I *loved* the boys," Glazier admitted.

"What?" Bayard's glass of wine slipped from his fingers; it splattered unnoticed to the floor. "What? That can't be true. All the girls wanted you."

"And they still do," Glazier replied smoothly, "but I don't want them, never did. My interests lie elsewhere." He shot a meaningful look at Harland, who grabbed his hand to show his support and love.

Bayard looked at Glazier's and Harland's intertwined hands and blindly groped for his glass of wine. "You dropped it, remember?" Glazier said, amused. "And yes, just so there's no misunderstanding, I'm gay."

"Big deal, so you're gay," Tamia retorted. "Get to why you partnered with Exor and turned your back on your family."

"I like you." His gaze took in Tamia's tousled hair, her full sensuous lips, and her natural beauty. "If I were into girls, I would so definitely do you." He blew her a kiss before continuing. "To be caught with a man was considered evil and was an instant death sentence. There wasn't the acceptance back then that there is now."

"You're gay?" Bayard mumbled, still stunned by the news. "I never suspected."

"Yes, he is," Harland quipped. "One hundred percent."

"But that still doesn't tell us why you did what you did," Dominic finally chimed in. Bayard and Carrington shot him double glares. He slumped back in his chair, knowing that he was a heartbeat away from being thrown out on his ass.

"I was chased out of the city by a mob with torches. They wanted to fry me. It didn't matter that I was in line for the throne, that I was going to be their king. I think that made it worse. Who wanted a king who bent over for other men?"

"But we were run out too," Bayard spat out, "and we didn't align ourselves with Exor."

"That's right, you were," Glazier said slowly, "but I bet you loved yourself. Even though you had your special powers, you never thought you were any less than any of those simple-minded monsters who ran you off with torches."

Bayard and Carrington didn't respond. They knew that they didn't have to. Glazier continued, "But I hated myself. I truly loathed myself and what I was. I felt less than human. I loved men." He laughed bitterly.

"They hated me because they caught me with a man—his name was Byron—in a rather compromising position. A group of homophobes—we didn't have a name for them back then, a gang of monsters—caught us. They did some unmentionable things to me, some very nasty and mean things," Glazier said quietly, then shuddered at the memory. He clenched Harland's hand. "After that, I hated everybody, and myself even more. And I wanted everybody, including myself, dead, and Exor promised me that he could do it. I wanted everyone in the hate-filled world to die."

The room was quiet as they absorbed Glazier's hurt masked as anger.

"Do you still want that?" Riley tentatively ventured.

Glazier chuckled. "Sometimes," he joked. "But times have changed. Nowadays gays can live openly without any hate. Oh, there are some places I wouldn't dare show my face in the middle of the night, but overall, it's a good time to be gay. And most important, I finally love and accept myself. It took four centuries, but I'm finally in love with myself."

"That's such a girlie thing to say," Harland teased.

"I'm just a girlie type of guy," Glazier quipped.

"Not hardly," Harland responded and they looked lovingly at each other.

Bayard watched the exchange between his brother and lover and wanted to leave the room. This wasn't the rough-and-tumble masculine brother he had grown up with, this was somebody else. A watered-down version of the brother he'd always known. Bayard forced himself to stay, mostly out of curiosity, as he wanted to know how his brother could assist them. But more than that he was curious to learn about Glazier Davenport the man.

"The real question is, where are your loyalties? With the Davenports or Exor?" Carrington challenged.

"With the Davenports of course. I severed ties with Exor centuries ago."

"Why haven't we heard about this?" Bayard snapped. "Exor's MO is to kill his defectors, so why did he let you live?"

Glazier yawned as though bored. "He saw that my heart wasn't in it." He laughed at everyone's shocked expressions. "I know, bizarre, right? I'm the one who wanted everybody dead. And that rage lasted for about a hundred years. I inhabited humans, I led an army that took over third-world countries, but after two hundred years, my heart wasn't in it anymore and Exor knew it. Exor isn't going to tell everybody that he let me go. Why would the mighty one admit to showing compassion? The rumor is that I'm on the run, and occasionally one of his soldiers shows up to capture me, but he's always dealt with.

"While I was with him, I learned a lot about him, his strengths, his weaknesses. I still keep in contact with a couple of demons in his inner circle who know the truth about our relationship. They can provide a lot of valuable information on Bradley."

"So why do you want to double-cross the demon who let you live?" Malik shot at his uncle.

Glazier shrugged. "Why wouldn't I? He's priming Bradley to wreak havoc on the world, and once Bradley's finished obsessing over Carter, he will refocus his attention. Exor wants Bradley to help him destroy mankind; we can't let that happen. This side would be so boring without humans." Glazier looked his brother squarely in the eye. "So do you still want to kick me out?"

chapter THIRTY - SEVEN

Riley glanced worriedly at Malik, who had tossed and turned throughout the night.

"Good morning," he said.

"How did you know I was awake?" she asked.

"I could feel you staring at me." Flipping over onto his back, Riley noticed that his eyes were almost blue-black.

"Are you okay? You were tossing and turning so much last night that I was half-expecting to see a bolt or two hit the ceiling."

Malik pulled Riley into his arms. "Never," he breathed softly in her ear. Riley smiled to herself before resting her head on his bare chest.

"Are you ready to talk about him now?"

Malik sighed. "Not really, but since he's here . . ."

"He seems nice," Riley said tentatively. Malik grunted. Riley rolled her eyes. "He and Bayard are identical twins, so how did Bayard end up being king and not Glazier?"

"They're both kings."

"What?" Riley raised her head. "That's not possible!" she protested.

Malik chuckled at her response. "After living here with me,

the first thing you should have learned was that anything is possible."

"That's true. But how did it happen? A country with two kings, I've never heard of such a thing!"

"When they learned that my great-grandmother was having twins, they decided on a caesarean section—"

"But that was centuries ago, how did they know she was carrying twins? They didn't have ultrasound machines back then."

"But they weren't dumb either, and it was common sense. She was much bigger than a pregnant woman carrying only one baby. And I was told that they both kicked like the dickens. So either she was carrying an octopus or twins, and they guessed twins."

Riley tweaked one of Malik's nipples. "Silly."

"It was decided that extra people would be on hand to help with the delivery. And when the time came, both of them were pulled out at exactly the same time. So technically they were both considered firstborn and were granted the power."

"How was that possible? How did they know where they both were in the womb?"

Malik shrugged. "I don't know, but it was a perfectly timed birth so that they both got equal powers. And when my great-grandfather was murdered, they were both named king of Ulgani."

"But how can Bayard and Glazier rule a country that they don't even live in?" Riley asked while letting the comment slide about his great-grandfather's murder, knowing she'd get the story when he was ready to talk about it.

"Easy. Bayard usually visits four or more times a year, but with everything that's happening with Bradley and Exor, he decided not to. So all his meetings are done with a video conference or over the phone. It can be done."

"Now that Glazier is back, maybe he can help him. Maybe this time, they can really share the throne," Riley suggested.

"We'll see how it works out," he said quietly.

Riley, Malik, Bayard, Carrington, Dominic, Glazier, and Harland crowded into the small library in the secure block. Although their normal living quarters seemed as secure as a virgin's chastity belt, Bayard had insisted on meeting in this part of the house. He told the group that they needed the privacy because he didn't want the kids to interrupt them. But Riley suspected he had chosen the secure block because he didn't want to risk an appearance of Exor. She had the feeling that the improved shield was no match for Exor and, if given a reason, Exor could smash it into a million pieces.

And Glazier's return could be that reason. Dominic heard from his sources that Exor was not pleased with Glazier's very public return to his brother's home. Lavastar was abuzz with the news. As long as Glazier remained neutral, he didn't pose a threat. But now that he was reknitting a tattered bond, action needed to be taken to stop the process. The only way to do that was to destroy the Davenports, and Exor was the only one powerful enough to do it.

Tao had set out a brunch that the group barely touched.

"You've really created quite the panic-room-type house," Glazier joked. "It has more security than the White House. And the walk just to get to this little gem, priceless. You really didn't have to do it."

"I wanted privacy," Bayard said stiffly.

"You wanted to make sure Exor didn't get me," Glazier snapped back. He leaned back in his chair and grinned at his brother. "Trust me, if Exor had wanted me, he would've gotten me long before this. I'm so off his radar, it's ridiculous. He's focused on something else, so I'm safe."

Dominic shook his head. "No, you're not. My sources are telling a different story. Exor is livid. He didn't mind your playing the former-demon-gone-good role, he found it amusing. But you joined forces against him, with his enemies, and he's pissed," Dominic said.

Glazier shrugged. "Thanks for the info but he'll get over it. Besides, you don't have to worry about me. But you do have to worry about her." He nodded toward Riley.

"We are well aware of the situation with Bradley," Malik retorted.

Glazier got up and went to the fake window that showed the yard. "Intriguing and beautiful. I feel like I'm looking outside. I can almost feel the breeze. Harland, come see."

Harland hurried to his side and Glazier slipped an arm around his lover's waist. "It *is* nice," Harland agreed while Bayard fumed.

"Do you love me?" Glazier called over his shoulder and everybody in the room knew that the question was directed at Bayard.

"Of course," he replied, his voice tight.

"Do you remember how close we were growing up?" Glazier asked. "We used to go hunting together; remember how we'd track pheasant and shoot them with our bows and arrows? And remember how scared you were of the dark and how you used to come into my room to sleep with me?" Glazier asked, his voice soft with memory.

"Of course I remember all that," Bayard said curtly. "We're brothers, we have a history, we shared things—"

Glazier snatched his arm from Harland and whirled around to face his brother, his blue eyes fiery with anger. "We share the Davenport blood! How can you forget that!" he shouted.

Bayard shot up from the table and marched over to his brother.

"Oh shit!" Malik muttered. Riley grabbed his hand.

Bayard stopped within inches of his brother. "How can I forget that?" Bayard repeated, incredulity lacing his words. "You're the one who barged into my home."

"What?"

Bayard held up his hand. "Let me finish. You're in *my* house." Glazier pressed his mouth together and nodded his assent. "You barged into my home as though you were Superman. You cut off communication with the family; for centuries we had no idea whether you were dead or alive. Then we hear that you're in cahoots with Exor. And you have the nerve to say that we share the Davenport blood, as if that would automatically erase all the wrong you've done, and make everyone fall in love with you. I wish you weren't a Davenport, you're not good enough to carry our name!" Waves of rage raced through him, so much so that they overpowered him. He reached out for a chair but groped air.

"Dad!" Carrington jumped up and raced to his father. Once he got to his father's side, he wrapped an arm around his shoulders and encouraged him to lean on him for support.

Bayard shrugged him off. "I'm fine," he said gruffly, embarrassed by his outburst. He calmly made his way to his seat.

"Whew! And I've been told that I'm a drama queen," Glazier quipped.

"Maybe we should do this another time," Carrington suggested. This meeting was proving to be a waste of time.

Glazier and Harland returned to the table. "No, let's talk. Bayard said things that needed to be said and I respect him for it." He looked at his brother. "I egged you on, and I'm sorry. We need to talk and we'll do it soon. Is that okay?"

"It's fine," Bayard replied tersely.

Glazier ignored his brother's tone and continued. "Let's get down to business." Gone was the teasing voice, in its place one all serious and businesslike. "Evil is permeating the world; we don't need our contacts from the other side to tell us that. We all watch the news, so we know what's going on. As far as Exor's plans, my sources say that he's going to simultaneously attack ten major cities." He quickly named them all.

Riley slumped back in her chair, reeling from the news. *This can't be happening.*

"When?" Dominic quizzed.

"Any day now," Glazier offered, "that's all I know. Sorry."

"You've given us more than we expected," Bayard said reluctantly. "How can we stop him? What's his weakness?"

"Like any demon, he gets his strength from hate. The more hate there is in the world, the stronger he becomes."

"So you're saying that we should all hold hands and sing a song? Or better yet, start hugging strangers?" Malik asked sarcastically.

Glazier chuckled and Bayard shot him a look. He quickly turned serious. "How long would the warm fuzzy feelings last? A day or two at most. We need to do something more permanent."

"Like what?" Dominic pressed.

"We need to take out his army," Glazier said quietly, "and all his top-ranking demons."

Riley inhaled sharply. "Destroy millions, possibly billions, of demons? How can we do that? We can't even destroy Bradley."

"Oh, we'll get him," Glazier replied confidently. "He's just a little flea and I can swat him with my eyes closed. Don't you worry about him."

"How are we going to do this?" Dominic asked. "Like Riley said, we can barely destroy Bradley. How are we going to get rid of a whole army?"

"I know it sounds impossible, but I think it can be done," Glazier said.

"How?" Carrington impatiently asked.

"We have to get them all in one place and blast them. I found out that waves of blue light can kill them."

"Interesting," Malik said, suddenly excited. "But how can we get them to congregate in one place and create a machine big enough to destroy them all?"

"Well, you know that a couple thousand of them are still plastered to the shield, and Dr. Imes should be able to create a machine," Riley suggested.

"That's only a couple of thousand. We'll still need to draw the top-ranking demons here. I'm not sure how we can do that."

Glazier picked up a bowl of grapes and grabbed Harland's hand. "It looks like you guys got the makings of a plan. I've told you all I know. Call me if you need me. I think that little pond is calling my name." He stopped in front of the metal door. "Can someone please let me out?" Dominic glanced at Bayard for approval, Bayard nodded, and Dominic sauntered over to the console, touched a screen, and the doors swooshed open.

The room was silent as Glazier and Harland made their exit.

"So are you happy now that Glazier's here?" Malik asked gruffly.

Riley stroked Malik's face and looked up at him, her eyes unreadable. "I'm not sure yet."

Carrington turned to his father. "Do we have an obligation to stop this war?"

"If we don't, there will be dire consequences," Bayard answered.

"Do you think it's as serious as Glazier says it is?" Riley asked.

Bayard shrugged. "Maybe, maybe not. Like I said before, Exor has been known to change his mind with the wind. He loves games, and right now he's playing one and we're the pawns."

Malik nodded. "I don't want to wait to see who's going to end up the winner, because it'll be me!" He got up and stormed out of the room.

chapter THIRTY - EIGHT

This is the perfect place for me to relax. Riley slid the door of the sunroom open and found Harland already there, clicking away on his laptop faster than a seasoned executive secretary. She braked on the threshold. "Oh, I'm sorry. I'm always walking in on people, first Bayard then you. I was looking for a quiet place to think. I can go somewhere else," she said as she began backing out of the room. "This house is certainly big enough."

"Don't be ridiculous," Harland said. "Come on in." He typed for a few seconds more before powering down his computer.

Riley stepped in and settled on a cream-colored sofa with green overstuffed pillows. She looked around the room. This was on her list as one of her top five favorite places in the house. With the exotic plants, floor-to-ceiling windows, consistent eighty-degree temperature, and bright sunlight, it was easy to pretend she was in the Caribbean.

"So what do you need to think about?" Harland asked.

Riley sighed. "I'm married to a demon slayer," she said, then looked him squarely in the eyes. "How do you do it? How do you survive?"

Harland chuckled. "It is interesting, isn't it? It's very different from being with a doctor. I never imagined falling in love with a demon slayer. I never even knew about it until I met Glazier. My my, what a sheltered life I lived," he joked. "I nearly pooped on myself the first time I saw Glaz fight," Harland confessed as he dramatically placed his hand over his heart. "I thought he was having a seizure."

"Well, I didn't do that. I guess I wasn't too scared since Bradley visited me."

"Oh, that must've been horrible!"

"It was," Riley said without adding anything else and Harland wisely let it go. "May I ask you something?"

"Ask away."

"How do you feel about getting old and Glazier remaining pretty much the same?"

Harland smiled faintly. "Ironically, when he finally admitted to me what he was, I walked out on him. Not because he destroyed demons"—he waved the thought away—"but because he wasn't aging at the rate humans age and I didn't want to be the old hag in the relationship. So I left him."

"Really?"

Harland nodded. "I know, how superficial. But he let me stew for a month before he pursued me." Harland giggled.

"Glazier chased you?" Riley asked, astonished. She couldn't imagine that man running after anyone.

"He did. And by then I missed him so much that if he'd told me he'd taken up with Exor again, I would still have taken him back, and that was twenty years ago."

"But doesn't it bother you?" Riley persisted. "You've aged since you met and he still looks virtually the same. Don't you worry? There are a lot of younger men around."

Harland nodded in agreement. "There are millions of younger men around and a couple thousand of them are prettier than a cover model, and I should be concerned, but I'm not. Let me tell you something about your uncle Glazier. He's not as shallow as he seems."

"I wasn't saying he was."

"Glazier took care of his last two partners until they were well into their nineties. He stayed with each of them and nursed them. And that gorgeous face of his was the last thing they saw before they passed over. And I expect him to do the same for me."

"Now explain to me how a fortyish-something man can be married to a ninety-year-old without raising eyebrows."

"When the age difference became significant, Glazier and his partner moved to another state and pretended to be father and son. No one was the wiser."

"Wow! You guys know all the tricks."

"And then some." Harland laughed. "Mother Nature didn't give me these fierce cheekbones, it was more like Dr. Stein. Hey, I'm not afraid that Glaz would leave me for a piece of eye candy, but I want him to keep licking this Tootsie Roll. I gotta keep it tight, girl."

Riley laughed. They enjoyed the tranquility of the room for a few minutes, then she sighed. "I'm just afraid of growing old while Malik stays gorgeous and wrinkle free. I don't want him to be repulsed by me when I get old."

"I haven't known Malik long, but I know that he isn't like that. That's something you don't have to worry about."

Riley's heart leaped with relief. "You think?"

Harland tapped his chest. "Trust this bitch. That man is crazy in love with you. You can tell by the way he looks at you."

"I know, and I am with him. I guess it's still hard to believe given our pasts." Riley gave him a quick synopsis of her and Malik's history.

"That's romantic, an unrequited crush flipped into love. And just wait until you're in your seventies. Everybody's going to be jealous of you. They're going to be wondering how you got such a pretty young thang."

"That's something to look forward to. Where is he? I haven't seen him in a while."

"Meeting with his uncle."

"Strategizing?"

"A little, but I think they're spending more time becoming reacquainted."

"That's good; I think there are a lot of unanswered questions and hurt feelings."

"They'll work it out," Harland said confidently. "Glazier is very persuasive, and besides, he loves his nephew. That's all he talked about."

"I think they'll work it out." They were quiet, then Riley finally asked the question that had most been on her mind. "Do you think Glazier can save us?"

chapter THIRTY - NINE

Riley paced back and forth in front of the leather club chairs. Earlier she and Tamia had decided to watch a movie in the media room, but now that didn't seem like such a good idea. Unfortunately, her sister thought differently. "I don't know how you can watch that with everything else that's going on," Riley said to Tamia, who couldn't tear her eyes from a Terrance Howard movie. Riley picked up the remote and pushed the off button.

Tamia met her sister's eyes. "I'm scared too, honest I am. But I don't know what else to do. This keeps me from thinking about what's going on."

"I know, it does provide a temporary respite."

"This is so much better than actually going to the movies," Tamia said with a grin.

"I know. This home theater is the truth! I don't even think that I can go back to a public theater." Riley glanced around the room. The theater was cozier than the cookie-cutter theaters they were used to going to. Two rows of leather club chairs in a semicircle faced the sixty-inch flat-screen TV. The sound system was so good that it seemed as if the actors were standing in front of them. "Even with all this, I still want to go *out* to the movies," Riley said before stuffing a handful of popcorn in her mouth followed by a handful of chocolate-covered raisins.

Tamia eyed her sister, then grinned slyly. "I'm sure a baby would love living here."

Riley started screaming. "You're pregnant? My little sister is having a baby?" she said excitedly, her angst long gone.

"Not me, silly . . . *you!*"

"What?"

Tamia pointed to her sister. "You're the one having a baby. You're pregnant!"

"Me?"

"Yeah, you're inhaling junk food just like you did with Brie and Carter, and you're sucking down that soda like it's liquid crack."

Riley slumped against the chair cushions. "I can't be pregnant," she said, shocked. "We were always so careful. Well, not all the time," she admitted.

"The way you and Malik are always all over each other, I'm surprised that you're not farther along than you already are."

"How can I be pregnant?" Riley muttered, dazed. "I can't be . . . I mean my last period was," she said, faltering for a moment, "oh shit! I can't remember my last period."

"Pregnant!" Tamia crowed.

Riley began looking around the room. "Is there a calendar here?"

"Pregnant!"

"Because if there is one, I can tell you that my period is probably due next week. As a matter of fact, I feel a little crampy." She cupped her breasts. "These feel a little tender, just like they usually do before my period."

"Pregnant!"

"Would you stop saying that?" Riley hissed to her sister. "Saying it doesn't make it real."

"But *not* saying it doesn't make it not real. So there," Tamia childishly retorted. "You're knocked up, so get used to it."

Riley turned stunned eyes on her sister. "What if you're right? What if I am pregnant?" she asked before letting out a loud sob.

Tamia swiped some stray popcorn out of the seat next to Riley before sitting down and pulling her into her arms. "Would that be so bad?" she asked quietly.

The movie played on as the sisters absorbed the news. Riley sniffled before answering. "No. But I feel a little strange. I'm having a demon slayer's baby."

"Damn, girl, I can't believe what I'm about to say, and even be impressed by it, but here it goes. You snagged a demon slayer, the *ultimate* demon slayer. Obviously, Malik is an extraordinary man who doesn't do ordinary things. I'd be disappointed if it happened any other way."

"What happens if my baby comes out all weird?"

"Weird like how?"

Riley glanced sheepishly at her sister. "I don't know." She thought for a moment before muttering, "It might be born with a third eye, right in the middle of its forehead."

Tamia laughed. "Now *that* would be weird. But a good thing about that is that you could make beaucoup money touring the country with your freak baby," she said before bursting into laughter.

"That's not funny," Riley said, then tossed a handful of popcorn at her sister. "Malik and I will make a beautiful baby."

Tamia dug her hand into her popcorn. "That's right, and remember that," she said before sticking the handful in her mouth then overturning the tub of popcorn over her sister's head.

Sputtering, Riley ran her fingers through her hair. Fortunately for her, Tamia didn't like butter or a lot of salt on her popcorn. As soon as she thought she had gotten it all out of her hair, she settled back in her chair. "I wonder how far along I am? I need to think about this. I'm so ashamed," she muttered. "I knew exactly when Brie and Carter were conceived. But now I don't have any clue as to when I conceived. That is so sad."

"No, what's sad is that you're tripping over something so inconsequential. This isn't the first time somebody had an oops baby and it won't be the last. Hell, you're still young, so it can happen again with you and Malik."

Riley clutched her sister's hand. "Oh no! My baby will never see the light of day. He'll never smell grass, he'll never get a chance to play in the ocean."

"If the baby was born today, it'd be able to go out and enjoy the sun," Tamia reminded her. "The force field is fixed."

"Yeah, but it will have Bradley peering down on it. He'll scare the bejesus out of him."

"If it's a boy, he'd probably kick Bradley's ass."

Riley grinned. "That's right, all firstborn sons have the special powers. We have months before the baby is born, and Bradley better be history by then."

Tamia frowned. "I know, I'm ready to see the world. This whole experience has made me appreciate life a lot more. Knowing that Bradley destroyed Daddy's spirit was a big factor," she confessed. "I just know that he would want me to live my life to the fullest. And remember the night you and Malik went out?" Riley nodded. "And you had to dive into the house, but Bradley still caught you and Malik, Carrington, and Bayard had to save you? That reminded me that tomorrow isn't guaranteed and that today I want to take a big-ass bite out of life."

"I guess you're right. Before all this, we were living a very vanilla life."

"Speak for yourself," Tamia joked. "I was out and about, doing things."

"Doing people doesn't count," Riley teased.

"In my book it does," Tamia answered with a laugh, then her voice turned serious. "Do you think Glazier can destroy Bradley?" Tamia asked, anxious to move on with her life.

"Harland seems to think he can, and after talking with him, Malik said they had a better chance now."

"I think that the four of them together can obliterate Bradley's sorry behind."

Riley nodded in agreement. "They're strategizing right now."

"Without us?"

"We don't have to be in the mix about everything. I prefer it that way. Sometimes, I get so mad at myself while I'm listening to them talk about Bradley. I still can't believe I was ever in love with that man."

"Don't be mad at yourself. He was very charismatic, he had us all fooled."

"Not you," Riley reminded her.

"It was easy, I'm a natural-born cynic. When are you going to tell your husband about the baby?"

"Now!" Riley decided.

"He'll be mad about the interruption of his meeting," Tamia predicted.

"Not when he hears the news. See you!" Riley raced through the house. The doorbell rang and she automatically opened the door.

"Hey, Riles, you're looking good and rosy," Bradley said, leering, "for a pregnant lady."

chapter FORTY

Bradley strolled into the house. "This place looks a lot better from the ground. Everything always looks so odd when you're flying over it; did you ever notice that?"

"Bradley?" Riley squeaked, fear paralyzing her throat.

Bradley sailed through the room, occasionally stopping to pick up an object to study before returning it to its original spot. "Yep, it's me . . . a new and improved version of me."

Riley couldn't take her eyes off her former husband. No longer transparent, he was as solid as a linebacker. His muscles rippled beneath a body-hugging sweater.

She planted herself behind a chair. "What happened?" she asked fearfully, still transfixed by his transformation.

"Amazing, isn't it?" He strutted over to a mirror and admired himself, preening more than a newly crowned beauty pageant winner. "When Exor promised that he could do it, I had my doubts, but he is all powerful and can perform acts that no one else can. Not even Him." He gestured to the ceiling, then chuckled. "I don't know why I do that, habit, I suppose, because he's everywhere. But I guess you knew that."

Riley kept her eyes glued on Bradley as he continued to roam around. "How did you even get in, we had the force—"

Bradley snorted. "Yes, the infamous force field. The first one didn't work, why would you think the second one would?"

"Dr. Imes—"

"Dr. Imes is stupid," Bradley said arrogantly.

"He created the force—"

"Fuck the force field!" Bradley shouted. "The force field," he mocked, "was made to deter demons, *weak* demons. It can't stop me or Exor."

"But how?"

"He gave me the ability to walk among you humans," he said with a sneer. "But his power is so much stronger than mine. Not only can he solidify but he can change his features so that you never know when you're going to come face-to-face with him. How cool is that? I can't do that, but I can do this—see?" In the blink of an eye he transformed himself into a demon and zoomed up toward the ceiling. He leisurely hovered above her. "I see you," he joked before floating down and solidifying himself again. "I don't like this form, it's so burdensome, so heavy. I don't know how I dealt with it like I did. So to make a long story short, while I'm in this form, I can walk right through the force field, just like you."

"Oh no!" Riley exclaimed.

"Oh yes," Bradley mocked and grinned maniacally. "And just so you know, your little crew has no clue. They think they know everything that's going on in Lavastar. If they did they would've been prepared. They're useless, just like their so-called informants, because if they knew what was really going on, they would be scared shitless."

"They know."

Bradley cocked his head. "They know what?"

Riley bravely stepped from behind the chair. "That you want to destroy mankind. They know about the ten cities."

Bradley raised his eyebrows in amusement. "I guess the crew isn't as useless as I thought. So are *you* scared shitless?" His eyes turned blood red and her stomach clenched with fear.

"Why are you doing this? Why can't you leave us alone? I don't understand why you can't let me be happy."

"I gave you the chance to be happy for eternity but you turned me down."

"You wanted me to stay in a place worse than hell."

Bradley shrugged. "It's all subjective. You say worse than hell, I say paradise. I'm done talking. I feel like walking." Bradley sauntered out of the room.

"Bradley!" Riley said, racing after him.

Bradley continued to breeze through the house with Riley right behind him. "Where is he?" he called over his shoulder and Riley stumbled.

"Who?" Riley asked, feigning ignorance.

"What are you, an owl? You know who I'm talking about. Where's my son?"

"He's out. Malik took him out on an errand," Riley said quickly.

Bradley whipped around, and before she knew it he was standing in front of her. She blinked up at him in surprise. "That's right, I'm faster than the blink of an eye. I'm Super Bradley," he said sarcastically. "And do you want to see what Super Bradley can do?" Before she could respond he jumped up toward the ceiling, flipped, and began swaggering across the ceiling. "Cool, isn't it? But this is just one of the fun things I can do. Wanna see something not so fun?" He brought his hands together and aimed them at a wall. A streak of black zipped down and blasted a hole through the sheetrock. Riley staggered backward. "I know, I know, it's only plaster and paper, but imagine what I can do to your body. Where's my son?" he growled, the teasing gone.

"You're not getting him," she shrieked as she raced down the hall. She glanced over her shoulder to see Bradley, with his hands stuck in his pockets, strolling after her.

"Oh, Ri Ri," Bradley called. "Why are you running away? We've always had such a good time, don't you think? Especially after your visit to Lavastar, or as you like to call it, the place worse than hell; we were practically inseparable. I was sad when you decided to leave."

Riley halted and faced him. "I didn't leave, I escaped, you loon. Not only are you an asshole but you're crazy!" she screamed as she continued to race down the hall.

"Name-calling is never nice. I'm sure your mother told you that," Bradley drawled.

Riley paused long enough to glance over her shoulder, then gasped. Although he hadn't changed his leisurely pace, it didn't seem like the distance between them was widening. She sped around a corner and slipped into the first room she saw. It turned out to be a small utility closet. She pressed against the wall and held her breath as she waited for Bradley to pass. After a minute, she slowly exhaled before cautiously pushing open the door. She peeked out and found the hallway empty. Relieved, she slumped against the wall. "Whew! He'll never get Carter."

Suddenly she heard a low chuckle, then it grew louder. "How cute, you thought you could escape me," Bradley said, amused.

Riley looked up to find Bradley hovering over her. Her mouth was so dry it felt as if she had stuffed it full of Brie's cotton socks.

"Nothing to say?" Bradley cackled. Riley screamed, dashed out of the closet, and darted down the hall. Bradley stayed close to her, drifting by her right shoulder. "I don't know why you won't save us both some time. I'm going to get what I want. I always do."

"You're not getting Carter," Riley vowed between pants.

"Oh yes I am. And you're taking me right to him," Bradley said smoothly. Riley instantly froze. "Don't stop now, I was enjoying the chase, please continue," Bradley said as he slowly transformed himself. A minute later he stood in front of Riley. "I know, I know, amazing, isn't it?" he mocked, feigning amazement.

"No, I won't."

"Oh, yes you will." While he was talking he had backed Riley against a wall. The smell of rotten fish exploded from Bradley, and Riley retched in response. She clamped her hand over her mouth. He hadn't smelled like that earlier.

"I smell delicious, don't I?" he asked. "Just one of the drawbacks of being able to walk among you. I tend to get a little ripe after thirty minutes or so. But hey, I heard P. Diddy has a new cologne, maybe I should check it out," he said as he put his fingers to his forehead and pretended to mull it over. In the blink of an eye, his demeanor changed. He grimaced and narrowed his eyes to little slits. He dragged his finger across her stomach and Riley thought he had cut it open. She let out a howl. Wild eyed, she looked down to find nothing amiss. "Listen, bitch, give me my baby or I'll take this one. That was just a warning; if I wanted to take it, I would've. Are you going to take me to Carter?" Tears streamed down Riley's face as she shook her head no.

"Oh yes you will." In a vicelike grip, Bradley snaked his hand around her forearm. "Where is he?"

"I'm not telling you!"

Bradley increased the pressure on her arm. "Where is he?"

Pain tore through Riley, knocking her to her knees. "Keep straight," she hissed between clenched teeth.

"Wonderful! I don't know why you enjoy making things so difficult. Now get up and walk like the lady I know you are," he ordered as he pulled Riley up.

"This is such a beautiful house," Bradley observed as they made their way down the hall. "Who would've thought that Malik Davenport was a warrior, and rich to boot. I never would've guessed. And the way he was always sniffing after you—"

Riley abruptly stopped. "You knew?"

"Of course, even a blind man could see it. Come on," he said, tugging her along, "let's not get distracted. Are we still on track?"

"Yes," Riley muttered. She was silent for a few seconds, then, "You didn't care that Malik was interested in me while we were married?"

Bradley snorted. "So what if he was, you weren't going anywhere," he said derisively. "I had you so whipped, literally and figuratively, that you never looked at another man. I was your everything," he said arrogantly.

"You're an asshole," Riley hissed.

Bradley chuckled. "You've turned into such a fighter. Why couldn't you have had this much fire in you while we were married? If you had, maybe I might not have cheated, or at least not as much!"

Nausea churned in Riley's stomach and bubbled up, but she swallowed hard, pushing it down. Ignoring his observations, she gave him the next set of directions. "Turn here," she said quietly. "It's the second door on the right."

They stood outside the door. "Hold on, Carter, Daddy's coming to get you. Open the door!" Bradley ordered. Riley shot him a timid look. "Do it, bitch!" Riley reached out and touched the doorknob. "Oh, can't you go any faster? Get out of the way!" Bradley shoved Riley to the floor and pushed open the door. Inside the room, sitting at a table, were Malik, Bayard, Carrington, and Dominic. Bradley quietly observed the scene, then drawled, "Hey, y'all."

chapter FORTY-ONE

The men were rooted to the floor; no one moved. "How did you get in here?" Malik finally asked.

"Where's Carter?" Bradley barked, ignoring Malik's question.

"Not in here," Riley said smugly.

"You fooled me. You get a point for ingenuity. How did that happen? You never had it in you before." Oblivious to the men in front of him, he chewed on the thought for a second. "Well, it doesn't matter; give me Carter and I'll leave," he said smoothly.

"When are you going to understand that you'll never get Carter? Never!" Riley yelled.

Malik stepped up to Bradley. "You're one bold asshole."

"Just one more thing that Riley loved about me." He nonchalantly walked toward the door and beckoned to Riley. "Let's go, we're not finished yet."

"She's not going anywhere. How the fuck are you going to come in my house and start making demands as if you were somebody?"

"That's just how I roll," Bradley drawled, fixing Riley with a glare. "You'd better take me to my son or you're going to lose that little bundle of joy," he said meanly as he gestured to her stomach.

Riley placed a protective hand over her stomach. "Don't you dare harm my baby."

"You're pregnant?" Malik asked.

Riley nodded. This wasn't the way she had envisioned telling him about her pregnancy. "I am—at least I think I am—but I'm pretty sure I am," she stuttered nervously.

Malik pulled off his shirt, exposing his muscular chest and arms. "You want to hurt my baby?" he asked. Malik shot out his hand and a white-lightning bolt hit Bradley in the chest.

Bradley laughed as though Malik had given him a friendly punch. "Don't waste your energy. I'm tired of playing games," he said, bored with Malik. "Where's my son?"

"Carter is mine now," Malik said, goading him, "he calls *me* Daddy."

"He's just confused," Bradley replied mildly. "I'll straighten him out."

"Don't mistake confusion for being smart. He knows who *isn't* trying to kill him."

Infuriated, Bradley thrust out his hands and two streaks of black energy blasted Malik in the chest, knocking him to the floor. Malik grunted before darting up and jolting him with two laser blasts.

With one hand Bradley brushed his shirt, as though he was wiping away a wayward piece of lint, and with the other hand he aimed at Malik. He zapped Malik's feet with a bolt of black. Malik yelped. "Jump, bitch," Bradley joked.

"Fuck you!" Malik said, aiming both hands at Bradley as though they were pistols and firing off laser after laser, each hitting its target: head, face, torso, and hands. Malik's eyes widened in shock when Bradley remained unscathed by his assault.

"Are you done yet?" Bradley asked. "All I want is my son. As soon as I get him, I'll scoot out of your lives, well, what's left of them," he added, then, using his hyper speed, he torpedoed in front of Malik. Before Malik could respond, Bradley picked him up, high over his head, and slammed him down on the floor. "When are you going to get it? Those methods don't harm me in this form." Malik thrashed around on the floor in pain.

"Just to make sure you stay down, let me do this." Bradley, reached into his pocket and pulled out a handful of black dust; everybody froze. The dust was as lethal as anthrax. Bradley held up his hand, drew it back, and was about to dump the dust on Malik when Dominic raced for him and tackled him, knocking him to the ground. Dominic knew he was safe. Even though he was a Davenport, he wasn't a firstborn, so the dust was as harmless as ash to him. A cloud of the dust went up in the air, causing the men to scatter for safety. Covering his face with his hands, Malik rolled away from the fatal dust.

"Everybody's trying to be a hero," Bradley said. He pushed himself up, grabbed Dominic by a leg and an arm, then swung him around before letting him go. They all held a collective breath as Dominic sailed across the room and thudded against a wall, narrowly missing a window. He slid down into a heap.

As soon as the dust settled, Bayard motioned to Carrington to check on Dominic and instructed Malik to stay where he was. "I'll take care of him." About to protest, Malik saw the steely determination in his grandfather's eyes and changed his mind. He stepped back. Bayard held his hands up toward heaven, and Riley gasped as rays of red energy rained down on Bayard's hands. He absorbed it all until his hands were fiery red and his whole body pulsed with power. With his hands splayed out, he rounded on Bradley, then pelted him with ray after ray of force. The smell of burned clothing filled the room. Bayard sucked in air as his arms dangled limply at his sides. When the smoke cleared Bradley glanced down at his clothing. "I do have to remember to get a nonflammable wardrobe," he said as he absentmindedly patted the small fires on his clothes. Other than his charred clothing, he remained unharmed.

Malik, Bayard, and Carrington surrounded Bradley. On cue they all simultaneously aimed their hands at him; bolts of light, white, blue, red, and green, all zeroed in on him. Shock made his face ugly. and he stumbled slightly when the deadly energy hit him. A second later he regained his footing and shook it off.

Bradley nonchalantly shot out his hands. "Black trumps you all," he said arrogantly. "And thanks for the practice, I wasn't sure if the bolts were powerful enough." The room seemed to vibrate as lasers the width of a fire hose hammered them to their knees.

The Davenport men rolled on the floor, groaning, each looking dazed. "Don't you dare go to them," Bradley hissed to Riley. "You should be kissing my ass right now for not killing them. You know I can. I hope my kindness won't come back and bite me on the butt."

"You are so horrible," Riley sobbed.

"All subjective, sweetie, all subjective," Bradley said smoothly as he sauntered toward the door. Riley reached out to her husband. "Don't you fucking dare!" he called over his shoulder. "If you so much as touch your husband, your baby will die. Come on." He pushed her out the door. "Let's go get my son."

"If you leave Carter alone, I'll live with you in Lavastar," Riley babbled as they marched down the corridor.

"Nope, don't want you, I want Carter. Discussion closed."

Riley stopped and faced Bradley. "Why do you want him? You didn't pay that much attention to him when you were alive. Why now?"

"I'm doing it simply because he's my son," Bradley stated as though that fact in itself entitled him to kill his own flesh and blood.

"Yes, and who kills his child? Why cut his life short? Let him live."

Bradley chuckled meanly. "You look at it as killing, I look at it as rebirth. Carter will ride alongside me and help me command my army. He'll learn and see things that he'd never have the opportunity to do here. So don't think of it as death, think of it as an educational opportunity."

Riley gasped. "You're crazy!"

"All subjective, sweetie. All subjective." He viciously grabbed her arm. "Let's keep it moving."

They walked in silence to Carter's room and stood outside the door.

"This had better be his room. If it isn't, I'm going to march back to Malik and rip his arms and legs off. You know I can do it," he said meanly. "Open the damn door!"

Tears raced down Riley's face and her hands were shaking when she pushed the door open. "I'm so sorry, baby, so sorry." Tears blinded her from seeing Bradley stalk into the room.

"Where is he?" Bradley called out.

"What?" Riley squeaked.

"Where the fuck is he!" Bradley roared.

With her heart pounding, Riley raced into the room and saw that it was empty. Overwhelmed with relief, she dropped to her knees. *Where is he?* Her eyes darted around the room. There was no sign of her little boy.

Bradley angrily leveled Carter's bed with a black bolt, turning it into a pile of wood. The closet door was his next target. It flew off its hinges, sailed across the room, and landed on the floor. "I could go through this house room by room until I find him," Bradley threatened, "but I don't have time."

Riley noticed that his odor had become more pronounced and that he was beginning to smell worse than a garbage dump baking under the hot Georgia sun.

He grabbed Riley by the arms and yanked her up over his head. She peered fearfully down at him, and what she saw in his eyes caused her relief to evaporate very quickly. They had turned a deadly red and were simmering with hate. "Why do you insist on playing games with me?" he roared, his voice shaking the room. "Where is he?"

"I don't know," Riley answered, her voice quavering.

Bradley jutted out his chin toward the wall farthest from them. "You know I can throw you through that fucking wall?" Bradley warned.

"I don't know where he is, honestly!"

"You must have a hiding place. Where did you go when my soldiers infiltrated this place?"

How would he get to the panic block? Riley tensed and Bradley saw her hesitation. "You know where he is, don't you?"

"I don't."

"Yes you do. I know you, Ri Ri, you're not a good liar, and you're lying now. I'm going to make you tell me where my son is hiding," he threatened as he squeezed her ankles together so tightly that Riley thought her bones would break.

"I'm not lying," she gasped.

"You make me sick," Bradley said before dropping her on the floor. Riley writhed with pain when she hit the carpet, her hands instinctively going around her belly.

"I can think of something I can do to expedite the matter. I think it's time for me to take full advantage of my newly acquired skills."

Bradley cupped Riley's face. The normally loving gesture felt as deadly as a boa constrictor's squeeze. "You know that I could crush your skull right now?" he murmured.

"Stop it!" Riley begged.

He continued talking as though she hadn't spoken. "Your bones are like saltines to me. All I have to do is squeeze," he said before demonstrating.

Riley howled. His hands were like a giant vice grip on her head. He continued squeezing until she thought she was going to explode. She was on the edge of a blackout when he stopped. Through half-closed eyes Riley looked up at him and saw his mouth moving. The ringing in her ears made it impossible for her to hear him.

"Huh?"

"Let's go get my fucking son!"

chapter FORTY-TWO

Bradley grabbed Riley and flung her over his shoulder. He stalked through the halls, retracing his steps to the conference room.

Malik, Bayard, Carrington, and Dominic were banded together as though waiting for them when Bradley barged in.

Malik marched up to Bradley. "Let her go!" he ordered.

Bradley narrowed his red-hued eyes. "Step back, asshole, we both know who'd win this. So rein in your testosterone and chill. I have a proposition for you."

Malik held his hands menacingly close to Bradley's face. "Let Riley go and then we'll talk."

Bradley looked at Malik in amazement, then he started chuckling softly, until it grew into a full-blown laugh attack and tears streamed down his face. "Whew! I needed that." He dried his eyes with the hem of Riley's blouse. "You're telling me what to do? The man who was granted powers by one of the most powerful beings of all time? I think not," he said with disdain. He flicked his thumb; the minuscule movement pushed Malik against the wall. Malik's eyes widened with surprise. "Oh yeah, baby, be scared. Just imagine what I would've done to you if I had waved my hand. No more playing with you all." He looked each man in the eye before resting his gaze on Malik. "Give me my son and you'll get to keep your baby."

"What's wrong with her?" Bayard asked; his granddaughter-in-law was as still as a corpse.

"She's resting," Bradley calmly said before dumping Riley at his feet.

"You asshole," Malik hissed, feeling powerless.

Bradley nudged Riley with his toe. "Now I see where Riley picked up her colorful language. You'd better tell her to tone it down, it's not very ladylike," he said as he toed her stomach. "So do we have a deal?"

"No fucking deal," Malik growled.

"That's not going to happen," Bayard calmly answered; his grandson was in no position to bargain. His emotions were running too high. "We can give you money and jewels; we're very rich," he said without sounding like he was boasting, but like someone who was very comfortable with his position on the totem pole of life.

"Oh, I know about the Davenports and all your riches. Bayard, you make Buffet look middle class. But I don't need your riches, I can take whatever I want."

"Everything except Carter," Riley mocked. She had wakened and was glaring up at him from the floor.

"I'm tired of playing games with you all."

Just then Glazier strolled into the room, saying, "Hi, Bradley." He pulled a pistol out of his pocket and tossed it to Malik.

"Say bye-bye, asshole." Malik pointed the pistol at Bradley's chest.

Bradley grinned at Malik, holding the weapon. "What's that supposed to do?"

"Kill you," Glazier answered.

"That won't do anything. It'll be like shooting through air. Your bullets can't hurt me."

Malik raised an eyebrow. "I would beg to differ."

"Why don't you try it! If you don't believe me, just try it."

Malik aimed the gun at Bradley's arm and fired. The bullet sliced through him and Bradley flinched. It embedded itself harmlessly in the wall behind him.

Bradley laughed as he eased in front of Malik. "So, do you want to waste any more bullets?"

"No, I think I'll get it right this time," Malik drawled.

"I don't know why you insist on trying to destroy me. Can't you see that it's a waste of time?"

Bradley snarled as the bullet tore through his shoulder.

"That felt like a fucking tickle. You're gonna have to do better than that if you think you're gonna kill me." Bradley advanced on Malik. "If I had the time, I'd pull the bullet out and stuff it down your throat."

"Are you sure that's the only thing you want to stuff down my throat?" Malik mocked before shooting; the bullet grazed Bradley's side but he continued moving forward.

He stopped in front of Malik an arm's length away. "When are you going to realize that I'm indestructible?" Bradley asked, his voice bored. The right side of his shirt was soaked through with blood, which dripped onto the floor. "None of you can do a damn thing to me."

"Sure we can!" Glazier called out and Bradley whirled in his direction. Being so intent on Malik he had forgotten about the others.

"How? How can you hurt me?" Bradley cocked his head and

curled his lips, like a dog on the verge of an attack. Riley shrank back in terror; Bradley's teeth had turned black. "This," Bradley continued, gesturing toward his wounds, "this only irritates me."

"Why, because it shows that you're almost human, almost vulnerable?" Carrington taunted and Bradley fixed him with a murderous glare.

"I'm not *almost* human," he spat out, "I'm better than human. Now I can travel from one world to the other as easily as you humans go from room to room. And I can shed this shell as easily as you humans take off your coats. Would you like to see?" Bradley ripped off his bloody shirt. A hole, big enough to push a small apple through, marred his shoulder and a flap of skin hung down. While glaring at Carrington, Bradley grabbed his right shoulder with his left hand and peeled the skin from his shoulder to his fingertips.

Riley leaned over and threw up. Bradley giggled crazily. "See that really did tickle." Then he refocused his attention on Malik. "If you're gonna shoot me, asshole, make sure you mean it."

"He's just playing with you," Glazier admitted. "He can take you out with one bullet."

"He just proved that he couldn't," Bradley said, reaching for Riley and dismissing Glazier.

"I see that Exor hasn't changed. He was never forthcoming with information."

Bradley scoffed as he ignored Riley and gave Glazier his full attention. "He wouldn't set me up," he said with false bravado. "I'm going to be his number one man."

"Do you feel your core?"

"Of course I do," he lied.

"Really? It's not there, is it? So that means Exor gave you a heart and you know what that means, don't you? You see Malik and I figured it out, Malik more so than I. He's so intelligent. He quizzed me on everything I knew about Exor. I told him about Exor's contempt for you and that he might give you a heart. And Malik latched on to that little bit of information. Then all we had to do was wait for you to show up. And you did, just like we knew you would, because you are so fucking arrogant and stupid that you couldn't resist showing off. Bye-bye, Bradley."

"No!" Bradley howled as he tried to transform himself back into a demon, but Malik was too fast.

"See ya!" Malik gloated before pulling the trigger. The gun exploded. He hit Bradley in the forehead, knocking him to his knees.

"I'm laughing so hard," Bradley gasped.

"Let me give you a rib buster," Malik said, his blue eyes icy. He hit Bradley in the heart and he fell face forward onto the floor. "Say bye-bye, bitch!" he quipped.

They watched in fascination as Bradley's body disintegrated into a pool of black slime before drying into black dust. Little spores shot up into the air then dropped into a neat pile.

"Oh my God," Riley said as she backed against a wall and slid down until she was sitting on the floor. "Oh my God," she repeated.

The men glanced in her direction, but no one offered her any comfort. They didn't have the time, as they still weren't finished. "What should we do with his remains?" Dominic asked.

Bayard backed away from the quickly decomposing body. "You know his dust is lethal to firstborns. If we get any of it on us . . ."

"We can use the salve," Malik quickly reminded him. With all the excitement, he had forgotten about it.

Suddenly Riley pushed away from the wall, stumbled over to the dark mass, and stared down at it. "So this is your soul? This is your essence? It doesn't surprise me, not one bit. It looks just as nasty and evil as I thought it would. Oh, by the way, are you laughing now?" she spat out.

"Don't get too close," Malik warned, "we need to get every particle; if not, we're in trouble. We don't need any extra dust floating around."

"Go get the salve," Bayard ordered and Carrington raced out of the room. Malik and Bayard stepped out until Carrington returned and they covered themselves with the antidote.

The next thirty minutes were spent with the Davenport men cleaning up and securing Bradley's remains. After placing them on a clay plate, Malik and Dominic went outside and dug a two-foot-deep hole and gingerly set Bradley's remains in it.

Malik reached into his pocket and pulled out a vial. He glanced at his cousin. "Take off the top," he ordered gruffly. Dominic quickly did so. Malik poured the contents of the vial over Bradley's ashes. The Davenport men silently watched as they bubbled, then sizzled until they evaporated into the air.

"Good work," Bayard said quietly to Malik and Glazier before making his way back into the house.

Hours later, Riley and Tamia were sitting in the den with the Davenport men and *everybody* had a drink in their hands.

"I love you so much!" Riley said to her sister for the gazillionth time. "You are so smart."

"I did what anybody would do," Tamia said modestly.

"But you didn't panic or anything; tell me again what happened." She never tired of hearing the story of how her sister saved Carter and Brie from Bradley.

"Almost a second after you left to tell Malik about your

pregnancy, I left too. And as soon as I was about to turn the corner, I heard Bradley's voice."

"And then what?" Riley asked excitedly.

Tamia rolled her eyes, but continued. "I backed up, then burned rubber; I was running so fast down the hall to Carter and Brie's room that I thought I was flying. As soon as I got there, I scooped them up and hurried to the elevator."

"With Carter fussing all the way," Riley confirmed.

"Yep. I was one second away from covering his mouth with duct tape."

"I've had those moments. That boy sure talks a lot at the wrong time."

"We made it to the room and I prayed that Malik had our DNA programmed into the security system. If not, we were in trouble."

"And he did," Riley said breathlessly, "it was programmed and you guys got in."

"Would you let me tell it?" Tamia said.

"Sorry."

"Fortunately, my DNA was programmed and I was able to make it in. I gave the kids ice cream and put them in Carter's room. Then I came out and watched everything unfold on the monitors. I was waiting for you to escape to the room," Tamia admitted.

"I wasn't even thinking about that. I was thinking about saving my children. And I don't know what I would have done if I had opened Carter's bedroom door and found him inside. I'm so glad that you rescued him," Riley said tearfully. Every time she thought about her sister's fast thinking she got weepy.

"And you saved us," Riley said to Malik, who grinned and rolled his eyes.

"Would you like to see my Superman cape?" he joked. Riley squeezed his thigh and blew a kiss at him.

"How did you know to bring a gun?" Riley wondered aloud.

"A Davenport is always prepared," Malik answered. "Glazier wasn't the only Davenport privy to Exor's secret. Somehow Kimball found out that Lucifer did the same thing to Exor. And he wrote about it. His journals are filled with so much info. Then I interrogated Glazier. Something told me that Exor would do the same thing to Bradley, but for different reasons. I found out through Glazier that Exor did the same thing to another one of his soldiers. He set Bradley up; he wanted to get rid of him. I found out there was talk that Bradley was trying to overthrow him. Not that he could. But he couldn't have his soldiers thinking that he could so easily be disposed of. So he banked on Bradley's arrogance and his desperation to get Carter. Exor knew that he would try to get him one last time," Malik said. "So when Exor turned his core into a heart, he knew it was only a matter of time."

"Do you think Exor would come after us?"

Bayard shook his head. "I doubt it, we were never his targets."

"But we might be in his sights for retaliation for destroying Bradley; he was one of his prized soldiers. He did things for him that not even his seasoned soldiers would attempt."

"Even so, I still don't think he's going to come after us. Remember, we were Bradley's pet project. Like Malik just said, Exor set Bradley up to be killed. He knew that we would find Bradley's weakness. Exor has a bigger potato on his plate."

"Yeah, world destruction," Riley said sadly.

"I think he's going to come after us," Dominic insisted.

"We'll soon find out, won't we?" Malik said ominously.

chapter FORTY-THREE

Riley glanced at Malik. "Is it over, for real?"

Malik nodded. "It is, baby, finally."

"Poor Daddy," Riley whispered.

Malik kissed her on the head. "I'm sorry, babe."

Riley smiled at him sadly. "I know you are."

After outfitting them all with pistols, Bayard had sequestered them in the house for an additional week just to make sure Exor wasn't coming after them.

And according to Dominic's contacts on the other side, Exor had put his plan of destruction on hold. It was becoming the most talked about secret of all time. He had decided that when he did it, he wanted to take everyone by surprise. Dominic's spies were saying that Exor was biding his time, waiting for the perfect opportunity to destroy mankind.

Riley was still getting used to being free. Over the last few days, she, Tamia, and the kids had spent the time rediscovering Atlanta and reclaiming their freedom. Whenever they saw a park, Riley parked the car, dragged everybody out, and they sat on the hood enjoying the fresh air and sun.

And they put a dent bigger than the Grand Canyon in Malik's

platinum American Express card. Even though Malik's paladins had bought them everything they needed, there wasn't anything like going into Neiman Marcus, Macy's, and Walmart to do your own shopping.

"Let's go outside," Malik suggested, "and take a walk."

"Do you think this is okay?" Riley asked, gesturing toward her outfit. She had on a wife beater that covered her growing belly and a pair of shorts barely bigger than a strip of tape.

Malik took in her appearance. If he hadn't known her age, he would have mistaken her for someone ten years her junior. "You look fine, and nobody's going to see you."

"Cool," Riley said before slipping her feet into a pair of flip-flops.

Malik grabbed her hand and led her down the stairs, through the house, and out by the pool. Riley breathed in the thick air. "I love it. It's nine o'clock at night and it's still as hot as it was at twelve o'clock today but I still love it," she said as she followed Malik past the swimming area and into the gardens.

"This is the same air you smelled from the balcony."

Riley shook her head. "No, that was the air of imprisonment, of fear and hopelessness. This is the air of freedom, sweet freedom," she said. And to prove her point, she took another deep breath of air, pulled out of Malik's grasp, and skipped away. "Freedom!" she called over her shoulder.

When Malik finally caught up with her, she was sitting in a chaise lounge enjoying the garden. "It's beautiful, isn't it?" He slipped in next to her and Riley snuggled in his arms.

"It is. And so peaceful."

"I really missed not being able to come out here and work on it. It's my stress reliever."

"So when are we going back to work? I'm eager to get back."

"I promised Pearl that I'd be back in the fall. Do you think you can take a year or two off after the baby is born?"

Her brow furrowed in confusion. "You mean be a stay-at-home mom?"

"Don't look like that, it's not a bad idea."

"Oh no," Riley said hurriedly. "It's a *wonderful* idea. It never crossed my mind. I never had the luxury of doing so. As much as I would love to get back to teaching, I would love to stay home with the baby." She peeked over at him. "Do you think that's selfish?"

"Not at all. Working with children is very fulfilling, that's why I do it. But I want you home taking care of our children; there's nothing like a mother's love."

"Thank you," Riley said.

"How are you feeling?" he asked, suddenly serious. This whole situation was stressful for anybody, even more so for a pregnant woman.

Riley grabbed his hand and tenderly kissed his palm. She had never felt so pampered in her life. Not only had Malik arranged for her to spend a day at a spa, he had taken her out on a dinner cruise and surprised her with a five-carat tennis bracelet. And he had already hired an interior decorator to design the nursery. "I was feeling a little nauseous a couple of hours ago, but I'm fine now."

Malik looked at her worriedly. "Did you have Tao bring you some crackers?"

"He did. I'm okay."

"Anything else?" Her obstetrician had examined her and declared her healthy, but Malik was a nervous first-time father.

"Nope, other than the morning puke session, I'm okay. It's nothing that'll kill me."

"I still can't believe I'm going to be a father," Malik said in wonderment.

"You never thought about it?"

"Of course I did with my first wife, but you know that story. She was killed before we could start a family. I feel so old," he admitted.

"But you look like you're only thirty. You look good for your age. You still get me hot," she whispered.

"Oh really?"

"Yes really." She tenderly stroked his face before pulling his head toward hers and nibbling on his bottom lip. Malik groaned softly. Cupping his face, she blew soft wisps of air on his lips before smoothly inserting her tongue.

Malik pulled away. "Are you trying to seduce me?"

"What do you think?" she asked before blowing in his ear and nibbling on his earlobe. Ever since she'd discovered she was pregnant, she'd been hornier than a teenager. She hadn't felt like this with her other two pregnancies; then she'd had twenty-four/seven morning sickness and did not want to be touched.

"I think you are," he said before leaning back on the chaise and letting Riley take control.

She looked nervously toward the house. "Do you think they can see us down here?"

"Not unless they have X-ray vision. It's impossible with the hedges and trees."

"Good! So they can't see me do this. We can have a quickie." She unzipped his shorts and tugged them down. His dick sprang up and she immediately wrapped her lips around it. Malik groaned softly. Riley ran her tongue up and down the length of him.

chapter FORTY-FOUR

Riley hugged Glazier to her. "I don't want you to go," she pouted. "Please stay, the kids love playing with you."

"And I them, but even though this house is as big as a cruise ship, I'm finding it a little claustrophobic."

"And maybe a little *homophobic*," Harland chimed in.

Glazier tittered. "You are so funny. That's why I love this man."

Riley knew what he was talking about. Every time Glazier and his partner showed any affection in Bayard's presence, he'd race out of the room as though Exor himself was after him. "He loves you, you know," Riley said quietly.

Glazier arched an eyebrow at her. "*Really?*"

"He does," Riley insisted, even though she wasn't sure if it was true. But she hated to see the two brothers fight. "You really should stay a little longer."

"Oh, you'll just get tired of me."

"Never!" Riley said with a laugh. He and Harland had brought more excitement into their lives than a touring drag queen show.

Just then Bayard strolled into the foyer. "I need to talk to you. Come with me!" he ordered Glazier before retracing his steps.

Glazier was about to snap something back when Harland shushed him. Instead he stood up and followed his brother.

"Would you like me to come with you?" Riley asked.

Indecision softened Glazier's face. "I'd like that," he said, suddenly timid.

Bayard didn't say anything as Glazier, Harland, and Riley stepped into his den. The trio sat down, Glazier in the middle and Harland and Riley lovingly flanking him. Bayard cleared his throat. "I just wanted to thank you again for all your help. I don't think we would have been able to destroy Bradley if you hadn't been here," he said gruffly.

"You're welcome," Glazier responded, just as gruffly. They glared at each other. "Is there anything else?"

"No. You may leave."

Glazier stood up, but Riley was faster. "Wait! This is it. No hug? No talking about what's really going on? You guys really need to talk."

"I'm here, aren't I? I came all the way from Brazil to help him. That's got to say a lot," Glazier said. "I didn't have to come."

"And I just thanked you," Bayard snapped.

"Bayard, stop it, he's trying!" Riley said sharply, momentarily forgetting that not only was she chastising her grandfather-in-law but two powerful kings who could easily burn her to a crisp if they wanted to.

"Okay, okay. I'll start," Bayard offered. "It's not the gay part that bothers me," Bayard said, "it's that you left the family, you left *me*," he admitted.

"I told you why," Glazier responded softly.

"But you still left me, you abandoned me," Bayard said, his voice cracking.

"So you're not disappointed or mad at me for being gay?" a stunned Glazier asked and Bayard shook his head. "How come any time Harland and I showed any PDA you walked off as if you were repulsed?"

"I was jealous."

"You wanted your brother to kiss you?" Riley asked, confused. "That's sick."

Bayard vehemently shook his head. "I was jealous of the closeness they shared. I wanted that closeness with my brother, definitely not the sex part, but the closeness . . . like what we had when we were younger."

Glazier's lips began to tremble. "That is so sweet. I just thought you hated me for being who I am."

"No, I hated you for the choices you made with Exor."

"Thank you," Harland said quietly. "It means a lot to him."

Glazier stood up and extended his hand to his brother. "Yes, thank you."

Bayard stared at his brother's hand. "You're still leaving?" he asked gruffly.

Glazier's hand dropped to his side. "Nobody asked me to stay."

Riley sniffled softly. *This is right out of a storybook.* She glanced at Harland and noticed that his eyes were shiny with unshed tears.

"I want you to. I want for us—" Overcome with emotion, Bayard paused. Embarrassed, he bowed his head and tried to compose himself; as soon as he felt in control, he looked up. "I want us to rule Ulgani together."

This time Glazier held his arms out for a hug. The brothers lovingly embraced.

Glazier was the first to pull away. "Bring me some champagne, y'all! 'Cause I'm staying!" he shouted.

chapter FORTY-FIVE

A sense of déjà vu washed over Riley as she stood at the front door. A set of Louis Vuitton suitcases was at her feet. "You know you don't have to leave."

"I know, but as much as I love it here, I want my freedom back. I want to be able to walk naked around my own place when I want to and drink orange juice out of the carton whenever I want."

"For Pete's sake, you're a woman over thirty, not a college coed!"

Tamia grinned. "But seriously, there is something to be said about having your own place and being able to do what you want. I can't do that here. And if I wanted to blast T.I.'s latest CD, I couldn't do it."

"You can in the secure room. You can do anything you want down there."

Tamia arched an eyebrow at her sister. "Now you're just being silly. It was fun living down there for a week or so, but let's not make it a lifetime."

Riley teared up. "I don't want you to go," she admitted, "I'm going to miss you so much." They had grown closer while living together, each gaining a new level of respect for the other.

"Would you stop it?" Tamia said, embarrassed by her sister's tears. "We'll still see each other, maybe not as much, but we will. You know you can visit me. You're not stuck here anymore."

"I know," Riley said. "I'm still getting used to my freedom. I can't believe what a big adjustment it's been for me." It was still hard for her to believe that her life had returned to normal and that Bradley was gone.

"I know, me too," Tamia said quietly. "The whole thing felt like a dream. I still find it hard to believe. You making love to a ghost, and then falling in love with a prince who happens to be a demon slayer."

"It sounds like it would make an amazing novel," Riley said.

"It'll have to be a novel because no one would believe me if I were to write it as nonfiction."

"The paladins would," Riley quipped.

Dominic strolled over and picked up the two largest pieces of luggage, leaving the small one for Tamia. "So what's going on with you and Dominic?" Riley asked as soon as she was sure he couldn't hear them.

"We're talking about moving in together," she divulged before blushing deeply.

Riley was speechless. Her sister avoided commitment more than an arachnophobe dodged spiders. "Wow!" she said, finally finding her voice. "I guess being forced to spend time together really was a good thing."

"It was," Tamia agreed. "I really got a good look at who he was. And he's a good man. At first I was attracted to him for his looks. But it was when he took action and got us to the secure room that I really appreciated him and fell in love. He was so different from the guys I used to date."

"Really? How?"

"He's a real man. He doesn't care about wearing the latest fashions or driving the most expensive cars."

"But he does," Riley pointed out. Dominic drove a Mercedes and had more designer clothes than she had.

"Yeah, but it's so understated; he makes the clothes, the clothes don't make him. And he doesn't need to flaunt his wealth. By the way, his Mercedes is five years old."

"Oh, that makes a difference," Riley said sarcastically.

"He's a real man. And I feel a hundred percent safe with him. I know he'll always take care of me."

Riley hugged her sister. "Okay, you're making a sound argument. I'm glad, girl. You finally found what you were looking for."

"Gotta love the Davenport men." Tamia stepped out of her sister's arms. "I'll call you as soon as I'm home." She picked up the last piece of luggage and walked out the door.

chapter FORTY - SIX

Months later

"Oh, baby, he's so gorgeous." Riley and Malik were seated on a love seat in her hospital's birthing room. After four days in the hospital, she was being released. The room was still filled with dozens of congratulatory bouquets of flowers and fruit baskets. Malik had taken home over a dozen bouquets and teddy bears already; he decided to give the leftover items to the nurses who had taken care of his wife and son.

"He's a boy, he's not gorgeous," Malik teased as he stared lovingly at his week-old son. "He's handsome."

Riley giggled. "Yes, he's very handsome, just like his father."

While the proud parents were admiring their baby, Omar intently stared at the ceiling and began kicking his legs and flailing his arms.

"Oh, isn't he cute," Riley cooed, "he loves to kick his little legs; he's going to be so strong."

Malik cleared his throat before answering. "He is strong," he agreed.

Riley noted her son's intent gaze and then his movements didn't seem so random after all. She slowly turned her gaze away from her son and to her husband. "Is he fighting demons?" she asked, her voice filled with disbelief.

Malik shook his head. "Not at all. He's just doing baby stuff."

"Whew! For a minute there, I really thought he was fighting demons." A ball of fear suddenly ran up Riley's spine. "He is a demon slayer; what happens when they *do* start coming after him? Who'll protect him then?"

Malik gently pulled his son from Riley's arms and proudly gazed down at him. "Nothing is going to happen to him. For the most part he will stay at home. When he goes out, my father, grandfather, or I will accompany him. And the same goes for his training; one of us or all three will be with him. Look at me, I've survived for over a hundred years."

"I know. I'm just scared. I didn't have to worry about this with Carter or Brie. My biggest worry was whether or not to use cloth or disposable diapers," she joked lightly.

"It'll be all right. I promise you." He nonchalantly hit the air before leaning closer to Riley. "You're my lady, right?" Riley smiled shyly, but she nodded. "Then don't you ever worry about anything, I always take care of my family. I love you."

"Thanks, baby. I love you too."

Malik passed his son to Riley. "May I present to you Malik Bayard Omar Davenport the second, the prince of Ulgani."